NORTH STAR

ARIA WYATT

North Star
Copyright © 2020 by Aria Wyatt
www.ariawyatt.com

Cover design by Lori Jackson Design
Photographer: Wander Aguiar
Editing by Silvia's Reading Corner and Eve Arroyo Editing
Proofreading by My Brother's Editor, Virginia Tesi Carey, and Amy Briggs
Formatting: Champagne Book Design

ISBN: 978-1-7359505-2-5

To Amanda Madsen:

This one is for you.
As always, thanks for your blunt AF feedback and for treating this book
like your own.
I appreciate the hell out of you for reading the manuscript until your eyes
bled.
Oh yeah, and for convincing me to get rid of THAT scene . . .
You're a badass and I adore you.
Never doubt what you're capable of.
(P.S. Garrett needs you.)

NORTH STAR

Warning:

If we're related, or you know me professionally, do yourself a favor and skip this one.
-or-
If you choose to proceed, do ME a favor and pretend someone else wrote the sex scenes.
You've been warned.
Let's not make this awkward, okay?

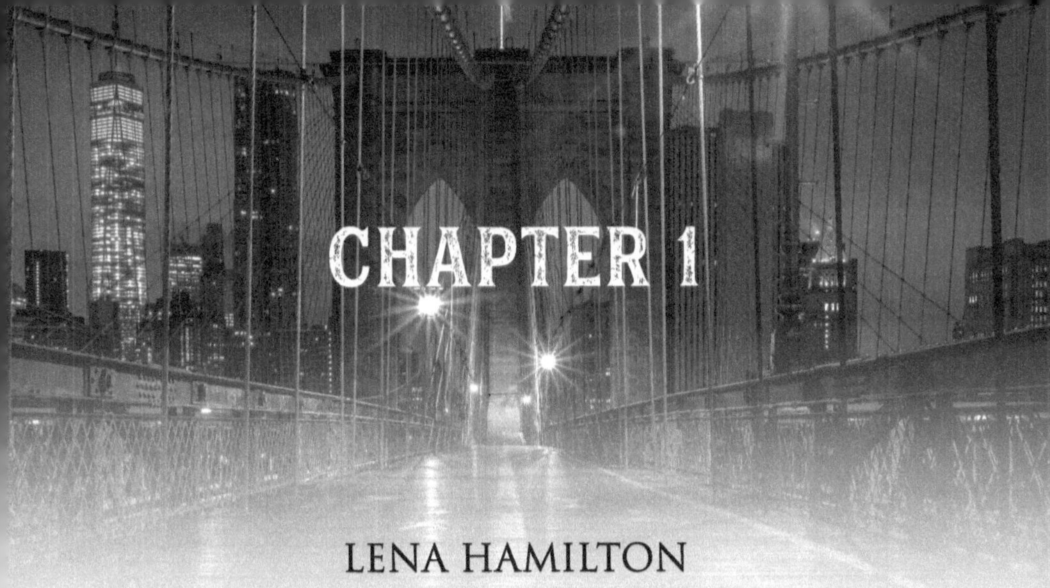

LENA HAMILTON

Internal playlist: "Awake" by Josh Groban

I press my forehead to the cool window of the hovering chopper. The swaying rope ladder was a bitch to climb, but I made it. On the tundra beneath me, Alaska State Troopers strap the man I love to a stretcher. Broken, battered, and on the fast-track to pneumonia, Wes Emerson is lucky to be alive.

We *all* are.

Alaska's Far North, with its raw beauty and untouched wilderness, was a brutal hostess. For three weeks, Mother Nature walloped us with unforgiving terrain, harsh elements, and deadly predators, but—by some miracle—we survived.

I glance at Wes's two best friends. Austin Pines is leaning against his headrest with his eyes closed, lashes resting on tear-stained cheeks. He clutches the edge of his seat as his lips move in a silent prayer. Beside him, a windblown Jake Bennett stares out a different window. With his gaze riveted to the scene below, he gnaws a hunk of caribou jerky, chewing in the way a distracted llama might.

The troopers signal to the medics on board.

"Okay, let's get him up here," a stocky, redhaired man says, gesturing to another medic. "He's got broken ribs, so we need to take it slow and steady."

"Please don't drop him," I blurt.

"Don't worry, Ms. Hamilton, we won't."

At six foot five, Wes is a mountain of chiseled muscle, and I know damn well how hard it is to move him. I hold my breath as the pair uses a rope harness to hoist the stretcher into the chopper. After what feels like an hour, it clears the entrance, and the medics close the door.

Wes grins. "I could've climbed the ladder, ya know."

I roll my eyes. "Now's not the time for your tough guy act."

"It's not an act."

He's right—it's not an act. "Tough guy" doesn't scratch the surface of his strength and will to live. Even the god of war, Wes's most renowned role, would've accepted defeat when thrown against jagged rocks and dragged beneath the John River's icy rapids. I still can't fathom how he endured the trauma. It wasn't Ares who survived—it was Wes. The *real* man who breached the walls I'd built around my heart.

Wes juts his chin at Austin. "Memphis, you all right, mate? You look like you're at a funeral."

"I'm still tryin' to wrap my mind 'round it, that's all." Austin slowly shakes his head. "I thought we were gonna die out there . . ."

Jake pats Austin's shoulder. "Me too, man."

The rotor blades spin faster, and the chopper lifts. Lost in the helicopter's deafening drone, I watch the troopers shrink beneath us. The medics tend to Wes as the pilot flies north to Anaktuvuk Pass, a remote village in the Gates of the Arctic National Park.

I relax my head against the headrest and take a slow, deep breath. *It's over.* We've finally been rescued, but that doesn't mask the desolate feeling that grips my chest. These men have become my friends. Correction, after what we've been through, they are like *family*. But now, our tight foursome will soon be split up. One question has been circling my mind since our rescuers found us.

What will happen with Wes and me?

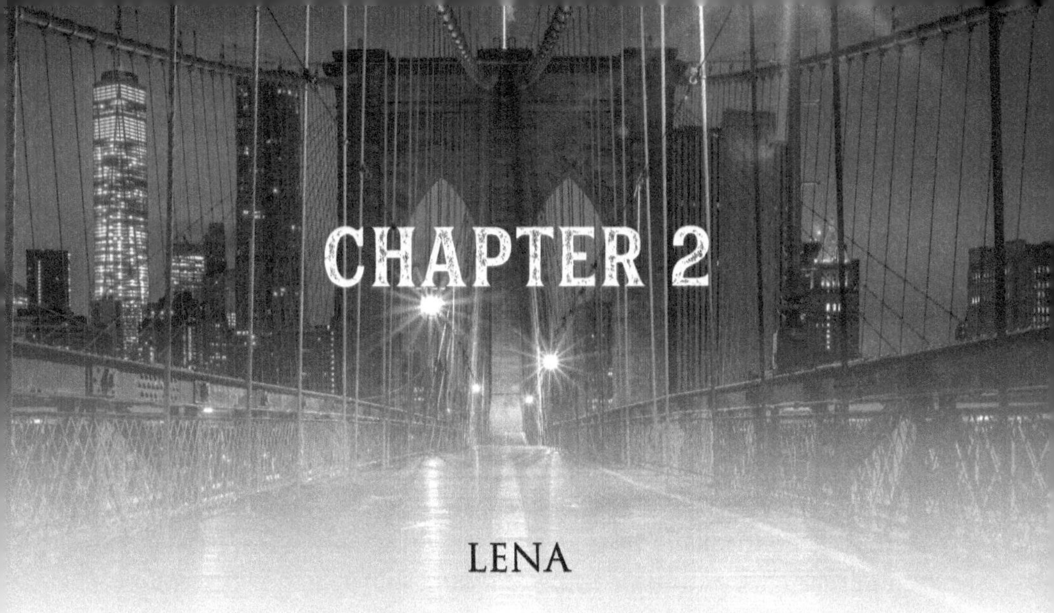

CHAPTER 2

LENA

Internal playlist: "Something Just Like This" by
The Chainsmokers & Coldplay

The Anaktuvuk Pass hospital is a one-story building, much smaller than the emergency department in New York General, where I work as a trauma nurse. Jake, Austin, and I disembark on the hospital's helipad. A blonde nurse waits with a gurney for Wes, and I peek at her name badge. Grace. A fitting moniker for the circumstances. If the doctor's name is Faith or Hope, I'm going back to church.

The medics transfer Wes from the stretcher onto the gurney and help wheel him in.

Grace touches my shoulder. "Don't worry, we'll take good care of him."

I nod my thanks and follow the group inside. It's a sterile, yet cozy facility. A handsome doctor is speaking with Wes in the hallway. He smiles and nods as I pass.

"That's Dr. Jacobs. He runs our hospital," Grace explains. "He'll see you soon. So, as you can see, Ms. Hamilton, we're a small facility. We service the Anaktuvuk Pass community and the occasional traveler who passes through. We have only three inpatient rooms, one of which is occupied. We'll need to room you with one of your companions. Do you have a preference?"

"Please put me with Wes." That's a given. He's the embodiment of certainty. Shelter and safety. He's my harbor. My haven. Ironically though, our future together is the most uncertain part of my life.

"We can do that. On the right is the ladies' room. I'm sure you'd like to get out of your dirty clothes and have a nice hot shower."

"Oh, God, yes." After nearly three weeks in the wilderness, a shower is more enticing than a winning lottery ticket. Even though we all took daily bird baths in fire-heated river water, I've never felt more repulsive.

"I laid out a hospital gown, slippers, and toiletries. Toss your dirty clothes in the bin and we'll wash everything for you. There are extra towels in the closet, along with lotion, disposable razors, and a blow-dryer if you're interested. You get freshened up while I deal with your friends."

"Excellent, thanks."

Grace smiles warmly. "You're so welcome, honey. After you get cleaned up, we'll work on getting everyone fed. Fortunately for you kids, we just had a supply delivery this morning, so we have fresh fruit and veggies to offer you."

I quickly latch the door, strip out of my filthy clothes, and toss them into the labeled bin. As I pass in front of a full-length mirror, I freeze at the sight of my battered face. My lower lip is lacerated and swollen like I'd undergone a botched lip-filler procedure. There is also extensive bruising on my cheek and forehead. Sections of my caramel-colored hair are matted to my scalp with dried blood, and the rest of it's a filthy, stringy mess. While I still have my hourglass-shaped figure, my breasts are smaller, and my hips and thighs have slimmed down. I've always been soft around the middle, but even that's flatter. I can't wipe the shocked look from my face at my transformation.

I grab some toiletries, turn on the faucet, and step inside.

Closing my eyes, I lean into the powerful stream of hot water as it flows through my hair, saturating my skin and cascading down my body. This is the most luxurious moment of my entire life. While I lather, the fragrant suds soothe my senses. Heat and steam relax my tired, achy muscles and melt away the tension that accumulated during the recent, merciless weeks. I shampoo my hair, my head falling forward as I rinse. Like a butterfly bursting free from her chrysalis, my metamorphosis from dirty to clean feels soul deep.

Through the thick steam, I watch as blood-tinged water flows down my legs before it circles the drain. The small crimson cyclone funnels down, washing away most of the physical evidence of the ordeal. Too bad the cuts and bruises won't go quietly into the night as well. I condition my hair and loosen any remaining knots and tangles, then get down to business with the razor.

Once satisfied, I dry off and dress in a hospital gown. I stare at my reflection as I floss and brush my teeth.

I'm a new woman—and not just physically. My impromptu Alaskan odyssey was supposed to be an escape from the chaos of New York, or more importantly, a reprieve from my stressful job at the hospital. In some ways, it was. But the universe had other plans when my treacherous journey to self-discovery culminated in falling for Wes.

I don't wear my heart on my sleeve for a reason. While I'm a math and science girl, I can appreciate history for what it is: a lesson. My history has proven love is a fusion of bliss and uncertainty. I learned *that* lesson the hard way.

As someone who operates on the anxious end of the spectrum, I don't do uncertainty well. My mind is quick to bolster my fears and give life to my insecurities, all while trivializing any reassurances. It's something I've been working on for years, but no matter what I do, I can't seem to get a handle on it. The unknown is my nemesis. If there's one thing I know beyond a shadow of a doubt, it's that I don't know shit about shit.

I slide on the hospital-issued slippers before exiting into the hallway.

Grace stands outside a patient room and waves me over. "Feel better?"

"There aren't even words."

"Good thing, since I'm pretty sure ya used up all the water north of the Arctic Circle," Wes calls from inside the room.

"Quiet, you." I wave him off and turn to Grace. "Where do you want me?"

"In here with Mr. Emerson, honey." She motions to the empty bed closest to the window.

His gaze sparkling, a lounging Wes sips from a glass of cranberry juice. He flashes his megawatt smile—the one that makes my knees weak every time. "G'day, roomie."

"Howdy, Ace." I kiss his cheek before flopping onto my bed. "Oh my God, a mattress." My head instantly sinks into the soft comfort of a pillow.

Wes gestures to my hospital gown. "Cute dress."

"Thanks. I scored the modeling contract with my greasy-haired, un-fed appearance."

He snorts. "I'm not allowed to shower until they check out the gash on my noggin, so you're stuck with a smelly Aussie."

"Spent the past few weeks in a tent with you. I think I'll survive." I point to the phone on our shared nightstand. "Did you call your family?"

"Yeah. I spoke with Mum, Dad, and Isla. I forgot about the time dif-ference and woke them up—Melbourne's like twenty hours ahead."

"I think hearing you are alive is an acceptable tradeoff for sleep, wouldn't you agree?"

"Mum and Isla were crying," he murmurs. "Made me get all misty-eyed."

"What about your brother?"

"Cora's mum has taken a turn for the worse, so Reed's at the hospi-tal. I'll call him tomorrow." He points to the phone. "You should call your family."

"I will in a bit."

Dr. Jacobs enters the room with Grace and introduces himself. Tall and fit, with olive skin and thick, dark hair that's slightly graying at the temples, he's the picture of sophistication. Brilliant emerald eyes light up his face.

"Let's get a look at your injuries." He motions to my thigh wound. "This looks good. I may give you some antibiotics just in case."

"She has pretty feet," Wes declares. "Her legs are pretty too."

Grace smiles and touches my arm. "Looks like the morphine's kicking in."

I nod in understanding. He's high as a kite, but I'll take it. Anything is better than knowing he's in agony. Throughout my career, I've tended to dozens of rib fracture patients and I've never encountered anyone as stoic as Wes. His pain tolerance astounds me. If I didn't know any better, I'd think he was superhuman.

"What caused these abrasions?" Dr. Jacobs asks, feathering his gloved fingertips over my thigh.

"I made an unsuccessful attempt to climb a tree. We were being followed by a grizzly, and when I slipped, the tree tore my leg open. It bled a bit, but I kept it wrapped. Unfortunately, the scab kept reopening."

"What about the gash on the side of your head?"

"I fell and hit my head on a rock."

"You do a lot of falling, Ms. Hamilton," Dr. Jacobs muses, examining my wound.

I chuckle. "Sadly, I'm not the picture of gracefulness I'd always hoped to be."

I tried ballet classes when I was a kid. Correction, my mother forced me into dance lessons. The teacher was this old French woman with leathery skin. When it came time for me to do a plié, I landed on my ass. I can still hear her voice. *Sacré bleu! Zat iz not how you plié. Bend at zee knees.* She and I didn't jive.

Dr. Jacobs gently presses on my cheekbone. "How about your facial bruising and split lip? This from one of your falls too?"

I open my mouth to answer, but Wes beats me to it. "I hit her."

Fuck.

Dr. Jacobs's head turns. "I'm sorry, what was that, Mr. Emerson?"

I silently plead for Wes to shut up, but he's oblivious, words pouring from his lips into a pool of self-incrimination. "She lied to the troopers. She told them she fell, but it was my fault. I hit her."

Dr. Jacobs stiffens and slowly turns back to me. His concerned eyes search my face. "Would you like to tell me what happened, Ms. Hamilton?"

I've gone through enough domestic violence training at the hospital to know the drill. This is the part where you ask the patient if they feel safe at home. Wes had unknowingly painted a dark picture of himself.

"We can speak in private if you'd like," Dr. Jacobs offers, mistaking my silence for fear.

I slowly inhale, exhaling like a deflated balloon. "No, here's fine. I know how this looks, but it's not what you think."

"I'm listening." He settles onto the edge of my bed.

"After we pulled him from the river, Wes drifted in and out of consciousness. Given the severity of his injuries, I should've expected him to be agitated when he came to. In any other circumstance, I would've been ready with lorazepam to sedate him."

His eyebrows shoot up. "You're a medical professional?"

"She's a nurse," Wes chimes in.

I jerk my head in his direction. "Wes, you need to keep your damn mouth shut before you make yourself look like a monster."

"I was just—"

I hold up a hand to silence him, then turn back to Dr. Jacobs. "I'm a trauma nurse in the ER at New York General in Manhattan. As I was saying, I should've expected his actions, but I was so relieved he was alive, my years of training went out the window. He backed away from us like a cornered animal."

"Then what happened?"

"Like an idiot, I tried to comfort him, but he came out swinging. He hit my shoulder and as I scrambled to get away, he struck my mouth too. Austin dove on top of him and Jake yanked me from the tent. You can confirm all this with them, by the way. When Wes was finally lucid, he had no clue what had happened to him and no recollection of attacking me. Once Austin told him about it, he became extremely distraught."

"You lied to the police?"

"Yes. And I'll tell you why. Wes is a good man. He selflessly put my life before his own on more than one occasion. Hurting me—or any other woman—is the last thing he'd ever do. It devastated him to learn what happened to my face. Obviously, he *still* hasn't forgiven himself." I glare at Wes. "He's an idiot like that." My eyes connect with Dr. Jacobs's again. "I'm fine. It was a fight-or-flight moment, and I was in the line of fire. I don't feel threatened by him, and I forgave him the moment it happened. I told Trooper Mayfield I fell because the last thing I wanted was the media to get ahold of the police report and twist Wes into an abusive man."

"You were protecting him." Dr. Jacobs nods in understanding. "Makes sense to me."

I turn and meet Wes's gaze. "Yes, because just like he'd never hurt me, I would never do anything to damage his reputation or threaten his career."

"Oh . . ." Wes murmurs. "I'm a bloody fuckwit."

"Normally I wouldn't condone lying to the authorities, but given the widespread media coverage of his disappearance, I think you made a wise decision. The tabloids would've eaten that up—especially with his next movie coming out soon. I can almost see the headlines, 'Hollywood A-lister Attacks Woman Who Saved His Life.'"

Exactly.

"So, you're not gonna rat me out?" I ask cautiously.

Dr. Jacobs smiles. "No, I'm not. I would've done the same for someone I cared about. Besides . . . HIPAA." He winks and pats my knee. I've never been so thankful for the privacy laws which govern health-care professionals and now keep our conversation safe.

Dr. Jacobs moves toward Wes's bed. "All right, Mr. Emerson, you're in rough shape. Let me see that shoulder."

I grab a magazine from the tray table and find Wes, Jake, and Austin on the cover. The issue features multi-page coverage of their disappearance. I scan the article and gasp when I discover my name in print.

Alaska State Troopers have located the bush plane chartered by Australian actor Wes Emerson, singer Jake Bennett, and pop star Austin Pines. The plane crashed seventy miles northwest of Fairbanks, a path nowhere near the one indicated by the flight plan.

Preliminary reports suggest bush pilot Charles MacGregor suffered an in-flight heart attack after leaving the passengers at an unknown location in the Brooks Mountain Range. New York trauma nurse, Lena Hamilton, 32, is also among the missing. Her association with the celebs is currently unknown.

Great, now everyone and their mother will be up in my business.

"You've got extensive bruising on your collarbone. I'm wondering if that's fractured. We'll get some x-rays to check. Ms. Hamilton, what type of dislocation did he have?"

I barely glance up from the article. "An anterior dislocation. Jake and Austin assisted with the relocation. The shoulder had begun to spasm, so we sat him up. Jake supported his torso and Austin applied traction to the arm while I used the scapular manipulation technique. An audible clunk accompanied the glenoid fossa's return."

"I love when she talks medicine," Wes swoons.

I roll my eyes before continuing, "I tested his range of motion and checked for numbness or tingling. He denied both."

"Never said I wasn't tingling." Wes waggles his brows.

I smile at Dr. Jacobs. "How much morphine did you give him?"

"He's opiate-naïve, but he's a big guy. I opted for mid-range dosing. Gave him seven point five milligrams."

"Excuse me?" Wes's face morphs into one of disbelief. "I'm not naïve."

"Jesus, does anyone have a gag?" I ask with a chuckle.

Wes leans forward and grins. "And here I thought you were joking about the whips and chains . . ."

"Keep it up, Wes."

"I don't have any issues in that department, love."

I can only shake my head at that truth bomb. Besides, I know better than to engage him right now.

"You kinda set yourself up for that one." Dr. Jacobs chuckles and checks the wound on Wes's head. "This looks great. No sign of infection. Nice work, Ms. Hamilton. I'm curious about how you learned shoulder reduction techniques."

I shrug. "My ex is an orthopedic surgeon. We work together."

"I don't like him." Wes curls his lip, and his eyes go squinty. "He's a real fuckwit."

"You don't even know Marc. You should thank him; otherwise, your arm would still be flopping around," I counter.

"All right, moving on to the ribs," Dr. Jacobs interjects with a grin. "Extensive bruising, several palpable fractures . . ." He listens to Wes's lungs with the stethoscope. "Lungs sound like they have some fluid. We'll confirm that with radiology and get you started on antibiotics. If this is the start of pneumonia, I want to nip it in the bud." He turns to me and I set the magazine down in my lap. "You performed chest compressions?"

"I did chest compressions and rescue breathing. Lost track of how many cycles. It didn't look good for a while . . . My colleagues would've called it, but I just couldn't." I swallow tightly, blinking back the tears threatening to spill over.

"Your persistence saved his life. You're a lucky man, Mr. Emerson."

"I know." Wes looks at Dr. Jacobs and gestures to me. "Isn't she beautiful?"

"Yes, she's a beautiful woman."

"She's mine," he growls. "I'm keeping her."

Dr. Jacobs grins. "I'm glad to hear that."

Wes cocks his head to the side in confusion. "Hear what?"

I finally succumb to the urge to laugh. "How about five milligrams next time, doc?"

Dr. Jacobs chuckles on his way out the door. "Duly noted."

"Do ya know what I wanna do to her?" Wes asks Grace.

Grace laughs. "No, but are you sure it's something you should be telling your nurse?"

"Why wouldn't it be?"

His indignant tone makes me snort. "Jesus, and *I'm* the one without a filter? Wes, do yourself a favor and zip it."

"I want to feed her," he announces. "I would feed Lena all kinds of food." He makes the declaration like it's part of his presidential campaign. Completely ignoring my advice, he continues, "I'd feed her pomegranates, bacon, and sausage. But real sausage. Not mine."

Grace laughs harder. "You're killing me, honey."

"I think she'd love Anzac biscuits and fairy bread too . . ." His voice trails off like he's caught in a reverie.

What the actual fuck is fairy bread, and where can I get some?

Grace motions to Wes. "Well, I was going to let you shower, but I'm afraid you'll get lost in the linen closet. I'll grab a basin and clean you up here."

"Oh, a sponge bath? That's bloody fabulous." Wes's eyes light up in mischief. "Hey, Lena's a nurse, she can do it."

Grace pats his shoulder. "I'm sorry, but I can't allow that."

He sticks out his lower lip in the cutest pout I've ever seen. "Why not?"

"It's my job as your nurse to take care of you. That's what I get paid for."

Wes is thankfully quiet for a moment before he perks up again. "Oh! I have an idea. How about I pay you to let Lena do it?"

"That brings me to my next reason. Something tells me you'd enjoy it too much if Lena were to bathe you." She winks and pinches his cheek before leaving the room.

"Damn right, I would." He sits up and motions to me. "Sunshine, can ya wash me sometime?"

"Sure, Ace. Maybe some other time," I placate him. "I'll even let you pick out the bubble bath."

Grace returns a few minutes later with a basin full of warm water and a washcloth. She gently cleans Wes's face and shampoos his hair. He babbles the entire time. They cover topics from kangaroos to wallabies and pumpkin patches. She finishes rinsing Wes's hair and towel dries it. "All right, mister. It's x-ray time. Come sit in this wheelchair."

"I can walk."

"Get in the chair, Wes," I command without looking up from my magazine.

"She's bossy sometimes," he stage-whispers, settling into the wheelchair.

"Because she knows what's best for you, dear."

Grace wheels him from the room, and I seize the opportunity to call my family. I dial my parents, but it goes to voicemail. Tears fill my eyes at the sound of Mom's voice. I choke out a message before I call Garrett.

"Hello?" My best friend's voice is gruff, deeper than usual.

I smile into the receiver. "Hey, good-lookin', what's cookin'?"

"Fuck . . . is it really you? Lena . . . my God . . . you're all right?" The questions tumble from his lips. "Oh my God, I thought I'd lost you . . . I thought—"

Garrett isn't usually overly emotional, so his strangled whisper brings tears to my eyes. They spill over as I speak, "Don't worry, I'm safe now. We're in a health facility getting checked out. They're bringing us back to the resort tomorrow or the next day, and then I'll be heading home."

Something crashes in the background. "Fuck. Hold on, I dropped my coffee." A rustling sound and several muttered curses follow.

"You all right, Gar?"

"Yeah, burned my thigh, but I'm good. I can't believe I'm hearing your voice. I love you so much."

"I love you too, Gar."

"I'm so sorry I talked you into that trip. Had I known—" His voice cracks.

"Gar, stop. Please don't blame yourself for anything that happened to me."

"But you wouldn't have gone if I hadn't pushed you." His tone tells me the guilt has been eating him alive. "Are you hurt?"

"Got some bumps and bruises, but for the most part, I'm fine. Our pilot changed our destination and then had a heart attack on his way back to the airfield. He never got the chance to tell anyone where we were." Remembering something the state troopers said, I straighten. "They never would've found us if it weren't for you."

"Yeah, but I—"

"*You* gave the police some clues about me that steered their search toward nature preserves. You helped them rescue us, so I don't wanna hear another thing about it, okay?"

His low chuckle warms me. "I didn't think it was possible, but you're feistier than when you left."

Garrett has seen me through my lowest of lows, so he's acutely familiar with my feistiness spectrum—and the total "absence of feist" when life gets to be too much. He'll forever be my rock, but I guess I took it for granted that he needs me too.

"You have no idea what I've dealt with." I wipe my cheeks. "I'll tell you everything when I get home. As soon as I know any details, I'll call you. Do you think you can pick me up at the airport?"

"Of course. Keep me posted. I love you so fucking much, Leens."

"Love you more, Gar. Bye."

I hang up and head next door to check on the other guys. Padding to their room, I pause in the doorway. Jake is sound asleep, hooked up to an IV bag.

I meet Austin's gaze and whisper, "What's that about?"

"They said he's dehydrated."

I nod, not at all surprised. Throughout our adventure, I frequently needed to remind Jake to drink. "How are you holding up?" I ask, approaching Austin's bedside. "Did you call your family?"

"I'm doin' all right, but I feel kinda weak and tired. I just got off the phone with Katie." He smiles and looks me over. "What did they say about your injuries?"

"Funny you should ask. Wes announced to everyone that he hit me, so that was fun."

His eyes widen. "Oh, fuck."

"Yeah, but don't worry. I took care of it."

"How's he holdin' up? He still in pain?"

"Currently, he's being x-rayed, but they've got him doped up on morphine. Hence the self-incrimination." I shake my head. "Austin, I gotta tell you, that man amazes me with his pain tolerance."

"He's always been pretty tough."

"This goes beyond tough. With my job, I've seen more rib fractures than I care to admit, and while I'm fortunate to have never dealt with one personally, I know they're *agony*. Patients have compared it to feeling like they're being stabbed with each breath."

Austin winces. "Damn."

"Right. Now I just need to make sure he follows all his discharge instructions when they let us leave."

He grins. "Don't you worry, baby girl. Me and Jake will ride his ass about it."

I squeeze his shoulder. "Knew I could count on you." I point to Jake. "Let me know when he wakes."

"Will do."

"All right, I'm heading back to my room. See ya."

"Later, darlin'."

Grace and Wes return a half hour later. His shoulder's perfect, his lungs have fluid in them, and as suspected, he has four fractured ribs and a hairline collarbone fracture. Grace inserts an IV into his left hand and hooks up a bag of fluids and antibiotics. She brings us turkey sandwiches and chocolate pudding, which we devour.

It's nearing nightfall and I'm fading fast. Thankfully, Wes is also losing steam. He quietly stares at his hands and picks at the tape that secures the IV.

"Don't do that."

Ignoring my reprimand, he continues to pick. "It's pulling on my hairs."

"You're gonna have to deal."

He gives me the side-eye. "Why're ya grumpy?"

"I'm exhausted."

"Then close your eyes and sleep, love."

I instinctively arch a brow. "I can't relax and sleep if I'm worried about you pulling your IV out."

"Okay, I'll stop. Sadly, no one's pulling anything out tonight." His devious grin stirs up memories of our sexy times together, and my body reacts instantly.

"No comment." I feel a smirk pull at my lips.

"Hey, sunshine?"

"Yeah?"

"I wanna kiss ya goodnight. Just not tonight."

"That's fine, Wes. Go to sleep."

"No, I said that upside-down." He furrows his brow, trying so hard to seem lucid. "I'm keepin' ya. And I wanna kiss you goodnight *every* night, not just tonight."

I meet his gaze. His cheeks are flushed, and his eyes shine a vibrant dark blue.

"We can start tomorrow if you'd like. That is, if you remember this conversation."

I would have flung myself into his arms and kissed him into oblivion if he'd made that commitment—hell, *any* commitment—while not under the influence.

"Sunshine, I love you."

"Love you too, Ace."

He melts my heart, even in his morphine-induced stupor. His slow, rhythmic breathing tells me when he's fallen asleep. I'm relieved he can finally rest without being assailed by pain.

God, I love him beyond words. What will happen now that we're back in civilization? We live on different continents and our lifestyles are worlds apart. Will he return to Australia or stay in New York for a while?

I know he has contractual promo events in Los Angeles that are scheduled for October and November. *The Aegean* will release in mid-November, so there will be interviews, appearances on late-night shows, and of course, the premiere. I can't help but wonder how it will all play out.

Will he still be part of my life? I can't fathom saying goodbye.

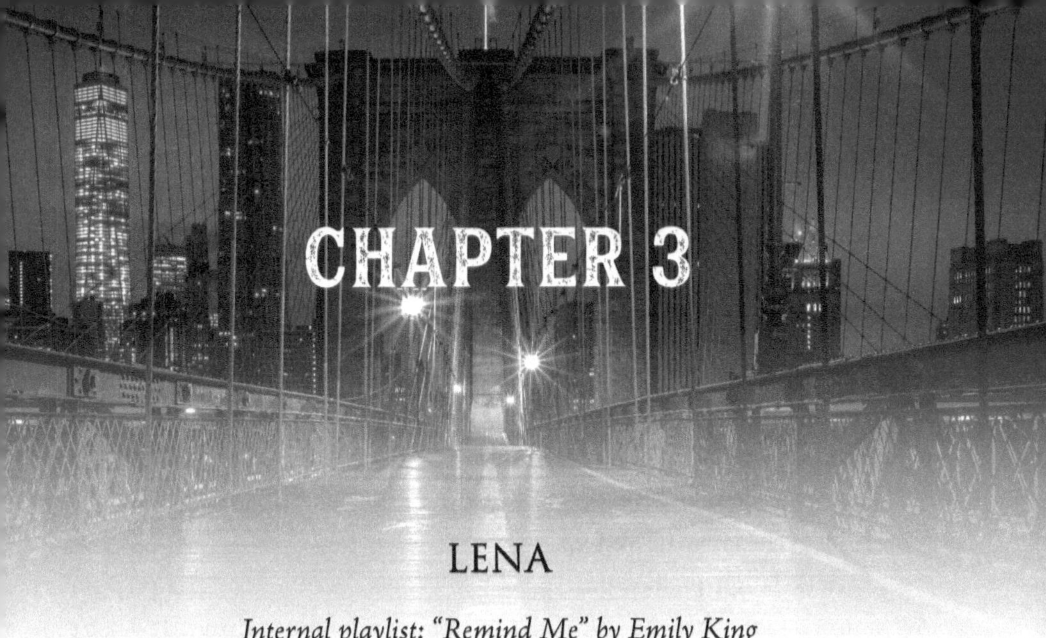

CHAPTER 3

LENA

Internal playlist: "Remind Me" by Emily King

I awaken the next morning to sunlight filtering through the blinds. I stretch and glance at Wes's empty bed. I didn't hear him get up, but then again, once I'd finally fallen asleep, I was comatose.

Maybe he's showering. My eyes flutter closed, and I allow my mind to take me on a sensual journey. Rivulets of water and soap suds sliding down his bare chest, over his rippling abdomen, and lower . . .

"Having a good dream?"

My eyes fly open and there he is at my bedside holding two steaming mugs of coffee. "Good morning. Strong, no sugar, with just a little cream." He smiles as he places one mug on my tray table. "I checked for caramel syrup, but they didn't have any."

My mouth drops open. "You remembered I like caramel?"

"I remember every detail about you, love." He cocks his head to the side. "Why ya givin' me a funny look?"

My gaze shifts to my mug as I shake my head. "It's nothing."

He softly strokes my cheek, and my eyes meet his. "Talk to me, sunshine."

"I guess it surprised me, that's all."

He sits on the edge of my bed. "Why would that surprise ya?"

"A history of forgotten details," I mutter. "But that doesn't matter now."

Wes nods, understanding immediately what I'm talking about. "He's a knob jockey. A total fuckwad."

"Yeah." I pick at my nails. "It was one thing to forget date night . . ."

"Whaddya mean?"

"I mean, sitting alone at a table reserved for two." I shake my head bitterly. "I remember forcing a smile, telling myself he'd be there. Like, maybe he'd gotten held up in surgery, or maybe there was traffic, or maybe his car wouldn't start. He didn't need to make his own excuses because I'd already made them for him." I sip my coffee and my eyes close in satisfaction. "This is perfect, thank you."

"You're welcome, love." Wes's warm hand touches my cheek. "Please tell me he eventually showed up."

A dark laugh pushes past my lips. "Nope. I remember the pity on the waiter's face when he informed me he'd comped my drink. It wasn't the embarrassment that got me, though. After a couple hours, I left the restaurant and went over to Marc's place."

"Was he home?"

"Yep. Lounging on the couch watching a baseball game." I roll my eyes.

"Seriously?"

"Dead serious. So, I stood there, fighting back tears. He was like, 'They're tied right now. May run into an extra inning.' There was no comment about my new dress, my haircut, any of that."

"What a dick!"

"So, I said, 'Marc, did you forget something?' and he kinda stared at me for a minute. Then it finally clicked. He didn't even try to make an excuse. I went home and cried."

"You should've given the ring back right then and there."

I look away, embarrassment softening my voice. "He hadn't given it to me yet."

"Are you *serious?* You agreed to marry the fucker *after* he treated you that way?"

"Like I told you, I was stupid for years. Finally got my shit together these past nine months."

"I'm shocked. When was this in relation to the proposal?"

"About a month before it. He proposed on Thanksgiving of last year." I wrap a strand of hair around my finger, unwrapping it just as quickly. "I feel like most women are overjoyed when someone proposes to them. I felt . . . dread . . . shame, even. I couldn't tell Garrett."

"You didn't tell him you'd gotten engaged?"

"Not right away, no. I was afraid of his reaction." I shrug at my lack of explanation.

"What *was* his reaction?"

"When I finally went over there, I wasn't wearing my ring. I sat him down and before I could say a word, he said, 'If you're here to ask for my blessing, I'll give it under one condition.' I asked what his condition was, and he said, 'Look me in the eyes right now and *swear* to me you're happy. Swear to me you want to live the rest of your life like this. If you can honestly say that, then you have my blessing.' I couldn't do it." I sigh and shake my head. "I was so pissed at him."

"Because you knew he was right?"

"Yeah. Part of me hoped Garrett would convince me I was doing the right thing by marrying Marc. Instead, he solidified what I'd known for ages—I wasn't happy. It was the slap in the face I needed, yet I was *still* too afraid to do anything. Would you believe Marc forgot my birthday last year? When I mentioned it, I was told it 'slipped his mind.'"

His brows pop up. "You're kidding me, right? Christmas Eve slipped his mind?"

"Apparently."

"Is that what finally did it for ya?"

"Yeah, that was my official breaking point. Christmas came. I kept waiting, thinking maybe he had something planned for my birthday. Even a dollar store card would've made me happy. Nope. Nothing. Then he was pissed that it hurt my feelings. I went to his place the day after Christmas and gathered up all my stuff. I spent a couple days downstairs eating ice cream on Garrett's couch and that was that."

"Jesus Christ, Lena."

"I know. So, can you understand why your attentiveness surprises me sometimes?"

Wes grips my chin and turns my head to face him. "I am *not* Marc."

"I know that, Wes," I whisper. "You're nothing like him. I guess I'm still getting used to feeling like I matter." I swallow hard against the lump forming in my throat. "You're so perfect. Sometimes it feels like you're too good to be true. I'm afraid I'm imagining you or this is some dream I'll wake from. My head tries to tell me I don't deserve you—"

"You deserve to be worshiped, loved, and respected. And I'll do *all* those things." He runs his fingers through my hair. "I love you, Lena. Even if it takes years, I promise to make you understand that. I'm not going anywhere, sunshine." His warm hands cup my face, and he kisses me, soft and sweet.

"I love you, Wes."

The pad of his thumb brushes against my lower lip. "Did ya sleep well?"

"Yes. How about you? Where's your IV?" I ask, noticing the absence of tape on his hand.

"I slept great, and Dr. Jacobs said I can take oral antibiotics."

"How's your pain?"

"About a six out of ten right now."

"I can't believe you're up walking around." I shake my head. "Rib fractures are agonizing."

"C'mon, love, you know me better than that—my legs still work. You think a little rib pain's gonna stop me?"

"You'd classify a six out of ten as a *little* pain?"

"Well, it was a twenty-three when it first happened, so yeah. Grace gave me a Toradol injection this morning. She said they'll discharge me with a few days' worth of pills and then after that, I can alternate between acetaminophen and ibuprofen. One thing's for certain—I'm not taking that other shit again." He shakes his head. "I felt like I was on a different planet."

"You were amusing." I chuckle at the memory. "At least you won't remember your antics."

"Oh, I remember them." He shoots me a sly smile. "I knew what was coming out of my mouth even though I couldn't control it. That must be how Jake feels with his lack of filter."

"There's no way you remember all that." I laugh. "You were hilarious, inappropriate, and thoughtful all at the same time. You almost got me in trouble with the cops and got yourself booked for domestic violence."

"I'm sorry. I didn't mean to make ya uncomfortable. And yes, I do remember everything I said."

"Don't apologize. It was funny." I brush my hair off my face and take another large sip. I can feel Wes's eyes burning a hole through me. "What?"

"You look beautiful this morning." His voice is soft, thoughtful, and the emotion in his eyes matches his tone.

Heat rises from my neck to my cheeks, thinking of my bruised face. *He's insane and blind, apparently.* "Thank you."

He slowly leans forward and presses his lips to my neck. My breath leaves in a rush as his mouth moves over my skin.

Kissing his way to my jaw, he whispers, "You owe me a goodnight kiss from last night. But I'm willing to accept a good morning kiss in its place."

Lips meeting mine, his thumbs brush my cheeks. I weave my hands into his hair and kiss him back. Every nerve ending in my body zings to life. All too quickly, he breaks off the kiss.

"Like I said, I remember." He straightens and sets his empty mug on the tray table. "I'm gonna shower now, love." He flashes me a broad smile before leaving the room.

I fall against my pillow, my lips still tingling from his kiss. How can he be so devastatingly sensual? How can he be so perfect? Does he really remember the things he'd said? We were alone in the room last night, so the only explanation is that he did, in fact, remember it all. Which means he intended to profess his commitment to kiss me goodnight . . . "not just tonight, but every night."

"Good morning, dear. Are you hungry?" I glance up and see Grace moving around the room.

"Good morning. I'm fine right now, thank you."

"All right, but make sure you eat something before the troopers arrive. Trooper Mayfield said they'd be here around ten to ask a few questions about the pilot. He said to tell you not to worry, that it's standard procedure. Then we'll work on getting you back to Aurora Borealis. Their concierge will make arrangements for your trip home," Grace says before she leaves the room.

I lift the blinds and stare out the window. I'm still mildly nervous about meeting the troopers. Hopefully, Wes will keep his mouth shut this time.

Speak of the Devil . . . I cock my head to the side. "You're back. I thought you were going to shower?"

Wes approaches my bedside with a shit-eating grin and both hands behind his back. "I am."

Not trusting what he's up to, I raise an eyebrow. "What's behind your back?"

I lean over to look, but he pivots. "Wouldn't you like to know."

"Wes, if you brought a spider in here, there's going to be a problem."

"No spiders." He shakes his head. "Won't make that mistake again."

"Then, what do you have?"

"Hungry, sunshine?" Eyes never leaving my face, he steps closer and drops a cluster of grapes onto my tray table. "They didn't have pomegranates," he explains, plucking a large one from the bunch. "So, these will have to do."

I blink, shocked he remembers his food dissertation from last night.

He holds a grape in front of my lips. "You took care of me, so now it's my turn to feed you. Open your mouth."

Heat shoots through my core at the command in his voice. I love when he takes a bossy tone, because it gives me an opportunity to push his buttons. I press my lips together in a sultry smirk of defiance.

"Always fighting me, sunshine . . ." Wes leans down and brushes his lips over my ear. "I'll let ya win later, but this round's mine." He strokes the side of my face with his thumb. "Open. *Now.*" My lips part, and he gently places the grape into my mouth. "Eat."

I bite into the plump, succulent fruit and its sweet juices fill my mouth. "Mmm . . ."

He smirks. "Taste good?"

My heart thumps against my chest. "Yes."

"Good. Keep eating. You'll need your energy for later." He flashes a wicked grin and leaves the room without another word.

I will never see grapes in the same light again. His words echo in my mind while I reach for another. The command in his tone, the intensity of his eyes. He looked like he wanted to devour me. Arousal floods my core at the thought of his lips on my body, his tongue tantalizing, tasting.

I can't wait until his body is healed.

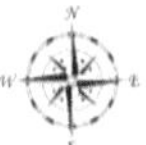

My mouth falls open as Wes saunters into the room after his shower. Clean-shaven and damp-haired, he's wearing his jeans that the hospital washed, and a snug-fitting white scrub top that molds to the muscles of his chest and shoulders. His attire is simple, but he simply cannot be sexier. He grins, and suddenly I lose the ability to think.

He winces as he slides his belt through the loops of his jeans. "Enjoying your grapes?"

"Yes, I've had a few, but for some reason, the first one tasted better."

My eyes dart to his jawline, his lips. Wes was ruggedly sexy with facial hair, but without it, he's a fucking Adonis. Looking at him right now, all gorgeous and perfect, is like seeing him for the first time. He's not the goofy guy who kissed me under the stars, he's Wes Emerson, Hollywood heartthrob. As my insecurities float to the surface, my chest tightens with a mixture of starstruck longing and deep familiarity.

He's mine. *For now.* How long will I get to keep him?

"How was your shower?" I ask distractedly.

"Glorious. I just made love to a bar of soap. I've never felt better."

"Lucky soap. When's my turn?" Never have I wanted to be soap that badly, to caress him, slide against his body.

He runs his fingers through my hair. "Soon, love." He plucks a grape from the cluster. "Shall we continue?"

This time, I automatically open my mouth for him and allow my lips and tongue to caress his fingertips. His gaze flares with a carnal intensity that steals my breath. No one has ever looked at me the way he does.

"Lena, my self-control's hanging by a thread, so I'd be careful with that eager mouth."

"Why?" I gaze up at him and lick the juice from my bottom lip. "Do you have something for it?"

"Damn right, I do," he growls.

My gaze comes to rest on his belt buckle. After weeks of partially clothed, stealth-mode sex, I can't wait to strip him naked in privacy. Of course, I'll need to be careful with him for at least six weeks, if not longer, judging by the winces he keeps trying to stifle. "Did I ever tell you I hate belts?"

"In general?"

"Personally, I don't like wearing them because they're too constrictive." I brush my fingertips over his belt buckle. "In your case, it has something to do with keeping your pants on."

"You undressing me with your eyes?"

"Maybe."

"Good." He steps closer to my bedside and rolls his hips for impact. The motion makes my nipples harden, lady bits quiver and clench, and him wince.

"You okay, babe?"

"Yeah." He chuckles. "Just don't sign me up for any dancing contests until I'm fully healed. Either way, my injuries can fuck off." He settles on the edge of the bed and brings his lips to my ear. "Because when I finally get you alone, that arse is *mine*."

"Or so you think."

"Oh, trust me, I *know*."

"We'll see about that." Feeling seductive, I slide my bare legs from beneath the sheet. "Are you hungry, Wes?"

"That's a loaded question." His gaze greedily wanders the length of my body as he rests against the pillows. "Do wolves howl at the moon?"

"I'm gonna take that as a yes."

"My answer for you is always yes."

"Good." I pluck two grapes from the cluster. "Now, open up." His lips part and I feed one to him. I pop the other grape into my mouth and bite down. "Sharing is caring," I murmur, leaning in to kiss him.

He groans as our lips and tongues meld, the sweet juices intensifying the kiss. After a few moments, I pull back. "We can't get too carried away until you're healed, but I promise you'll be the one howling."

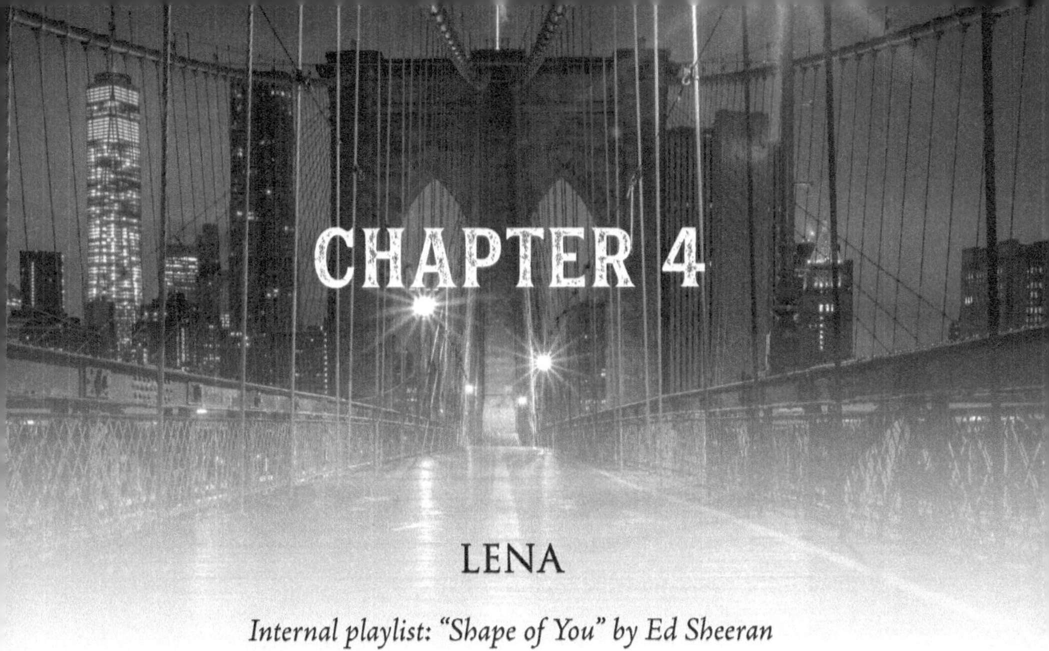

CHAPTER 4

LENA

Internal playlist: "Shape of You" by Ed Sheeran

I clutch the armrest between Wes and me during takeoff. After our meeting with the troopers, and Dr. Jacobs gave us the all-clear for discharge, our group prepared for the flight back to the Aurora Borealis Resort—the place where it all started.

Wes's warm palm settles atop my hand and squeezes. "Relax, love. We're on the home stretch now."

I nod, but I can't relax until both my feet are firmly on the ground. Unfortunately, my entire viewpoint on flying has forever been altered.

After a couple hours in the air, I can finally see the lodge in the distance. It seems like ages since we were there. I've learned a lot can change in three weeks' time—including the seasons. Gone are the reds, burnished golds, and yellows that greeted us upon our arrival. Now, the tundra grasses glisten with frost and a blanket of snow covers the trees. The Brooks Range looms in an ominous reminder of all we endured. The plane lands in a field and everyone disembarks.

In August, when we first arrived at the exclusive lodge, we were the only guests. Since our original two-week reservations were at the tail end of their season, it wasn't a hardship to store our belongings in our rooms while we were missing. Aurora Borealis has since closed for winter, but management insists on accommodating us while we finalize our travel itineraries. We'll make our journeys home sometime tomorrow or the following day, depending on flight schedules.

Resort staff wait at the clearing with a large golf cart. We all pile on and ride to the lodge in relative silence. The resort's concierge, Ellen, meets us at the door and leads us inside.

The aroma of freshly baked bread and pies makes my mouth water. Ellen informs us the kitchen is preparing a feast for dinner this evening. She lists off filet mignon, lobster tails, and various sides.

I grin at her. "You had me at the meat. I'm looking forward to it."

Wes flashes a cheeky smirk. "That's what she said."

Austin rolls his eyes. Jake snorts and shakes his head.

"Everything should be ready around five, so if you want to relax in your rooms until then, you have plenty of time to do so," Ellen says with a smile.

"I could use a shower. See you guys in a bit." I trudge upstairs, the weight of our ordeal making my limbs heavy.

Turning the knob to my room, I enter into the lap of luxury. It's incredible what a queen-size bed—with a real mattress—can do for one's spirits.

I spend a blissful fifteen minutes in the bathroom, under the hot stream. After drying off, I slide the plush robe over my still-pink skin and tie the belt. I pad into my room while I towel dry my hair.

I've always been one of those women who hates blow-dryers. Even in the dead of winter, I'll venture outside with damp hair. Throughout my childhood, my mother would ride me about it, but I have my reasons. For one, my hair is thick, so it takes forever to dry. I just don't have the patience required. Also, the motion aggravates my old shoulder injury—something I try to avoid when possible. Not to mention, it's a waste of electricity.

A knock sounds on the door.

I toss the towel onto the bed and flip my damp hair behind me. "Just a second." I open the door to find Wes in the hallway, holding the twisted sling. "Hey, Ace."

He holds out the sling, pain written across his beautiful face. "This fucking thing's already pissing me off."

I study the tangled mess, making no move to take it from him. "What the hell did you do to it?"

"I dunno." He sighs.

I motion for him to enter my room. "Give it to me."

He follows, closing the door. "Been a while since I've heard you say that."

I peer up at him in time to see his signature smirk. "You're injured, Ace."

He drops the sling onto my bed with a muted thud. "What does that have to do with anything?"

"It means I'm not gonna let you overdo it."

"Doesn't have to be a tango," he murmurs, moving closer. "We can waltz."

I press a finger to the middle of his chest, halting his movement. "I already told you, I don't waltz."

"If we can't dance," he reaches for the belt of my robe, "then at least let me see that luscious body of yours."

My fingers curl over his. "Can you control yourself?"

He grins. "Of course not."

"I'll let you look, but that's it. *Your* body needs to heal."

He unties the belt, slides the robe off my shoulders, and tosses it onto the bed. "Turn around."

I slowly turn in a circle. Two months ago, if someone told me I'd be standing butt naked in front of Wes Emerson, I would've died laughing. Even getting to meet him would have seemed like an impossibility. But here he is in *my* room, admiring *my* ass cheeks, while his cock tents the material of his jeans.

"That arse," he says, his voice husky. "God, I want you." He strokes his fingers through the wetness between my thighs, making me gasp. "And you want me too."

Understatement of the fucking millennium.

"Tell you what, Ace," I turn to face him and flatten both hands on his chest, "how about I help with the healing process?"

I back him to the door and reach for his belt. Meeting his gaze, I slowly pull the leather from the loops and unzip his jeans. "Relax and let me love you."

CHAPTER 5

WES EMERSON

Life lesson: I've been worshiping the wrong deity.

Air refuses to fill my lungs as Lena shoves my jeans and boxers down, springing my erection free. She slowly sinks to her knees. Her heated gaze locks with mine as she brushes her lips over the head of my cock and swirls her tongue through the bead of moisture at the tip.

In one smooth motion, she takes me to the back of her throat.

My hips jerk. "Oh, *fuck*."

She moves with one hand gripping my shaft while the other cups my balls.

"God, Lena," I groan. "Your tongue feels so good . . ."

My breath comes in harsh bursts as I watch her suck me. Head bobbing, her tongue rubs the underside and flicks over the tip. I can't control the moans and groans that leave my chest. I weave my hands into her hair and grip the silken strands. She hollows out her cheeks and sucks me harder.

"Yes . . . just like that, love."

Her eyes never leave mine. With her hands, lips, and tongue, she brings me to the edge faster than I would have liked. Legs shaking, it's all I can do to remain upright.

"You gotta stop." Gasping, I push her head back. "I'm gonna come."

Of course, she doesn't listen. Instead, she brushes my hand away and increases her pace and suction.

"Oh, *fuck*." My cock pulses, then releases. "Lena . . ." She keeps going until she milks every last drop of my sanity. Until I can't take it another second.

"Feel better?" she asks, pulling back with a smile.

"I'll tell ya right now, sunshine—"

A loud knock rattles the door.

"Lena-Bean, you coming down for dinner?"

Fucking cock-block Bennett.

Lena smirks. "In a minute, Jake."

"Okay, see you there." Luckily, his footsteps retreat down the hall.

I grip Lena's shoulders and haul her to her feet. "Injured or not, I'm gonna give it to ya after dinner."

With four broken ribs, I don't know how I'll do it, but I'll die if I can't be inside her soon.

Note to self: load up on pain meds before dinner.

She wipes her mouth and flashes a sultry smile. "We'll see about that one, Ace."

"There will be no seeing, love." I grip her shoulders. "Just fucking."

She shakes her head. "Once again, I'll remind you you're injured. I honestly don't know how you're walking around right now."

"Even if they'd put me in a full-body cast, you'd be in my bed tonight."

CHAPTER 6

LENA

Internal playlist: "Lioness" by Sarah Fimm

Blow jobs are like riding a bike. I was way out of practice, but as soon as I gripped his handlebar, my skills resurrected themselves. Now the training wheels are off, and my sparkly streamers are blowing in the wind. Knowing I pleased Wes so much satisfies me. His desire for me makes me feel like a goddess, and his growled warning turned me on. Now, I just need to make it through dinner without combusting.

I choose a jade dress from my suitcase and step into it. Though it's a looser fit, the delicate fabric still hugs my curves and accentuates my breasts. I slip into my favorite black, knee-high boots and study my flushed reflection in the mirror.

My hair cascades over my shoulders and down my back. Other than my bruised face, I look pretty damn good. *Thank you, Garrett.* He forced me to pack the dress. Am I overdressed? Probably. Do I care? No, not one bit.

I sashay down the hallway, then descend the stairs to the great room like a puma in heat, my movements slow and deliberately sensual.

Eat your heart out, Ace.

The three men gape at me. I smile coyly as I approach the table and purposefully take the seat across from Wes, who is staring hard. His expression is raw, his desire far from secret. Wanton heat courses through my body, and I press my thighs together at the flood of arousal. Without fail, I could change panties after less than one minute in his presence.

"Hot damn, li'l lady," Austin drawls.

"Looking pretty fancy there, Lena-Bean."

"Wes inspired this outfit," I quip. "Plus, my jeans no longer fit. It was this or a bathrobe."

"Well, it suits you." Jake sips his ale. "Don't you think so, Emerson?"

Wes studies me for a moment but doesn't say anything. He doesn't have to, though. His eyes do the talking as they roam over my body, down the column of my neck to the curve of my breasts. His gaze is so intense, I can practically feel his hands caress every inch of me.

Jake chuckles. "You gonna answer my question or sit there and eye-fuck her?"

"The latter." Wes flashes a wicked grin. "And the bathrobe would've been preferable."

Two resort staff approach with freshly baked rolls and butter. They inform us the meal will be served shortly.

Wes snatches a roll, breaks it apart with his fingertips, and spreads a generous amount of butter on both halves. While his friends aren't looking, he gives me a lewd reminder of his intentions and deliberately drags his tongue through the butter, eyes never leaving my face. *Holy fuck.* I bite my lip to contain the moan that wants to burst free.

The chef appears with a platter of filet mignon, which he places on the buffet table. Lobster tails, rice pilaf, and several other sides follow. Once the kitchen staff leaves, Jake and Austin rush toward the food table, loading their plates with generous helpings of everything.

I slowly rise and approach the table after Jake and Austin return. Wes pursues me, stalking like I'm his prey. With a shaky breath, I stab a piece of filet with my fork. It's hard to think with him so close, but somehow, I place the tender, juicy meat on my plate and reach for the serving spoon in the rice.

I feel Wes's body heat directly behind me. He lingers for a moment, then grabs my waist and pulls me against him.

His erection presses into my back as his lips find the shell of my ear. "Load up that plate, sunshine, because you're gonna need your energy." He slides his hand to the juncture of my thighs. "Tonight, this is *mine.*"

Before I can react, he releases me and fills his plate as if nothing happened. I can't move, frozen in place with lust. Glancing over, he smirks and piles another piece of filet onto my plate, then leads me back to the table with a warm palm at the small of my back. His fingertips brush the upper curve of my ass and squeeze. Then, he lightly slaps the other cheek. No one sees it happen, but I feel it down to my toes.

An inferno of lust consumes me. I want nothing more than for him to strip me naked, toss me over his knee, and spank me . . . ravage me . . . fuck me senseless.

Broken ribs, my brain reminds me.

Taking a deep breath to cool my senses, I slide into my seat and drape a napkin over my lap.

Austin holds up his glass. "Here's to our survival, our resilience, and our friendship. That means you, too, Lena. You're one of us now." He smiles warmly and clinks his glass against mine.

I do the same with Jake, and then, Wes. His eyes are fathomless pools of royal blue. I ache to drown in him. He clinks my glass and takes a slow, sensual sip of the amber liquid.

After that, everyone digs in. The food is phenomenal. Wes inhales his meal, tearing the filet apart with his teeth like a starved man.

"Hungry?" I snort.

He pins me with his desire-darkened gaze. "You have *no idea.*" His unspoken message makes my inner muscles clench again.

Two can play this game. I eat my meal slowly, my movements sensual.

Jake and Austin go up for seconds. Once they move out of earshot and turn their attention to the buffet, Wes leans in close and snags one of my hands. He presses a tender kiss to each knuckle, then lifts his eyes to mine. "Tonight, I'm gonna fuck you boneless."

My lady bits spasm, and I clutch the edge of the table with a gasp. "No, you will not. You're injured."

He ignores my protest. "Brainless and senseless too. By the time we're done, you'll feel me inside you for days."

Whether or not he's willing to admit it, the man is in pain. There will be no fuckery. No matter how much the idea turns me on.

"Maybe I'm not in the mood?" My shaky whisper betrays me.

"You sure about that?" His gaze drops to my hardened nipples in challenge.

I stiffen my spine. "Never mind my boobs. I'm worried about your ribs."

"Good thing I'm not."

I roll my eyes. "You aren't fooling me—I'm a nurse. I *know* you're in pain, Ace."

"It's nothing I can't handle."

"Never said you couldn't handle it. I said we aren't having sex."

"You wait and see. I'm gonna—"

The guys are on their way back, so he clamps his mouth shut. Despite my better judgment, my body is on fire for him. I'm talking straight-up forest fire inferno. Fuck the match, he's using a blowtorch. I force a few calming breaths and attempt interaction with the other guys.

Once Austin settles in, I lean over toward him. "How's Kate feeling?"

"Nauseous and tired, but her doctor told her it should get better now that she's starting her second trimester. I can't wait to see her. I swear to God, I'm never lettin' her go."

Austin dissolved into tears and revealed his girlfriend's pregnancy news after our near-death experience with a grizzly bear. Shit got real for us that day. It broke my heart to see him so distraught over the possibility of leaving Kate to raise their baby alone.

"She flying up here?" Wes asks.

"No way! The last place I want her is on a plane. I told her to sit tight, cause Daddy's comin' home." He grins. "And I have an important question for her . . ."

"Hold on, you're not waiting for your Riviera trip like you planned?" I ask in surprise.

"I'm not waitin' a second longer than I have to. Hopefully, I'll make it through the front door."

Wes's eyes widen in shock. "You're gonna propose?"

Jake mirrors his expression.

"The moment I lay eyes on her," Austin declares.

I look over at Wes and grin. "He already has the ring."

Wes's gaze bounces from his best friend and then back to me. "You knew about this?"

I smile and nod. "Sure did."

It was only our second day in Alaska when Austin told me about his proposal plans. We'd taken a walk to the men's campsite to gather supplies. He didn't want his friends to tease him for the whole trip, so he asked me to keep my mouth shut. Austin wasn't the only one to whom I lent my ear—Jake also shared some juicy morsels.

I've been told I'm easy to talk to, and I've always considered it an honor when someone confides in me, so I take their privacy seriously. And since I rarely divulge my secrets, I expect the same courtesy when I open up.

"I can't believe you didn't tell me," Wes murmurs.

I smile. "Wasn't my news to share."

"That's awesome, Memphis," Jake says with a broad smile. "Congratulations."

"Thanks, man. It's time, you know? I can't imagine my life without her. I should've made her Katie Pines two years ago, but I didn't wanna rush it. After all this, I'm done wastin' time. She's everything to me and it's high time I show her."

"Teach the class, Austin," I say. "For real . . . do it."

"What class?" Wes asks.

"Lena told me I need to teach a class on how to romance a woman," Austin explains with a faint blush.

Jake snorts. "Wes can be his first student."

"Nah." I shake my head. "Wes already has that part down." I meet his swirling cobalt gaze with a small smile.

"What's next for you two?" Jake asks.

I freeze. The question has been circling my mind for days. I wanted to ask Wes, but a deep-seated fear of his answer silenced me. What if he suggests we go our separate ways? How can we make it work with an ocean between us? Will we fall back into our old routines?

Reality comes knocking . . . hard.

In the wilderness, we were just a pair of campers with a common goal—survival. Without the distraction of our careers, distance, or other people, we fell in love. Mother Nature leveled the playing field. But what will happen now? Our lifestyles are worlds apart. Can our love withstand the noise, chaos, and media attention? Can I survive a long-distance relationship? I know there would be plenty of time alone. Am I ready to love him from afar? *But Wes isn't Marc.* Wes never makes me feel like an afterthought. Wes listens and hears me. He treats me like a goddess. Will that change? Will I still be a priority in his life?

I look over at Jake, my voice soft and uncertain when I speak, "That depends on Wes."

Wes drops his fork. "What the hell does that mean?"

I sigh and meet his gaze. "It means we need to talk," I glance at the other two, "in private."

"You worry too much, sunshine." He reaches across the table and squeezes my hand. "We'll figure it out as we go."

"I need more than that," I whisper. "We'll talk later."

"I've gotta call my brother and get my shit together. Then we'll have our talk."

After dinner, we all part ways and head to our rooms.

Wes stops me outside my door. "We'll talk, love. First, I need to pack my stuff and call Reed. It'll probably be a while because I'm sure he'll want to make a game plan for his wedding next month and my work schedule. I've already missed a few contractual events."

"Can they hold that against you?" I ask. "I mean, your circumstances were extreme."

"They definitely can, but most people are reasonable. I'm sure I'll be bombarded with appearances to make up for everything I've missed. As my manager, Reed takes care of all that shit for me—he's much more organized. Plus, now the media will be demanding interviews about Alaska," he mutters. "Let me iron out the details with him."

"Take your time and do what you need to do." I gesture to my room. "You know where to find me."

"Lemme take care of business first. Like I said, it'll take some time. But then, I'm coming for ya." His eyes flash with dark promise, a carnal foreshadowing of how he thinks our night will play out.

As much as I'd love a romp in the sack, it's not feasible with his broken ribs. He doesn't know it yet, but I'm planning an encore blow job instead.

I lick my lips and allow my gaze to travel the length of his body. Standing on my tiptoes, I brush my lips over his ear. "You got that right, baby. I'm gonna make you howl . . ." I kiss his neck, flash a sultry smile, and softly shut the door in his face.

I rest against the closed door and salute my brazen inner goddess. This feeling of power as a woman is new. Knowing Wes craves me as much as I crave him, seeing how I affect him, has changed me. I'm alive and reborn in ways I never thought possible.

I freshen up and slip into my pajamas, settling on my bed. With my luxe comforter draped over my body, I lounge in that sexy way a woman reposes when sexily awaiting her lover.

LENA

Internal playlist: "Tapes" by Alanis Morissette

I'm warm and comfortable. A welcome change from the past few weeks. I know it's morning by how the shade eclipses my window. I glance at the clock on the nightstand. Nine-thirty. *Wow, I must've passed out.* Which means I missed Wes's knock. *Shit. I hope he's not mad.* I throw the covers off, then quickly shower and dress before heading downstairs.

Jake is at the table reading a newspaper with our faces on the front page.

"Good morning," I call.

"Morning, Lena-Bean. Sleep well?"

"I passed out. How about you?"

He nods and sips his coffee. "Same."

"Where're the other two?"

"Austin's on the phone with Katie. I heard him talking when I walked past his door. Wes is sleeping in, I assume," he scratches his chin, "which is weird for him. He always rises with the sun."

"He had to call Reed last night," I explain. "Told me it would be a while. I guess they had a lot to discuss."

He chuckles. "Reed's very structured, so he probably droned on for hours and put Wes to sleep."

"Well, he needs to rest." I walk toward the buffet table. "Oh, pancakes!" I place several on my plate and load them with syrup, before returning to my seat with a grin. "I'm ridiculously excited to eat these."

Jake eyes me. "You forgot coffee."

"Holy shit. I guess I got used to not having caffeine. But now that you mention it . . ." I rise and stride to the coffee station.

At that moment, a young resort employee enters the room with a fresh carafe. "Here's some more coffee for you guys. The decaf is still brewing."

"Thanks, perfect timing." I pour myself a cup and turn to Jake. "Need a refill?"

"I'm good, thanks."

I smile and sip the delicious life-giving nectar. "Damn, that's good. I forgot how much I love it. I need to pace myself or there won't be any left for Wes."

The employee pauses near the table. "Mr. Emerson left hours ago."

My scalp prickles, and ice fills my lungs. There's no way she said what I think she said. Wes wouldn't just leave. I open my mouth to speak, but no sound comes out.

Jake drops his newspaper. "Did you just say he *left?*"

"Yeah. I gave him a ride in the golf cart before dawn. He was in a real hurry to leave."

My mouth goes dry. There it is—the other shoe. I've been waiting for it to drop for weeks. Looks like my intuition was on to something.

He's gone.

He left without saying goodbye.

It's over.

"Where the hell did he go?" Jake asks in confusion.

"He boarded a bush plane headed for Fairbanks, but I dunno his plans after that. He didn't say much," she informs us. "Do you guys need anything else to eat?"

"No, thank you." Jake rises from his seat.

"All right, enjoy the rest of your stay." She smiles and leaves the room.

"That doesn't make sense." Jake shakes his head. "I'm gonna go talk to Memphis."

I struggle to expand my aching chest enough to breathe, let alone speak. Tears threaten to spill over.

Jake squeezes my shoulder as he passes. "Don't worry, Lena-Bean. I'm sure there's a logical explanation." Then, he bounds up the stairs.

I clench my jaw. There's a logical explanation, all right. He ran out of here under the cover of darkness.

A brilliant escape.

Bitter thoughts swirl around my head as the house of cards begins to crumble. No longer hungry, I rise and trudge upstairs.

Down the hall, Jake pounds on Austin's door. "Memphis, open up." He glances at me. "Where're you going, Lena-Bean?"

Without a word, I retreat to the safety of my room and close the door. I collapse onto my bed and curl into a ball on my side. My tears come freely, each sob cutting deeper.

Every single one of my insecurities rears its ugly head, offering desolate scenarios to explain Wes's departure. I try to beat them back, but the ordeal has me exhausted. Negative emotions consume me. Their whisperings become a reality in my mind.

We were no longer an arrangement of circumstance.

Wes had the freedom to cut ties with me.

I turn my head to the soft knock on the door.

When I don't answer, Jake opens it a crack. "Lena-Bean, I'm coming in. I think Memphis is showering," he mutters on his way over to the bed. He sits on the edge and touches my shoulder. "Talk to me."

"I'm so stupid," I sob.

"Why do you say that?"

"Because it's true. I knew going into this it was more than likely a fling. Thought I was okay with that, but I was wrong." I furiously wipe my tears away. "I allowed myself to get carried away in the fantasy of him wanting more."

"You're reading too much into it. I promise, you're not alone in your feelings."

"How do you know?"

"Because I'm a man and his friend. I know how Wes operates. I know he loves you."

"Maybe he thought he did—"

"Why are you using past tense?"

"Because he just ran off in the middle of the night without saying goodbye."

"He also said nothing to me, which is why I'm gonna see if Memphis knows what's up." Jake studies me for a moment. "Let me ask you something. You don't have to answer if it's too personal."

"Go for it."

"Did you have your talk last night?"

"No. He said he needed to call Reed first. He promised to come to my room afterward. But he never came."

"You should try calling him."

"For one, I don't have cell service here. Beyond that, he never gave me his fucking number. Or *any* way of contacting him. Probably intentional," I mutter.

"Lena, stop."

"Don't you get it, Jake? You said Reed's all business. Well, maybe he gave Wes a reality check. Convinced him I'm not worth his time. Or maybe Wes finally realized how different we are and seized the opportunity to cut his losses. I told him I needed more than 'figuring it out as we go,' and that freaked him out. Why would he commit to someone like me? Why would he settle for *ordinary*?" The word leaves my lips in a bitter whisper.

"Ordinary?" He frowns. "What the hell is that supposed to mean?"

"Look at me. I'm nothing like the women he's used to. I was so stupid to let myself fall for him." I sniff. "He said he loved me, and I believed him. Meanwhile, it was all an act—"

"Stop." He shakes his head. "You can't truly believe that."

"Think about it."

"Look, as much as I love to fuck with Wes, I'll come to his defense here. Does Reed keep his life in order? Absolutely. But that doesn't mean Wes takes his orders. Emerson's a free agent. He does whatever the fuck he wants. If he wanted to cut ties with you, he would've told you to your face. Can he be a hotheaded asshole? Yes. But he's no coward. That man loves you. I knew it long before he had the balls to tell you."

"Then, where is he?"

"I dunno. But I guarantee there's a reason for this. Let's see what Memphis has to say. Please don't cry. You'll hear from him."

"Doubtful."

"Then why don't you cut him off at the pass?" He cocks a brow. "I'll give you his number right now."

I shake my head slowly. "I won't chase after him and humiliate myself any further."

"Isn't he worth chasing?"

"Of course he is. I love him, Jake," I whisper. "But I won't put myself in that position. This hurts bad enough. I won't beg for his attention. I spent four years like that. You're more than welcome to give him my number if he asks for it. If he wants me, I'm his—mind, body, heart, and soul. But I'll never beg for someone's affection or attention again." Tears stream down my face at the thought.

"Fair enough. Do what you think you need to do. But don't hide behind your past. You're stronger than that and you know it."

A door slams.

"Yo, Bennett!" Austin shouts over the loft railing.

"In Lena's room," Jake calls out.

Austin appears in the doorway waving a brochure. "You talk to Wes?"

"No, man. Where the fuck is he?"

Austin marches into the room and thrusts the paper in Jake's face. He points to something scrawled on the back. "He left this note. I just found it on the floor inside my room."

Jake snatches the brochure and reads it aloud, "Reed needs me. I have to leave. Tell Lena I'll be in touch." He shakes his head. "Could he be any more fucking cryptic?"

Austin turns to me. "Don't cry, baby girl. We'll figure out what's goin' on." He taps the note. "Stupid fuck coulda left us more than a riddle."

Jake motions to me. "Lena thinks he ghosted her."

"That's crazy talk, darlin'," Austin scoffs, brushing the hair back from my face. "He loves you."

But he couldn't leave a note for me? Or wake me?

"I tried callin', but he didn't answer. If he left this morning, he's probably on a plane. I tried Reed, too, with no luck. Hopefully, he's okay." He turns to Jake. "Do you have Isla's new number? Not the one from Sydney, but the one after that. The *new* Melbourne one."

Jake stiffens. "No. I've never had her number."

Austin cocks his head. "Seriously?"

"Yep."

"I thought you two were tight?"

Jake shakes his head. "Clearly, I'm not inner-circle material."

"That's bulls—"

"Not now, Memphis."

"But I think—"

Jake holds up a hand. "Dude, please just stop. I don't wanna talk about it." He turns back to me and squeezes my knee. "Like I said, there's an explanation. We'll figure it out."

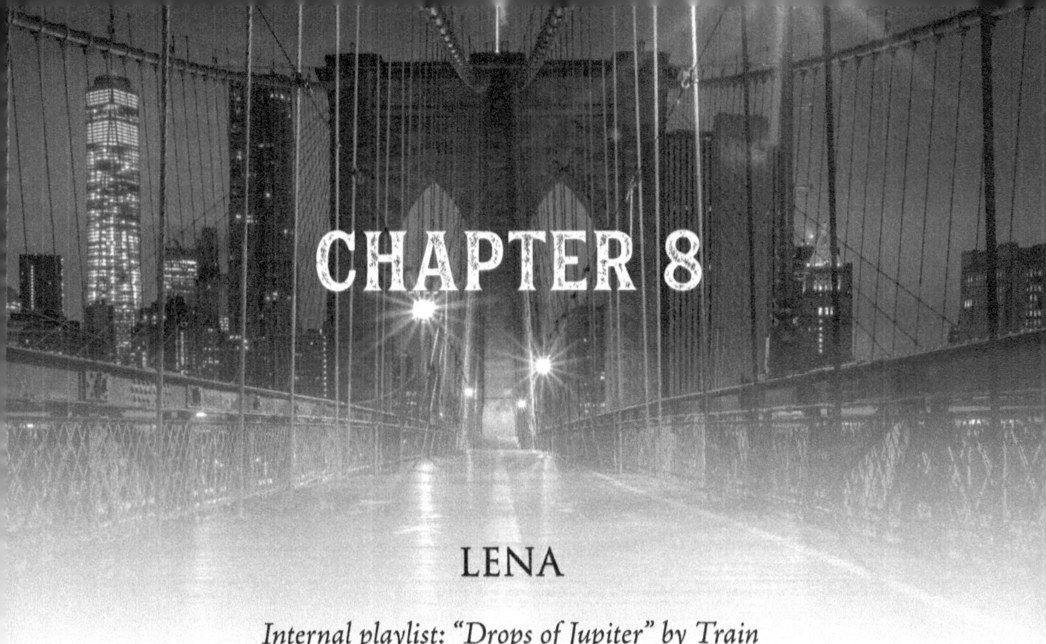

CHAPTER 8

LENA

Internal playlist: "Drops of Jupiter" by Train

Jake and I trudge up the jetway at JFK airport in New York. We parted ways with Austin in Seattle as he was heading for Tennessee.

He glances at me. "I never thought I'd live to see this moment, Lena-Bean."

"Same here. I still can't believe we survived."

"It feels so surreal. I keep thinking I'm going to wake up in that tent again."

A shudder courses through me. "I hear you."

Airport staff direct us to a private reception area. I see Garrett before he notices me. He stands beside a petite, middle-aged woman with a kind face and silver waves that fall to her shoulders. Her resemblance to Jake is uncanny.

Looks like Garrett's been hitting the gym. Dressed in dark jeans and a charcoal sweater, he looks nothing short of gorgeous. Inky waves accentuate his golden-amber eyes. His trademark stubbled jawline is in full effect. He laughs at something Jake's mother says. *God, I missed that laugh.*

"Ahem," I announce our arrival.

"Leens!" Garrett's face lights up, and he charges in our direction, wrapping me in a tight hug.

"You're crushing me, Gar," I grunt.

"Sorry." He relaxes his grip. "I'm just—" Eyes misting, he swallows tightly.

"I missed you too." I kiss his cheek and melt into his warm, strong embrace. Over the years, his hugs have never failed to soothe.

Garrett kisses my forehead. "I'm so happy you're safe."

Jake hugs his mother and consoles her as she weeps. She clings to her son like any mother would, no matter what age their child. He makes eye contact with me and smiles.

"Mom, I want you to meet the fiercest, most *extraordinary* woman on the planet. Besides you, of course." He chuckles and leads her by the hand to where Garrett and I stand. "This is my dear friend, Lena Hamilton. Lena, this is my mom, Donna."

I take Donna's hand. "A pleasure to meet you, Ms. Bennett. Your son is a gem."

"Thank you, honey. Nice to meet you too." Donna wraps me in a hug. "Jake told me everything you did for his friend. *You* are the gem, my dear."

"Jake, this is Garrett," I say.

"Nice to meet you, man. I've heard a lot about you. Lena tells me you auditioned for *Prodigy?*" Jake shakes Garrett's hand. "Which part?"

Prodigy is the upcoming Broadway production certain to shatter precedents. Garrett auditioned for the controversial show on the day I left for Alaska.

"Funny you should ask . . ." Garrett beams. "They've selected me to play the male lead, Xavier Crane."

Jake smiles. "Congratulations. That's impressive. I read the script and it looks phenomenal."

"Gar, I'm ridiculously proud of you," I squeal, hugging him.

"Thank you. Broadway has always been a dream of mine. I'm shocked. Everything sort of fell into place. I need to focus and start memorizing my lines now that I'm not paralyzed with worry." He gives me the side-eye. "I've been distracted to say the least. I can't tell you how relieved I am that you guys are okay. It's been a living hell."

"For us too, man. I still can't believe we survived. There were moments when I truly thought it was over. This woman is incredible." Jake points at me. "I watched her bring my friend back from the dead. I'm sure she'll fill you in."

"I'll tell you everything later, Gar. I don't have the energy right now."

"So, I mentioned this to Lena on the plane, but I wanted to tell you as well. I'm hosting a benefit gala in Manhattan on the second Friday in November. I want you two to come. I'll arrange for a car to pick you up. I'd like to introduce you to some of my theater people," Jake says.

Garrett's eyes light up. "Thank you so much. We'll be there." He elbows me. "Right, Leens?"

"Yes. I can't thank you enough, Jake." I embrace him. "You helped me keep my sanity."

"Likewise, Lena-Bean. Listen, don't be a stranger. I'll hunt you down if I have to."

"I won't," I promise, kissing his cheek. "We'll schedule some lunch dates too."

We say our goodbyes and part ways. Once again, I'm bereft. The throbbing ache in my chest makes it hard to breathe. Too many goodbyes. Austin first, and now Jake. *Yet nothing from Wes.* A glimmer of hope flickers to life.

Maybe it wasn't goodbye.

CHAPTER 9

LENA

Internal playlist: "Cosmic Love" by Florence + The Machine

I stare at Harry and Hermione as the purring pair of felines weave through my legs. My fur-children certainly didn't suffer during my absence.

"Garrett, they're fat."

"Well-rounded," he corrects me with a grin. "Uncle Garrett bought them lots of goodies. Right, guys?"

Hermione chirps and rubs her plump self against his leg. Harry stretches and slow blinks.

"Thanks for watching them."

He nods and heads for the couch. I follow, sinking into the cushions with a heavy sigh. It feels so good to be home. So good, I almost forgot my sadness. *Almost.* During the ride to our shared Brooklyn brownstone, I told Garrett every detail of the forsaken Alaska adventure.

"Want me to help you unpack? I can order Chinese?" he offers. "Or if you need some alone time, I'll head home."

"Please stay." I scratch Hermione's ears. She found my lap the moment my ass hit the couch. "Sesame chicken."

Garrett smiles, places the order, and then turns on my laptop. "I need to respond to a few work emails."

"Do your thing. I'm gonna unpack." Reaching across Hermione's portly frame, I unlock the tiny padlock on my luggage, then pull out my belongings and sort them into piles. She "helps" by stretching and mashing her paws into the assorted fabrics, purring like a motorboat. Across the room, Harry squints at me, clearly pissed that I abandoned him for so long.

I glance at my wardrobe with a sigh. Most of the clothes are too big now. Looks like I'll be sporting yoga pants for the foreseeable future. I freeze when my hand brushes the material of the jade dress. I pull out the garment and swallow past the lump in my throat. It's as if every fiber singes me with memories. I can almost smell Wes, feel his hands all over my body. A wave of pain crashes into me. I crumple the dress before dropping it onto the living room floor.

"What's up?" Garrett peers over the screen. I point to the dress, and he nods in understanding. "He'll call you, Leens. Just give him a chance. It's a long flight and there's a huge time difference." My best friend is always so rational, which pisses me off sometimes.

"I know," I mutter. "Obviously, I hope his brother is all right . . ."

"But?" Garrett sees right through me, his lion-like gaze sharp and assessing. There's no hiding from him. He lifts a brow. "I know there's more, so keep going."

"Maybe I'm just being selfish."

"How?"

"For feeling like I deserved a note."

"No. I think your feelings are justified. But if he's spent the past fifteen years believing he's responsible for his brother's accident, then that's where his focus is right now. Communication's on the back burner. At least he left a note, period. You'd be a lot more upset if he vanished into thin air."

"I know." I sigh, rubbing my throbbing temples. "But what if . . .?"

"What if, what?"

"What if it's all a con?"

Garrett cocks a brow. "A con?"

"Jake and Austin are his best friends. They've known him forever. What if he wanted to end things with me and got them to cover for him by staging a mysterious exit?"

He scrubs a fist over his face. "Do you really believe that?"

"I don't know what to believe," I whisper. "What if it was us? What if I needed your help to get out of a situation? You'd have my back."

"Leens, I have your back no matter what. But that doesn't mean

I'd let you be an asshole. Austin and Jake care about you, and not just because you saved Wes's life. From what you tell me, they're genuine dudes."

"But Wes is their best friend."

Garrett throws his hands in the air. "All the more reason not to let him walk away from a woman like you."

I hold my head in my hands. "I'm so confused." The sudden blare of my ringtone makes me jump. *What if?* I lunge for my cell and topple my water. Scanning the screen, my eyes flutter closed.

"Who is it?"

"My mother."

"Good. Ask when her train's coming so I know what time to leave tomorrow. I assume she's taking the Amtrak out of Hudson?"

I nod and mop up the water with a sweatshirt. "Hello?"

"Oh, my sweet girl, I'm so happy to hear your voice!"

"Hi, Mom."

"Are you all right? Are you hurt? I've been a nervous wreck."

"I know. I'm sorry. I should've told you where I was going."

"It's in the past. What matters is you're safe."

"Yeah. Garrett wants to know what time your train gets in."

She sighs heavily. "Honey, listen . . ."

"Mom, what's wrong?"

"I won't be able to make it down for a while."

"Why not?" *I was just lost in the fucking wilderness.* I stiffen when she doesn't answer. "Dad's drinking again, isn't he?"

"Yes."

"There's a big shocker," I snap.

Garrett sets down the laptop and raises an eyebrow. I shake my head.

"Sweetheart, I'm sorry . . ."

"Whatever, Mom," I say bitterly. "Do what you gotta do."

"Dad's in jail."

"For *what?*"

She sighs. "He got a DWI."

I clutch the phone. "Again?"

"Yes. I'm meeting with the lawyers tomorrow."

Hope surges within me. "Divorce lawyers?"

"Of course not," Mom snaps. "I need to see what we can do about the charges."

"Go ahead, Mom, enable him more." Disgusted by the situation, I don't bother suggesting she come the following day—mainly because I'm afraid if I *do* see her, I'll say something I'll regret. "I gotta go." I hang up and toss my phone on a couch cushion.

Garrett eyes me. "What's up?"

"My piece of shit father got another DWI."

"Another? That's his third!"

"Yep. They locked him up this time. Apparently, bailing his ass out takes precedence over one's own daughter."

"What do you mean?"

"Mom's not coming." Tears stream down my face. "First, Wes can't leave me a note. Now, I'm my mother's fucking afterthought too."

Garrett pulls me into his arms. Like I've done so many times over the years, I bury my face in his chest and weep.

It's after ten. Garrett just went home. Exhausted, I finally summon the strength to peel myself off the couch. I head to the bathroom to wash my face, and stare into the mirror. Haunted, puffy, red-rimmed eyes with dark circles stare back. My bruises and split lip stand out against my pale skin. Truth is, I'd take the physical pain over the suffocating ache in my chest any day. Once again, alcohol has driven a wedge in my relationship with my mother.

An icy, throbbing numbness settles in my heart and claws its way to the lead weight in the pit of my stomach. While Garrett's reasoning was sound, I can't help but feel like Wes ghosted me. And now Mom isn't coming to visit.

So glad I'm a priority.

The faded wraith in the mirror traces her fingertips down the column of her throat, but it's Wes's hands I feel, his lips and tongue gliding over my skin. For years, no one could touch my neck—not Garrett, not even my mom. *Wes is the only one.* The memory brings me to my knees.

Only Wes.

Pressing my forehead against the cool tile of the bathroom wall, torrents of hot, bitter tears spill over and splatter onto the floor. My shoulders shake with silent sobs as I break down for the second time today.

CHAPTER 10

WES

Life lesson: Those who don't communicate . . .

I yank my suitcase from the baggage claim and rush through the airport in Sydney, Australia. Several people call out to me, but I ignore them and keep walking. Now is not the time for fucking autographs. Reed needs me and I'll be damned if I fail my brother this time.

I approach a taxi idling at the curb and throw my shit into the back, wincing as the move tweaks my ribs. After telling the driver my destination, I stare out the window and pray I make it in time. Traffic is heavy, but the driver weaves in and out, switching lanes, and pushing well past the speed limit.

Finally, the hospital is in sight. The taxi screeches to a halt, and I pay the driver and grab my luggage. I spot Isla near the hospital entrance and wave. She shrieks, charging in my direction. We've always been incredibly close, even more so after I gave her one of my kidneys ten years ago. I'll never forget the day we learned she needed dialysis. At the time, she was only twelve. It fucking killed me to see her hooked up to all those machines. When my organ compatibility testing came back positive—the only match in our family—the surgery was a no-brainer.

"Oh, God, Wes. I love you so much." She throws her arms around me and clings to me for dear life, whispering her thanks on a shaky prayer.

"Easy, Isla," I say, gasping. "My ribs."

"I'm sorry, I forgot. Did I hurt you?" she stammers, peering up at me. Wet lashes fringe a pair of eyes the same vivid blue as mine. Her golden-brown hair is piled into a messy bun and, somehow, she seems taller and more grown up than when I last saw her.

"Not at all," I lie.

"I'm so happy you're home." She touches my cheek. "I didn't think I'd ever see you again."

I kiss her forehead. "I know. Wasn't so sure I'd make it home. More about that later. Where're Mum and Dad?"

She swipes at her cheeks. "Upstairs. Hurry, Father Gene's waiting in Gwen's room."

The lift doors slide open and we step into the waiting area. Mum bursts into tears at the sight of me. I stride across the room and embrace my parents, Luke and Rhea Emerson.

"Don't cry, Mum. I'm home now," I whisper to the top of her head.

We're a tall family, but Mum is the shortest Emerson. I've towered over her since I was twelve. Even Isla has her by a few inches. She strokes her hand over my cheek. Another sob escapes as she holds on to me.

"Missed you, son." Dad firmly squeezes my shoulder and I beat back my wince. He's unflappable like Reed, but even his eyes are wet. "Your mum has been falling apart."

She hugs me tighter when he says it, making me gasp in pain.

"Don't hurt his ribs, Mum," Isla warns, misty-eyed again.

"Oh, that's right." Mum loosens her hold and fixes my shirt. "Sorry, love. C'mon, your brother's waiting."

I follow my parents and sister to a patient room. Inside, Reed and Cora speak with the Catholic priest we've known since our baptisms, while Gwen lays prone in a bed. Cora's sister, Dana, dabs Gwen's face with a cloth. Cora is the first one to see me. Her mouth drops open and she clutches Reed's arm.

Reed spins around, relief flooding his face. I step forward and embrace him, ignoring the pain in my ribs.

"Welcome home, mate." Reed clings to me, his shoulders shaking. The tears streaming down his cheeks soak into my T-shirt. My brother is the stoic one in our family. Other than when he was a baby, I can count on one hand the number of times I've seen him cry. My chest tightens and my eyes burn, but I'm trying to keep it together.

Once Reed finally releases me, I hug Cora and Dana, greet Father Gene, and clasp Gwen's hand.

"You made it," Gwen says, her voice little more than a wheeze. "Thank God you're safe. I prayed every day for your return."

"C'mon, Gwen, you know me better than that. Do ya honestly think I'd miss my baby brother's wedding?" I smile softly at the dying woman.

She winks and forces a smile. "I had faith in you, Wesley. We all did."

I squeeze her hand and fight back a wave of emotion. I was convinced I wouldn't make it in time. The hours since Reed alerted me of Gwen's imminent demise are a blur. *Cora wants her mum to see her get married before she dies. And I need you by my side.* His words echoed in my mind during the entire flight from Fairbanks.

"All right, folks, we should get started." Father Gene motions for me to stand by Reed. I loop my good arm over his shoulder. Dana takes her place beside Cora and holds her sister's hand. Everyone else stands nearby.

I watch as my brother exchanges vows with the love of his life at her dying mother's bedside. Cora can barely speak through her tears and leans against Reed during the entire ceremony. I glance at Gwen. Despite her pain, her eyes shine with love. She meets my gaze and smiles. I return her smile and decide the wedding is as perfect as it could be.

After the ceremony, my parents, Isla, and I return to the waiting room. I exhale heavily as I plop into a chair beside my sister.

"Tell me everything," Isla says, her voice breathless. "I want every detail."

"Let Wes get settled before we bombard him. He's been through a lot." Mum turns to me. "Are you in pain? How's your shoulder? Aren't you supposed to be wearing a sling?"

"Yep. It's in my suitcase."

"That's a good place for it," Mum chides.

"Who's bombarding him now?" Isla quips.

"My shoulder's all right. I can deal with the pain of it. It's the ribs that're bloody killing me."

Dad returns from the vending machine and hands me a water and a Twix bar.

"Thanks, Dad."

"Figured you were running on the smell of an oily rag by now." He settles beside Mum.

"Been running on fumes for a month," I mutter, twisting the cap from the water.

Mum nods. "I can tell, love. You're far too thin for my liking."

"Maybe you'll have to make me some pie, Mum," I suggest with a grin.

Isla nudges me. "How are the guys? Is Austin still seeing Kate?"

I chuckle and glance at my watch. "If my estimation's correct, they're engaged by now." I keep Austin and Kate's pregnancy news under wraps—that's theirs to share.

"Um, I'd *better* be invited to that wedding."

"That's their call, not mine." I laugh and elbow her. "But I'm sure ya will be."

"How's Jake?"

"Still single."

Her brows pop. "Really? I thought he got back with Nadia?"

I shake my head. "Nope. That'll never happen. She's an ice queen. I wouldn't piss on her if she were on fire."

"Wesley!" Mum shoots me a glare.

"She treated him like shit, Mum. I'd rather him be single than stay with someone like her."

Isla grins. "He can be my date to Austin's wedding."

"Bennett's too old for ya. Find someone in your circle and leave my friends alone, you imp." I laugh. "That reminds me . . ." I dig through my carry-on and pull out my phone, which I realize is still on airplane mode. I switch it on and stuff it into a pocket, only to withdraw the device a moment later. The thing dings, buzzes, and chimes with a barrage of texts, missed calls, and voicemails.

"You're popular," Isla remarks. "Haven't you called them yet?"

"Nope." I shake my head. "I was so worried about getting here, I didn't even think about it."

"That was dumb." Her eyeroll reinforces my idiocy.

Mum nudges Isla's shoulder. "Leave your brother alone."

"It's all right, Mum. I've missed the little imp. But I should reach out to the guys and Lena."

"Wait, you didn't tell *her* you were leaving?" Isla gapes at me.

"It was after midnight by the time I got off the phone with Reed. I knocked on her door, but she was asleep. I didn't want to wake her—"

"So, you vanished?"

"I didn't vanish," I protest lamely. "I left a note for Austin."

"Did you at least leave *her* a note to explain?"

"No." Realizing my stupidity, I stare at my hands. "I figured the guys would fill her in." Except I really didn't explain much to them, either.

"You'd better call that woman immediately."

No shit.

"I don't have her number." And like the bloody fuckwit I am, I never even gave her my contact information.

"God, Wes, when did ya become such an idiot?" Isla climbs to her feet. "I'm getting a cuppa," she announces. "Any takers?"

I hand her a wad of cash. "Please bring me the largest size they have."

Jet lag is no joke. Combined with the physical and emotional trauma, I'm fried. And *clearly*, my brain isn't functioning to its full potential. While I wait, I scroll through the text messages and listen to my voicemails. My mates are pissed.

I dial Austin. No answer. He's probably busy with Katie, and the last thing I want to do is interrupt anyone's "welcome home/engagement" sex. I leave him a quick message explaining myself.

Isla returns with the coffees and I take a generous sip. "Thanks, Imp." The dark roast warms me as I dial Jake.

"Oh, good. You're alive." His sarcastic tone makes me chuckle. "Guess I can scrap the eulogy I've been working on."

Jake is a professional worrier. He battles obsessive-compulsive disorder and generalized anxiety—something I only just discovered when we were lost in Alaska. While we've been friends for decades, Jake kept his struggle hidden from Austin and me. Just like he keeps it hidden from the rest of the world.

"I'm sorry, mate. Reed needed me." Then, I quickly fill Jake in on the details of the call at the lodge, my trip home, and the bedside ceremony.

"I get it. Your note was shit though. Total shit. We were all thinking something terrible happened to Reed. Then we couldn't get ahold of *anyone* in your family. You can't do shit like that, Wes. It's fucking inconsiderate."

"Sorry. I was in a hurry and not thinking straight. Did Lena make it home all right?"

"I assume so. Garrett picked her up at the airport."

"I bet she was happy to see him. Did she give you her contact information?"

"Yup."

"That's good. Otherwise, I'd need to get creative and hunt her down." I grab a pen and paper from one of the end tables. "Okay, I'm ready."

"Ready for what?"

"Her number."

"Who said I'm gonna give it to you?"

"Don't fuck around, Bennett."

"You fucked up big time, dude. Austin was on the phone with Katie all morning, so Lena didn't know about your shitty note until later. A resort employee dropped the bomb on us over breakfast."

"Damn . . ."

"Gotta tell you, man, she completely fell apart. Ran up to her room and cried."

I scrub my hand over my face. "I'm such an idiot."

"Yeah, I won't argue with that one. You left before having your talk and she thought you ghosted her."

"Son of a bitch." I'd never ghost anyone. It's a cowardly move. It kills me to know Lena thought I'd do that to her.

Jake sighs. "She came up with some crazy shit."

"Like what?"

"First, it was that Reed convinced you she wasn't worth your time."

"That's bullshit—"

"Then she thought you took off because you didn't want her. You realized she was 'ordinary' and didn't wanna settle. Her words, not mine."

"Jesus fucking Christ," I snap, knotting my hands in my hair. "She's off her bloody rocker if she thinks that's true."

"Wesley James!" I catch my mum's glare.

"Sorry, Mum." I usually try not to swear in front of my mum, but right now, I don't give a fuck about my language. Lena is my number one concern—too bad I didn't factor her in when I left the resort like a bat out of hell. I can't believe my stupidity.

"Not for nothing, but what did you *think* would happen?" Jake demands. "You know she's got all those insecurities bottled up inside her and you went ahead and threw a lit match. Like I said, she fell the fuck apart."

"I wasn't thinking."

"No shit. And tell Mrs. E that I say hello."

"Jake says hi."

Mum smiles. "Hello, Jake." She nudges me. "Tell Jake we're so happy he's safe. Ask when he's coming to see us."

"Did you hear her?" I ask Jake.

"Yeah, tell her—"

"I don't have the patience for this back and forth shit. I'm putting you on speaker." I press the icon. "Go ahead, Bennett."

"Hi, Mr. and Mrs. E. Thanks for the invite, but I'm stuck in New York for a while—work obligations and all that. But if you ever want to visit the city, your family's always welcome to stay at my place in Brooklyn."

"Thank you, love," Mum says warmly.

"Hi, Jake." Isla leans in. "Does your invitation include me?"

"Isla . . . hello. Uh, yeah . . . of course it does." Jake clears his throat. "I'd be happy to show you around the city, Sprite."

She grins at his nickname for her. "Really?"

"Yes, really. Hotel Bennett's always open, and anytime you wanna make the trip up here, consider me your personal tour guide."

Jake has always had a soft spot for my sister. He took it so hard when I told him she needed dialysis. Years back, when he and Austin came to visit one summer, Jake spent his time building sandcastles with five-year-old Isla instead of learning to surf. Most fifteen-year-old boys would want nothing to do with a little girl, but Jake was super-attentive. He's an only child, so I think he enjoyed the chance to have a sibling for a few weeks. I *know* Isla did. She had the poor bloke playing Barbies with her by the end of the trip. Even now, she's twenty-three, but Jake *still* checks in with me to see how she's doing. It's a shame his parents didn't have more kids. He would've made an excellent big brother.

Isla's smile lights up her face. "I'm gonna hold ya to that, Jacob Bennett."

"Please do."

"Leave my friends alone, Imp," I say, turning off the speaker. "All right, Bennett, it's just me again. Back to Lena. You told her that *ordinary* shit was bull, right?"

"Yep, but that doesn't mean she believed me. I still don't understand why you didn't wake her."

I clench the phone. "Bennett, I'm sorry. I wasn't thinking and acted like an idiot. Satisfied? I know that's what you're waiting for. Now, *please*, give me Lena's number."

"I dunno if you deserve it."

"Don't fuck around, mate," I mutter darkly. "I'll beg all day if I have to."

"That's what I was hoping you'd say." Jake chuckles and reads out the number.

Cora's anguished wail echoes down the hallway, making me jump.

"What the hell was that?" Jake asks.

"Cora. I think Gwen passed. I gotta go." I hang up the phone, fold the scrap of paper, and tuck it into my pocket.

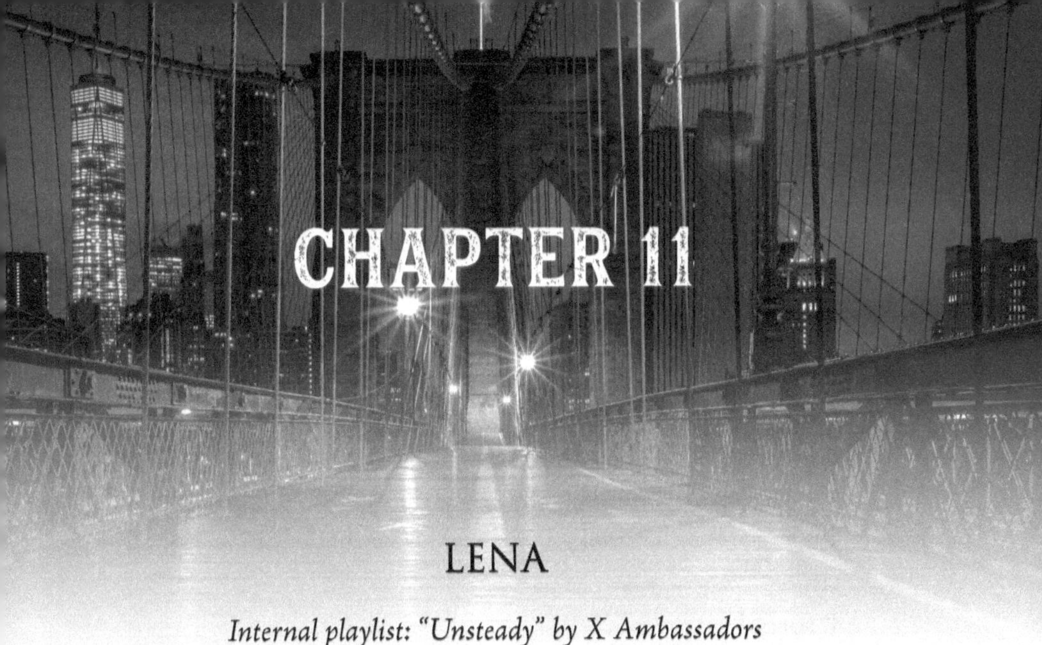

CHAPTER 11

LENA

Internal playlist: "Unsteady" by X Ambassadors

"Lena! What the fuck?" Garrett kneels over me with his hands clamped on my shoulders.

I twitch and roll to my side, peering at him from beneath a curtain of hair. He roughly shakes me, his face drawn in terror.

"Fucking answer me." His snarl makes me jump.

"What's wrong, Gar?" I ask groggily.

Why's he in my bathroom? And what's he doing on the floor? Wait, why am I on the floor?

I push myself up and glance around the room. I'm still in yesterday's clothes and a bath towel lies beside me. An open prescription bottle is tipped over on the vanity. Chalky white tablets litter the floor.

Oh, right. Panic attack.

Heartache had morphed into a clawing terror that stole my breath and robbed my ability to think. Haunted by flashbacks of wolves and rivers, I remember grabbing the bottle and sitting on the floor. I must've fallen asleep after taking the Xanax. Good thing I only took one tablet. Evidently, my malnourished state intensified the drug's effect. Realizing the dark picture the scene paints, I reach for Garrett and wrap my arms around him.

"I'm okay, Gar. I was sleeping."

"You're gonna be the death of me," he wheezes. "I swear to God, it'll be a miracle if I live to forty."

"I'm sorry."

"Why the fuck were you sleeping on the bathroom floor?"

"I must've passed out after taking a Xanax. I had a panic attack."

Garrett sighs and hugs me. We've been down this road before. After a work incident, when a patient assaulted me, my panic attacks were a regular fixture.

"Why didn't you call me? You know I would've been here for you."

"I didn't even have the strength to pull myself off the floor. With the exhaustion and all of yesterday's drama, I was tapped." I motion to the pill bottle. "I realize how that looked, but you know that's not me, right?"

"Yeah."

"I'm sorry I scared you."

"It's all right, Leens. Let me help you up. I brought bagels from Nicolai's." He hauls me to my feet.

He eyes me and I glance down at myself. "What?"

"Why don't you take a hot shower and get dressed? I'll fix your bagel. No offense, but you look rough."

I peek at the mirror. *He has a point there.* I look like a washed-up, train-wrecked shitshow. I nod and turn on the faucet.

GARRETT CASEY

Even though I *know* Lena would never off herself, the sight of her on the floor was a knife to my chest. Probably has something to do with my history of finding women sprawled out in the bathroom. I beat back the images of my dead mother and retreat to the kitchen.

Sick to my stomach, I attempt to distract myself with the plump, doughy wheels of divinity. In all my life, I've never tasted a bagel as good as Nicolai's. It's a wonder I'm not four hundred pounds. With shaking hands, I open the fridge and withdraw the container of chive cream cheese—Lena's favorite. I toast her bagel and spread a generous amount on each half.

Then, I pour myself a mug of coffee and stare out the window as I take my first few sips. The gray skies typical of October are in full force, cloaking the neighborhood in a dismal fog. A squawking murder of crows circles overhead, making me wonder what has drawn them to the area. I'm not a fan. As far as birds go, they are far too loud and obnoxious for my taste. Lena has several feeders, all of which are currently occupied by the obsidian fowl.

I glance up as she enters the kitchen dressed in black socks, black yoga pants, and a long-sleeved black thermal.

"Don't you look like a ray of sunshine this morning," I snip, handing her a large cup of coffee. Her expression morphs into one of sadness, and I backpedal. "I mean, you're beautiful as always. I'm talking about all the black."

"I know what you meant. Wes called me sunshine." She holds out a hair tie and settles on a stool.

"Right. Sorry, Leens." I accept the elastic and gather her locks in my hands. "Your hair got long."

"You just haven't braided it in a while."

"Good point." I weave her hair into a French braid the way she'd shown me when we were kids. Lena braided her hair all the time, but couldn't do a French braid on herself, so I perfected my technique over the years. It's also a comfort thing for her. She always wants her hair played with when she's upset. "That too tight?" I ask, wrapping the elastic around the end of her braid.

"No, it's fine. Thanks, Gar."

"No prob." I search her face. "You sure you're all right?"

"I'm fine. I'm done melting down, I promise." She sips her coffee. "I knew this was a possibility all along. I swore to myself I'd keep my eyes wide open, but I screwed up. I let myself fall for him. I ate the cake and now I want more."

"Stop. Don't get all worked up without knowing the details. He'll call."

"But what if he doesn't?"

"Then you'll deal with that too."

She sighs. "I'm just—"

"Pissed you fucked him before getting a commitment?" I offer.

While I'm the master of casual sex, it was never Lena's thing. *Ever.* She made her first boyfriend wait well over a year before letting him fuck her, so it shocked the shit out of me to learn she slept with Emerson.

That's where we differ. I don't have the capacity for romantic love. For me, sex is purely a physical need. I keep it separate from emotion, mainly because I'm not capable of most normal human emotion. Except pain. Nothing can numb the throbbing ache in my soul, a fact I accepted years ago.

Lena doesn't work like that. For her, it's a package deal—sex and emotion go hand in hand. She isn't someone who uses sex like a drug. That's my game.

She shakes her head. "I don't regret the sex, even if he never calls. It was a relief to find out I'm not broken."

"Broken?" I raise a brow in question.

"Sex was never on my radar, so I thought there was something wrong with me. My libido, my ability to orgasm, intimacy. . . shit like that."

I shake my head. "No, you just have a habit of involving yourself with limp-dick pussies. It's been years since someone fucked you properly."

"Gar, before this, I'd *never* been fucked properly. That's what pisses me off. Turns out, I'm more than capable of orgasming from sex. Marc just didn't know what he was doing. But what really bothers me, is that nobody will ever compare to Wes. I feel like he's ruined me for all men. Like, how can I go from Godiva truffles to sugar-free, store-brand chocolate syrup?"

I snort. "I see your analogy game's still strong."

"Seriously, though. I'm just . . . I dunno."

"So, he's hung. Plenty of us are," I say with a smirk.

Lena rolls her eyes. "You men and your dicks. I'm sure if I had one, you'd be trying to compare."

I laugh and tug her braid. "Yeah, probably. But for the record, I'm in Godiva territory."

"No kidding, you tool. I've seen you naked."

I'm sure most best friends haven't seen each other naked, but we have. Many, many times. But it was never in a sexual context. And it never will be. While I admit, Lena is one of the most beautiful women I've ever seen, she's sacred. I figured that out a long time ago. If there was ever a forbidden fruit, it's her. While I may have a "borderline sex addiction"—whatever the fuck that means—I'd die before I tainted her with my darkness. Besides, she's like a sister to me and incest isn't my thing.

She punches my shoulder. "And I'm not just referring to size. It's the overall experience. I mean, at this point, I'm giving up and joining the convent."

"Until Wes calls . . ."

"*If* he calls," she mutters.

"Why don't you get his number from Jake? I understand the pride thing, but you should call the fucker out."

"If he contacts me, I'll give him another chance. I'll wait for him, but I won't chase him. I deserve to be chased for once."

"Been telling you that for years," I mumble.

She sighs. "I know."

I glance at Lena. *To mention or not to mention . . .*

"What?" she asks. "Why are you making that face?"

I smirk because she can always see right through me. "Limp-Dick-Pussy Numero Uno called me while you were gone."

"Marc?"

I curl my lip at his name. "The one and only."

Her eyes widen in shock. "What the hell did he want?"

"He wanted to know why I *let* you go on a wilderness trip by yourself."

Lena arches a brow. "*Let* me?"

"Yep. Said I was irresponsible and reckless." My anger bubbles to the surface just thinking about the stupid fuck. "Said you weren't equipped to handle yourself out there. And *he* would've never let you do something like that. Apparently, I don't care about your well-being."

"He's unbelievable," she sputters. "I handled myself just fine. Who the fuck does he think he is? He never cared about me when we were together. Why the sudden concern?"

"Guilty conscience?" I offer. "Anyway, he demanded I keep him in the loop."

"Did you?" She gives me a look, already knowing my answer.

"Fuck no." I shake my head. "I told him I'd send his regards when I saw you."

"I wanted his regards last year. He missed his opportunity."

For years, I stayed out of her relationship with the big-shot doctor because it wasn't my business, but if Donnelly thinks he's going to fuck with her head some more, I'll make it my business. "Don't you dare let him come crawling back. I'm telling you right now, Leens, I will sabotage the fuck out of any rekindling."

Lena grips my chin. "I'll *never* allow someone to treat me like that again. I'd rather be alone."

"Good, because I won't *let* you go there."

"If Marc thinks I take orders from any man, he clearly never knew me at all."

"Did you take orders from Wes?"

"Nope." She smirks. "But it was hot when he tried."

I grin and squeeze her shoulders. "That's my girl. Now, I'm gonna *let* you sit your ass down and eat a fucking bagel."

CHAPTER 12

WES

Life lesson: Hindsight is twenty-twenty.

Isla clasps my wrist as I reach for another orange wedge. "Why ya look so sad?"

"Oh, I dunno, we just left a funeral?" I offer. "Would ya prefer I dance a jig or something?" I snatch the fruit, peel it from the rind, and pop it into my mouth.

"No, arsehole. You know what I mean."

We sit at the bar in a Sydney restaurant. Family and friends had caravanned from the cemetery to gather for a memorial luncheon for Gwen.

After I finish chewing, I take a long sip of ale and meet my sister's laser blue gaze. She stares unblinkingly for a few moments, and I sigh. "Lena won't return my calls."

"Can ya blame her?"

"I've left voicemails trying to explain myself. Had I known this would happen, I would've broken down her door."

"Why didn't you wake her, again?"

"Because she was exhausted, and I wanted to let her sleep. The woman saved my life, then sat vigil for days, taking care of me."

"She's a nurse, right?"

"Yeah, but this went beyond any nursing I've ever experienced. She kept me as comfortable as she could, given the circumstances. She even helped me out of the tent when I needed to piss and shit."

Isla grimaces. "Please tell me she didn't have to wipe your arse . . ."

"No, but she would've done it if I needed her to."

"That must've been embarrassing."

"You have no idea, Imp." I chuckle at the memory of the argument we had when Lena insisted I tell her about my bowel movements. *I'm a fucking nurse, Wes. Bodily functions don't faze me. Now, did you poop or not?* Lena's version of tough love sucked at times, but I'm grateful for her.

"She sounds amazing."

"That wasn't the half of it. She cleaned my wounds, fed me, and made sure I was hydrated. She forced me to cough every hour, so I wouldn't get pneumonia. She washed and dressed me when all I wanted was to lie there and rot." I meet her gaze. "Isla, that first night, the pain was so bad, I begged them to kill me. Every single breath felt like I was being stabbed. Lena never left my side. Her voice, her eyes, and her soft touch kept me going. After everything she did for me, she deserved a decent night's sleep."

"I get it. And I love her for taking such good care of you." She shakes her head. "But I still don't understand why you didn't leave a more detailed note."

"I was *exhausted*, likely still doped up from the morphine, and in a shitload of pain. Clearly, my decision-making skills were fucked. Of course, I can say that after the fact. At the time, the only thing on my mind was getting to the hospital as soon as possible. I fucked up Reed's entire life—the least I could do was make an appearance at his wedding."

"He wouldn't have met Cora if the accident never happened, Wes. In some crazy way, it was all meant to be."

I snort. "You sound like Memphis."

"Well, it's true. You need to find the silver lining here. Even with Gwen's passing . . . I mean, as terrible as it was, at least she's no longer suffering. If she'd been well, Reed would've gone to Alaska and you would've never met Lena."

"I know. But she's angry with me and it's ripping me apart."

She smiles softly and pats my hand. "That's because you love her."

"I'm lost without her."

And it's true. I can't eat, can't sleep. I've been pacing my flat like the more steps I take, the better my chances of earning Lena's forgiveness will be. I've never considered myself an anxious person, but ever since Alaska, my nerves are shot. With all my pacing, I've probably climbed Everest by now. Twice.

"I'm surprised by all this. You don't date women who aren't in the industry, and I thought ya didn't want anything serious." Her lips curve into a smirk.

"I didn't, but she opened my eyes. Lena changed everything I thought I knew about life." I meet my sister's gaze. "I need her, Isla."

"Then make sure *she* knows that."

"But she's avoiding me . . ."

"Then become *un*avoidable." Isla leans in close. "C'mon, Wes. You've always been the man who gets what he wants."

"You don't know Lena—she's a fighter," I mutter. "My playbook doesn't apply. She battles me every step of the way."

Isla grips both sides of my face. "If you truly love her, then I suggest you put on your war paint, *Ares*."

GARRETT

It's sometime after eleven when I finally get home. I study the contents of my fridge, but there's nothing appealing, and I don't feel like cooking. I grab the container of milk. Me thinks it's a cereal-for-dinner kind of night. I glance at my watch.

More like a midnight snack at this point.

As I crunch on a colossal bowl of Lucky Charms, I chase a shamrock with my spoon and aimlessly tap the counter. I need to eat better. Sure, I work out, but without proper nutrition, I fear I'll run out of steam. I bite into a shooting star and vow to do better tomorrow. Yeah, tomorrow I'll go to the grocery store and maybe pick up some quinoa or something. Lena eats that shit all the time and she's usually pretty healthy. A muffled scream interrupts my musings.

Lena!

I leap from the stool, toppling it. I snatch my keys, run into the shared foyer, and grab the baseball bat Lena had stashed. If someone's trying to hurt her, I'll beat their fucking brains in. I rush upstairs, taking the steps two at a time, then thrust my key into the lock and sprint to her bedroom.

I freeze in the doorway, watching Lena kick and thrash, her legs tangling her sheets. She flings out her arms and wails something incomprehensible.

I gently place the bat on her dresser and walk over to her bed. Sweat-drenched, her hands claw the material of the fitted sheet and she screams again.

To wake her or not to wake her?

After some lunatic at her job attacked her, nightmares and panic attacks were regular events. Sometimes, she'd wake up screaming, and others, she'd drift back into a fitful slumber. I lost track of the number of times I held her in her sleep.

She moans something about a wolf and thrashes some more. She spends her days battling anxiety, and I hate that she can't escape the torment during sleep.

"He can't run," she wails.

I sit on the edge of her bed and firmly grip her shoulders. "Wake up, Leens. It's just a dream—you're safe."

"They're coming! He's gonna die!"

"Nothing's coming, you're safe," I repeat softly.

Her eyes flutter open and her gaze settles on my face. "How'd you get in the tent? Where're the wolves?" she whispers, her eyes darting around the room.

"You're safe. The wolves are gone."

My voice must have finally registered because she sits up and wipes the sweat from her brow. "I was dreaming?"

"Yes."

She flops against her pillows. "I'm a fucking mess."

"Do you want to talk about it?" I brush the hair off her face.

She untangles her legs. "No."

I know she'll talk when she's ready, so I stand and shuffle back a step. "Okay, I'm gonna head home now. Do you want a drink of water or anything?"

"Wait," she whimpers, scuttling to the edge of her bed. "Can I please come with you? I can't be alone right now."

I pull her into a tight hug. "Of course."

She melts against me, her breathing slowly coming back to normal. "I fucking hate wolves."

"I know. But you guys escaped them. Try to remember you're safe." I bring my lips to her ear. "Please call Dr. Turner tomorrow."

She doesn't acknowledge my plea. At all. That's the thing about Lena. She doesn't do anything until she's ready. While I've accepted that I need to see my shrink on a regular basis, she thinks she can handle everything on her own. We both know that's bullshit—she's been home five days and hasn't left the house once.

Lena trails behind me as we enter my apartment. She settles on my couch as I move to the corner of the room. "Here's a blanket. I'll go turn up the heat."

"Thanks, Gar. Love you."

"Love you too, Leens. Please, try to rest. Remember, there are no wolves in Brooklyn."

CHAPTER 13

LENA

Internal playlist: "No Light, No Light" by Florence + The Machine

I smell coffee. The aroma is a harbinger of bliss. I stretch and yawn. Garrett's couch is too warm and comfortable to warrant rising, so I snuggle beneath the blanket instead. He mills around in the kitchen, talking to someone. I crane my neck to listen.

"Just forward the files when you get a moment. Thanks, Jules."

Juliana. I wonder why he bothered to call his secretary when he'll be seeing her in—*Wait, what time is it?* I squint at the cable box. *Nine forty-five. He's running late.*

Garrett enters the living room with two cups of coffee in hand. "Morning."

"Hey," I mumble, eyeing his T-shirt and green plaid pajama pants. "Aren't you running a little late?"

"Working from home today. Didn't get enough sleep to deal with actual humans."

Guilt squeezes my chest. "Sorry."

"Don't apologize, Leens. I'm still working." He runs a hand through his unruly black waves. "Besides, you saved me the trouble of shaving."

I accept the mug and take a sip. "Mmm . . . How do you make the coffee so damn good?"

Garrett settles on the couch by my feet and turns on his laptop. "Pixie dust." He stretches out his legs, resting his feet on top of the coffee table. "I mix a little dark roast with a little breakfast blend and *voila.*" He wiggles his fingers.

"Okay, Peter Pan. Care if I watch the news for a minute?"

He tosses me the remote. "Go for it."

I sip my coffee while flipping through the channels. "Ugh. I forgot it's an election year. I hate politics."

Garrett chuckles. "It was an election year before you left for Alaska. Pretty sure you were only gone a month."

I glare at him playfully. "Yeah, and I hated them then too."

The news segment switches to a commercial for one of my favorite late-night shows.

"Tonight, on Aidan McDowell, we catch up with Australian actor, Wes Emerson, as he recounts the tale of his Alaskan wilderness survival nightmare. Join us at ten for our exclusive interview with the Aussie heartthrob."

I freeze, staring at Wes's face on the screen, my hand inches from the remote.

Garrett jerks his head in my direction. "Leens?"

I have a history of avoidance in times of heartache. Out of sight, out of mind is my go-to coping method. Dr. Turner always told me I need to face my pain, confront it head-on, but I'm the quintessential ostrich. Since my return, I've buried my head in the sand and willed the hurt to disappear. I know I'm not doing myself any favors trying to purge all memory of Wes. Especially since I love him so deeply. I'm not stupid; I know I can't exist in this world without stumbling across his face—be it on television, in a magazine, or on the big screen. Wes Emerson is ubiquitous. Even more so since his return from Alaska. No matter how hard I try to hide, his memory finds me. No, Wes isn't going anywhere even though he vanished from my life.

GARRETT

I touch Lena's knee to get her attention. "Do you want me to watch it with you?" She turns to face me. If she were a fucking basilisk, I'd be dead. I throw my hands up in surrender. "Okay, okay. Don't shoot daggers at me, it was just a question."

"I'm sorry," she mumbles, lurching to her feet. She rushes into the bathroom without another word.

Once she's out of sight, I program my DVR to record the show. She doesn't have to watch it, but I'm curious to hear what that fucker has to say for himself. Will he mention the woman who saved his life? Or will he pretend she doesn't exist—like she's trying to do with him—and move on?

Lena reappears, wordlessly settling onto the couch with her back to me. She burrows into the cushions.

"Try not to suffocate, okay?"

Lena has been in the same position all day. She's so quiet, I almost forgot she was here. If not for her breathing, she could be mistaken for an odd lump of decorative throw pillows.

She's in shelter mode now.

I know better than to engage her because she'll only retreat deeper into herself. But every once in a while, I squeeze her ankle, just so she knows I'm here.

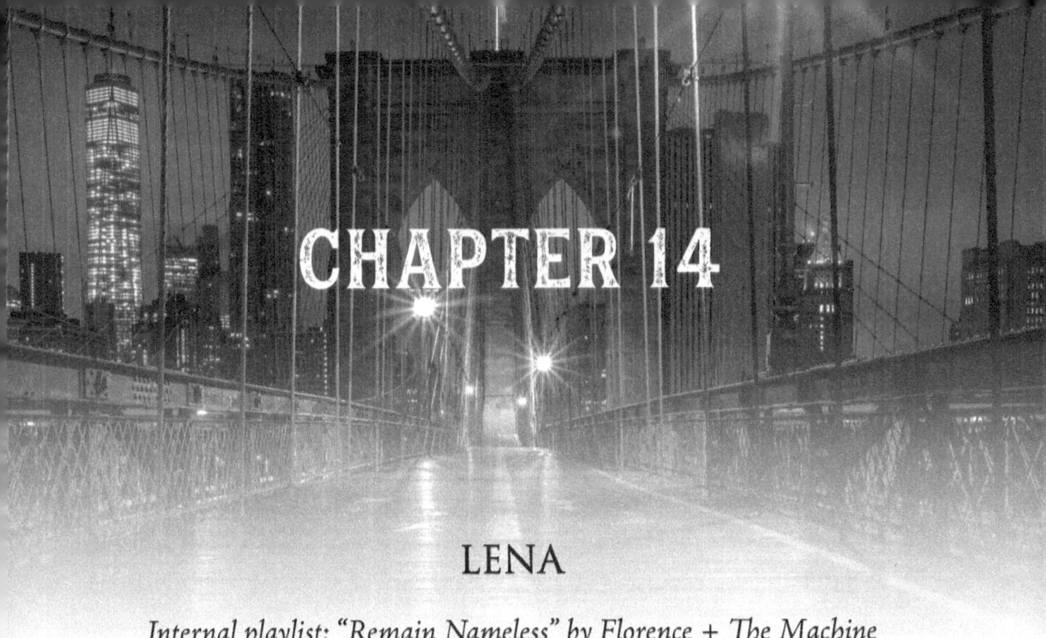

LENA

Internal playlist: "Remain Nameless" by Florence + The Machine

Six days later, I look up as Garrett walks into my living room. He just got home from work and still has his tie on.

I set down my novel. "Hey."

"Hey, Leens." He plops on the couch beside me and presses his lips into a grim line.

I watch him nervously. "What?"

He holds up a magazine.

I freeze, my gaze locked on a photo of me on the upper corner of the cover. I snatch it and gape at the picture—my hideous employee photo from New York General. The magazine is a celebrity gossip publication I often read on the subway. This issue features a story about Wes, Jake, and Austin, entitled "Arctic Survival." Beneath my photo, it reads, "Who is Lena Hamilton?"

"What the fuck?!"

"Saw it on a newsstand near Bryant Park," Garrett explains. "You're famous, Leens." He flashes me a cheesy smile.

I huff as I scan the table of contents and locate the article.

Manhattan trauma nurse, Lena Hamilton, age 32, accompanied the celebs on their wilderness trek. The Brooklyn resident's association with the men is unclear, but sources hinted

at a possible love triangle. According to a
source close to Jake Bennett, Hamilton is ro-
mantically involved with both the singer, and
Aussie heartthrob, Wes Emerson.

I drop the magazine. "Are you fucking kidding me?"

Garrett wags his brows. "You never mentioned participating in a
ménage a trois."

"Because I didn't," I grit out.

"Relax. I'm just fucking with you. You know this shit's all fabricated."

"They have my picture, Garrett. And they know where I live." I lurch
to my feet.

"Where are you going?"

I quickly close the blinds, panic chilling my veins. "I'm probably being
watched. Next thing I know, my fucking boobs will be on a billboard in
SoHo."

Garrett chuckles. "I think you're getting ahead of yourself. I imagine
they'd be on the side of a bus first."

My eyes well up and I wrap my arms around myself. "I don't like this.
I don't want people scrutinizing my every move."

"Hey, calm down, honey." He walks over and hugs me. "Don't worry,
it'll blow over quickly. I wasn't gonna grab it, but I figured you should be
informed. You know, in case someone from high school reaches out or
something. At least this way, you know what's out there. Right?"

"This is what they deal with all the time," I mutter against his chest.
"I don't know how the fuck they do it. Wes told me that some chick he'd
never met tried to get child support from him for a kid he supposedly
fathered."

Garrett moves back to look at me. "Have you heard from him?"

"No," I whisper.

My cell rings and my stomach lurches—like it does *every* time the damn
thing makes a sound since my return. I turn off the kitchen faucet and

quickly dry my hands. Snatching the phone, I peer at the unfamiliar area code. My heart flutters on a glimmer of hope.

"Hello?" The breathless greeting is unintended.

"Lena, what the fuck were you thinking?"

Fucking Trevor. My heart sinks. Again. With him being nine years older, my brother is more like a second father—there for the criticism, but little else. At best, our tumultuous relationship is a thorn in my side.

"Hello, Trevor." I glance at the calendar on the fridge. "Wow, I'm surprised it only took you eleven days to acknowledge my existence. So nice to hear your voice—"

"What made you think it was wise to go to the fucking wilderness by yourself?"

I pull the phone away from my ear as I fill the kettle and place it on the stove. "I never claimed to be wise." I flick on the burner and grab my favorite mug. Hopefully, a cup of tea will rid my body of the chill that clings to me, although a wool sweater and cranking the heat hasn't helped yet.

"Cut the shit, Lena. I asked you a question."

I clench the phone. "What, are you my keeper?"

"Well, someone ought to be."

"Look, if you're calling for your pound of flesh, now's not a good time—I don't have the energy."

"Get the energy, Lena," Trevor sighs, "because this is getting old."

"What the hell are you talking about?"

"Your shitty life decisions."

I pace the kitchen and nearly trip on Harry, sending him scurrying down the hall. "Tell you what, Trev, next time I make a vacation decision, I'll run it by you first."

"You know what I mean," he says in a gentler tone. "No one even knew you were going to Alaska."

"Garrett knew," I correct him.

"I'm talking about your *family.*"

My eyes tighten as anger simmers in my veins. "Garrett *is* my family." My voice is low and dangerous. "I'm fucking sick of you undermining my relationship with him."

There's a pause before Trevor has the balls to speak again. "Whatever, Lena. He didn't think to stop you, or at the very least, inform the rest of us?"

"Pretty sure he called Mom—"

"*After* you fucking went missing. Then, we had to see your face all over the news," Trevor sputters. "I mean, why would he let you do something so reckless?"

"Gar's not my keeper. In case you've forgotten, I'm an adult. I do what I want, when I want, and I don't need your—or anyone else's—permission."

"Goddammit, Lena. Sometimes you act like such a petulant little brat."

"Did you call to insult me, or did you have a fucking purpose?" I snap.

"Mom's a nervous wreck . . . said you won't return her calls."

"Maybe I don't feel like talking to her. Come to think of it, I don't feel like talking to you, either."

Trevor sighs heavily. "Stop being childish."

"Setting boundaries isn't childish."

"Boundaries?"

"Yeah, I'm blocking out all enablers and instigators. I'll give you a hint . . . you're the second kind."

"Who do you mean by enablers?"

"Who do you *think* I mean?" When he doesn't respond, I add, "I'm talking about Mom, obviously."

"What happened with Mom?"

"You don't know?"

"Lena, please tell me what's going on."

"I guess some other news didn't make it to your little sanctuary in Tokyo. But I'll fill you in. Dad got another DWI."

"Another?"

"She bailed him out of jail instead of coming to see me after I got home, so, yeah, that kinda stung."

"Jesus Christ," Trevor mutters. "When will she open her fucking eyes?"

The kettle's shrill call fills the room. I pour hot water into my mug and settle on a stool. "Your guess is as good as mine, Trev. With everything I went through, and the fucked-up state my head's in, I'm keeping my distance. I can't be around the drama. I can't fix her life." I realized years ago I can't parent my parents.

"I can't believe she didn't tell me."

"Of course she didn't tell you. She's ashamed, Trevor. I only found out because Garrett was supposed to get her from the train station."

Trevor grunts. "What's going on with you and those men?"

I shake my head. "Holy subject change, Batman." He's always been super random, but I find it jarring today. Might have something to do with the men in question. Or, rather, the *man* I can't stop thinking about.

"Are you involved with them?" he asks.

I release a dark laugh. "You make it sound like my life's one big orgy."

"Seems that way. I saw a magazine article—"

"That's bullshit tabloid gossip and you know it. None of it's true—I'm not involved with anyone. I gotta go." I hang up and rest my head on the island. I'm too damn tired to explain it to Trevor, especially since I know he'll only yell at me for my "poor life choices."

I haul myself up the stoop and retrieve the mail. I walked a few blocks to clear my head after dealing with Trevor. The blustery October wind helped numb the ache that has settled in my chest. Nearly two weeks have passed since my return, and Wes hasn't called.

As much as it pisses me off, his influence extends to my perspective on time and direction. I finally have a concrete picture of what holds the most importance for me, and as a result, made some decisions for my life's path. These choices hold true even in his absence.

Eager to restore some normalcy, I called my boss, Dr. Soteris, to set up a timeline for my return to work. I declined the promotion he'd offered on my way out the door for my medical leave. I need to fill my tank—not drain it. After I described my physical injuries and alluded to my emotional state, we agreed that an extended leave of absence would be appropriate. I'll return to work part-time after the first of the new year. Dr. Soteris also urged me to reconnect with Dr. Turner, my old psychiatrist.

I've already suffered several panic attacks and multiple nightmares, my body thrumming in a constant state of anxiety. Nearly ten years ago, when my psychiatric patient assaulted me, fracturing my collarbone and nearly strangling me to death, PTSD and panic attacks reigned supreme. Dr. Turner helped me cope with the aftermath of the workplace incident, so he is more than capable of dealing with this fallout.

Now I face what has become my new normal—being alone.

Sure, I have Garrett, but he's busy. He spends his days at the office while preparations for *Prodigy* fill most of his evenings. He has a lot to learn before the production debuts next year.

I enter my apartment and leaf through the mail. A thick envelope catches my eye. It's addressed to me in peculiar, scrawled penmanship. Leaving the rest of the stack on the end table, I plop onto my couch with the mysterious letter. I open the envelope and withdraw a formal invitation to Jake's gala, along with his handwritten note.

Lena-Bean! I hope all is well. It's been EXTREMELY challenging for me to readjust to the real world, how about you? I miss your jokes and can't wait to see you guys in a couple of weeks. Garrett seems awesome. I look forward to introducing him to my theater contacts. (Not that he needs the help.) So AMAZING that he scored the lead in Prodigy! Enclosed is your invitation for the gala. I will send a car to pick you up at your place at six that evening.

Much love,

Jake

PS: See? I told you everything would work out..

I furrow my brow, refold the letter, and tuck it into the envelope. *What is he talking about?* I wonder what line of bullshit Wes is feeding his friends.

The buzzer to my front door rings, making me jump. I glance at my watch. Garrett isn't due home for an hour. *Who could this be?*

"Hello?" I say into the speaker.

"Hey chicky, it's me. Let me in," Rita commands.

I bound to the front door and hold it open for my coworker, who's carrying a gorgeous floral arrangement. "Hey, Rita."

"Hey, girl." She kisses my cheek and follows me upstairs.

"Thanks for coming to see me."

"Of course. These are for you." Rita places the vase on the kitchen island.

"They're gorgeous," I gush, eyeing the pink and white stargazer lilies interspersed with red roses. "Thank you."

"They're not from me." Rita tosses her obsidian locks over a shoulder and chews her lip. "Marc sent me over with them."

My lip curls. *Why would Marc send flowers?*

"We're all so relieved that you're safe," she explains, as if reading my mind. "You know how he is with words. He's been a mess since you went missing. God help him if he were to attempt to express his feelings."

She has a point there. Although, he could've delivered them himself. *Limp-Dick-Pussy.* Turns out, Garrett's nickname for my ex is fitting. However, it's still a sweet gesture and I'm not such a bitch that I can't appreciate some kindness now and then. Smiling, I send Marc a quick text thanking him.

"How're Javier and your boys?" I set my phone down.

"Driving me crazy, but everyone's good. How are you holding up?" Rita settles onto a stool at the island.

"I dunno." I sigh. "I feel anxious all the time. And I've been down."

Rita studies me with warm, gingerbread-colored eyes. "You need to do something fun, chicky. You can come willingly, or Garrett and I can force you."

"I'll come willingly," I concede with a laugh. "I'm just exhausted on every level."

"Did you call Dr. Turner yet?" Her knowing gaze burns into me.

"No."

"Garrett said you had a panic attack?"

"I've had several since my return."

"Lena, I know you think you're being strong by trying to deal with this on your own, but we're worried about you. There's strength in asking for help."

"I know. He's in the office tomorrow. I'll call him."

"Good." Rita smiles. "What are we doing for dinner?"

"Uh, I haven't shopped in a while. Do you wanna go out?"

"I'm down. What do you feel like?"

"Well, I've had Chinese three times this week, so not that."

"What about Ralph's?" Rita suggests. "You love their burgers. And we can walk there. You need to get your ass out of this house."

Ralph's Tavern is a few blocks from the brownstone, and we work with the bartender's sister. I suppose a field trip with a friend is exactly what the doctor ordered.

"I haven't seen Teddy in ages," I say. "Yeah, let's do it."

Teddy is a burly, bearded man with a jovial demeanor. He hooks us up with extra appetizers and wine, and soon enough, we're stuffed. After several hours of laughter, we hug him goodbye.

"It was great to see you, Ted," I say.

"You too. Tell Garrett I said hello."

"Will do."

Teddy gestures to us. "Don't be strangers."

"We won't." Rita elbows me. "Right?"

"Right."

On the way back to the brownstone, Rita fills me in on some hospital gossip. When we round the final corner before my home, a camera crew stops us.

The fucking local news.

This is exactly why I haven't been leaving the house much. It was only a matter of time before they found me.

"Excuse me, Ms. Hamilton," an attractive blonde reporter says. "We just wanted to ask you a couple questions. What was it like, being lost in the Alaskan wilderness?" She holds her microphone out to me with a bright smile.

"It was terrifying."

"How did everyone else feel about it?"

"I won't discuss anyone else."

"*Celebrity Buzz* reported that you're in a relationship with Jake Bennett and Wes Emerson. What do you have to say about that?"

"I have nothing to say about that," I reply coolly. "Perhaps instead of butting into our lives, the media should allow us to get back to them."

Her eyes glitter with intrigue. "Sources tell us you hold Wes Emerson's attention in particular."

"That would be a question for Mr. Emerson. Now, if you'll excuse me—" I move to step around the reporter.

Unfortunately, she's quicker and blocks my path. "What was it like out there with three megastars? How did an ordinary girl like yourself get mixed up with them?" She shoves the microphone in my face again.

Rita steps in. "Nope. We're done here."

I hold up my hand. "No, I'll answer that one. What's your name?"

"Brooke Burns, *News Nine*."

"Well, Brooke, let me enlighten you," I snap. "In the wilderness, we were *all* ordinary. Mother Nature didn't give a damn about the number of lives I've saved. And she certainly wasn't concerned with album sales or box office records. We were four people fighting for our lives. We held on—even when it seemed impossible—and somehow, we survived. All three megastars, as you called them, are quality human beings who treated me like I was one of them. I will not discuss any details, because unlike the media, I respect their privacy." I narrow my eyes at Brooke. "And I'd appreciate it if you'd respect mine."

CHAPTER 15

WES

Life lesson: Assumptions will bite you in the arse.

My phone buzzes. I tap on the screen and open Austin's message. I furrow my brow as the video clip loads.

"Who ya texting?" Isla asks.

We just finished lunch at my flat. Since my return, Isla has been my little shadow. She and Mum follow me around like they're afraid I'll go missing again. In truth, I don't mind. I appreciate the company. My family is more comforting than the bourbon anyway. Reed is still dealing with the aftermath of his mother-in-law's passing, but I hope to see more of him soon.

"Memphis sent me a video. Said it's from a coupla days ago."

"Of what?" At my raised brow, she adds, "Yeah, yeah, I know. I'm nosey." She leans over my shoulder, nevertheless. "Lemme see."

I press play and we watch a New York reporter approach a pair of women. I clench the phone as all my breath wooshes out of me. "That's Lena in the blue coat."

"She's beautiful."

My eyes never leave the screen as I smile. "I know."

I replay the clip four times.

The fifth time I reach for the play icon, Isla stops me. "Enough. Now, you're obsessing."

"That would be a question for Mr. Emerson?" I knot my fingers in my hair. "What is she not understanding? How much fucking clearer do I need to make myself?"

Isla touches my shoulder. "It doesn't sound like she watched the interview, Wes."

"Because she's fucking stubborn."

"Whaddya mean?"

"I mean, she's hiding. 'Retreat and hide' is her MO."

Isla cocks her head. "Thought you said she's a fighter?"

"She's both." I sigh. "She likes to push buttons—especially mine—but then she reaches a threshold where she shuts everyone out."

"Why don't you fly to New York?"

"Isla, I can't. *The Aegean's* press tour is about to start. I have all these stupid fucking obligations."

"Fuck the press tour."

"I wish I could," I mutter. "They've got me flying all over the world, until the damn movie comes out next month." I straighten and meet her gaze. "That reminds me. Do ya wanna be my date for the premiere?"

"No, thank you." She says it like I offered her a piece of old broccoli.

"*Seriously?*" I thought she'd jump at the opportunity to attend a red-carpet event.

"While I'd love quality time with my favorite brother, you know how much I hate the spotlight." She cocks her head. "Besides, I thought you wanted to ask Lena."

"In case you couldn't tell from that clip, she also hates the spotlight. I'm sure the fuckers are harassing her." I rub my jaw. "I was going to ask her, but Bennett invited her to his gala before I had a chance . . . and now it seems like she doesn't want anything to do with me."

She grips my wrist. "Wait . . . Jake's having a gala?"

"Yeah, it's in Manhattan on the second Friday in November. It's a benefit for his foundation. He's trying to raise money to build a community center for the arts."

"Wow, that's amazing. You mean, like theater?"

"*All* the arts. He wants kids to have a safe place to be creative. Whether it be performing arts, music, fine arts, fashion—"

"Fashion?" she squeals.

"Yeah, there'll be costume design workshops and such. He was rambling about a bunch of sewing machines when I last talked to him."

"Consider yourself warned—I'm marrying Jake."

I snort. "Says the girl who brings home a different bloke every Christmas and won't sign a lease because she can't stay in one place for more than a few months."

She gives me the finger. "Unlike *you*, I haven't found one worth settling for."

"I'm not *settling* for Lena."

She shakes her head. "That's not what I meant. I'm referring to *my* life, and I mean settle in the literal sense. Why should I commit to a lease—or a man, for that matter—when I'm not sure that's where I wanna be? Why cage myself when I can fly free?"

"Even birds get tired, Imp. A home doesn't mean a cage."

"Like I said, I haven't figured it out yet. I'll settle when I'm ready. It's gotta be the right time, the right place, the right circumstances, you know?"

"Yeah . . . I know."

"I know you're not *settling* for Lena, but you're willing to make concessions and sacrifices to be with her, right?"

"Absolutely."

"I haven't found that, yet. I haven't found *my* person." She punches my arm. "But if all else fails, I'm marrying Jake."

I snort. "Jake is definitely *not* your person."

"How do you know?"

"Because you're *my* little sister. He's smarter than that."

She cocks a brow. "Are you insinuating I'm stupid?"

"No. I'm saying he's not interested in you."

"Again, how the hell would *you* know?"

"Because he's my best mate." I level a glare at her. "And he's way too old for ya, anyway."

"Age is only a number," she snips. "Besides, you don't own me . . . or him."

"You're at different stages in life—*you* can't give him what he needs." I grip her shoulders. "I'm serious. Jake is off-limits."

She rolls her eyes. "Whatever, Wes."

"Bennett knows better than to cross that line with me."

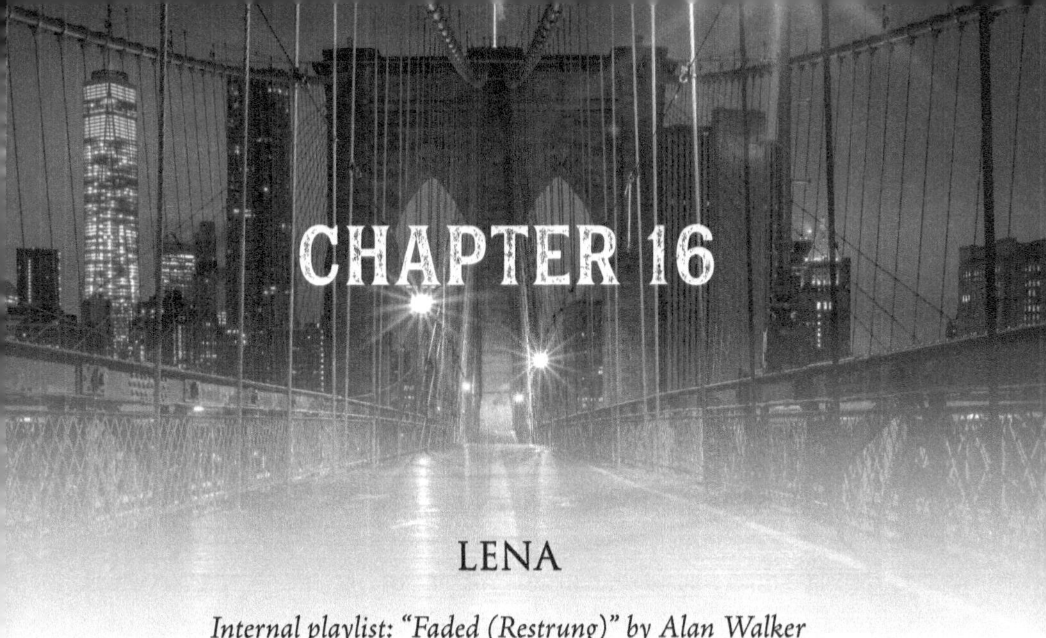

CHAPTER 16

LENA

Internal playlist: "Faded (Restrung)" by Alan Walker

I glare at Garrett and cross my arms over my chest. He's the most persistent bastard on Earth. "I really don't see the point."

I just returned from my second appointment with Dr. Turner. He agreed to see me twice weekly for the time being. Garrett met me in the foyer and dragged me into his living room. He's been trying to get me to watch Wes's interview for over a week now, but it took some convincing from Dr. Turner to get me to finally concede.

"Do you think I'd tell you to watch it if I thought it would upset you?" he demands. "I'm not *that* much of an asshole."

"No," I sigh, "go ahead."

"Good. Now, sit your ass down." He presses play on the DVR and plops on the couch beside me. He fast-forwards through the beginning of Wes's interview. "The first part is where he goes on about what happened, injuries, yada-yada-yada. You already know all that shit. I want you to watch the end."

I focus on the screen. Wes lounges in an armchair across from Aidan McDowell—clean-shaven, wearing khakis, and a white linen shirt with the sleeves rolled to his elbows. The phoenix tattoo on his wrist is visible, but he's not wearing his goddamn sling.

"Wow, Mother Nature really did a number on you," Aidan exclaims.

"Yes. Yes, she did." Wes nods. "But she was overruled."

"How so?"

Wes pivots his body and stares directly at the cameras. "The only reason I'm sitting here today, is because I happened to cross paths with an extraordinary force of nature who, with their stubborn refusal to let go, kept me tethered to this life."

I gape in disbelief. Garrett flashes an I-told-you-so look in my direction.

"Who is this force of nature?" Aidan asks.

"They know who they are and what they've done for me."

"So, you're saying it was all a matter of chance? A serendipitous twist of fate, perhaps?" Aidan muses.

"What I'm saying is that I owe this person my life—my everything. They hold my eternal gratitude and affection, and I'll do whatever it takes for them to understand how I feel." His solemn gaze fixes on the lenses in front of him. "I think we both learned a lot about ourselves."

I struggle to pull air into my lungs. I stare into Wes's eyes on the screen as the tears silently roll down my cheeks.

Then where are you, Ace?

It's true, I did learn a lot about myself in Alaska. I discovered the depth of my perseverance and my will to survive. I realized I'm stronger than I ever thought possible. And I unearthed the core of my womanhood. No, Marc had not destroyed me for all men. I'm still very much alive, very much a woman.

I glance at Garrett and reach for my phone. I dial Jake's number, but it goes to voicemail.

"Jake, it's Lena . . ." I grip the phone tightly. "Please call me when you get a chance." I hang up and wipe my tears.

"Why'd you call Jake?" Garrett asks.

"Because I need to know what the fuck is going on."

I spot Jake at a corner table in Ralph's Tavern. The impromptu dinner date was his suggestion when he returned my call from earlier. I smile and make my way over to him.

"Lena-Bean!" He stands and wraps me in a tight hug. He's one of the best damn huggers I've ever had the joy of hugging. "How the hell are you?"

"I'm . . . adjusting." I settle across the table from him. "How about you?"

"Same." He runs a hand through his chestnut waves. "It's crazy—I expected to feel relieved to be back to reality. But I'm not."

"What do you mean?"

"I'm anxious as fuck and my OCD is out of control."

"Did you go back on your meds?"

"Yeah, and I've been in Lola's office three times this week, but it's not helping."

Jake and Garrett both see Dr. Lola Ortiz, one of Manhattan's most renowned psychiatrists. Years back, she saved Garrett's life when I nearly lost him to his battle with alcoholism. During one of our heart-to-hearts in Alaska, Jake confided that she'd brought him back to life after a particularly rough patch in his teens.

"I finally called Dr. Turner. Had my second appointment today."

"Good." He flashes a crooked smile. "On the plus side, I found a floor cleaner that smells like an almond Danish . . . so there's that."

"Ah, so you're an anxious cleaner?"

"Yep. I clean and organize incessantly. Nearly asphyxiated myself with spray bleach the other day." He leans back in his chair. "I guess you could say I'm livin' the dream."

"How are you sleeping?" I ask.

His dark brows knit together. "When I actually sleep, I wake up in the middle of the night and don't know where I am. My friend Jesse keeps calling to make sure I eat. The dick has even forced me out of the house a few times."

"I've been having nightmares and panic attacks, so I totally get it."

"I guess since I mostly held it together out there, I figured I was in the clear." He sips his water. "I didn't expect to fall apart at home."

I nod. "Our adrenaline's worn off now."

"Austin's been on edge too. Katie told me he won't let her out of his sight. He keeps pacing the house, which is odd for him. Wes is the one who paces all the time. How's he doing, by the way?"

Pain shoots through me. "Who, Wes?"

"Yeah, I haven't talked to him since a couple days after I got back. Are his ribs any better?"

"I have no idea, Jake. He hasn't contacted me."

Jake stares, his chocolate-brown eyes going wide. "At all?"

"Nope," I say, popping the 'p.'

"That doesn't make any sense. He asked for your number."

"Oh? When was this?"

"The day we got home." He shakes his head in disbelief. "He called me from the hospital in Sydney."

My heart sinks. "Is Reed all right?"

"Reed is fine, but his mother-in-law passed away. That's why Wes left. Cora wanted her mom to see them get married, but Reed wanted Wes by his side and begged him to come home."

"Wait, Wes left the resort like a thief in the night—scaring the shit out of *all* of us—for a *wedding*? He asked for my contact info the day we got back, and here it is, two weeks later, and I *still* haven't heard from him?"

Jake gives me a sheepish look. "It sounds pretty fucked-up when you put it that way."

I cross my arms over my chest. "Because it *is* pretty fucked-up. Well, did he make it in time?"

"Barely. Gwen passed away when I was on the phone with Wes a few hours later." He shakes his head again. "I assume there was a funeral and all that, but like you said, it would've been two weeks ago… I don't understand. He literally *begged* for your contact info."

"Other than his cryptic note and the interview—"

"Clearly, I've been living under a rock. What interview?"

"He was on Aidan McDowell last week." I meet Jake's gaze. "He said he 'owes his life to an extraordinary force of nature who holds his eternal gratitude and affection.' I kinda figured that was me."

"Of course it's you." Jake rubs his jaw. "Something's not jiving, here. I'll call him later to see what I can find out." He squeezes my knee. "Don't worry, Lena-Bean."

WES

I'm washing dishes when my phone buzzes. It seems the bloody thing always makes a noise when I have wet hands. I snatch a towel and glance at the screen to find a text from Jake.

Jake: Get your shit together, dude!

What the hell is he talking about? Since I don't feel like fucking around with texts, I call instead.

Jake answers on the first ring. "Wes, what the fuck? I thought you were gonna call Lena?"

"I've called her a dozen times, mate. She never answers her damn phone. She's avoiding me."

"I had dinner with her tonight. She said you never called. Read me the number you've been dialing."

"555-555-5548"

Jake chuckles. "Well, I see the problem . . . That's not her number."

"That's the one ya gave me!"

"You switched the last two digits, man. Try 8-4, instead."

"Holy fuck. I gotta go." I hang up and stare at the phone, my hands shaking. Taking a deep breath, I dial the correct number this time. Praying I'm not too late, that I didn't fuck this up just because I can't write numbers correctly.

It goes straight to voicemail.

Fuck.

CHAPTER 17

LENA

Internal playlist: "Hear Me" by Kelly Clarkson

*S*eriously? I just dozed off when my phone vibrates on the nightstand. I yawn and reach for it. Unknown number. I silence it, but they immediately call back. I groan and silence it again. Then, my phone pings with a text.

Unknown: Answer your goddamn phone, sunshine.

I lurch upward and switch on the light. The phone rings a third time. My heart races as I accept the call. "Hello?"

"Oh, thank fuck," Wes blurts. "I didn't think you'd answer."

"Where the hell have—"

"I'm gonna FaceTime you. I need to see your face." He hangs up and my phone immediately chimes again.

Shit. I frantically smooth my hair and fix my shirt before answering. "Wes Emerson. Thought you fell off the face of the Earth."

His face is a mixture of agony and relief. "I'm sorry, sunshine."

"You're sorry? That's all you've got?" I shake my head. "You disappeared and waited over two *weeks* to call me."

"I'm sorry. I'll explain everything." He gestures to his screen. "Did I wake ya?" He's wearing a plain white T-shirt and I see cabinets and a fridge in the background, so I assume he's in his kitchen.

"No," I fib.

"My God," his grin overtakes his face, "it's good to hear your voice."

I glare at him. "Spare me the pleasantries."

"I know you're angry—"

"I'm heartbroken." I clench my jaw to keep the tears from spilling. "You promised we'd talk things over and then I woke up and you were *gone*."

"I left you a note."

"No, you left *Austin* a note. I wasn't too high on your list of priorities since all *I* had to go by was a cryptic, indirect message. So, I allowed myself a glimmer of hope. Thinking, okay, if Reed needs him, it makes sense he'd rush out. I'm sure I'll hear from him soon. I'm sure it wasn't goodbye . . ." I knot a hand in my hair, the other gripping my phone tighter. "I was so worried something happened to your brother. I kept praying for his safety and hoping for an update from you." I shake my head. "But then, over two fucking *weeks* passed. You have no idea how that felt, Wes. But I guess it shouldn't surprise me—my mom couldn't bother to get on a train either."

"What?"

"They arrested my father for drunk driving. She decided her time was better spent with him. I'm so tired of being everyone's fucking afterthought."

Wes shakes his head. "You're not my afterthought."

"I've been falling apart. Panic attacks, nightmares. I needed you, Wes," I whisper, my eyes welling, "but you were gone."

"Lena, listen to me," he commands. "I—"

"No, *you* listen to *me*. If you wanted to cut ties, you could've had the balls to tell me. I'm a big girl, Wes, I can handle it. I deserve better than being ghosted. I deserve better than a fucking slow fade. I gave myself to you . . ." I wipe a tear. "I gave you every part of me and I believed you wanted me. I believed you loved me." My voice breaks at the end, and I have to avert my eyes instead of looking at the man who broke my heart.

"I *do* love you! Listen, Reed called and said Gwen was dying."

"Jake filled me in. I heard all about the emergency wedding," I snip. "Did you catch the garter belt? What about the girl who caught the bouquet? Was she pretty? Did you guys dance?"

"The ceremony was in Gwen's hospital room, Lena. She died shortly afterward." He scrubs a hand over his face. "Look, I realize I was stupid—"

"I'm sorry for everyone's loss and I hope Gwen is at peace." I stiffen my spine. "Jake told me you asked for my number the day we got back. That was over two weeks ago, Wes." I wipe my tears again. "It didn't occur to you to call me?"

"Lena, I—"

"I figured you wanted to cut ties. So, I finally started coming to terms with everything, and then I saw you on Aidan McDowell—now my head's in a fucking tailspin again."

"Lena, I know I fucked up and hurt you, but I swear to God it wasn't intentional."

"Oh, so, calling me slipped your mind, then?"

"I'm trying to explain. For fuck's sake, shut your trap and *listen.*"

"I'm listening."

"I was on the phone with Reed until around midnight. I knocked on your door, but you didn't answer. I didn't wanna wake you." He clenches his jaw and begins to pace. "Had I known how hard it would be to reach you, I would've ripped the fucker off the hinges. I realize I should've explained my departure. You deserved a fucking note, and I'm so sorry I didn't write one." He rubs the back of his neck, the phone moving closer so just his face fills the screen. "No, I should've woken you up."

"Why the hell didn't you?"

"After all the shit we went through in Alaska—and how you went days without leaving my side—I wanted you to recover too. You needed your rest just as much as I did. I was trying to keep your best interests in mind, but I was so fucked-up with pain and fatigue, my mind wasn't working.

"I'm so sorry I gave you the impression you don't matter to me. That couldn't be further from the truth. Lena, in that moment, I was so worried about being there for Reed that everything else went by the wayside. I almost forgot a note entirely. The bush plane arrived, and I ran back into the lodge and scribbled my note. I asked Ellen to give it to Memphis. I *couldn't* let Reed down again . . . and I made it just in time."

I release a slow breath, feeling some of my anger start to dissipate. "I get it, but that doesn't explain the delay."

"I'm getting there, sunshine. Gimme a minute, would ya?"

"Go ahead."

"Anyway, after the ceremony, my parents, sister, and I gathered in the waiting room. I was on the phone with Jake when Gwen passed away." He begins to pace again. "So, I went from best man to pallbearer within three days. And then, you wouldn't return my calls. I went out of my mind trying to reach you."

"Uh, excuse me? I didn't receive a call from you until now. Believe me, I didn't let the damn phone out of my sight."

"I realize that, love. My roos were loose again, and I copied the number down incorrectly. Cora screamed when her mother passed, and I mixed up what Jake was saying," he explains. "I called you over a dozen times and left a bunch of voicemails, never realizing I had the wrong fucking number until an hour ago when I double-checked with Jake." He knots a hand in his hair. "I'm *such* a fuckwit."

"Oh my God. Here I thought you wanted nothing to do with me," I whisper in relief.

"Quite the opposite, love. I've been going insane." He rubs his jaw. "But I thought I would've heard from you after you received the flowers."

"What flowers?"

"I sent flowers to your job a few days ago." He smiles. "Roses and stargazer lilies for my stargazer. Did ya like them?" His face looks soft and unsure, disarming me of my remaining hostility.

"Wait, they were from *you?*"

"That would be why I had the florist sign my full name on the card and add my phone number. I hoped to hear from you . . . unless there's another Wes Emerson in your life?"

"Oh my God." I shake my head in disbelief. "Yes, I received them. They were gorgeous, thank you. But there wasn't a card. I haven't been at the hospital, so my friend Rita brought them over after work." I replay the day in my mind and stiffen. "Marc told Rita they were from *him*." My voice vibrates with anger. "I even sent that asshole a thank you text."

A dark expression passes over Wes's features. "No, love, they were from *me*. Told ya I didn't like that fucker."

I'm going to strangle Marc. And poison him. And beat him with a stick.

"Here I thought you seized the opportunity to cut ties with me because you didn't want to settle for someone ordinary. Or maybe Reed convinced you I wasn't worth your time. Then I thought after you saw me fully naked, you know . . . with actual lights on, that maybe I turned you off."

Wes gapes. His expression is almost comical. "Turned off by—" he mumbles, narrowing his eyes. "First of all, you're lucky I can't reach through this phone right now. I'm so fucking tired of hearing the word ordinary come out of your mouth."

"But what was I supposed to think, Wes? You know how insecure I am. I told you all the shit Marc put me through."

"I realize my behavior fucked with your mind, and I'm so sorry." He shakes his head in disbelief. "But to think I don't want you? Lena, you couldn't be more wrong. Do you know what would've happened after dinner if I'd woken you up?" He doesn't wait for a response. "After I'd finished with my brother, I would've taken you to my bed and ravaged you. Let me paint that picture for ya, sunshine . . .

"First, I would've stripped the clothes from your body. Then, I would've carried you to my bed and caressed every inch of your body with my hands and my mouth. I would've spread your legs wide, settled between your thighs, and devoured you. I would've held your hips in place and licked you up, down, and sideways. And when you couldn't take it any longer, I would've buried my cock deep inside you." He clenches his jaw and inhales slowly. "Lena, I would've made love to you all night long until your voice was hoarse from screaming my name. Until I had marked every inch of you and there was absolutely *no doubt* in your mind that you were mine and I was yours. And when you were too worn out to continue, I would have held you as you slept." He plops onto a stool and gestures to his lap. "I'm hard just thinking about it. So, don't you *dare* question my desire for you."

Speechless, I feel the heat of his gaze through the screen.

"And *never* doubt my love. Lena, I'm crazy about you. I went out of my mind trying to reach ya. Once I get you in my arms, I promise I won't let go."

Tears stream down my cheeks.

"I miss you," I whisper, "so fucking much. When can I see you again?"

"My press tour starts tomorrow," he mutters. "I'll be in Europe for most of the week." He perks up. "What're ya doing the following week? When do you go back to work?"

"I took a leave of absence until January, so my schedule's open."

His brows pop. "What about your promotion?"

"I turned it down . . . it's not for me."

"Are you happy with your decision?"

I straighten. "Yes. Life's too short to put that kind of pressure on myself. I need to fill my tank, not drain it."

Wes smiles. "I'm proud of you, sunshine."

"Thanks."

"I want you to meet me in Los Angeles the Thursday after next. I'll be there for a few days. I have a bunch of shit going on, but my evenings are free. Please come stay with me."

"I don't want to interfere with your work—"

"I'll have a hotel room in Beverly Hills. You can stay there, explore the city, or come with me to events—totally your call. We can go for dinner, order room service, I really don't care . . . I just need you in my arms at night."

"Of course I'll come. Send me the details and I'll book my flight."

He shakes his head. "I'll take care of everything. Text me your email address. Your boarding passes will be emailed to you within the hour."

"Thanks."

"No, thank *you*. You have no idea how happy this makes me. I wanna introduce you to my sister and costars."

"I thought Isla lives in Melbourne?"

Wes chuckles. "She does, but the little imp's been up my arse since I returned. I told her if she left me alone for an hour, I'd let her come to LA when I'm there. I booked her a room near Rodeo Drive so she can check out the fashion scene."

"I can't wait to meet her."

"Trust me, the feeling's mutual. I spoke to Alainna yesterday and she's eager to meet my 'off-screen Aphrodite' too. Maybe we can join her and her fiancé for dinner one night."

Alainna Baker, Wes's on-screen Aphrodite, is a goddess among mortals. I know I shouldn't feel jealous, but I can't help it—Alainna is perfection. Perfect hair. Perfect body. Perfect smile. She's a talented actress with a formidable Hollywood presence. Plus, she gets to kiss Wes on a regular basis. I wonder how I'll stomach *The Aegean's* erotic content.

"I'd love to."

He laughs. "If my clairvoyance ever shits itself, your facial expressions will do the trick."

"What are you talking about?"

"Your look at the mention of Alainna's name. Did ya miss the part where I said her *fiancé?*"

I feel the heat crawl up my neck and cover my cheeks. "No, I heard you, Ace. I'm just—"

He grins and cocks his head to the side. "Jealous?"

"Yeah, maybe a little."

"Don't worry, sunshine. My heart is in your hands. And my mind, body, and soul."

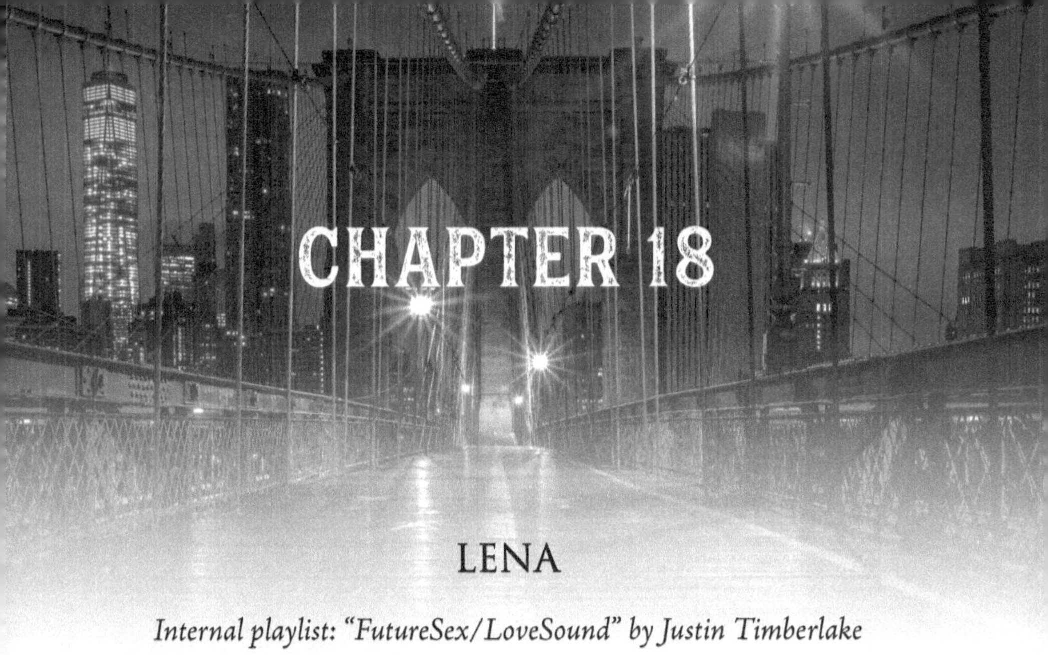

CHAPTER 18

LENA

Internal playlist: "FutureSex/LoveSound" by Justin Timberlake

11 days later

I scan the bustling Los Angeles airport. With its palm trees and sunshine, LAX is nicer than JFK, but just as busy. The drivers for various car services linger on the sidewalk with signs indicating their intended passengers. A brutally handsome man in a tailored navy suit, who's built like a tank, holds one that reads, "Adele Montclair."

Bingo.

In hopes of maintaining my anonymity, I asked Wes to have the driver use my mother's maiden name. I cautiously approach the man, whose resemblance to the fictional renegade veteran, John Rambo, has me reciting lines from *First Blood* in my mind. Garrett loves the Rambo movies, which means I've seen them more times than I care to admit.

With his rigid stance and how his thick arms stretch the material of his suit, the guy makes me wonder if I'll need to show ID. I hadn't considered that possibility. Not that it matters. My on-the-fly decision to impersonate my mother didn't leave me any option. It's not like I could've driven to Windham and sifted through stacks of documents.

Hopefully, Rambo doesn't give me any shit.

The driver's dark hair is cropped short and slightly graying at his temples. His inviting smile contrasts with an ice blue gaze. "Are you Adele?"

I grin. "I am."

"I'm Paul. Welcome to Los Angeles." He reaches for my luggage. "Let me have your suitcase." He grabs the handle and leads me to where he's parked across the street in the lot.

I thank him and settle in the back seat of a luxury SUV while he stuffs my overpacked red suitcase in the back.

Paul climbs into the driver's seat and fastens his belt. "Do you want to stop for coffee or anything?"

"I just had some, thank you."

"All right, make yourself comfortable . . . the traffic's intense."

Paul smoothly weaves through the lines of vehicles. My eyes widen at a passing Ferrari. A hideous lime green, with tinted windows, it's almost as obnoxious as the red Lamborghini that revs its engine beside us. I peer at the driver—some young punk with spiky hair and tattoos.

I trace the vehicle's sleek lines with my eyes. "Do the doors really open like wings?"

Paul chuckles. "Sure do. This your first time in LA, Lena?"

"Yes." I meet his gaze in the rearview mirror. "Wait, you know who I am?"

He winks. "Of course I do. What the hell kind of bodyguard would I be if I didn't?"

Bodyguard? Oh, right.

"Normally I follow Wes around, but I've been given a dual assignment for the next few days." In a mock Australian accent, he adds, "All right, mate, do ya think you can handle my little sister *and* my woman? One's a flight risk and the other's feisty as hell."

I laugh. "You do that perfectly."

"I know." He chuckles. "It pisses him off, so I've honed my craft."

"It sounds like you and I will get along just fine, Paul. And don't worry . . . I'll save the feistiness for Wes."

Paul and I laugh and chat the whole way to the hotel. I learn he's been working for Wes ever since the first *Olympus Fire* movie came out nearly eight years ago. He's familiar with Austin and Jake as well.

"So, what's on the agenda for today?" I ask as we park. "I know Wes mentioned he's pretty booked."

"He did some rearranging." Paul grins. He hops out and makes his way around to my door, pulling it open for me. "By that, I mean, he took today off. I believe his exact words were, 'Your job is to pick up Isla and keep her occupied. Don't come around until tomorrow—I need to *reacquaint* myself with my woman.'"

Oh my God.

My face heats, and arousal floods my core. "Oh." My knees buckle as I step out onto the pavement.

Paul grips my arm to steady me. "You okay?"

"I'm good. Just a little nervous."

"That's understandable." He chuckles and moves to the back, opening the SUV's hatch. He lifts my suitcase out and extends the handle. "Especially since he followed it up with a warning about firing me if I so much as *thought* about knocking."

Holy. Fuck.

I force a swallow as my legs turn to rubber. I follow Paul inside, where we take the elevator to the top floor.

"There's a great view of the Hollywood sign from up here," he informs me as the doors slide open. "Make sure you take a look. Or ask Wes to take you to the Griffith Observatory."

"Uh-huh."

We walk to the end of the hall and I glance at the placard outside Wes's room.

Mother of God, he booked the honeymoon suite.

Paul hands me a key card and his business card. "Here's your room key and my contact information. Save it in your phone. If you need me—any time, day or night—I'll be there. I'm so glad to finally meet you, Lena. He's been talking about you nonstop."

"Thank you, Paul. Nice to meet you as well."

Hands trembling, I stare at the key card. Truth be told, everything trembles, including my insides. I'm one big fluttery mess.

Paul holds his card to the magnetic panel. "He's waiting for you." The light on the panel turns green, and he pushes the door open. Setting my suitcase on the floor, he ushers me inside with a wink. "See you tomorrow."

"Bye." My voice is barely above a whisper. I've never had anticipation grip me like this—where it zings through my veins like a drug. Probably because I've never shared a hotel suite with Wesley Emerson. After weeks of discreet tent sex, we'll finally be alone.

In a bed.

Naked.

Paul leaves, the door softly clicking behind him.

I see the trail of rose petals first—dozens of them, their deep red color bathed in candlelight. Soft music reaches my ears as I tentatively enter the suite.

"You here, Ace?"

"Damn right, I am." His booming voice rumbles through me, drawing me deeper into the room. "Get your sweet arse in here."

Wes leans against a far wall in the living room, holding a single red rose. Clean-shaven, with tousled hair and a devilish grin, he's so devastatingly gorgeous, it hurts.

"Hey."

"Hey, yourself." He straightens his tie. He's wearing a black suit—no doubt custom made for him—that molds to the hard musculature beneath. Muscles I can't wait to get my hands on.

"We match." I wipe my sweaty palms on the material of my royal blue dress. I wore it on purpose because it matches his eye color, but I didn't expect him to wear a shirt the same shade.

"We do. You look stunning, love." He gestures to my suitcase. "But you overpacked . . . again."

I chew my lip. "You said three days."

His gaze darkens. "Yes, I did," his voice grows husky, "but you won't need clothes for most of them."

My breath wooshes out of me and every nerve ending flares to life. My lady bits throb in response to his words, growing wetter than I thought possible.

Wes steps closer and holds out the rose. "Come dance with me, sunshine."

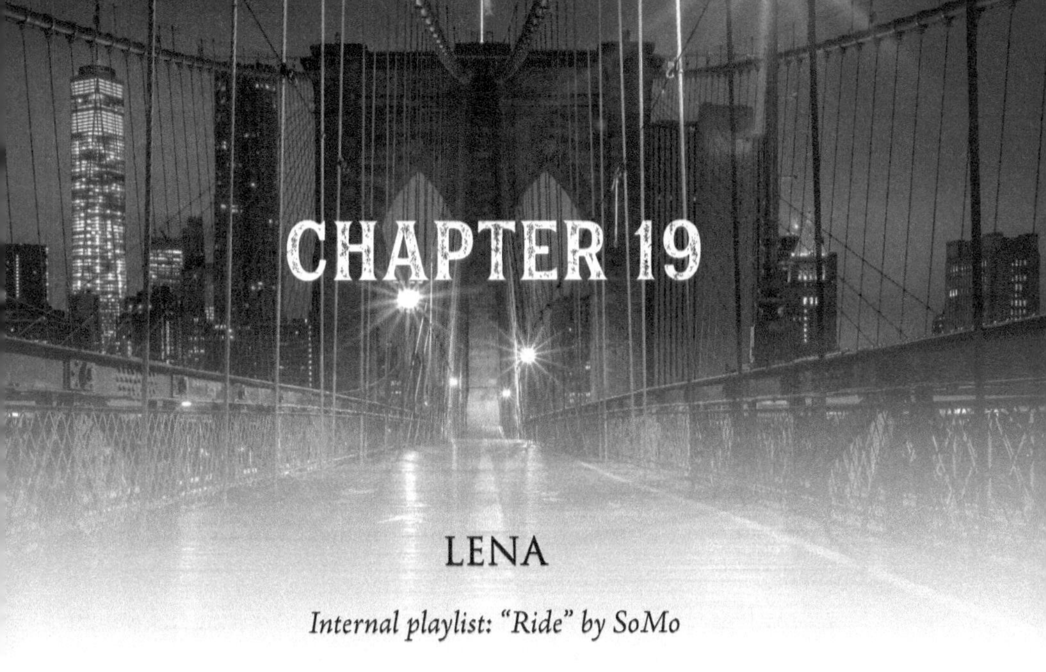

CHAPTER 19

LENA

Internal playlist: "Ride" by SoMo

I rush forward and throw my arms around Wes's neck. "I missed you so much." Eyes misting, I bury my face in his chest and cling to him, careful not to put pressure on his ribs. The time spent apart, the distance, it all evaporates.

Wes hugs me tightly. "I missed you too. More than you know." He holds me, his chin resting on top of my head as we sway to John Legend's "All of Me." He kisses my forehead. "These lyrics remind me of you."

I melt into his embrace and listen to the ballad, his heartbeat, and the breaths filling his chest. Being in his arms feels like home—warmth, shelter, and love. I'm beyond grateful I didn't lose him in Alaska.

Wes threads his hands in my hair, rubbing strands of it between his fingers. "Your hair feels like silk," he inhales deeply, "and smells like warm vanilla."

He smells glorious. Woodsy, spicy, and clean. Everything about the man is an aphrodisiac for me.

I peer up at him. "I like you clean-shaven. It's sexy."

He brushes his lips over my ear, sending goose bumps across my neck. "I didn't want my stubble to scrape your skin."

I draw in a shaky breath. He tightens his arms around me, sliding a warm palm to the upper curve of my ass.

"I love dancing with you, Lena."

"At first, I didn't realize you meant dance in the literal sense."

He chuckles. "I mean it in every sense. First, we'll dance, then we'll *dance.*" He tilts my chin to face him. "Tango . . . Salsa . . . Waltz."

I laugh. "I don't waltz, remember?"

"You will, tonight."

"Is that a promise?"

"Too fuckin' right, it is." He brings his lips down over mine. Hard. Possessive. His tongue surges into my mouth, claiming me.

A soft moan escapes my chest. I clasp the back of his neck and pull him deeper. He slides his hand lower and squeezes my ass cheeks. Without breaking our kiss, he backs me into the bedroom and nudges me onto his bed.

I part my legs, and he slowly settles between them, resting his weight on his forearms. I weave my hands into his hair and tug gently, needing him closer. Deeper. I just *need* him.

A groan rumbles in his chest. He drags his lips from mine and meets my gaze. "I missed these lips," he brushes his thumb over my lower lip and kisses it, "so fucking much."

"Missed yours too, Ace. Now, shut up and kiss me some more." My breathless demand makes his eyes heat.

He kisses my cheek and jawline. I gasp when his lips find my neck. He works his way down my throat, nibbling and swirling his tongue over my skin. Kissing me, loving me, the way only *he* can.

"Oh, God, Wes . . ."

"I love when you say my name," he whispers, his breath tickling my ear. "No holding back tonight—let me hear ya."

I loosen his tie and pull it off. Wes presses himself into a kneel and shrugs out of his jacket with a wince.

I blink through the lust-filled haze in my vision. "Are you okay? If your ribs are too sore, we can skip this."

"I'm fine, love. Just tweaked my shoulder a bit taking off the jacket. Don't worry. I'm back to normal for the most part."

"You sure?"

"I'm good, love. I promise." He starts to unbutton his shirt.

"Wait." I reach for his hands. "Let *me* do it." He lowers them to his sides, and I take my time unbuttoning his shirt, tracing my fingertips down his chest and chiseled abdomen. Candlelight flickers on his golden skin. I swear, the body on this man ought to be carved from granite. Pushing the material off his broad shoulders, I flatten my palms on his sculpted pecs and indulge in his warmth. His heartbeat throbs against my hand nearly as fast as my heart races. "I want you *now*."

"And you'll have me, love," he finds my dress's hemline and shoves it to my waist, "but not until after I've had my fill of you." I gasp as he slowly slides my panties over my hips, trailing his hands down my thighs. He tosses the silk thong over his shoulder and meets my gaze. Swirling pools of blue lava burn into me. "You made me wait this long to taste you, so I'm gonna take my—"

His cell rings.

"Mother. Fucker." He yanks it from his pants pocket and glances at the screen. "Hold that thought."

"If that's Jake, I'm gonna reach through the phone and choke him."

"No, this time it's cock-block Isla. I made her promise to call when she landed. I'd better answer, or she'll freak out." He holds it to his ear. "You landed?"

I take a moment to catch my breath.

"Paul will be waiting by your gate—he'll take you to the hotel. Call me tomorrow morning." He squeezes his eyes shut. "No, I'm fine . . . just a little *busy*."

Wes usually acts like Isla hung the moon, so his gruffness is out of character. Clearly, she noticed.

"Yes, good busy. Now, leave me alone. Love you. Call tomorrow." He hangs up and turns off the phone. "I'm sorry. I just wanted to make sure she got in safely."

I nod. "Don't apologize, I understand."

He tosses his phone aside. "Now . . . where were we?"

CHAPTER 20

WES

Life lesson: There's no such thing as too much of a good thing.
(Unless your ribs are fractured)

"I think you were about to make me moan." Lena brushes her fingertips down my happy trail. "At least, that's what I was hoping for."

"No hope necessary." I grip her knees, spread her legs apart, and carefully lower myself onto the mattress between them, hiding my wince. If Lena had any idea how much pain I'm in, she wouldn't let me touch her.

I swear to Christ, if anyone knocks, calls the room phone, sets off the fire alarm, or calls in a bomb threat, I'll fucking explode. I've never wanted Lena this badly. The time apart, the worrying, only intensified my need for her. I'm desperate. Starving. And so damn hard, my dick hurts. But first . . . I'm going to lick her until she screams.

I kiss my way up her creamy porcelain thighs and slide my hands beneath her arse. I palm each lush cheek and pull her body closer to my mouth, stifling a groan. Needing a minute to breathe through my discomfort, I hover, my lips mere inches from her pussy. Her scent calls out to me. While I'm dying to taste her, I refuse to rush the act—I waited too damn long for this. I rain kisses on her inner thighs, brushing my lips and nose over her soft flesh, which glistens with her desire. "You're so wet for me."

Lena gasps and flexes her hips upward. "Stop teasing me."

"I'm not teasing you, love," I kiss her lower belly, my chin grazing her clit, "much." I lick my lips and trail damp kisses over her pussy.

"Wes, I want—" Her hips buck.

I squeeze her arse. "Tell me what you want." No way am I letting her get away with being shy. I want to hear her every desire, wish, and fantasy so I can make damn sure I give them to her. "What do you want me to do to you?"

"I want—" Her words are cut off when I drag a slow, torturous lick through her slit. "Oh, fuck . . ."

I spear my tongue inside her, then pull back. "I'm listening."

"I want *that*." She grips my shoulders, making me clench my jaw. "Please don't stop."

I suck her clit between my lips, lightly flicking my tongue. "You like that?"

"Yes . . . Oh, God, *yes*."

When we were lost in the wilderness, my fingers had explored, stroked, and thrust inside her. I cradled Lena in my warmth while I made love to her on the hard, cold tundra, but she refused to allow me a taste of her. Now, we're in a real bed, nestled against crisp sheets. Warm. Safe. *Alone*. This time, I'll keep my hands off, and she'll writhe beneath my lips and tongue.

I press against her legs. "Spread wider for me."

Her thighs fall open.

I lick up one side of her and down the other. "You're so sweet, Lena. Just like butterscotch." I alternate sensual swirling licks with thrusts and flicks of my tongue, leaving no part of her untouched. I know I'll become addicted to her heady nectar and won't be able to wait to get my fix. Again and again.

"Wes . . ." Her hips thrash. "You're gonna make me come."

I seal my mouth over her clit and suck, flicking my tongue on the bundle of nerves. Lena is paradise—her scent, her taste, her throaty moans. I can't get enough.

"Oh!" She knots her hands in my hair and presses herself to my mouth as she climaxes. "Oh, Wes . . ."

Her moans are a siren's call. My cock throbs, begging to sink into her wet heat, but I need more of her taste.

"Fuck me," she pleads, tugging the strands of my hair.

I lift my head. "I'm not done—"

"Yeah, you are . . . I need you inside me."

The desperation in her eyes undoes me.

I ease off the bed and stand, ignoring the throb in my chest. I unhook my belt and shed my pants and boxers. I point to Lena's dress. "Take this off."

She rises to her knees and turns. "Unzip me."

I lower the zipper and remove her dress, my fingers featherlight against her spine. She shivers as goose bumps bloom on her skin. Next, I unhook her bra and toss it aside. I love Lena's breasts—so full and soft. I ache to touch, lick, and kiss them.

Or watch them bounce as she rides my cock.

I grab her around the waist and bring my lips to her ear. "I want you on top of me." The position will be much easier on my ribs.

"We can do that." Lena flashes a sultry smile and points to the bed. "Lie down."

I settle with my head resting on the pillows. She straddles my hips and lines up the head of my cock with her pussy. Closing her eyes, she slowly lowers herself onto me, inch by rock-hard inch.

"That's it, sunshine," I groan, "take all of me in."

Lena rolls her hips and slides all the way down, causing us both to moan. She leans forward and meets my gaze, hands clamping on my biceps. "Giddy up, big boy." She circles her hips in an invisible hula hoop.

"Oh, fuck . . ." I grit my teeth and bite back the urge to flip her over and mount her. I grip her hips as she slides up and down my shaft. My balls tighten and release with each stroke. It amazes me how well she handles my considerable length and girth. "You're so tight . . . I love feeling you squeeze me."

"Can I tell you a secret?" She gasps and grinds her hips.

"Anything," I say.

Lena kisses my neck. "I love when you talk dirty to me."

I pull her ear to my lips. "Then ride my cock like you mean it."

She thrusts herself downward and moans against my neck. "Oh, Wes . . ."

"Sit up so I can watch your pussy take me deep."

She straightens and tosses her hair over her shoulder. Arching her back, she uses her thighs to move her body up and down.

She's like a fucking flower.

With each downward stroke, I clench my jaw and watch as my cock, glistening with her nectar, disappears into the soft petals of her pussy. I let her set the pace with slow, rolling thrusts of her hips, even though I want to flip her over, press her shoulders into the mattress, and pound inside her. I want to fuck her senseless, plow into her addictive wet heat until we both forget our names. I want. I want. I want.

She's making me crazy with these deep, languid strokes, but I know by their trembling, her legs are getting tired.

"Help me," she says on a gasp.

I hold on to her hips and pull her down, hard. My ab muscles protest, so I try to use my arms as much as possible to lift and lower her onto my cock. She cries out and clutches her breasts. I can't decide what's hotter—me touching them, or watching Lena roll her dusky pink nipples between her thumb and forefinger. I love her curves. Breasts, hips . . .

That arse.

"Actually, turn around." I nudge her and she spins into reverse cowgirl. "Damn . . . Lena, you're so fucking hot." Gripping her hips, I lift and lower her onto my cock, watching it slide inside.

Christ, she's everything. Her lush arse on display for me is the hottest thing I've ever seen, so I give it an open-palmed slap. Her moan tightens my balls. "Lean forward and hold my ankles." I pump my hips upward, meeting her thrust for thrust. "I love fucking you, sunshine."

She digs her nails into my ankles and picks up her pace. "Wes . . ."

"I've got you, love. Come for me."

"Oh! Yes!" Her pussy flutters around my cock, squeezing me as she orgasms with a wail. "Wes . . . fuck." She sags forward, her face hitting my shins.

I slap her arse again. Harder this time. "Oh, we're not done."

She dismounts, flops onto her back, and pulls me on top of her. "You take over."

Ignoring my rib pain to the best of my ability, I settle between her thighs and sink my cock deep inside her.

Home. She feels like home.

I pump my hips and bury my face in her neck. "I love you."

"I love you too, baby."

I close my eyes and let my body take over. Lena orgasms a second time, loudly moaning her release. I tilt her chin and kiss her, my tongue in rhythm with my thrusts. She tightens her legs at the back of my thighs and pulls me deeper.

"Oh, *fuck*. Lena . . ." My cock pulses and I lose myself inside her. My hips keep moving until I finally collapse on top of her with a loud groan. Chest heaving, ribs throbbing, heart racing, and head spinning.

Lena lightly strokes my back. "I hope you didn't jostle those ribs."

"*You* jostled them." They hurt like a bitch, but I'll never admit that to her. I don't care. The pain is worth it. But it's a damn good thing I loaded up on ibuprofen before she arrived.

"Well, you started it."

I press myself up and peer into her eyes. "Are you all right?"

She smiles softly. "I'm more than all right."

"I know it's been a while—I wasn't too rough, was I?"

"Not at all. While I enjoy slow, tender lovemaking, I'll take a hard fuck from you any day. I love when you get carried away and give me your beasty side."

I smirk. "That wasn't a hard fuck. Not by any means."

"Oh." She flexes her hips and squeezes me with her inner muscles. "Then sometime in the near future, you'll have to give me one." She pinches my arse. "Had a feeling you were holding back."

I let out a harsh exhale. "You're gonna wear me out."

She laughs. "I'm hungry. How about you?"

I give her my standard answer, "Does a bear shit in the woods?"

Lena snorts. "Pretty sure I stepped in some in Alaska."

"I know *I* did." I laugh. "Let's order room service. What do you feel like eating?"

"Meat," she says it with a straight face, but I wait. Sure enough, the corners of her lips twitch into a smirk. "Preferably a *big* serving."

Lena sits cross-legged on the comforter, organizing her toiletry bag. We finished our meal and spent the afternoon lounging.

I study the beauty products strewn across the bed and scratch my head. Miniature bottles of shampoo, conditioner, and body wash mingle with face wash, face cream, and body lotion. Then there's the makeup—lip gloss, blush, and eye shadow. So many eye shadows. I open a palette called "gold rush" and press the pad of my pinky to the powder.

"Uh, excuse me, but that goes on my eyes."

"Yeah, I figured that out by the sticker that reads eye shadow."

"As in, keep your grubby paws out of it."

"My paws aren't grubby." I close the lid. "And you don't need any of this shit." I pick up a tube of something—eye cream, apparently. "How many damn creams do ya need?"

"All of them." She holds out her hand. "Especially that one."

"Your eyes are perfect, sunshine."

"Thanks, Ace," she points to the outer corners, "but I'd like to stave off the haggard thing I've got brewing over here."

I raise a brow. "Haggard?"

"Fine lines, dark circles, and such."

"You don't have any of them, so . . ."

She cocks her head to the side. "Are you trying to flatter your way into my pants?"

"I don't need flattery for that." I flex my biceps. "I'm fairly certain ya want me."

Lena laughs and leans over to kiss my cheek. "Always."

I reach for her hairbrush. "Let me have that." She hands it over and I settle behind her. "For the record, I thought you were beautiful in Alaska—even when you were elbow deep in fish guts."

She grimaces. "I can honestly say if I never eat another salmon, I'll be fine with that."

I remove her hair tie and unravel her braid. "We were both so dirty, sweaty, stinky—"

"Who you calling stinky?"

I grin. "Well certainly not you, my delicate flower."

She snorts. "If someone had told me four months ago, I'd be sharing a tent with *you*—greasy-haired, makeup free, and un-showered—I would've died of embarrassment."

"That's what I'm saying. I was attracted to you even then." I gesture to the beauty products. "You don't need any of this shit. Your beauty's natural and soul deep."

She leans against me with a sigh before she straightens again. "You always know the right things to say."

"Comes easily when it has to do with you." I gently run the brush through her hair. Her posture softens and her head falls back. "Your hair's so silky. I love touching it."

"I love having my hair played with, so please, don't stop."

"Is this your natural color?"

"Yes."

"It reminds me of caramel."

Lena laughs and looks over her shoulder at me. "Thought you were gonna say butterscotch."

Instant hard-on.

My fingers clench in the strands. "Same thing."

"Nope." She shakes her head. "Caramel is made with white sugar and a little butter. Butterscotch uses brown sugar and *lots* of butter."

I bite back a smile and stare at her for a minute. "You know an awful lot about sweets."

"My sweet tooth knows no match."

"Dunno about that, love. I'll see your sweet tooth and raise you mine."

"Also, it goes beyond color—white sugar is just sugar crystals, which means it's refined and free flowing. Brown sugar, on the other hand, has molasses in it. You gotta get your confections straight first."

I chuckle. "So, it's *unrefined?*"

"I was gonna say, 'raw,' but unrefined works. It's generally wetter and stickier than white sugar."

"Ah, so my butterscotch comparison still applies."

She flushes a beautiful pink. "Are we still talking about desserts?"

"You're goddamn right we are." I slide my hands to her hips and pull her up against me, my stiff cock pressing against her lower back. "Trust me, sunshine . . . I know everything I need to know about confections." I kiss the side of her neck slowly, licking it like a favored treat. "And my appetite for desserts is *insatiable*."

"Not now, Ace. I need a shower first."

I reach around and palm her breasts. "No, you don't."

"Yeah, I do."

Despite her weak protest, she leans against me, shoulders rapidly rising and falling with each breath. I fumble for the buttons on the front of the shirt she's wearing. My shirt. Seeing her in my clothes makes my inner caveman growl in satisfaction. The material parts as I work my way down. Her bra lays abandoned on the floor from earlier, so her soft, lush breasts fill my hands. I thumb over her nipples as I kiss her neck.

"You've got a thing for my boobs."

"I've got a thing for *you*." My lips find the triangle of skin beneath her ear and I whisper, "All of you . . . Just like the song."

Goose bumps spread over her skin and her nipples grow even harder. She presses her knees together and squirms against me. I trail my fingertips over her hips, between her legs, and slip a hand inside her panties. She moans when my knuckles brush against her clit, making me even harder. I slide a finger inside her silken pussy.

LENA

Sitting between Wes's bent legs, his hard, jean-covered cock pressing against my lower back, I couldn't move if I wanted to. He holds me in place with his thighs while he pleasures me. He adds a second finger and curves them in a come-hither motion that makes my toes curl. He kisses my neck and shoulders, my ears, my jaw. Any place his lips can reach.

He buries his face in my neck and lightly sucks on my skin.

"You'd better not give me a hickey."

"What're you gonna do about it?" I can feel his smile against the sensitive skin.

"Cover *your* neck in them so your press-tour interviews get really awkward."

A laugh rumbles deep in his chest. "Unfortunately for you, I'm immune to awkwardness." He resumes sucking for a moment. "And if you wanna mark me, sunshine, I'm happy to let you."

"You're impossible."

He slowly pulls out his fingers. "Actually, I have a better idea . . . Come dance in the shower with me."

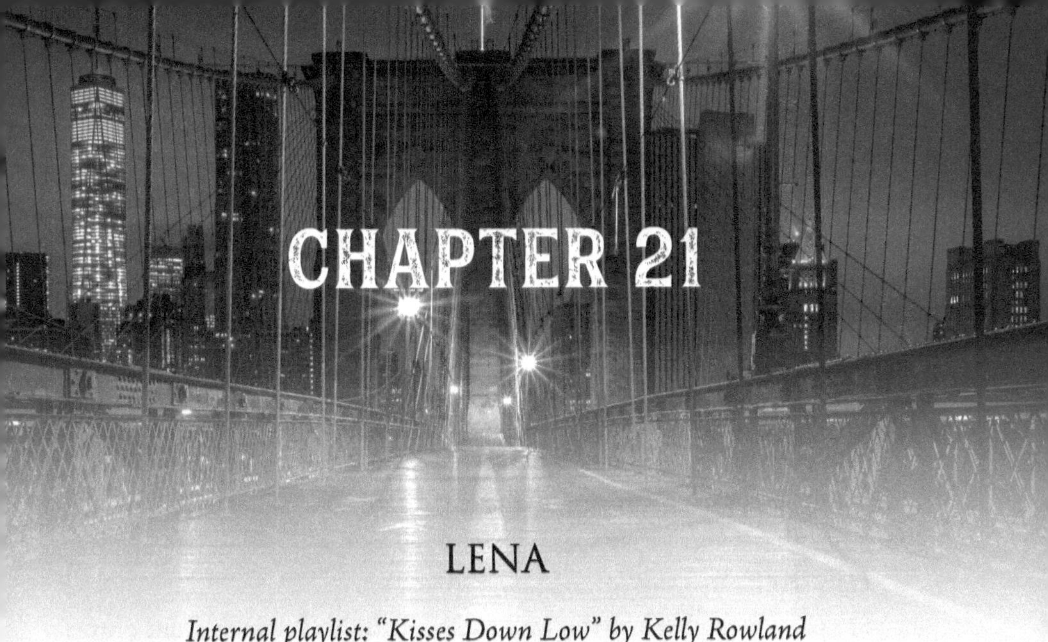

CHAPTER 21

LENA

Internal playlist: "Kisses Down Low" by Kelly Rowland

This is one of those fancy doorless showers with a giant rain showerhead. Wes sets a couple towels on a black marble vanity and turns on the water. I catch a glimpse of his backside in one of the several mirrors.

Lord have mercy.

"Did I ever tell you your ass is to die for?"

He grins over his shoulder. "Not with actual words, but I got the idea with some of the looks you've given me."

"Seriously, how did it get this perfect?" I come up behind him and clench both cheeks in my hands. "I can't help squeezing it, and I almost wanna bite it."

He laughs. "Squats. More squats than you can imagine."

"I hate squats—they hurt my thighs."

"You'd have less trouble on top if ya did some squats," he points out.

"Who says I have trouble?" I squeeze his ass hard. "Maybe I like letting you do all the work? I mean, why have ass cheeks like these if you're not gonna use them for thrusting?"

"Here's a little anatomy lesson for you." He turns to face me and grips my hips. "I've got hips," he slides his hands to my thighs, "and a strong set of quads and hamstrings, which work in tandem with my glutes." He squeezes my butt. "So, it isn't *just* my arse that powers those thrusts."

I bite my lip coyly. "A package deal for your package thrusting." I pinch his ass again. "Also, I'm a nurse, so I don't need any lessons on anatomy. That is, unless you're ready to give me a demonstration . . ."

"You have a way with words, love." He laughs and pulls my lower body up against him. "Which is another reason I love you."

I wrap my arms around his neck and kiss him. "I love you too."

He backs me into the shower, beneath the hot waterfall. "I'm hoping to render you speechless in a minute."

"Speechless?"

"Yeah, before I spend the night thrusting my cock inside you, I'm gonna lick that sweet pussy again."

Holy. Fuck.

He presses my back to the wall and sinks to his knees in front of me, never breaking eye contact. "Use my lips and tongue to make you scream my name. Over and over and over again." He clamps his hands on the backs of my thighs and yanks me to his lips. "Trust me, by the time I'm done with you, that sassy mouth of yours won't have any words left." He licks up my center. "Let me show you how *I* eat sweets."

"Wes . . ." My eyes flutter closed as I absorb the sensations.

It is an understatement to call Wes Emerson a generous lover. The man is a fucking sex philanthropist. He lavishes pleasure on me like it's his born destiny. He moves his lips and tongue like he can't get enough of me, like he'll *die* if he doesn't taste me. He worships my body like he truly enjoys the act. Pleasure altruism is something I'm not used to. I can't stop my moans and gasps as he brings me to the edge. My legs tremble. No amount of squats could prepare me for the knee-buckling ecstasy.

"I'm gonna hold you. Put your legs over my shoulders."

He lifts my body, and I swing my legs up. Wes nestles his face between my thighs. Water droplets glisten on his forehead, eyebrows, and eyelashes. The shower turns his tawny surfer hair a dark brown, with pieces falling in his face. He meets my gaze through the steam. His eyes, swirling pools of blue lava, burn with lust, passion, and reverence. There's no question in my mind that this man loves me. I mouth the words.

The corners of his eyes crease on a smile. He tightens his grip and gives my clit a swirling lick.

"Oh, Wes," I clutch his shoulders, "I'm so close."

He increases his pace and I fall apart. My hips jerk in his hold. Wanton moans escape my chest.

But he doesn't stop.

I orgasm a second time. And a third. It's a damn good thing I didn't let him do this to me in Alaska. I would've awakened every hibernating creature north of the fucking Arctic Circle.

"Wes, fuck!"

Number four.

He pulls back slightly, lips curving in a cocky grin. "My last name is not fuck."

"It should be," I say, gasping. "Put me down—I can't take it."

"Thought I'd try for another," he slowly lowers my feet to the floor, "but lucky for you, my cock's not the only thing that's stiff." He rises to his full height. "Next time, remind me to bring kneepads."

"Will do." I wrap my arms around his waist, sagging against him. I close my eyes and listen to his heartbeat, the water from the showerhead, and my own gasping breaths.

CHAPTER 22

WES

Life lesson: Nurses know best.

I don't hear Lena's whispered "I love you." I *feel* it in the flutter of her lips against my chest and the way she clings to me.

I kiss her forehead and pull her close. "I love you too."

I love everything about her. From the emotion swimming in her soulful eyes, to the snark that tumbles from her luscious lips. While her sassiness and fiery spirit ignite me, her presence soothes the restless beast inside. A goddess of fire, passion, and love—*my* Aphrodite. I close my eyes and savor the embrace.

"Thanks for letting me come see you," she murmurs. "It feels so good to be in your arms again."

"Feels so good to have ya here." I tighten my arms around her. "You belong in my arms."

Lena reaches for a washcloth and squeezes bodywash onto it. "I seem to recall I promised to wash you sometime." She reads the label. "Does French lavender work for you, Ace?"

I grin. "I forgot about that."

She gently soaps my chest and shoulders. "Well, I didn't. And you've been a very dirty man, Wesley." She washes my arms, back, and abs. She grips my cock with warm, soapy fingers and begins to stroke me, moving her hand until the suds rinse away.

"I thought you liked when I talk dirty?"

"No, I *love* it." She sinks to the shower floor in front of me. "It turns me on."

I pull at her shoulders. "Stand up or you'll hurt your knees. I don't expect you to—" She takes me to the back of her throat. "Oh . . . *fuck.*"

She uses both hands—one moving up and down with her mouth, while she traces circles on my balls with the other.

"Lena," I groan, "you're killing me."

She pulls back. "Do you want me to stop?"

"Fuck no."

"Then close your eyes and relax." She brushes her lips over the head and my cock jerks in her hands.

"I wanna be inside you again."

"You will, but right now, I wanna give you some lovin'." She flicks her tongue. "So, back to our conversation about confections," she meets my gaze, "let me show you how *I* enjoy a popsicle."

She takes the head into her mouth. She moves slowly, drawing each sensation out. Advancing a little, then pulling back. Teasing me. My hips instinctively flex toward her.

"Hey, sunshine," her gaze flickers to mine, and I flash my most wicked grin, "suck my cock like you mean it."

I stretch and wince. My ribs and shoulder throb in tandem, and it hurts to breathe. I open a bottle of ibuprofen, pop four into my mouth, and swallow them with a swig of water. Admittedly, I have an *extremely* high pain tolerance. My doctor can't understand how I've been functioning so well with my injuries. He told me sex was out of the question for at least six weeks post-injury. It has only been about a month. Oops. But would I be me if I did what I was supposed to?

Lena comes out of the bathroom wearing a white terry robe. She points to the pill bottle. "What did you just take?"

"Ibuprofen."

"On an empty stomach?" she scoffs.

"We had lunch."

"Yeah, like five hours ago." She retrieves some pretzels from the room stash. "Eat these. I don't want you giving yourself a bleeding ulcer."

I crunch on the pretzels. "I may have overdone it today."

"You think? Is it the ribs or your shoulder that's hurting?"

"Both, but the ribs hurt more. I'd say the pain's a dull roar at this point."

She touches my shoulder gently. "Where's your sling?"

"In my suitcase."

"Because *that's* a good place for it." She walks over to my luggage and pulls out the sling. "You need to wear this." I put it on, and she adjusts the straps. "I'm gonna get some ice for your ribs."

"I'm all right—"

She holds a hand up. "With only the candles in here, I didn't see the bruising when you first took off your shirt. Your job for the rest of the night is to relax and let me take care of you. I'm sorry I let you overdo it—there's a reason we nurses shouldn't fraternize with our patients."

I grin. "I love when you fraternize with me."

She stands on her tiptoes and kisses me. "I love *you*, which is why you're gonna get on that bed and rest."

I settle against the pillows. "Yes, ma'am."

She steps into her shoes.

"Wait, where ya goin'?"

"Getting ice from the ice machine."

"This is a suite—we've got a full kitchen."

"Oh, right." She laughs. "This is my first time in a five-star hotel. Apparently, there's a learning curve. Do you always book a suite for yourself?"

"No. I upgraded the room when you agreed to join me. I don't need the fancy shit, but I thought you might like it."

Lena smiles. "Thank you, but moving forward, you don't need to do all that. As long as I'm with you, I don't care where I stay. Please don't fuss over me. You may have noticed in Alaska, I'm not the diva type."

"Come here." I hold out my free arm in invitation.

She pads to my bedside.

I pull her close and stroke her cheek. "I realize you don't need luxury, but I wanna give you the world. Please let me pamper you, sunshine. It makes me happy."

"I'll allow a little pampering, but nothing too extravagant." She kisses my forehead. "I don't want money or glitz—I just want *you*."

I interlace our fingers, kiss her knuckles, and press her hand to my heart. "I'm all yours, love."

CHAPTER 23

LENA

Internal playlist: "Hurts 2B Human" by P!ink

I stretch, roll over in bed, and glance at the clock. *Nine-fifteen.* Paul and Isla are due to arrive at ten. I'm mildly nervous about meeting Wes's sister and hope to make a good impression. I know from his stories how close they are, and the fondness in his gaze when he talks about his "little imp" warms my heart. While Wes has given her the gift of life, their bond goes deeper than the transplant. It's clear he'd give his life for her. His devotion to his family is one of the things I love most about him.

Wes is sound asleep beside me, dark lashes resting on his cheeks. I trace my fingers over the scar on his abdomen and think of my brother, who wouldn't give me the time of day, much less his kidney. Garrett, on the other hand, would gladly give me an organ. Our friendship runs deeper than the blood I share with Trevor. They say you can't choose your siblings, just your friends, and it's true. Garrett is my chosen family. The man who will always love me and have my back.

Unlike Roger fucking Hamilton.

I grimace at the thought of my father. His lies. The abuse. Drunken rages. Thousands of dollars wasted on bail and legal fees. Empty promises. Shame. I picture my mother, a spineless enabler, and anger courses through my veins. I know it's wrong, feeling resentment over my mother's choices, but I can't help it. In contrast with Wes's loving one, my family dynamic is a complete and utter shitshow.

I jump at the feel of Wes's warm fingers tracing my shoulder. "If you're so worried about fine lines and wrinkles, maybe you'd better stop scowling."

"I didn't realize I was scowling. Sorry."

He sits up. "What's on your mind?"

"I was thinking about my idiot father's DWI," I mutter.

"You said your mum bailed him out, right?"

"She always does." I shake my head and sigh. "I understand wanting to stand by the person you love, but where do you draw the line? Do you watch them spiral out of control over and over again? Is it right to continually put them back on their feet? His behavior is not only self-destructive, but it hurts our family. Trevor's in Tokyo, so he doesn't have to deal with any of it."

"Does he know?"

"Yeah, *I* was the one who told him. Mom strategically left out those details when she talked to him."

He furrows his brow. "Why wouldn't she tell your brother?"

"Mainly shame. I mean, he witnessed a lot of shit when we were growing up. I remember him getting between our parents when my father was in one of his drunken rages. She once promised us she'd leave him . . . but that never happened."

Wes peers at me with soft eyes. "Your dad was abusive?"

"*Is* abusive. Mainly verbal abuse, but he does escalate." I stare at the comforter's jacquard pattern. "And Mom just takes it. She *lets* him treat her like shit."

"Do you mean he hits her?"

"I've seen it happen."

"Was he abusive to you?"

I clench my jaw and squeeze my eyes shut.

"Lena, look at me."

I meet his gaze and swallow. "Once."

"What happened?"

"Most of my childhood was great because Dad stopped drinking when I was born. Mom stayed home with us while he worked, and there was a time when he was a decent father. He fell off the wagon when I was in middle school. That's when the fighting started. Alcohol brought out the worst in him, but like Jekyll and Hyde, he still had his good days—as long as we all walked on eggshells. At that time, Trevor still lived at home. He buffered a lot of the arguments, stepping in when necessary. Then he got a job in Tokyo. He moved to Japan when I was fourteen, got married, and then my nieces were born. He's stayed there ever since. As much as I understand why he left, a part of me will never forgive him for leaving Mom and me behind."

Wes squeezes my hand. "I think your feelings are justified, love."

"Once Trev left home, Dad redirected his anger at Mom, usually in the form of a drunken tirade. He frequently shoved her around, but I hadn't seen him hit her at that point." I swallow tightly. "Garrett lived with us for a while, courtesy of some awful shit that went down at his place. Anyway, we were seventeen and he'd just gotten his license, so we went for a ride in an old beater car he'd saved for. We got home and heard my parents fighting. When we went inside, we saw Dad hit Mom in the face." Bitter tears prick my eyes and spill over. Wes tightens his grip on my hand. "I got between them and told him I was calling the cops. Bad idea. He slapped me and threw me up against a wall so hard I bit my lip."

"Jesus Christ." Wes breathes.

"He was about to hit me a second time when Garrett, in all his lanky, teenage glory, jumped on his back and put him in a headlock. I remember cowering on the floor while they thrashed around. Garrett kept yelling for me to run, but I knew my father would kill him when he got free. Meanwhile, Mom had called the cops. She held the phone up and said, 'Roger, the police are on their way.' The fight went out of my father and he slumped to the kitchen floor in shock. He actually started to cry," I scoff. "Garrett released him and dragged me to his car. We got inside and he just kept driving—with me bleeding and the both of us crying."

"Where did you go?"

"North. We wound up someplace in the Adirondacks. He probably would've taken us across the Canadian border if the car was in better shape. We stopped at a little diner in a Podunk town for pancakes. They had boysenberry syrup, and I swear, I can still taste it." I give a sad smile. "That day was a game changer. High school graduation was months away, and we'd both planned to attend a nearby community college in the fall. Over breakfast, we scrapped those plans and made a pact. Come hell or high water, we were getting the fuck out of Windham. Garrett has nicknames for everyone and everything, so he calls that little dive 'the breakfast club,' and jokes about how our careers were birthed from soggy pancakes and runny eggs."

"So, what happened after that? Did you go back home?"

I shrug. "We had to. Neither of us had packed anything, we were too young to get a motel room, and it was too cold to sleep in his car. After we made our plan, we headed home. The cops were waiting for us."

"So you could press charges against your dad?"

"No. They'd already arrested him. My mother was worried and told them Garrett and I disappeared. Meanwhile, my asshole father claimed Garrett *took* me."

His eyes widen. "Like . . . kidnapped?"

"Yep. Dad's best friend is a lawyer, so they concocted a scheme implicating Garrett in the attack."

Wes shakes his head in disbelief. "You've gotta be kidding me."

"I wish." I clench my jaw. "I'll never forget the look on Gar's face when they tried spinning the tale that *he* hit me. Thank fuck we were both minors, or my father's scumbag lawyer would've played the statutory rape card too."

Wes raises a brow. "You were dating?"

"Hell no. We spent every minute together, so they assumed ours was a sexual relationship. We've never had sex. We've never even kissed. He's like my brother—except *he* didn't move to another continent and leave me there."

"Instead, he came to your defense."

"Right. Then was accused of hurting me."

"What about your mother in all of this? She saw it happen. Why didn't *she* defend Garrett? Please tell me she wasn't trying to implicate him."

"Mom was a spineless mute that day. I don't know what threats my father made after we left, but she played the typical battered wife role. I looked at her and said, 'Clear this up or I'll never speak to you again.' She finally came to her senses, but Garrett was devastated. He packed up his shit and went to stay elsewhere."

"What happened with your father?"

"He spent a month in jail." I shake my head bitterly. "Wanna guess what happened when they released him?"

"Your mum took him back?"

"Yep," I say, popping the 'p.'

"Wow. I don't even know what to say."

I force a dark laugh. "Neither do I. But in case you were wondering about my family dynamic . . . well, there you have it."

"I'm assuming you and your dad are still on bad terms?"

I nod slowly. "We don't speak. Things between us got even worse after my grandmother died."

"Why?"

"He can't get over the fact that she left me the brownstone and most of her fortune. But she wasn't stupid—she knew how he squandered his money. There were provisions in her will stating he wasn't supposed to get *anything*, but I felt bad and gave him all my grandfather's jewelry, which he subsequently hocked at a pawn shop. Then he had the balls to ask for Gram's jewelry."

"Did you give it to him?"

"Hell no, and I never will."

"I'm sorry you went through that shit, Lena. I'm thankful to Garrett for being there when you needed him."

"He always is." I meet his gaze. "Listen, I realize our closeness may be foreign to you, but I need you to understand we're a package deal. He's as much a part of me as I am of him. Our lives are interconnected, and as far as I'm concerned, *he* is my family."

"You've made that quite clear, love. I look forward to meeting him."

"Garrett is the only family member you'll meet. I won't introduce you to my parents because, quite frankly, I'm embarrassed. Your family seems so loving while mine's a shitstorm. Besides, I don't want their toxicity anywhere near us." I bite my lip. "I guess I'm just . . ."

"Just what?"

I look up at him shyly. "Nervous about meeting your sister."

"You have nothing to worry about. You saved my life—my family loves you by default and they haven't even met you. Isla was by my side when I sent your flowers. She was like, 'Put your goddamn number on the card, you idiot. How the hell's she supposed to reach ya?' I was just going to send an obscene amount of stargazer lilies. She suggested I add the roses because they symbolize love. I got the delivery confirmation email . . . and waited."

"And here I thought I was the only one sitting by the phone," I murmur.

"Definitely not. Isla was also instrumental in my decision to go on McDowell's show. Originally, I wasn't planning to do any interviews about Alaska—despite Reed being up my arse about it. Isla said, 'Send her a message. Be direct and make sure she knows it's about her.' I figured after you'd seen it, you would've called me. But then Austin sent me a video of your little news clip. I played it over and over, until she took the phone from me, telling me it didn't sound like you'd seen the interview."

"I hadn't. I was on Garrett's couch when I saw a commercial announcing that you'd be on the show. Seeing your face knocked the wind out of me because I—"

"You were avoiding anything that reminded you of me," Wes says knowingly. "Hiding like the stubborn, fiery goddess I know and love."

"Yeah. I refused to watch it and spent the day on his couch. Garrett must've programmed his DVR when I was in the bathroom or something. *He* watched the interview, then spent over a week trying to convince me to watch it. One day he met me in the foyer, dragged me into his living room, and gave me a 'Do you think I'd make you watch if it were bad?' speech. He fast-forwarded to the good parts." I chuckle. "The bastard had his classic I-told-you-so smirk plastered on his face the whole time. Told me to stop being stubborn. So, I met Jake for dinner and the rest is history."

"Wow, I have an ally in Garrett? I figured he'd hate me."

"While his opinion of you isn't exactly high, he doesn't hate you, either. He's an excellent judge of character, but he's calculating—gathers all his facts before making a judgment. He won't make any decisions about you until *he* meets you. As you can imagine, he's extremely protective of me. He *hated* Marc and made damn sure I knew it."

"Was your ex physically abusive?"

"God, no. Marc wouldn't hurt a fly. I wouldn't call him abusive at all . . . he was just neglectful."

"Neglect is a form of abuse, sunshine."

"Now you sound like Garrett."

"Well, it's true. Marc's neglect hurt you. And I wouldn't say he'd never hurt a fly. That shit he pulled with the flowers hurt you. The fucker hurt *me*, and I don't even know him." Wes's features darken. "Doctor Whatever-the-fuck better hope we never cross paths."

I smirk. "Garrett offered to slash his tires."

"Christ, I can only imagine what he wanted to do to me."

"I was upset, so he checked boxes in the 'no' column. At the same time, he insisted I was missing part of the story. That's the thing about Garrett—he has my back unconditionally, but he's not afraid to tell me when I'm being an asshole."

"He thought you were being an arsehole?"

I snort. "I believe his exact words were, 'Leens, you know I love you, but I'm about to fuck you up with some realness. *You* are choosing the uncertainty. You could easily get Emerson's number and find out what the fuck's going on, but you *choose* not to. Get off your stubborn ass and *do* something.' He was absolutely right—I was hiding."

"You refused to seek me out because you felt like my afterthought."

"Right."

Wes pulls me into his lap. "Sunshine, you are at the forefront of my *every* thought. Every wish, every hope, and every dream. All I see is you. There's no 'after' about it."

I clasp the back of his neck and kiss him slowly, absorbing his warmth, his security. "I'm sorry I doubted you," I whisper against his lips.

"You didn't just doubt me . . . you doubted *us*. And while I understand the whys of it, I don't get your heart's uncertainty. What do I need to do to make you feel secure? I want you to trust me. I *need* you to trust my love for you. I need you to trust our bond. I need you to believe in it, no matter what life throws at us."

"I do trust you, baby. My insecurity's a reflection on me—my history, my vulnerabilities. Old habits die hard, some shit's deep-rooted, but

I'm trying. I'll get there. You just keep doing what you're doing. *But . . ."* I grip his chin to make sure he's listening. "We have to communicate better. *Never* do the whole 'vanishing into thin air' shit again."

"I won't." He grimaces. "Consider that a lesson learned."

"I don't need to know your every move, but please don't make me worry about your safety any more than I already do. And I shouldn't have to wonder about the integrity of our relationship because I haven't heard from you."

"It won't happen again, love. I promise." He touches my cheek. "Listen, I don't want you to worry about Isla—she's already designing her bridesmaid dress."

Oh my God.

Floored he's alluding to a wedding, I open and close my mouth, unable to articulate a sentence. I imagine my arm linked with Garrett's, as he, forever my rock, escorts me down the aisle to my groom. I picture myself focusing on the vivid blue of Wes's gaze, absorbing his warmth, security, and love, seeing my future reflected in him. My hopes. My dreams. Our family. I envision my dream gown—mermaid-style with a sweetheart neckline. Luxe ivory satin with bead and lace details. I line up the wedding party in my head. Reed, Austin, and Jake at Wes's side. Garrett would be my man of honor, and Rita and Isla, my bridesmaids. The ceremony would be short and sweet, with vows we'd write ourselves. The reception, a celebration of love, with music, dancing, and laughter. Wes as my *husband.*

"What's on your mind, sunshine?"

"You," I whisper. "It's always you."

"Likewise." He presses his lips to my neck. "Now, get your arse in the shower before Isla and Paul show up."

"How about you join me?"

He glances at the clock. "We don't have time for that."

"Sure, we do." I stick out my lip. "There's always time for a quickie."

Wes trails his fingertips down my neck. "While I loved our frenzied forest fuckery, I'm in the mood to take my time with you. Now that we've got real privacy, I wanna hold you in my arms and make love to you . . . not fuck you."

"Can we do both?"

He laughs. "You're insatiable. Go shower."

I climb to my feet and pad to the bathroom, pausing outside the door. "Hey, Ace?"

He looks up. "Yeah?"

"Make me."

CHAPTER 24

WES

Life lesson: Set appropriate ground rules.

I slowly shake my head. "You're playing with fire, sunshine."

Lena peeks her head out the bathroom door. "And what do I always tell you about that?"

"Trust me, if my sister wasn't due in twenty minutes, I'd give you hot and *then* some."

"Promises, promises." She turns and goes back inside the bathroom and I hear the shower start.

I chuckle to myself. I'd love nothing more than a quickie, but now isn't the time. Paul is known for punctuality and the last thing I need is my little sister walking in on us bonking.

I can't believe Lena is nervous to meet Isla. There's absolutely nothing threatening about her. Beyond that, Isla is busting at the seams to meet her.

Reed, on the other hand . . .

My brother carries himself with a gravity that defies his years. Our mum called it "middle child syndrome," but his moodiness goes deeper than birth order. Whereas Isla and I are pranksters with solid senses of humor, Reed is all business. On the rare occasions when he lets down his guard, he has a dry humor and quick wit, wielding sarcasm like it's his profession. One thing is for certain, he doesn't do the warm and fuzzy thing well. That's not to say he's cold—just standoffish. I decide to hold off on introducing him to Lena. The last thing I want is to scare her away.

The familiar wave of guilt washes over me. The same wave that threatens to drown me, even after close to fifteen years.

I didn't cause the accident. It's not my fault.

I repeat the mantra in my head, but it does nothing to assuage my conscience. No, I didn't *cause* Reed's accident, but I was responsible for the events that led up to it. *I* yielded to Rachel's guilt trip and went to her cousin's party instead of the joyride I'd originally planned. *I* convinced Reed to go in my place. *I* provided the motorcycle. No, I wasn't the drunk driver who T-boned Reed, but it should've been me on that bike.

Reed's accident not only ruined his acting career before it started, but it nearly cost him his life. It irrevocably changed him. Physically, his injuries robbed him of the ability to run and surf. Even now, he walks with a significant limp and battles residual pain. What bothers me most, is the shadow that has taken up residence in his heart.

A loud knock interrupts my train of thought.

"Come in," I say, since I have a clear view of the suite's main door.

Paul pops his head inside. "You decent?"

"Fuck no. But I'm wearing clothes."

He laughs and holds the door open for Isla.

I grin. "G'day, Imp."

She races through the living room and meets me in the bedroom. "Hi. Where's Lena? Please tell me you didn't fuck things up again."

I snort. "She's showering."

"Oh, thank God. I was worried." She flops onto the bed beside me.

"You make it sound like I'm an eternal fuckup."

"No, you're not a fuckup. Just the occasional fuckwit."

"How was your flight?"

She smirks and nudges me. "Oh, *now* ya have time to talk?"

"I swear, you and Bennett are kindred spirits with your timing."

Paul follows Isla into the bedroom and leans against the dresser. "How's cock-block Bennett doing, by the way?"

"He's all right—readjusting to the real world like the rest of us. Lena said he seemed down during their last dinner. Anxious and such. He gets lost in his own head sometimes, and I think the whole experience really fucked him up. I should probably check in with him more often."

"What about Austin?" Paul asks.

"He's happy to be home with his woman."

"I bet. Everything going well with the pregnancy?"

"What pregnancy?" Isla chimes in.

"Fuck," Paul mutters. "I thought it was out in the open now."

I glance at Isla. "Kate's pregnant, but they're keeping it quiet."

"My lips are sealed."

I turn back to Paul. "Yes, Kate's doing great."

"Good. What's your game plan for today?"

I stretch. "I figured you could show the girls around while I deal with *Aegean* shit."

Paul nods. "When's your dinner with Alainna and Sal?"

"Tomorrow night." I perk up. "Why don't you swing by the studio this afternoon so I can introduce Isla and Lena to everyone? That way they already know them before the dinner."

"Wait, is the whole cast going to the dinner?" Isla asks. "I thought it was a double-date thing."

"Yeah, that was the original plan. But people heard us talking about it, and I think Alainna felt bad for excluding them. It's not the whole cast, but a good number of us. She reserved a private room at some fancy restaurant."

Isla grimaces. "I may sit that one out. You and Lena have a date night."

"Will ya come to the screening at least?"

"When's that?" she asks.

"Tonight."

"I'm not sure I wanna watch you fuck Alainna."

"It's *acting*, Imp."

"Yeah, but I have no desire to see your arse cheeks."

Paul laughs. "I'm with you on that one."

"You're both missing out. I've been told wonderful things about my arse."

"Gross," Isla mutters. "Paul, let's watch a movie or something."

"Tell me which one and we'll make it happen."

I perk up when I hear the water turn off. "Listen, before Lena comes out, I want to set some ground rules."

Paul arches a brow. "Ground rules?"

"Yeah." I grab my wallet from the nightstand, pull out my credit card, and hand it to him. "She's proud and feisty as hell, so I'm giving this to you now. I added your name as an authorized user."

A slow grin crosses Paul's face. "Your ground rules are a shopping spree?"

"Whatever Lena wants . . . it's hers. I don't care about the price."

"You sure about that? She was eyeing a Lamborghini when we left the airport."

"If she wants a Lamborghini, get her one. Get whatever the imp wants too."

"I have my own money." Isla rolls her eyes. "And you just called Lena proud. I doubt she'd let you buy her a coffee, let alone some stupid car. Don't overdo it—that's a surefire way to piss her off. Christ, I haven't even met her, and *I* know that."

"I know, but sometimes it's fun to piss her off." I gesture to them. "In all seriousness, she mentioned wanting to look for a gown for Jake's gala. If she sees something she likes, buy it."

Paul straightens. "Why don't you just give *her* the card?"

"She'd refuse it."

"What if she won't let me pay for the dress?"

"Then have them put the dress on hold."

Isla snorts. "Why? So you can ride your chariot over there and get it?"

"No. I'll send Paul back later."

"What if she insists on paying?" Paul asks. "I'm not about to wrestle a wallet from the woman."

"Listen, I don't care how ya do it, just make sure I pay for the dress. No excuses."

Isla chuckles. "You're gonna get your arse kicked. You know that, right?"

I grin. "Yeah, and I look forward to it."

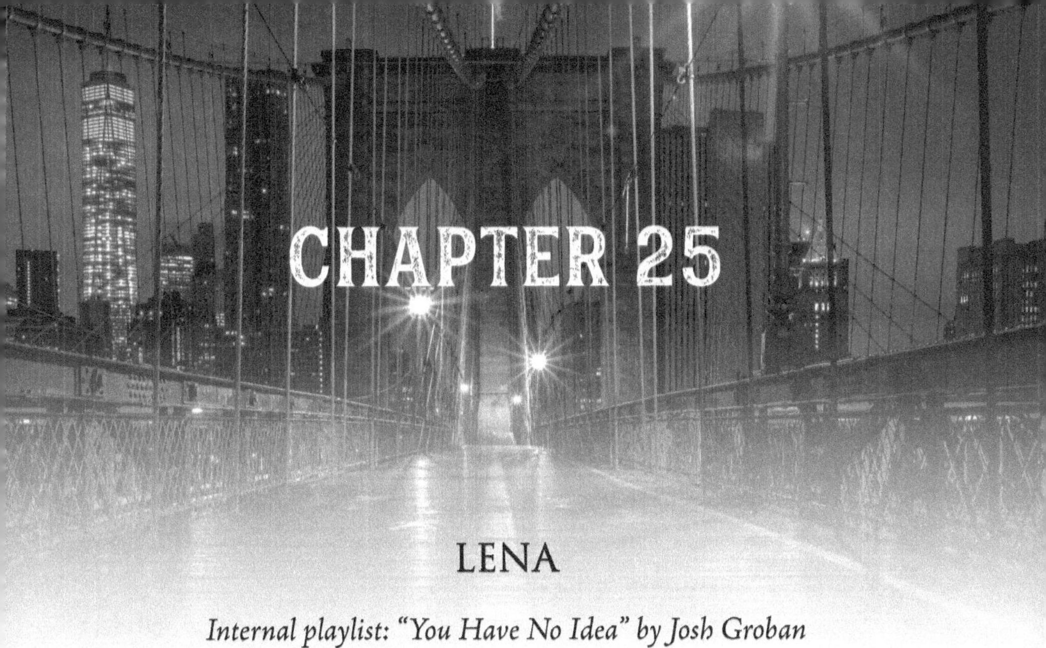

CHAPTER 25

LENA

Internal playlist: "You Have No Idea" by Josh Groban

I check my reflection once more. Lip gloss, a coat of mascara, and a swipe of blush does wonders for my features. I leave my hair down. Hopefully, it won't be humid later and get all frizzy. Wes mentioned a high of eighty-five, which is much warmer than October in New York. Satisfied with my jade sundress and sandals, I emerge from the restroom and walk into the living room.

"Any hot water left for me?" Wes teases.

I smile. "I saved you a few drops, Ace."

"Lena, I'm thrilled to meet you," Isla gushes, rising from the couch. With beachy golden-brown waves and legs to her neck, Wes's sister is gorgeous. As in, straight out of a fashion magazine gorgeous. She's wearing a purple maxi dress and gladiator sandals. Vibrant blue eyes shining, Isla crosses the room in a few long strides and hugs me. "I feel like I already know ya."

Holy shit, she's tall.

I smile and return her embrace. "Likewise, Isla. Wes speaks fondly of you."

Isla snorts. "Yeah, *sure*, he does." She gestures to her brother. "As long as I'm not cock-blocking him."

Wes laughs. "I don't take kindly to cock-blocking of any variety."

I greet Paul. "Howdy, Rambo."

Paul raises a brow. "Rambo?"

"Yep. Your charisma's laced with a healthy dose of 'I'll fuck you up' *First Blood* style."

"I'd call that an accurate assessment." Paul laughs.

Wes grins at me. "You're familiar with those movies?"

I giggle. "Familiar? Courtesy of Garrett, I know every line."

Isla cocks her head. "I haven't seen them."

"Not your cup of tea, Imp," Wes says. "Rambo's nothing like Olaf."

"That's it!" Isla wraps an arm around Paul's shoulder. "Rambo and I have a date with Sven tonight."

Paul scratches his head. "Who the hell's Sven?"

Wes claps him on the back. "Don't ask, mate."

"Speaking of Sven," I turn to Isla, "did Wes tell you we saw reindeer in Alaska?"

"They were caribou, love," Wes corrects me.

"Reindeer *are* caribou. Get your deer species straight, Ace."

"You tell him, Lena." Isla laughs and hugs me. "I fucking love you already."

"Jesus Christ, now they're gonna tag team me," Wes mutters, waving us to the door. "Goodbye, ladies. Go buy some things and think of ways to antagonize me."

Paul snickers. "*I*, for one, am loving this, Emerson."

"Of course you are." Wes smirks and crosses his arms. "Keep them safe, mate."

"Will do. What time do you want us at the studio?"

"Aim for five." Wes snags me around the waist and kisses me. "Have fun, love."

"We will," Isla singsongs, tugging me with her.

"Later, Ace." I follow Paul and Isla into the hall.

"Where to, ladies?"

"I'm good with wherever," I say. "Isla, Wes said you wanted to see fashion stuff?"

She nods. "As long as you're on board with that."

"How about we check out Rodeo Drive?" Paul suggests. "You two can shop and I'll trail behind like a lost puppy."

I nudge him. "More like a lone wolf, Rambo."

Isla holds up the most exquisite gown I've ever laid eyes on. Forest green, covered in intricate beadwork and sequins, it scintillates in the light. "Did ya see this one? The color would be amazing on you."

"There's no way I could do that dress justice."

"I'll be the judge of that." Isla grips my arm. "Come with me, you're trying it on."

Paul stands across the store, but his watchful gaze follows us. He raises a brow. Isla gestures to the fitting rooms and he nods.

She ushers me into a room and closes the velvet curtain. "Come out when you're ready."

I undress and slide into the gown with the fluidity of a mermaid easing herself into a lagoon. The style hugs my curves, accentuating my hourglass figure. The plunging halter neckline reveals the alabaster skin of my neck, collarbone, and shoulders. A slit up the front exposes my left leg to mid-thigh, and the back dips below my bra line, stopping in a V-shape near my waist. I open the curtain.

"Oh. My. God. You look like a fucking *goddess*."

I bite my bottom lip, unsure. "You think?"

"I don't think—I *know*." She circles me. "You're getting this dress."

I smile at my reflection. "I wish Wes was coming to the gala."

"Trust me, so does he. And once he sees you in this dress, he'll be cursing *The Aegean* and just about everything Greek." She points to my feet. "You need gold shoes. A seven, right? Be right back." Isla scurries toward the shoe display.

I glance at the price tag and feel myself blanch. *Two thousand dollars? Nope. Not happening.* I wouldn't even spend that on a wedding dress.

Isla returns with a pair of gold stilettos. "Here, try these on."

"Uh, I may need to look for something else . . ."

Isla holds up her hand. "No way. That dress was made for ya. You have to get it."

"I can't justify spending—"

"Wes will pay for it."

"I'm sure he'd be glad to, but I'd rather look for something that's within *my* budget."

Isla smirks. "I like you, Lena. A lot. So, I'm not gonna beat around the bush here. Wes already gave Paul his credit card with orders to buy you a dress."

I shake my head. "I'm not letting him spend two grand on a gown for an event he's not even attending."

"You know how Wes operates, right? Either you *let* him buy it or he'll figure out a way to do it behind your back." She grins. "Trust me, I know my brother."

"Let me guess, he called ahead and told them to decline my card?"

Isla snorts. "No, but he'll have them refund yours and charge his instead."

"Then I'll pay cash."

"He'll just have them mail you a refund check. He's relentless."

"I don't want his money, Isla."

"I know that, and *he* knows ya love him—not the shit that comes with him. But he's an alpha to his core, which is why he wants to protect and provide for you, regardless of your ability to do so yourself."

"I guess I'm not used to being treated this way."

Isla smiles warmly. "Let the man buy you a dress. You deserve it for putting up with him."

"Fine," I concede with a sigh. "But I'm paying for the shoes."

Isla chuckles. "Just don't be surprised if he gets the price refunded to you."

"He's impossible sometimes."

She laughs. "I give you credit. I could *never* date a man as alpha as him."

"Let me change so we can get something to eat. I'm starving."

"I feel bad Paul's sitting in the corner," I say, stuffing a forkful of penne into my mouth.

We ducked into an Italian restaurant for lunch and to cool off for a bit. Plus, Isla mentioned her skin needing a break from the sun. I've been craving carbs and this place boasted several enticing pasta dishes, including gluten-free options for Isla.

"I told him he could eat with us, but he didn't wanna listen to 'girl talk,' " Isla replies using air quotes. "Then he mumbled something about having a clear view of the surroundings."

"Does Wes always arrange for a bodyguard?"

She places her dark sunglasses on top of her head. "Only when he travels. Back home, people are generally more respectful. They treat him like one of the locals. Here in the States, they swarm like vultures. It's sickening, honestly."

"If Paul's with us, then who's protecting Wes?"

"No one."

"That makes me anxious."

She nods. "Me too. I mean, no one knows who I am, and although you've been linked to Wes, you haven't been seen with him yet. I told him we'd be fine on our own, but he wasn't having it."

"I imagine there was some foot stomping involved?"

"Yep, and some chest pounding too." Isla sips her water. "Are ya ready to be seen with him?"

I chuckle. "I dunno, is *he* ready to be seen with *me*?"

"He's used to the attention. It's you he's worried about."

I tilt my head to the side. "He's worried?"

"Absolutely. Said you hate the spotlight as much as I do."

"Yeah, I'm a 'fly under the radar' kind of gal."

"That's why he's nervous. I'll warn you . . . your days of anonymity are numbered. Is that something you can handle?"

I meet Isla's gaze. "I truly don't know *how* I'll deal with the attention, but I love him with all my heart, so I *will* handle it."

"I want that kind of love," Isla says wistfully. "The type that tramples obstacles that dare to arise. You two are fierce about each other, and it shows. I'm so happy he found you, Lena. You make him a better man."

"We found each other," I correct her. "And I'm a stronger woman having met him. He taught me a lot about myself in Alaska and showed me the way I deserve to be treated."

"And now you need to hold on to one another."

"We will. The long-distance thing sucks, though."

"You guys will figure it out. At least he's in a financial position where the cost of a plane ticket's not an issue, ya know?"

"Good point. Travel's an acceptable expenditure. But the material stuff? Not so much."

Isla laughs. "You're gonna have to get over that sooner rather than later. If he had his way, he'd shower you with gifts."

"I know he would." I touch Isla's arm. "Thanks for talking me into the dress. Refusing it would've probably offended him, and it's easily the most beautiful thing I've ever worn."

"You looked drop-dead gorgeous in it. And look at it this way—if Wes can't be your date, then at least you're wearing something from him."

"I like how you think."

Isla taps her temples. "My noggin works on occasion." She sighs and stares at her plate for a moment.

"You all right?" I ask, around a mouthful of bread.

"Yeah, I just wish *I* could go to the gala."

"You should come."

"I wasn't invited—"

"Jake would *love* to have you there."

Isla bites her lip. "I highly doubt that one."

I cock my head. "What makes you say that?"

She toys with the edge of her napkin for a moment before responding. "Because he keeps his distance." The sadness in her tone is a punch to the gut.

"He *does* live across the ocean, so I guess that's distance."

"It goes beyond geography," she sighs, "and it's my fault."

"What do you mean?"

"I mean, he's different toward me ever since Wes's thirtieth birthday." She shakes her head. "I was so fucking stupid."

The waiter arrives with the dessert menus and informs us he'll return shortly.

"What happened on Wes's birthday?" I ask, perusing my options. "Wait, are you getting dessert? I'm having the chocolate caramel torte."

She peers at the list. "Yeah, I'll try the coconut mango pie."

"Sorry about the interruption, but desserts are top priority for me."

She chuckles. "Believe me, I get it. Anyway, Reed and Austin planned a huge party. It was a beach bash that went all day and night. People swam, surfed, and played volleyball. Music was blasting, and everyone danced and drank to their hearts' content."

"That sounds like a good time."

"It was amazing. I technically wasn't invited, but Wes said I could come." She flashes a grin. "Which pissed Reed off—something I try to do on the regular. Anyway, I felt so cool hanging out with my brother's mates. I was wearing a bikini, I'd finally gotten some boobs and my braces had come off, so the teeth were straight too. It's funny, I think they were still expecting dorky, awkward Isla, but I'd changed a lot during the years between fifteen and eighteen."

"Ugh, didn't we all? I shudder when I see teenage pictures of myself."

The waiter returns, and we place our dessert order.

Isla waits until he's out of earshot before speaking. "Me too. Anyway, they didn't think Jake would make it because he was still on tour, but he surprised Wes and flew in from New York. I hadn't seen him in a few years, and let me tell you, I wasn't prepared for the tidal wave of longing."

"Like butterflies?"

"More like a flock of albatross. Or a mob of emus. Or a bunch of drunken roos."

"The roos were loose in the top paddock?" I snort. "That's my second favorite Wes-ism."

"It's a good one to know." Isla laughs. "My roos weren't just loose, they were having a fucking stampede."

Our waiter reappears, setting plates in front of us before leaving once more.

"Everything about him was warm and inviting. That day, I noticed the flecks of gold in his chocolate brown eyes and how the corners crinkle when he smiles. And good God, those dimples . . ."

I squeeze her hand. "Jake is adorable."

"He's perfect," Isla swoons. "I love his unruly hair and the way his waves fall into his face. That day on the beach, he seemed taller and he'd filled out." She takes a bite of pie, smiling as she chews. "I'm a sucker for muscles."

"Oh, same here, girl."

"Anyway, I'd crushed on Jake my whole life, but up until then, it was an innocent admiration—mainly because he was the one who paid attention to me. That night was the first time I saw him as a *man*, not just my brother's best mate." She meets my gaze. "And I wanted him. Desperately."

"And how did Jake react to you?"

"He didn't recognize me at first."

"Seriously?" I stuff some torte into my mouth.

She nods. "I went up to him and gave him a seashell—I used to give him shells when I was little."

"I heard about the sandcastles too." I murmur. "Can you say heart-melting?"

"I know. Don't get me wrong, I love Austin, but Jake's always been my favorite. He spent time with me when the guys surfed and did guy things."

"So, what happened when you gave him the shell?"

"He literally did a double take. Then his ears turned red and he started talking really fast, jumbling his words."

I press a hand to my heart. "Gah! He's *ridiculously* adorable."

"Yeah, he is." She smiles. "He was definitely nervous, but it was the way he looked at me that got me. It felt like . . ." She flushes and stares at her plate.

"Like you were the most beautiful woman he'd ever seen?"

Isla's eyes flick up to meet mine. "Yes."

"I completely understand the effects of that look." At her raised brow, I add, "That's how Wes looks at me."

"In your case, it's legitimate. *I'm* just an idiot." She shovels a large bite of pie into her mouth.

"Trust me, you're not. What happened next?"

She finishes chewing and sips her water. "We all huddled around a huge bonfire after dark. Everyone was laughing and singing, sharing stories from childhood and summers past. I remember sitting on a log, watching Jake across the fire. Every time our eyes met, I felt like my heart was gonna bust through my ribs. I'd had my share of crushes, but this was different, almost like a bone-deep awareness of him." She wraps her arms around herself. "It was chilly after the sun went down and I must've shivered or something. He walked over, removed his Brooklyn hoodie, and told me to put it on." Her eyes close as if savoring the memory. "I pulled it over my head and looked down at the blocky maroon lettering. It was so warm, and it smelled like his cologne . . . I can't explain it, but I felt like *he* was keeping me warm, not the shirt. He told me to keep it when he left. Sometimes I still put it on when I feel lonely. I've washed it plenty, so it doesn't smell like him anymore, but it still warms me."

My heart flutters with the romanticism of her story. "Does *he* know that?"

"I doubt he remembers."

Oh, I beg to differ.

Isla sighs. "But it doesn't matter."

"Why? What happened?"

"He had to head back to the States for the rest of his tour, so he left early to get some sleep before his flight. As he walked toward the beach's parking area, I realized he'd forgotten his keys in the pocket of the sweatshirt I had on, so I followed him. Besides, I didn't want him to leave without knowing when I'd see him again. I caught up to him outside the Jeep he'd rented. Being clumsy like always, I stumbled over a rock, but he caught me and held me to his chest. It felt so fucking good to have his arms around me, so I . . . I kissed him."

My eyes widen at her whispered admission. "You kissed him? Like *really* kissed him?"

"Yes."

"And did he kiss you back?"

"He froze at first. Then, he gripped my face and kissed me like he'd *die* if he didn't. Like he'd been waiting his whole damn life to kiss me, and his Earth stopped turning when our lips met. Lena, when I tell you sparks were flying, I mean fucking lightning bolts. It wasn't my first kiss, but I wish it had been because in that moment . . . I knew what I'd been missing."

"But Wes said you've had a lot of boyfriends in the past few years?"

"Yeah, but I don't keep any of them around for long."

"Why not?"

"To this day, *no one* has ever kissed me like that. No one's come close. I cycle through guys, hoping I'll find someone who compares. Hoping I find one who ignites me, makes me feel alive, but they barely even flicker." She squeezes her eyes shut. "Jake felt like a raging storm, a fucking inferno."

"Then what the hell happened?"

"He suddenly seized up and broke the kiss. His expression was this awful mixture of shock and horror. He apologized to me, then left abruptly. I've only seen him a handful of times since then. He's always distant, not the funny, hair-pulling guy I grew up knowing. The one who laughed with me, teased me, played Barbies without hesitation. I know he regrets kissing me, but it hurt to see it on his face, and his distance hurts even more."

"I *guarantee* he doesn't regret it."

Isla narrows her eyes. "What're ya saying?"

I smirk. "How old were you then?"

"I'd just turned eighteen."

"So, that means Jake was . . .?"

"Nearly twenty-nine."

"Think about it, Isla. What could've possibly crossed his mind in that moment?" When she doesn't respond, I lean in close. "I'll give you a clue. Six foot five, muscles carved by the gods, hotheaded as fuck. One doesn't freely make-out with the little sister of a man like that."

She curls her lip. "Why the hell would he think about my idiot brother when kissing me?"

"Because he's one of Wes's best friends. He respects him. He respects *you*, Isla."

"Are you saying you know something I don't?"

I try to hold back my smile, but it's a lost cause. Though I can't see it, I *feel* the Cheshire cat grin cross my features. I stuff some chocolate caramel torte in my face and avert my gaze.

Isla leans in and grabs my hands. "Tell me *everything*."

"Oh, you know, little things here and there."

"Tell me."

"Let's just say his body language was a dead giveaway for me. I noticed a change in him every time you came up in conversation."

"Whaddya mean?"

"He'd go from his usual wise-cracking, dirty-minded, filthy-mouthed self to a damn mute."

Isla shakes her head. "Jake doesn't have a dirty mind or a filthy mouth—"

"Maybe around *you*, he doesn't." I grin. "But I spent three weeks in the wilderness with him. He's a big perv, which is why we get along so well."

She flushes a deeper shade of pink. "I'd love to see that side of him."

"Seriously, Isla, the second you came up in conversation, he'd switch gears. Someone would mention your name and he'd tense, shoulders stiffening, jaw clenching. Then, he'd stare into the distance, or at his hands, or whatever random thing he held—anything to keep from making eye contact with Wes."

"Maybe he was ashamed—"

"Shame was the *farthest* thing from his mind."

"How do ya know?" Isla breathes.

"One day, he had a migraine, so we couldn't hike. Wes and Austin went looking for saplings to make traps. Jake and I stayed behind and talked."

"About what?"

"Everything—relationships, love, finding the right person. I noticed the distant look in his eyes again, so I decided to test my theory and called him out."

"Called him out, how?"

"Lena-style." I grin and pat myself on the back. "Blunt and subtlety-free. Poor guy—I shocked the shit out of him."

Isla clutches my hand. "Please tell me what you said."

"I asked him if Wes knew he was in love with you. After he finished choking on his water, I got my answer."

"What did he say?" she asks, her lower lip trembling.

"So, first I'll say that I love Jake dearly. He asked me not to tell anyone, so I already feel like a shitty friend for breaking his trust. Because of that, I can't tell you *what* he said." I touch Isla's shoulder.

"Of course," she murmurs sadly.

"If you hadn't confessed to feeling the same way about him, I never would've opened my mouth at all. While I feel shitty for breaking his confidence, I couldn't sit back and watch you both suffer."

"You really think he loves me?" The hope in her eyes tells me I'm doing the right thing.

"Let's put it this way . . . he didn't deny it."

Her eyes well. "He's been so distant."

"He's got reasons."

"Like what?"

I cock a brow. "Nice try. *My* lips are sealed. But perhaps you should dig out the *Shades* album and give tracks seven and eleven a listen . . . Jake says plenty."

"Hold on, 'Desert Rose' is about *me?*"

"No comment."

Her eyes widen. "Oh my God. Wait, which one is eleven? I downloaded the album before the CD shipped, so the order's fucked-up."

"Number eleven is 'If Only.'" Her jaw drops open, so I lean in closer. "Maybe you're his forbidden fruit. Maybe maintaining an ocean's distance between you helps him control his attraction." I cover my mouth. "Oops, I've said too much."

"If he feels that way, why not tell Wes to fuck off and come after me?"

"Again, he has his reasons. Keep in mind, Jake's not an alpha like Wes—he's a gentleman. He *knows* he wants you, but he's not gonna act on it. His wants and needs take the back burner to things like respect and loyalty."

She spears some pie with her fork. "Fuck respect and loyalty."

I laugh. "I knew you'd say that."

"Well, it's true. I'm not a child anymore and Wes doesn't run my life—I do."

"He doesn't run Jake's life either." I steeple my fingers in front of my lips. "But Wes *is* on the forefront of Jake's mind when it comes to you. Like I said, he's a gentleman. He'd sooner pine from a distance than risk the friendship—and the last thing he'd want is to drive a wedge between you and Wes."

"So, in *his* mind, I'm off-limits?"

"Exactly. You're the embodiment of forbidden fruit."

"You're *sure* he wants me?"

The uncertainty in Isla's gaze breaks my heart. I've been in her position—burdened by insecurities, worry, and longing.

I squeeze her hand. "'Desert Rose' and 'If Only' aren't the only songs he's written about you, Isla. *Shades* came out after your kiss. If you listen closely, you'll discover that several tracks hold and hide your name." I flash a grin. "I know this, because I came right out and asked him."

"Oh my God, is 'Crave' about me?" she whispers.

"Crave" is a dark, sensual song. Jake's intoxicating voice caresses each word of the hidden bonus track. It's just him and a piano, and he sings with a seductiveness not typical of his music. It's the kind of song one would add to their sex playlist. In fact, if the thought of Jake serenading mine and Wes's lovemaking didn't wig me out a bit, I would add it to *my* sexy soundtrack. But that's not happening. It would be way too weird. Because it's Jake, my favorite cock-block.

I smile coyly. "He's a gentleman, but he's a *man* first."

"Holy fuck." Isla's face turns beet red.

"Like I said, don't expect the foot-stomping, claim-staking, chest-pounding antics you grew up with. Jake won't come after you because he's not an alpha."

"Let me tell you something about the Emerson family . . ." A slow smile transforms Isla's features, and she drags her spoon through some whipped cream on her plate. "We're *all* alphas."

CHAPTER 26

LENA

Internal playlist: "Surrounded" by Chantal Kreviazuk

Paul and I pull up outside the film studio. Isla had no desire to rub elbows with movie stars, so we dropped her off at the hotel first. Truth be told, I'm not keen on rubbing elbows with anyone other than Wes. Small talk isn't exactly my forte, and here I feel like an orphan from the wrong side of the tracks, ringing some rich lady's doorbell.

"You ready?" Paul asks.

"As ready as I'm gonna get. What does one talk to these people about?"

He chuckles. "Just be yourself. I've met the cast and they're all really cool. Besides, if you can handle Mr. Hollywood himself, you've got nothing to worry about."

"It's not *Mr.* Hollywood I'm worried about."

Paul cocks a brow. "I take it Aphrodite's got you on edge?"

I flush. "Yeah. You could say that."

"Why?"

I roll my eyes at Paul as he parks in front of the building. "Because she's Alainna Baker. Because she's gorgeous enough to make *me* want her. Because I'm insecure as fuck and she's everything I'm not."

Paul jumps out, greets a security guy, and holds the door open for me. "While I agree that she's gorgeous, rich, and famous, you're missing a key factor."

"And that is?" I step inside the studio.

"She's his *on-screen* love. People pay them to act the part." He smiles and nudges me down a hallway. "The kissing, the sex scenes, the lovey-dovey shit . . . all fake."

"I know," I mutter.

"I understand your insecurity but know this . . . when it comes to you, none of it's an act." He pauses outside a door. "I've worked with him for years, and he's the real deal with you. I talked to him while you were getting changed this morning, and he's just as nervous as you. He wants to let you in, show you his day-to-day life, but he's afraid the lifestyle will scare you off. He knows this is uncomfortable for you and you'd rather be sequestered in a hotel somewhere, but he needs *your* reassurance too. His heart is in your hands, kiddo. And that's something she'll never have."

I smile up at him. "Thanks for the pep talk, Rambo."

Paul winks. "Now get in there and draw first blood."

I enter a room with a large viewing screen and cushy, red theater chairs. A group congregates at the far end of the room. I spot Wes over the top of the crowd, as he's the tallest one here, standing near a woman in a white pantsuit.

Aphrodite.

Tall. Curvy, yet slender, her body is perfection. With flowing, gold-spun waves and piercing green eyes, she is every bit the goddess I imagined. Alainna Baker is fucking radiant. Easily ten times more beautiful in real life. Suddenly, I feel like a prairie-marm spinster reject, dressed in ill-fitting petticoats with pieces of hay in my hair and horse shit on my shoes.

Alainna is all smiles and standing *way* too close to Wes. She leans in and whispers something to him. He laughs heartily in that booming laugh I love so much. My scalp prickles and my palms begin to sweat. Alainna giggles, a girlish, tinkling fairy laugh, and my innards churn.

This was a mistake.

Paul appears at my side. "Get out of your head and go over there."

"Gimme a minute. I'm working on it," I mutter.

Just then, Wes spots me. A megawatt grin appears on his face.

"Time's up," Paul murmurs.

Wes reaches me in a few long strides. Wordlessly, he grips both sides of my face and kisses me passionately—like he doesn't give a fuck who's in the room—and suddenly, neither do I.

I clasp the back of his neck and return the kiss with newfound ferocity. Someone makes a howling sound, and a few people clap.

"Are you gonna introduce her to us or suck her face off?" Ronan Flynn, the actor who played Zeus throughout the *Olympus Fire* franchise, teases.

Wes breaks the kiss. "I'd rather suck her face off than bother with any of you." He laughs and addresses his castmates, "Everyone, this is Ms. Lena Hamilton, the extraordinary force of nature who saved my life and stole my heart."

I flush and give a weak wave. "Hello, everyone."

Wes snakes an arm around my waist, leading me over to the tall, muscled hunk with russet hair and forest green eyes. "Lena, this is Ronan Flynn, aka the Z-man. He's one helluva guitar player and he knows his way around a kitchen. He's got a mean left hook and a soft spot for Hallmark movies."

Ronan playfully shoves Wes. "Dude, that was our little secret." He turns and shakes my hand. "Nice to finally meet you, Lena."

"Likewise, Ronan. I also have a soft spot for Hallmark movies," I reply with a giggle.

"They're the shit, right?" He bumps fists with me.

I nod and grin. "The absolute shit."

Ronan laughs, revealing adorable dimples on his cheeks. "I hear you're a New Yorker?"

"Guilty as charged."

"We're neighbors. I grew up in Cali, but I just moved to Manhattan last month."

"I was born upstate though. People hear New York and automatically assume the city, but I'm originally from the Catskills. Now I live in Brooklyn, but the hospital where I work is in Manhattan. Welcome to the Empire State."

"Thanks!"

Wes leads me over to a beautiful woman with caramel-colored skin, bouncy chestnut curls, and amber eyes. "Lena, this is Maribel Rodriguez, who I'm sure you recognize as the lovely Athena."

"Hi, Maribel, it's wonderful to meet you."

"Lena, I can't tell you how awesome it is to finally have a face to go with your name," Maribel gushes. "Wes talks about you nonstop."

"He does?" I ask, peering up at Wes.

He interlaces our fingers and presses a gentle kiss to my knuckles. "Damn right, I do."

Maribel giggles and nudges me. "He's got it bad for you, chica."

"I feel the same about him." I pinch his cheek and wink.

We work our way down the line with Wes making introductions, until I've met all but one—Alainna. My gut churns as we approach her.

"And last, but certainly not least, my on-screen Aphrodite, Alainna Baker." Wes touches her arm as he introduces us. "Alainna, this is my real-life Aphrodite, aka the woman who puts up with all my shit."

Alainna laughs her fairy laugh and hugs me. "Thank God *someone* puts up with him. So great meeting you, Lena. I feel like I know you already."

"Nice meeting you as well," I reply, returning her hug. "He puts up with *my* shit too."

"Something tells me he's a much bigger pain in the ass though," Alainna remarks. "He told me how he went after you with a spider."

I chuckle. "Yeah, I nearly throat-punched him."

"I nearly throat-punch him most days on-set." She purses her lips and cocks a brow at Wes. "Right, Emerson?"

"Oh, c'mon, Baker." He snorts. "I'm not *that* annoying."

"You know what he did to me in the first movie?" Alainna says to me, not even acknowledging Wes.

"Oh, would you let it go already?" Wes laughs.

"We had to film a kiss scene," Alainna jabs a finger in his chest, "and this asshole ate *four* cloves of garlic."

"She hates garlic," Wes explains with an impish grin.

"Raw garlic?" I ask.

Wes's eyes twinkle with mischief. "Yep."

I grimace. "I can deal with cooked garlic. But raw? Not so much. Were you having Italian food for lunch?"

Alainna meets my gaze. "No, he did it to mess with me. Then, he followed it with a cayenne ginger kombucha and some kimchi."

Wes nudges Alainna. "Don't forget the tuna."

"Right. How could I forget the nasty ass can of tuna?"

I crinkle my nose. "Gross."

"I know! He came out of his trailer with a shit-eating grin and, at first, I didn't think anything of it because he always has a smirk on his punk face. Then, he got within five feet of me, and I was like, 'What the hell's that smell?' He laughed, which gusted his dragon breath at me, and I literally gagged." She shakes her head. "The director was like, 'You're supposed to love him, not look like you want to puke on him.' and I was like, 'But the asshole reeks of vampire repellant.' I made him eat half a tin of Altoids."

I laugh along with Wes.

"Then, *I* literally threw up," Wes says with a snort. "Turns out, garlic, tuna, fermented cabbage, and spearmint makes a shitty combination."

"Served you right," Alainna says.

"I think I've got a pretty good picture of what it's like on-set with him," I muse.

Alainna shakes her head. "You have *no* idea. He's like the younger brother I never wanted." She points to me. "You're a better woman than most—I'm so happy he found you."

"He's worth it." I smile and tuck my arm around Wes. "Even when he smells like a dumpster."

Wes stiffens when a dark-haired man approaches us with a scowl. I recognize him as the fashion model, Salvatore Bonavito, Alainna's fiancé. A native of Rome, he's gorgeous in a broody mafia prince kind of way.

He grips Alainna's elbow. "I need to talk to you."

Alainna gives Wes and me a wave before following Sal out of the room.

CHAPTER 27

WES

Life lesson: When a woman tells you she's fine, she is definitely NOT fine.

So *far, so good.* I'm grateful my castmates have welcomed my woman with open arms. Not that I doubted they would.

The tension that radiated from Lena upon her arrival has finally dissipated. I'm well aware of the reason behind it—her insecurity, even though it makes no sense to me. I enjoyed seeing Lena and Alainna laughing and chatting amicably, but I wish dickface Sal hadn't cut things short. I hate that stupid prick.

I glance over at Ronan, who stares after Alainna's retreating form. The pain and longing on his face tightens my chest. He and Alainna have been best friends since childhood—much like Lena and Garrett—except Ronan's secretly in love with her. It gutted him when she and Sal got engaged last month, so much so, he moved across the country. Alainna has no idea why he left California. None whatsoever. Too bad Ronan doesn't have the balls to tell her. I wish someone would stop her from marrying that stupid prick. Fuck Sal and his underwear modeling career. Fuck his shitty attitude. She deserves someone with a heart of gold. Someone like Ronan Flynn.

Ronan meets my gaze and shakes his head slowly, clenching his jaw before he looks away.

The film screening is due to start soon, and I'm looking forward to viewing the finished project. The *Olympus Fire* films changed my life, but the trilogy has been a long-haul and I'm ready to have my life back.

I glance over at Lena. She looks incredibly sexy in her little jade sundress and cardigan, so different from the jeans and flannels of Alaska. I like her in both, or better yet, nothing at all.

I touch her shoulder. "Are you hungry, love?"

"I'm okay right now. We had a late lunch." She cocks her head. "I just realized you aren't wearing your sling."

I smirk. "I forgot."

"No, you didn't. Wes, we've been over this. If you want the collarbone to heal properly, you need to wear your damn sling."

"I know."

She grips my chin. "Then. Wear. It."

Alainna, who returned a few minutes ago, laughs. "Don't waste your breath, Lena. He's as stubborn as an ox. If I didn't know any better, I'd peg him as a Taurus."

Lena purses her lips. "I dunno, I'm thinking the warlock Scorpio bit fits."

I give an exaggerated grin. "Trick or treat."

Even though the holiday is a much bigger deal in the States, a Halloween birthday still has its advantages. Namely, the lollies and sweets I adore, but I enjoy a good costume. Maybe I'm juvenile, but I also love a good trick.

Lena laughs and nudges Alainna. "Speaking of his birthday, he won't give me any gift ideas. Help a sister out."

"I don't need any gifts, love. I have you."

"You two are adorable," Alainna swoons, placing a hand on each of our shoulders. "Gift-wise, I'd suggest a toothbrush, Listerine, and a ball gag. He also loves to eat, so anything food-related works." She glances at me. "I can't remember our press-tour schedule. Will you guys get to be together for your birthday?"

"No, but at least I'll be in Australia. My mum's excited for that. I haven't spent a birthday at home in a few years."

Lena touches my arm. "How long will you be home?"

"Four or five days."

She nods. "I'm going to mail you something. We'll celebrate when you come to New York after the premiere."

"What're ya sending me?"

Lena flutters her lashes. "You'll have to wait and see what I figure out."

Alainna turns to Lena. "Wes said your birthday's Christmas Eve. That's cool you're both born on a holiday."

I snort. "Yeah, but Lena's a gift and I'll rot your teeth."

Alainna punches my shoulder. "Well, you burned my nostrils, so I guess that's to be expected."

Sid Warner, *The Aegean's* director, asks everyone to take their seats for the screening. I guide Lena to a chair in the front row with a hand on the small of her back. She settles to my right and I wrap an arm over her shoulders.

Alainna sits on my other side and whispers, "Seriously, you two are so cute. I really like her. Don't fuck it up."

I laugh instead of answering. *Ye of little faith, Baker.*

"All right, people, I admit—I cheated and watched our movie already," Sid says with a grin, "and I gotta tell you . . . it's our best one yet. Give yourselves a round of applause because we're about to break some fucking records."

Everyone claps and cheers.

Lena's hand settles on my knee and squeezes. "I'm so proud of you, baby."

"Thanks, love." I kiss her forehead. "But you probably shouldn't praise me until *after* you've watched it."

"I already know your talent, Ace."

"Everyone sit back and prepare to be amazed," Sid says with a flourish of his hand.

I glance at Lena as the credits roll.

"Wow," she shakes her head, "just . . . wow. I don't have any other words."

"Did you like it?" I ask, literally terrified to hear her answer.

It was one thing to act out a scene, but to see it on a big screen, when it seems so *real*, is unnerving. At times, the graphic violence was hard to watch. The sex, even more so. There were a few scenes that bordered on explicit. If it made *me* uncomfortable, I can only imagine how Lena felt. Beneath my arm, her body had turned to stone—shoulders stiffening, fists clenched in her lap. At one point, she averted her eyes and panic flared in my gut. Alainna had shifted beside me too.

Lena meets my gaze. "It was . . . intense."

The lights come back on and Sid reappears in the front of the room. "How about those sex scenes?" He gestures to me and Alainna. "You two were amazing. Your on-screen chemistry is fucking *sizzling*." Lena tenses and turns her focus to her hands. Sid continues, "I felt like I was in bed with Ares and Aphrodite."

Shut the fuck up, Sid.

Alainna clears her throat. "Well, you hired us to *act*, did you not?" Her gaze darts to Lena as she downplays the director's remarks. "We did our jobs."

Thanks, Baker.

She'd confided in me earlier that she was apprehensive about her fiancé watching the film. Turns out, she had good reason. Salvatore is currently shooting eye-daggers in my direction. I've been nothing but pleasant to the guy, but he's always hated me. That's fine. I hate him too.

Ronan, also eager for a topic change, chimes in, "Yo, that final battle scene was epic."

I wonder if the sex scenes get under his skin. He's never mentioned it, likely because he knows Alainna is just my friend, but I can't imagine they're easy for him to watch. Especially since the poor bastard plays her on-screen father. I consider Ronan a good friend, so I hate the thought of causing him pain.

Everyone chats excitedly. I tighten my arm around Lena's shoulder.

She peers up at me. "I know I've said this before, but you're extremely talented."

"Thank you." I touch her cheek. "Are you all right?"

An unnamed emotion flashes in her eyes before her poker-face takes over. "I'm fine."

Fine. I fucking hate when she says "fine."

"Night, Wes." Alainna grasps Lena's hand. "Lena, it was nice meeting you. I look forward to seeing you tomorrow night."

"Nice meeting you too. And congratulations. Your acting was incredible."

"Thank you. See you tomorrow," Alainna says before following dickhead Sal out the door.

"Wow." Lena stares after them. "That guy hates you."

"Ya think?" I rub the back of my neck. "He seems to forget we're only acting." I tilt Lena's chin to face me. "You know that, right?"

She nods, but her eyes tell me otherwise, making my stomach twist.

"You remember my clairvoyance?"

She cocks a brow. "Thought you left it in Alaska?"

"Well, I got some of it back." I pin her with my gaze. "Between that and my crystal ball—"

"I'm fine, Wes."

Liar.

"We'll talk later, sunshine."

Sid approaches, shaking his head appreciatively. "Emerson, once again, you blew my mind. Your acting gets better with each film."

"Thanks, mate."

He eyes Lena. "What did you think?"

"It reinforced my stance that Wes is the cream of the crop in this field. I'm extremely proud of him and impressed by the entire cast's talent. This film will shatter records and redefine the genre."

Sid's brows pop. "Those are some powerful words, Lena."

"I speak the truth, Mr. Warner. Congratulations, and bravo for spearheading the production."

He grins. "And what did you think of the sex scenes?"

I send Sid a warning glare. *Seriously, mate?*

Lena stiffens and forces a smile. "Profound authenticity, which further proves my point about Wes's talent."

"What did you think of Alainna's performance?"

Are you fucking kidding me?

"She exceeded my expectations."

Sid nods. "How about when she—"

I step forward and pat Sid's shoulder. "We're gonna head out now, mate. See you tomorrow."

"Leaving so soon?"

I narrow my eyes. "Not soon enough, actually." I grip Lena's hand and usher her outside to where Paul waits with the car.

"How'd it go?" Paul asks, opening the door for us.

"Bloody fabulous," I mutter.

"You going for dinner?"

I shake my head. "Room service tonight."

Paul nods. "Isla's settled in for the night too." He glances at Lena, who still hasn't said a word. "What did you thin—"

I put my hand up. "Not now, mate."

Paul's gaze flickers between us before he slowly nods. "Got it."

We ride to the hotel in heavy silence. *Fucking Sid Warner.* Clearly, Alainna's engagement and my relationship mean nothing to the guy; he's been trying to push us together since the first movie. I wonder if Sid would've pulled the same shit if Alainna's fiancé had still been there. Salvatore looked like he wanted to rip my face off when they left. He probably would've thrown a punch.

I look over at Lena, who stiffly stares out the window. I know better than to push her, so I clench my fists in my lap. I meet Paul's knowing gaze in the rearview mirror. Paul's ability to read me is one of the things I love most about my bodyguard.

He drops us off in front of the hotel. I quickly move around to open the car door for Lena, but she's already emerged.

I guide her into the lobby and press the lift call button. Lena stares at the floor numbers as we ride up in silence. We walk down the hall in silence too. I hold the suite door open for her and close it behind me.

She walks into the bedroom and sits on the edge of the bed. "Before you say a word, know that it's not you I'm upset with."

"I know, love." I settle beside her and take her hands in mine. "He's a bloody fuckwit and I'm sorry."

"You don't need to apologize for him."

"Yeah, I do." I tilt her chin to meet my gaze. "I'm sorry I put you in that position."

She nods. "I think your film is incredible. I won't lie to you and say it was easy for me to watch—because it wasn't—but I refuse to let *my* discomfort cast a shadow over your accomplishment. I'm truly proud of you, Wes."

"Thank you, love."

She squeezes my hand. "I admit, the sex scenes made me uncomfortable. It was hard to watch you be intimate with another woman. But what bothered me most was your director's inability to conduct himself appropriately. His behavior cut me to the quick. I'll be polite and respectful, but I will *not* pretend to like that man. I hope you understand where I'm coming from."

"Believe me, I do. He was about three seconds from getting punched."

"And I appreciate Alainna's attempts to downplay his idiocy. She seems like a wonderful person, and I'm sorry I preemptively hated her."

"You hated her?"

Lena holds up her thumb and forefinger. "A smidge," she shakes her head with a small smile, "but I'm over it."

"I thought you'd hate her *more* after seeing the movie."

"Like I said, it was hard to watch, but I won't hold her job against her—or you." She touches my cheek. "I don't want to put a damper on your night, and I'm sorry I got all quiet and moody. You should be celebrating, not reassuring me."

"I appreciate that, love, but reassuring you takes precedence. I'm sorry about Sid. He's a knob jockey."

"It seemed like he went out of his way to make me uncomfortable, which makes no sense."

I sigh. "Yeah, it does. He's been trying to push me and Alainna together for years. 'For publicity's sake,'" I explain with air quotes. "But it didn't work out that way and I think he's still bitter about it. I'm just glad Alainna and Salvatore left before Sid started his shit."

"I saw the look Salvatore gave you."

"He's extremely jealous and possessive. She's confided in me over the years and, to be honest, she deserves better. I don't like how he treats her. I can't believe she agreed to marry him."

Lena chews her lip. "Sometimes we women make shitty choices. I'm sure people said the same things about Marc. Actually, I *know* they did."

"He's a bloody wanker. So is dickwad Sal. I'm sure he's giving Baker a raft of shit right now, which pisses me off. *She* should be celebrating too, you know?"

"Absolutely." Lena shakes her head. "It's funny how the media paints them as this picture-perfect couple, but after spending five minutes with them, it's clear they're not."

"The media shows the public what they want them to see. They get a lot of shit wrong—dead wrong."

I lurch awake to Lena's muffled scream. She kicks and thrashes beside me, clawing the fitted sheet.

"He's not breathing," she wails. Though she's squeezed them shut, tears stream from her eyes. "Oh, God . . ."

I grip her shoulders. "Lena, wake up."

"The current's too strong." Her back arches off the bed. "Wes, please . . ."

I shake her firmly. "Wake up."

Her eyes fly open. "Where's Wes?"

"I'm right here, love." I pull her to my chest. "I'm right here."

Lena's arms find their way around me. Her entire body trembles. "I was doing CPR and when I looked down, you weren't there," she sobs, gasping for breath.

I tighten our embrace and kiss her forehead. "I've got you. I'm here. Just breathe for me."

She buries her face in my chest, dampening my skin with her tears. "I don't want to lose you again."

"Look at me." I wait for her to meet my gaze before I continue, "Look into my eyes and trust me."

"I do trust you," she whispers.

"I need you to trust this—trust *us*." I kiss her lips and stroke my thumbs over her cheeks. "I'm not going anywhere, sunshine."

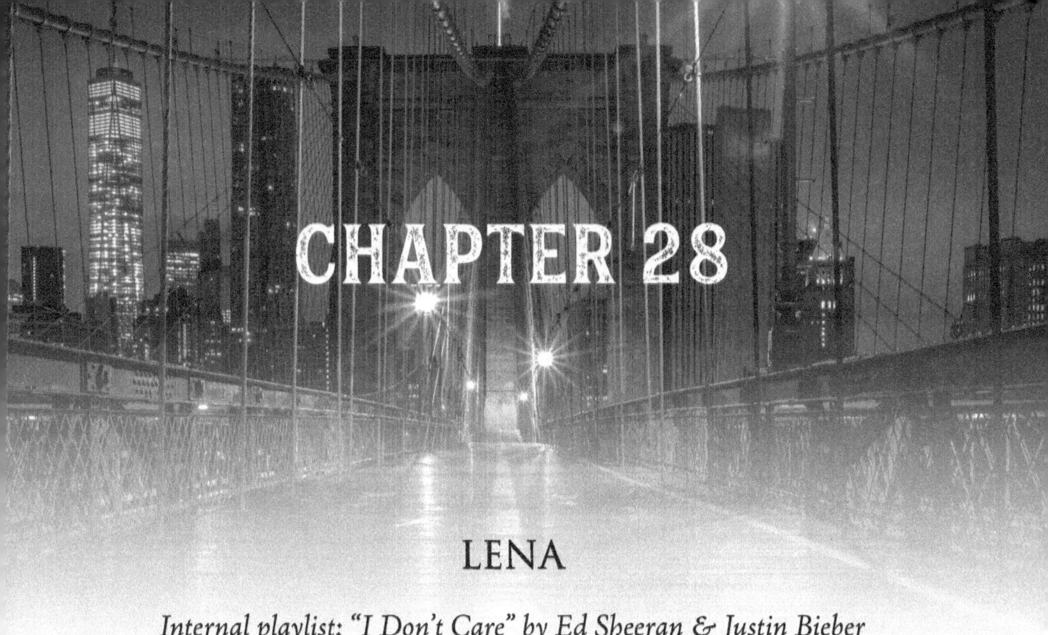

CHAPTER 28

LENA

Internal playlist: "I Don't Care" by Ed Sheeran & Justin Bieber

I glance up from my novel as Paul enters the suite—twenty minutes early as Wes had predicted.

"Greetings, love birds."

"Howdy, Rambo."

"Where's Hollywood?"

"Showering." I stretch and place my book on the nightstand. "He was on the phone with Reed for a while and got a late start."

"Ah." Paul leans against the dresser. "Makes sense. The grand master spares no details."

"Grand master?"

He rubs his chin. "Clearly, you haven't met Reed."

"Nope. Not yet." I cock my head. "Why? Is he a dick?"

Paul snorts. "You have a way with words, Lena."

"Been told that before." I study his face. "No, seriously, is he?"

"He's not a dick, per se. Just . . ." He sighs. "Reed is different from Wes and Isla. Very different."

"Wes said he's moody and all business."

"He's a hard shell to crack."

I roll my eyes. "Then I'm sure he'll *love* me."

"He will . . . eventually. But don't expect anything warm and fuzzy right off the bat."

"I'll keep that in mind. What's Isla doing today? Is she dragging you to that fashion expo she mentioned?"

"No, she's resting, so I'm following you two around today."

"Is she all right?"

He frowns. "No. She said she's having a flare."

I nod in understanding. While Isla lacks the telltale physical signs of lupus, like thinning hair and a butterfly facial rash, she hadn't escaped the joint pain, weakness, and fatigue. She never once complained, but I knew she was uncomfortable when we were shopping. It was the subtle winces and shifting of weight that tipped me off. By late afternoon, her pace slowed considerably, and when I suggested we rest, Isla jumped at the opportunity.

"Her feet are bothering her?"

Paul shakes his head. "Today it's her ankles and elbows. She's staying in her hotel room to crochet something."

"Won't that aggravate it?"

"She said her wrists are fine."

I peer through the bedroom doorway as Wes emerges from the bathroom with a towel wrapped around his hips, upper body glistening with water droplets. He makes his way over to his suitcase. "Where's Imp?"

"In bed," Paul replies.

Wes tenses. "Another flare?"

Paul nods sadly. "She said to tell you she'll see you tomorrow for breakfast."

Wes presses his lips in a grim line and pulls out jeans, boxers, a belt, and a T-shirt. "Maybe if she'd try the new medicine, she wouldn't have as many flares," he mutters, heading for the bathroom again.

"You never mentioned she's resistant to taking medication."

Wes pops his head out the door. "She takes a slew of anti-rejection drugs, but she refuses to try some of the newer biologics that could help with her pain." He zips his jeans and slides a belt through the loops.

"She said she's on a special diet?"

"Yeah, a strict low-sodium, anti-inflammatory one. She also takes certain blood pressure meds to protect her transplanted kidney. She doesn't have high blood pressure, so I think they make her dizzy. She hates taking the meds and feeling like she's reliant on them." He pads across the room, shrugging on his white T-shirt. "But, obviously, she *is* reliant on them."

"You think that's why she's flighty?" Paul asks.

"Some of it. She hates being tied down, trapped, dependent—you name it. She was *miserable* when she had to have dialysis. Now, she chases freedom like it's a high she can't let herself come down from. She jumps from guy to guy, and it scares me sometimes."

"Why?" I ask.

"I don't want her getting a reputation for being promiscuous."

I cock a brow. "So, it's all right for guys to play the field, but when a girl does it, she's slutty?"

Wes crosses his arms over his chest. "Not what I said."

"You didn't have to . . . you implied it, Ace."

"I mean, I want to see her happy and secure—not burning through men like a fucking brush fire."

"Do you think she's unhappy?" I ask. "Or insecure, for that matter?"

"I dunno what she is."

"You should ask her. Maybe she'll surprise you."

Wes glowers. "I'm not big on surprises."

I poke the middle of his chest. "You're not big on *anything* you don't agree with."

Paul smirks. "Hit the nail on the head there, Lena." Wes gives him the finger, and Paul's smirk widens to a grin. "She's young yet—she'll settle down. Give her time."

Wes snorts. "Doubtful. I'll be a grandfather by the time she finds someone she'll commit to."

Buckle-up, Gramps.

I smile to myself. Wes would shit a brick if he knew about Isla's crush on Jake. He'd shit a concrete block if he knew Jake felt the same way about her. *What big brother doesn't know, won't hurt him.*

Wes tilts my chin to meet his gaze. "What's on *your* mind, sunshine?"

"Oh, nothing," I chirp. He'd shit a fucking two-by-four if he knew what I know.

Paul rubs his belly. "I'm starving. Where do you two wanna eat?"

"I'll eat anything, mate. Maybe someplace with patio seating?"

I stiffen. "You want to be all . . . exposed like that?"

"This is LA—I'm exposed no matter where I go."

"What about that one with the rooftop bar you like? The place we went last time," Paul suggests. "You can get some fresh air, but it'll be more private than being on the sidewalk."

"Yeah, let's go there." Wes stands and pulls his aviators on. "You on board with that, sunshine?"

I'd prefer room service.

"Sounds good." I glance down at my outfit. The sage green floral dress is more boho-chic than I'm used to, but Isla convinced me to buy it. I left my hair down and layered a denim jacket on top in case it's breezy. "Am I dressed appropriately for a rooftop bar?"

Wes grins. "It's a restaurant, not a black-tie gala."

"Yeah, but you're gonna be seen with me . . ." *And I don't want to embarrass you.*

Wes kisses my cheek. "You look gorgeous, as always, love."

I study the drink menu. "You know what? I'd love a blood orange mojito." I had a similar cocktail when Rita and I visited the Turks and Caicos a few years ago. I remember lounging by the pool at our resort without a care in the world. I could use another girls' trip.

Our waiter nods his approval. "An excellent choice." He turns to Wes. "And for you, sir?"

"I'll take the Shiraz, please."

"I'll be back with those shortly."

I peer across the table at Wes. "Shiraz, huh?" On our first night at the Aurora Borealis Resort, he'd poured me a glass of an Australian vintage Shiraz. I love how all my memories involve food and drinks. Gluttony for the win.

"I enjoy a spicy vintage," he winks, "but I'd rather sip you."

Heat floods my core. "Maybe later, Ace."

He reaches across the table and grabs my hand, interlacing our fingers. "There's no *maybe* about it," his gaze darkens, "consider it a promise."

"I love when you make promises."

Wes squeezes my hand. "I love *you.*"

My breath leaves me in a rush, like it does every single time he says it. "I love you too, Wes."

He smiles and lifts my hand to his mouth, brushing his lips over my knuckles. The waiter reappears with our drinks. "Thanks, mate."

"I'll give you more time with the menus," he says before leaving.

I peruse the options, feeling the weight of Wes's gaze. "Pick your food, Ace. You can eye-fuck me later."

"I already know what I want," he flashes a wolfish grin, "and what you're gonna get."

"Hmm . . . I think I'll take the meat. Well-done, this time."

"Damn right, you will."

I laugh and point to the menu. "I mean the filet mignon panini."

"You can have that too." He grips my knee beneath the table, sending a shock wave of desire through me. "Consume those calories, love. We're gonna burn 'em later."

"In that case, I'll have fries instead of salad." I drag the tip of my shoe up his calf. "I love burning calories with you."

He laughs. "Good. Then we can do some squats."

I snort and curl my lip. "Nope. Fuck those."

He traces circles on my knee, each one reverberating to my clit. "You already know my answer to that."

A dark-haired young woman approaches our table, making no attempt to hide her ogling of Wes. She touches his shoulder and squeals, "Oh my God, it *is* you!"

Paul appears out of nowhere, positioning his body between them. "Can I help you?"

"I . . . uh, I wanted to get his autograph."

"Can you not see the man's eating?" Paul growls.

"He didn't have his food yet, so I figured—"

"You figured wrong." With his icy tone and unyielding stance, he's every bit John Rambo, the lone wolf ex-patriot who will fuck up anyone who crosses him.

I glance at Wes, who bears a conflicted expression. He sighs and touches Paul's elbow. "It's fine, mate."

Paul steps aside and points at the woman. "You can get your autograph, but don't let me see you touch him again." He crosses his thick arms over his chest and glares.

Wes peers up at the woman, who nervously twirls her hair. "Hi. What's your name?"

"Lacey."

"Hi, Lacey. Where ya from?"

"New York."

"Ah, so's my beautiful girlfriend." He smiles and points at me.

His girlfriend.

I feel the woman studying me, so I meet her gaze.

"Sorry I interrupted your lunch. I've been a huge fan for years," she says sheepishly.

"No worries. Wes appreciates all his fans."

"Where in New York?" Wes asks. "Not that I'm familiar with any place other than the city."

"Plattsburgh. It's near the Canadian border."

"Nice. What would ya like me to autograph, Lacey from Plattsburgh?"

The woman fishes in her purse and withdraws a planner. "This is the only paper I have." Her hands shake as she passes it over and rummages in her purse again. "Shit. I don't have a friggin' pen."

I reach for my bag. "You can borrow mine." I pull it out and hand the pen to Wes, whose fingertips brush mine as he takes it.

"Thanks, love. Always prepared." He smiles and scrawls his name in Lacey's book before returning the pen.

"Thank you so much." She glances at me. "Again, I'm sorry for interrupting your date, and thanks for letting me use your pen."

"It's all right and you're welcome. We New Yorkers need to stick together in Cali, am I right?"

Lacey grins. "Absolutely." She peers at Wes shyly. "Thank you."

"While you're here, how about we get a picture, Lacey from Plattsburgh?" Wes offers.

"Oh my God. Yes, please." She holds out her phone to Wes.

"I can take the picture," I offer.

"Nope, Paul will. You're gonna be in it." He rises and hands the phone to Paul. "Lena, come here."

He lightly loops an arm over Lacey's shoulder. He snakes the other one around my waist and tugs me close. "Wait. Do I have any herbs in my teeth?" He flashes a grin at us both.

Lacey laughs. "No, you're good."

I peer up at him. "No bats in the cave, either, Ace."

He laughs. "Oh, thank fuck for that. Where would I be without you to check for boogers?" He kisses my forehead. "All right, everyone, smile."

Paul takes the picture and returns the phone to Lacey.

"Thank you so much," Lacey gushes. "It was nice meeting you both."

"You're welcome. Take care of yourself, Lacey from Plattsburgh."

She giddily retreats to her table.

Paul eyes Wes. "I give it seven minutes before that shit goes viral."

Wes shrugs. "What else is new?"

The waiter returns for our orders. "I'm so sorry about that, Mr. Emerson. We can move you to a more private area—"

"No worries." Wes shakes his head. "Here's fine."

Paul steps in. "I'd like a closer table though."

The waiter nods and points to the one beside ours. "I'll clear this one." He leaves after we all order our meals.

Wes studies me, his royal blue gaze locking on to mine.

"What?" I ask.

"You handled that better than I expected."

I smile at him. "I'm full of surprises."

He snorts. "No kidding. But in all seriousness, are you all right?"

"I'm fine."

He curls his lip. "Get a new word. I hate fine."

I shrug. "She was pleasant, not too pushy. And you made her life."

"I'm not asking about her, I'm asking about *you*."

I smirk. "Like I said, I'm fine."

"Christ Almighty," he mutters, running a hand over his face.

I sip my mojito and bite into a piece of orange. "Damn, this is amazing. Taste it." I hold the glass to his lips.

"Wow. I'm having that next."

"Getting your drink on today?"

"I'm a bit apprehensive about dinner," Wes confesses. "I could use a few drinks."

I cock my head. "Why? Because of me?"

"Yes and no. Mainly, Sid's dumb arse."

I squeeze his hand. "Relax, Wes. I'll tune him out. Drink if you want to, but don't get wasted because of me. I want you to enjoy yourself tonight. You deserve it."

CHAPTER 29

WES

Life lesson: My inner compass works perfectly.

I smile at Lena. She truly surprised me with the Lacey encounter. Aside from her initial tensing, she reacted with grace and patience, something Rachel was incapable of. It gives me hope for our future and a sense of pride. Pride in my woman, my choices, and my accomplishments. Rachel always robbed me of my pride. She'd robbed my freedom and peace of mind too. Not Lena—this radiant goddess lifts me up. Praises me. *Loves* me.

"Thank you for being supportive of me." My words may be simple, but they hold more meaning than she could ever realize.

"That's what one does when they love someone." She traces my jaw. "I love you, baby."

"I love you too, sunshine." I press my lips to her knuckles, kissing each one separately. "More than you know."

Paul leans over and nudges me. "Paparazzi at two o'clock."

I flash a huge smile at the fuckwit on the adjacent building's rooftop before turning my attention back to Lena. "Fuck 'em."

She stiffens, and I know she's caught sight of the photographer. "He's *blatantly* taking pictures of you."

I chuckle. "He's paparazzi. That's what they do, love."

"No, I mean, switching in a fucking zoom lens and everything."

"Well, at least I haven't got any boogers." I squeeze her hand. "I can guarantee I'm not the only one in the frame, so you may as well give him a smile too."

She clenches her jaw. "How do you deal with this shit?"

"I'm used to it, love." I rake a hand through my hair. "It bothered me in the beginning, but it really doesn't faze me anymore. That's a prime example of why I left LA, though—it's not like this back home."

"What about in New York?"

"It's a different vibe there." I shake my head. "It's hard to explain."

The waiter arrives with our meals. Lena pushes the meat around her plate and gnaws a fry.

I nod to the filet. "Thought you were hungry?"

"Lost my appetite," she mutters. "It's hard to eat with fucking eagle eye over there."

"Ignore him."

"I'm trying. But he's literally zooming in on my pores."

"Good thing you use all those creams," I point out. "Soon you'll have the cream companies calling you to do a commercial for beauty serums."

Lena snorts. "Or I'll be featured on *What Not to Wear*."

I furrow my brow. "What's wrong with your outfit?"

"Everything. Nothing. I dunno." She sighs. "I'm sorry—I feel really self-conscious right now."

"Would ya feel better if we got our food as carryout?"

"Yes," she whispers. "I'm sorry."

"Lena, I don't want to hear sorry again today." I flag down our waiter and request carryout containers.

"I'll wrap it for you," the waiter insists. "Be back with your check in a few."

Lena picks at her nails and gnaws her lower lip. Every bit of relaxation plummeted to the ground when the paparazzi showed up on a neighboring rooftop. Now, she sits statue-still with a steely spine and creased brow.

"Look at me," I command. Her wide, green gaze meets mine. "I love you." I know I say it a lot, but I need to chase away her doubts and fears.

She smiles, long lashes fluttering against pink cheeks. "Love you too."

I pay the tab and hold my arm out for her. "Let's get out of here."

She rises and loops her arm through mine. "I'm ready."

Paul returns from the bar. "There're a bunch of people on the front sidewalk. Bartender said we can use the back exit."

Lena stiffens. "There's a crowd on the sidewalk?"

"Yeah, word got out that he's here."

I peer down at her. "Just stay close to me, love." I turn to Paul. "Why don't you get the car and call me when you're out front."

He nods. "Sounds good. Stay here until my signal."

Lena watches Paul leave and then turns to meet my gaze. "I don't like this, Wes. I hate that people swarm you."

I shrug. "Goes with the territory."

"It makes me worry about your safety."

"I can handle myself. Besides, I've got Paul. No one in their right mind would fuck with him."

I glance at the paparazzi fucker who's lurking in the adjacent rooftop café. The guy twists his lens, likely zooming in some more. I cock a brow and the bastard smiles. *Dick had the nerve to ruin our lunch. Now, he's fucking smiling at me?* I tighten my grip on Lena. The guy had no doubt snapped dozens—no, *hundreds* of pictures. Knowing the gossip magazines, they'll find the least flattering ones to publish. I don't give a fuck, but I know it will bother Lena. *Let's give him something he can't refuse. If you're gonna publish something, publish this, fucker.*

I abruptly dip Lena, who squeals, and I seize her lips in a passionate, old-style Hollywood kiss. She gasps and throws her arms around my neck to keep from falling. I lay it on thick for several reasons. Mainly because I want to kiss her. More than that, I want to make damn sure everyone knows she's mine. If she's going to make her spotlight debut, why not blind the fuckers?

I break the kiss and straighten her.

"What was that for?" she asks, gasping.

"Do I need a reason to pash my woman on a rooftop?"

She blinks several times, confused. "Pash me?"

I grin. "Pash now and root later."

"Root? Hang on, Imma need to Google that right now."

"Use your imagination," I say with a chuckle. "If you're lucky, I'll let you get me in the nuddy, and we'll have some nookie." She loves when I use random Aussie slang, so I usually ham it up for her benefit.

Lena's face lights up with laughter. "Easy, Ace. Don't get a hard-on yet. We're in public."

"The proper term is, 'crack a fat.'" I waggle my brows. "As in, when we get back to the hotel, maybe I'll crack a fat and you can give me a gobby."

She laughs and punches my arm. "That's it, I'm officially using Aussie slang for all our future communication."

"Don't use me as a gauge. I don't know what I'm talking about." My phone buzzes. "C'mon, Paul's ready for us." I lead her to a door near the bar, where we descend several flights of stairs to the ground floor. We pause inside the door. "You ready?"

She takes a deep breath. "As ready as I'm gonna get."

I hold the door open for Lena and usher her to the SUV idling at the curb. Down the sidewalk, shouts of my name and camera flashes erupt. She slides into the back seat and I hop in beside her.

Paul speeds away from the curb. "You two all right?"

"We're good, mate, thanks." I kiss Lena's forehead. "You all right?"

"I'm fine."

I grip her chin. "Perfect example of why I *hate* fine. I know you aren't fine, and I'd appreciate your honesty."

She sighs heavily. "Lunch was great, the fangirl didn't bother me, the kiss was incredible, but I'm . . . rattled."

"I know, love."

"Like, I get that you're famous and ridiculously sexy, but you're a fucking person. Don't these people realize that?"

"They don't know me. To them, I'm more of an idea or concept—*not* a person. Loss of privacy, objectification, idolism—that's the tragedy of fame. That, with the influx of cash, is a lot to handle, and I think that's why so many turn to booze and drugs."

"You're so much more than any of that to me."

"I know, sunshine. That's why I love you so much. You see me, the *real* me, and love me just the same."

"It's times like these when I wish we were still in Alaska," she murmurs.

Me too.

Lena peeks out the bathroom door. "You ready for me?"

"I'm always ready, love. Let's get a look at that dress." My breath catches as she prances across the room, forest-green gown glinting in the light. "Christ Almighty . . . you look gorgeous."

She raises a brow and poses with a hand on her hip. "You like?"

"I don't have words." I shift in the desk chair and adjust myself. And, of course, she notices.

She bats her lashes. "Cracking a fatty already?"

"Goddamn right, I am." I shake my head. "You're so beautiful, Lena."

"Thank you for the dress." She twirls and makes her way over to me. She lifts a stilettoed foot to my knee. "And the shoes."

My cock throbs against my zipper. "You're welcome." I trail my fingertips up her calf, resting them on her thigh. Then, because I can't help myself, I slide both hands beneath the dress and yank her hips toward me.

"How about you take this off me so I can get busy slobbing your knob?"

I laugh and squeeze her arse. "You mean, give me a gobby?"

"Yeah, that's it." She shimmies her hips. "Give you a gobby . . . Play your skin flute . . ."

"Now, *that's* a new one." I slide her panties down over her hips. "But I'd rather you ride me."

She unzips my jeans, springing my cock free, and strokes my shaft with both hands. "Then let's make it happen, Ace."

I shove the dress to her waist and pull her into my lap. Hips straddling mine, Lena slowly eases down onto me, gasping as I fill her. No woman has ever fit me so perfectly. She is paradise. A warm, wet heaven I can't get enough of.

She rolls her hips and moans. "You feel so good inside me."

My balls tighten, hips flexing upward to meet her. She lifts and slides back down, her tight pussy gripping me.

I groan into her neck and clutch her hips. "Lena . . . fuck."

She clings to my shoulders and gasps with each downward stroke.

I love her like this—face-to-face, bodies fully clothed, save for where we join. Breasts pressed to my chest, her hair hanging loose around her shoulders. I tangle my fingers in the silken strands and breathe in her scent—warm vanilla like always.

"Look at me," I groan. Swirling pools of frosted emerald meet my gaze, more beautiful than the Gold Coast tidepools. Her eyes move something deep inside me, tightening my chest. "You're mine, sunshine."

She threads her hands in my hair and kisses me, slowly and passionately, like she needs to be just as deep inside me. Like the world could crumble around us and we'd be fine. Like I'm everything to her.

I pull her closer as her lips unravel me. She tugs strands of my hair and rides me. Moans mingle with her kiss. Her thighs tighten around me as she increases her pace.

I'm so fucking close. It takes every ounce of my energy to hold back. Finally, she goes over the edge. She breaks the kiss and wails my name, nails digging into my scalp, pussy fluttering around me. I grip her hips and pull her down hard. My cock pulses with my release. My grunts and groans mix with her gasps and sighs of pleasure. She collapses against me, burying her face against my neck, hot breath gusting my skin.

I squeeze my eyes shut and hold on to her. Lena. My goddess, my muse, my true north.

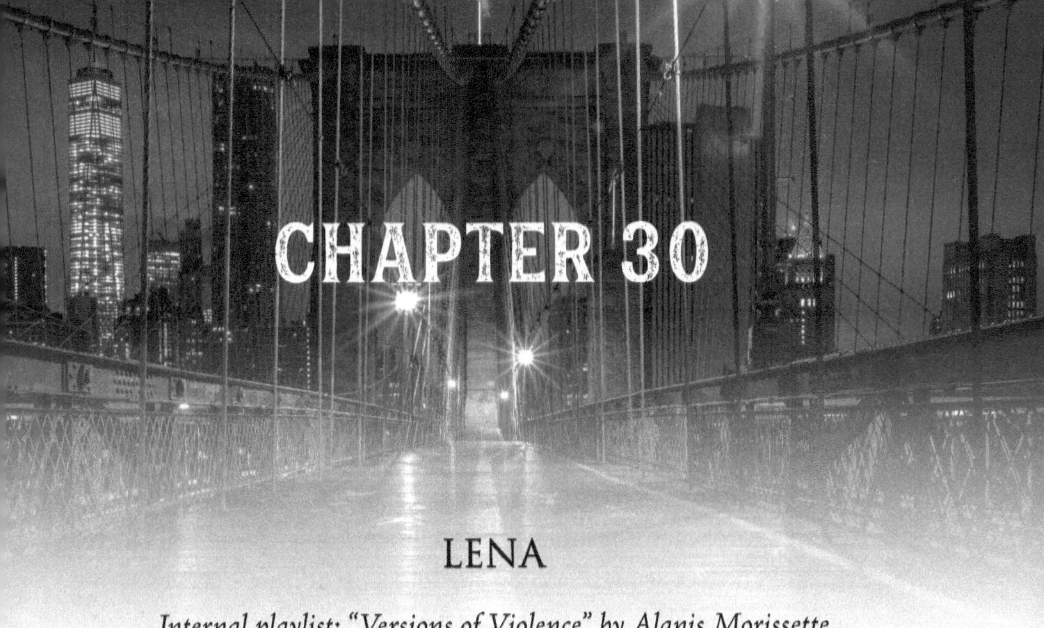

CHAPTER 30

LENA

Internal playlist: "Versions of Violence" by Alanis Morissette

I settle beside Wes at the table we share with a few of his castmates. He steered us away from his dumbass director, which works for me.

Alainna plops into the seat beside me. "I'm starving."

"Me too."

"Wes said you guys relocated your lunch date to your hotel?"

"Yeah. I'm still getting used to the whole paparazzi concept. I don't know how you guys deal with it. The guy was literally zooming in on us, watching us chew our food. It was so fucking intrusive."

"That's kinda the norm around here. I feel like I can't leave the house for a quick Target run without making sure I'm photo-shoot ready. I swear, they get off on exposing dark circles and frumpy clothes."

"That would make me insane."

"I've gotten used to it, but sometimes the comments are pretty hurtful. When I had the flu last year, I stopped at CVS to pick up my prescription and load up on tea and cough drops. Some asshole in the parking lot took pictures, and the next thing I knew, people were saying I looked like a washed-up junkie. I cried over that one."

I nod. "I would too. I'm sure they'll publish pics of me stuffing my face or something."

Alainna grimaces. "It wouldn't surprise me. Prepare yourself—now that you two have been seen together, people will develop an extreme fascination with you. Some will idolize you and others will hate you out of jealousy." She touches my arm. "Try to ignore it, but beyond that, you've gotta grow a thick skin. Don't let the haters shade your sun." She pulls out her phone. "Let me have your number. I'll send you a text with my contact info in case you need to talk."

"Thank you. I'm sure I'll be calling you for tips." I rattle off my number and feel my phone buzz a few moments later.

"Please do. Make sure you get Maribel's number too. She's mastered the art of not giving a fuck."

The more time I spend with Alainna, the more I like her.

Ronan approaches our table, his gaze lingering on Alainna. "I'm getting drinks. Who needs one?" When she looks up at him, his eyes soften. He quickly turns to Wes. "You want another bourbon?"

Wes grins. "Sure, mate. Why the hell not?" He squeezes my knee. "Would you like more wine, love?"

"No, thank you. I'm cutting myself off after this one."

"But that's only your first," Ronan says with a chuckle.

"I've got a love-hate thing with alcohol, Ronan. But thanks."

"Bad experience?" Alainna probes.

I nod. "That's an understatement."

Throughout the evening, I mingle with Wes's castmates, laughing and chatting like we're old friends. Ronan is hilarious—he reminds me of Garrett, and if my gut isn't fooling me, he has a thing for Alainna. He reacts much like Jake does when someone mentions Isla. Every time she speaks, his eyes soften. Then, when Salvatore adds something to the conversation, Ronan clenches his jaw. When asshole Sid asked Alainna about wedding plans, Ronan's nostrils literally flared. Yeah, there's definitely some backstory there. I'll have to ask Wes about it later.

Maribel is a firecracker like Rita. Saucy and spicy, it's clear she doesn't take anyone's shit. I'd like to categorize myself that way, but I'm definitely guilty of being a doormat.

I never expected to feel at home among Wes's costars, but I do. Even with Alainna. I feel like an asshole for my preemptive hatred.

Wes squeezes my knee beneath the table. "Thank you for being here, sunshine."

"Thanks for inviting me," I peer up at him, "and for letting me see the ways of your world."

"*You're* my world."

Across the table, Ronan makes a barfing sound. "Don't make me publicly swoon, Emerson."

Wes laughs. "You're just jealous, mate."

Ronan turns to me. "You don't need Hallmark movies with this guy around." He says it with a smile, but there's a deep sadness in his tone that tugs at my heart.

"True story. But, let's be real, he's not Hallmark material. Says fuck too much."

"Good thing you love my filthy mouth."

I grin and place my napkin on the table. "Damn right, I do. Now, if you'll excuse me, I'm gonna grab a refill. Anyone want a drink?"

"I'm good, love. Thanks."

I nod and make my way to the bar. My throat is dry from talking too much and the ice water just isn't cutting it.

"Hi, what can I get for you?" the bartender asks.

"I'll take a cranberry and seltzer, please."

"You got it."

I lean against the gleaming bar and wait. I'd been so worried about not fitting in with these people, but it was all for naught. Everyone is friendly, accepting, and just plain fun.

Alainna's fiancé sidles up to me and leans against the bar. He's tall and lean, muscled but not bulky. "Enjoying dinner?"

I peer into his espresso-colored eyes. "Yes, actually. How about you?"

Sal shrugs. "Don't have much of an appetite, but I'm surviving."

"Are you sick or just not hungry?"

"Something like that." He grabs an orange wedge and peels off the rind. "It doesn't bother you at all?"

"I'm not sure what you mean, Salvatore."

He jerks his head toward the table. "Them . . . *together*."

"I admit, the screening was hard to watch, but they're just friends."

"Oh, so *that's* what he told you?" Sal swigs his drink. "Apparently, he skipped the benefits part."

I narrow my eyes. "What do you mean?"

"I mean that during the first two movies, they hooked up on the regular. Their *chemistry* as Sid called it, isn't an act," he mutters, snatching another orange wedge. "They're experienced fuck-buddies."

I force a swallow. "Oh."

He runs a hand through his inky hair. "Granted, Alainna and I weren't together then, but it makes me *crazy* he's had her."

Thankfully, the bartender places my drink in front of me. "Here you go."

"Thanks," I croak, chugging the cool liquid.

Sal eyes me with something that resembles pity. "I take it Emerson failed to mention that part?"

I cast a glance at the table. Wes is laughing at something Alainna said, and my chest tightens. "Yes, he conveniently left that out."

He swirls his glass of whiskey. "Yeah, I had a feeling he would."

"But that was in the past."

"I wouldn't be so sure of that. Last year, I surprised Alainna on the set of *The Aegean*. Their trailers were side by side and I saw him leave hers one morning. She claimed he stopped by to bring her *coffee*, but I don't buy it."

"Do you trust Alainna?"

Sal rubs his jaw. "Yeah."

"Really? Because it doesn't sound like you do."

He crosses his arms over his chest. "*He's* the one I don't trust."

I pin him with a hard glare. "Well, I guess it's a good thing I trust Wes."

"Be careful with that," he murmurs. "You seem like a sweet person and I'd hate to see you get hurt."

"Thanks for the warning." Eager to escape his negativity—and more than a little miffed Wes kept the fuck-buddy tidbit a secret—I turn and march to the table, resettling between Alainna and Wes.

Wes eyes my glass. "Fruit punch?"

"No. Cranberry and seltzer."

He furrows his brow. "You all right, love?"

I sigh heavily. "Just had an interesting conversation."

Wes glances at the bar where Sal chats with the bartender and stiffens. "Fuck."

That's right, Ace. Your secret's out.

CHAPTER 31

WES

Life lesson: For the love of Christ, communicate.

I know damn well where Lena's sudden iciness stems from. Fucking Salvatore Bonavito. The jealous fuck who can't get over mine and Alainna's past. God only knows the shit he filled Lena's mind with.

Should I have kept it from her? No, probably not. But it wasn't Sal's place to run his fuckwit mouth. Now Lena's eating her meal in silence.

I discreetly text Paul to bring the car around. I need to get us the fuck out of here and talk to her.

My phone buzzes a few minutes later. "All right, mates. Lena and I are gonna call it a night."

Her surprised gaze flashes to mine. "We don't have to leave . . ."

"I'm not feeling well. Think I had too much to drink," I lie.

We say our goodbyes and meet Paul out front. Lena slides into her seat.

I close the door behind me and lean against the cool leather. My phone buzzes with a text.

> **Alainna: Are you all right?**

I don't reply. Lena picks at her nails beside me. No, I'm not all right, and neither is Lena. I can only imagine how Sal spun the tale.

> **Alainna: Never mind, I think I know what's up. I'm sorry.**
>
> **Wes: You have nothing to be sorry about, Baker. But this reaffirms the fact that your future husband's a dickhead.**

Lena eyes me. "Who are you texting?"

"Just telling Alainna her fiancé is an arsehole."

She nods and turns toward the window. Her purse buzzes on the seat between us. She pulls out her phone, glances at the screen, but doesn't open the message. I can see it's from Alainna.

I meet Paul's gaze in the rearview mirror and slowly shake my head. I should've taken his advice when he told me to be open with Lena about my past with Alainna. Why don't I ever listen to those older and wiser than me?

We arrive at the hotel and walk inside. Lena doesn't make eye contact with me once during our awkward lift ride. My bourbon-filled gut churns. Thankfully, I only had two. I hope to God she'll listen to my side of things. Rachel certainly never gave me the benefit of the doubt.

I close the suite door behind us and kick off my shoes. Lena leaves her stilettos by the bed and retreats to the bathroom in silence. I hear her turn on the shower.

I sit on the edge of the bed and wait, head resting in my hands.

After forty-five minutes—a colossal waste of water since she wasn't dirty in the first place—Lena emerges wrapped in a towel.

She pads to her suitcase, retrieves her pajamas, and heads for the bathroom to dress.

"Really?" I knot my fingers in my hair in exasperation.

She stops in the doorway. "What?"

"I've seen you naked."

"I'm aware."

"Then why're ya hiding in the bathroom?"

"I'm not hiding, Ace. I need to get dressed and brush my teeth— toothbrush is in here." She closes the door behind her.

"Fuck this." I scrub a hand over my face and climb to my feet. I stalk to the bathroom and yank the door open.

"Uh, excuse me. Do you mind?" she says around her toothbrush.

"Actually, I do."

She rolls her eyes and continues to brush.

For five minutes.

"You're gonna brush off your enamel."

She spits and rinses her mouth. The stubborn ox of a woman swishes mouthwash until her eyes water.

"You can rinse all night, sunshine, but I'm not going anywhere until you talk to me."

She spits out the mouthwash and reaches for the floss, then painstakingly weaves it between her teeth. Every. Single. One.

"I think you got it."

"Oral hygiene's important, Ace."

I snatch the length of minty string and toss it in the trash. "And so am I." Her julep eyes widen as I grip her shoulders and steer her to the bed. "Talk to me."

"Make me."

"You know I can and will, but I'd rather you do it willingly." I press on her shoulders until she sits. I stand in front of her and wait.

And wait some more.

Finally, she sighs. "Why didn't you tell me?" Her voice is small and she's staring at her hands.

"Tell you what?" I bend to try to catch her eye. "We gonna play a game, or are you ready to talk?"

Her gaze snaps to mine and narrows. "Don't play stupid with me. You *know* what I'm talking about."

"Yeah, I think I do, but I'd like to hear what's on *your* mind first."

She crosses her arms over her chest. "You didn't tell me you and Alainna are fuck-buddies—"

"*Were.*" I lean in close, nose touching hers. "I can assure you, it's past tense."

"Whatever."

"No, it's not *whatever*. There's a huge distinction."

"But you made a conscious decision not to tell me."

"Yeah, I did," I grip her shoulders, "because I didn't think a meaningless fling would matter. It's in the past, Lena."

"I realize that, but I felt blindsided by Sal."

"It wasn't his place to tell you."

"No kidding, but *you* didn't—"

"You want full disclosure? I'll give it to you." I plop onto the bed beside her. "Yes, I've slept with Alainna. Many times. But there isn't, and never was, any kind of emotional attachment. We're friends and we trust each other. At the time, we were both single and lonely. *Nothing* has happened since she started seeing Sal—despite what he thinks."

"He said he saw you leaving her trailer one morning."

"I brought her a cup of coffee, you know, because friends do nice things for one another."

"Are you still attracted to her?"

I sigh heavily. "Listen, I won't lie and tell you I don't find her attractive. I'd be blind if I didn't. But I will say this—I don't have romantic feelings for her. And since I've met you, I *only* have eyes for you." I rake a hand through my hair. "I kiss her and act out sex scenes for work, but I don't want more from her."

"Did you ever?"

"Want more, you mean?"

"Yeah."

"Maybe I did at one point, but we never connected in that way. What we had was purely physical—the emotional aspect was always missing. Don't get me wrong, I care about her as a person, but that's the extent of it."

"Thank you for your honesty."

"Lena, what I feel for you goes beyond anything I have ever felt. I need you to know that. Believe it and trust it. I need you to trust *me*."

"I do trust you, Wes," she whispers.

"I truly hope so, love," I take her hands in mine, "because you're everything to me. I'm so sorry you were sucker punched like that. I didn't tell you ahead of time because I didn't want you to feel even more uncomfortable around Alainna. She's a great person and I guess I hoped you could be friends."

"To be honest, I don't feel uncomfortable around her at all. I actually really like her."

I smile. "She likes you too. I'm sure she feels like shit about Sal opening his big fuckwit mouth."

"Speaking of Sal, I noticed you aren't the only one who hates him."

"Yeah, well, he's a dick, so—"

"No, I mean, Ronan. He was mean-mugging Sal like it was his fucking job. Does he have a crush on Alainna or something?"

"Not a crush," I mutter. "They've been friends since primary school. The poor bloke is desperately in love with her."

She nods. "I thought so. He looks at her like—" She clamps her mouth shut. "Never mind."

"Looks at her like what?"

"Does she know?" She clears her throat. "I mean, does Alainna know how he feels?"

"She has no clue, and Ronan would never jeopardize their friendship by telling her."

"So, he gets to sit back and watch her marry that moody bastard?"

"Yep." I rub my neck. "That's why I always feel guilty about the sex scenes. Not because of Sal—I don't give two fucks about him. I feel bad for Ronan. I hate knowing I contribute to his pain."

"Have you guys talked about it?"

"Yeah, a little. He doesn't hold it against me, but I know it hurts him. He moved to New York after they got engaged because he couldn't take it anymore. He had to place some distance between them before he lost his shit."

"Ugh, how sad. You should visit him when you come to see me after your press tour."

"Good idea." I touch her cheek. "Please don't hold our past against Alainna. I don't want you to hate her again."

"Wes, relax. I'm over it. I'll text her back in the morning."

CHAPTER 32

LENA

Internal playlist: "Seven Devils" by Florence + The Machine

Wes and I just got back from breakfast. I'd left my phone in the room while we ate. I peek at the screen out of habit, and frown.

"What's wrong?" Wes asks.

"Two missed calls from Garrett. I hope everything's all right."

He touches my shoulder. "Call him back and—"

My phone rings.

"It's him. How's that for timing?" I press the icon on my screen. "Hey, Gar, what's up?"

"Did you forget to mention something?" Garrett asks.

"Uh . . ." I run down the list of possibilities in my mind and come up empty. "No."

"The guy's here to clean the furnace."

"We had that done already." I remember the day clearly because the fucker almost let Hermione out when he left the front door open.

"When?"

"They came before I left for Alaska. I forgot to have it done the previous year, so I scheduled it early this time. August third."

"Well, the dude's here now. Told me you called last week to set up an appointment?"

I stiffen, my scalp prickling. "Gar, I didn't call anyone to do anything. I wouldn't have set something up if I was going to be out of town."

"Are you sure?"

"Of course I'm sure. I know my head's been up my ass lately, but that's not something I'd forget."

"I called the heating company, but they wouldn't tell me anything because my name's not on the account."

"Your name *is* on the account. I added you like five years ago when we got the new furnace." I shake my head in frustration. "You called Heritage Furnace?"

"No. I called Eco-Heating. That's what his badge said. They said they'd charge your account two hundred bucks for a missed appointment, so I let him in."

The hair on my arms rises. "We use Heritage—I've never even heard of Eco-Heating."

"Fuck! Gotta go."

"Garrett? Hello?" I glance at the screen. He hung up. "What the hell is going on?"

I dial his number. No answer.

"Is everything all right?" Wes asks.

"I dunno. Some guy's there to clean my furnace, but I didn't schedule anything. Garrett just hung up and now he's not answering."

"Call the company."

"I don't even use that heating company."

I try Garrett again, but he still doesn't answer, so I Google Eco-Heating and call them.

After waiting on hold for twenty minutes, a female voice finally answers, "Good morning, Eco-Heating. How may I help you?"

"Hi, my name's Lena Hamilton and I'm calling regarding a service appointment." I rattle off my address and phone number.

"Ms. Hamilton, it doesn't look like you have an account with us."

"I don't, but one of your guys is at my place right now."

"That's not possible. All our guys are in Manhattan today."

Bile rises in my throat. "Then who the fuck is at my house?"

"I don't know, but it isn't one of our employees."

"Thank you." I hang up and dial Garrett. Still no answer. I turn to Wes. "The company has no record of me or anyone going to my house."

"What the hell?"

"And Garrett isn't answering."

"Call a neighbor," Wes suggests.

"Good idea."

I call the people next door, but they don't answer either. I try the elderly neighbor who lives across the street. She only leaves the house for bingo night at the church, and that was yesterday.

"Hello?"

"Hi, Joan, it's Lena."

"Hi, honey. Is everything all right?"

"I don't know. I'm not home right now. Can you please look outside and tell me if you see Garrett's Jeep?"

"I'll take a look. Give me a minute."

Joan is one of the few people I know who still has a phone with a cord. I hear her set the receiver down and shuffle across the room. I press the phone to my ear. Joan yells something. My hand clenches the device as I wait for her return.

"Lena?"

"I'm here."

"Honey, Garrett's Jeep is here and so are the police."

Ice fills my chest. "The police?"

"There's a big white van outside and two cop cars. An ambulance just pulled in. Funny, I didn't hear sirens . . ."

"Oh my God!" I leap to my feet. "Did you see Garrett?"

"No, I didn't."

"Thank you, Joan. I have to go now." I hang up and turn to Wes. "The cops are at my place."

"What the hell's going on?"

"I don't know." My hands shake violently and my eyes well with tears. "Joan said there's an ambulance too. What if someone hurt Garrett?"

Wes wraps his arms around me. "I'm sure he's all right. Try not to think like that, love."

I try Garrett again—still nothing.

"I can't believe this. Who would want to get into my house?"

"Your ex?"

I shake my head. "No. Marc has no reason to do something like this."

"I dunno, Lena. He pulled that shady shit with my flowers."

"Yeah, but that was more of a win-me-back type of thing. Breaking into my home doesn't make sense. Besides, Garrett knows him."

My phone rings and I eye the 2-1-2 area code. "Hello?"

"Ms. Hamilton?"

"Yes."

"This is Officer Shane McDermott with the NYPD. We're responding to a call at your residence."

"What happened? Is Garrett all right?"

"Mr. Casey is fine."

"Oh, thank God." I breathe a sigh of relief. "Did you catch the guy who was in my house?"

"The suspect is in our custody, yes. Does the name Andrew LaGrange mean anything to you?"

"No. I've never heard that name."

"All right. We'll question him after he receives medical attention."

"Medical attention?"

"It appears that Mr. Casey worked him over before we got here."

LENA

Internal playlist: "The Hard Stuff" by Justin Timberlake

I sit on the bed, hugging my bent knees to my chest. Wes settles beside me and pulls me into his lap.

"I changed your return flight to tomorrow morning. It was the earliest available. When you hear back from Garrett, see if he can get you from the airport. If not, I'll hire a car service."

"I'm sorry."

"Please don't apologize—figuring out this mess takes precedence over lounging around with me."

My eyes well with more unshed tears. "But I won't see you until mid-November."

"And then I'm off for a few months, so you'll see plenty of me, love."

I bury my face in his chest, tears flowing freely now. "I'm so sorry for all the drama."

He tilts my chin to face him. "Stop. Apologizing."

"I know. I'm sorr—" I squeeze my eyes shut. "You deserve better than me."

"Lena, for the love of Christ, stop." He tightens his arms around me. "I love you, drama and all," he wipes at my tears, "but I want you to get a security system installed."

"I will."

"I have Paul looking into Andrew LaGrange. Paul's a former military intelligence officer. If anyone can find stuff out, it's him. You're sure the name doesn't ring a bell?"

"Not at all. I'd ask Garrett if he'd fucking call me back."

"Well, if he beat the shit out of the guy, he's probably tied up with the police now."

"I'm so freaked-out," I whisper.

He rubs my back. "I know, love."

My phone rings, causing us both to jump. Wes glances at the screen before handing it to me. "It's Garrett."

"Hello? What happened? Are you all right?"

"Yeah, I'm fine, Leens."

"The police called me. Who is Andrew LaGrange, and what does he want from me?"

"*He* isn't the one who wants something from you."

"What do you mean? I'm putting you on speaker. I can't fucking think right now and don't want to repeat everything to Wes." I press the icon.

"Howdy, Emerson."

"Hey, mate. You all right?"

"I'm good. Got blood on my favorite shirt, but I'll survive the disappointment."

"Are you hurt?" I ask.

"No. Fucked him up pretty good though." He releases a dark chuckle. "He's probably gonna press assault charges."

Garrett is an avid boxer with an MMA background. I've seen him in action and his fists are lethal weapons.

"Oh my God," I squeak. "That's the last thing you need with *Prodigy* coming up."

"I'll deal with it. Anyway, I called you when he first got here because you didn't mention the appointment and that's not like you. When you didn't answer, I told him I needed to check with the heating company. He gave me his business card and I called that number. I talked to some dude who told me about the two-hundred-dollar cancellation fee. I figured that since you've been out of work, you wouldn't wanna pay it, so I let him in and showed him where the furnace was."

"And that's when you called me," I finish.

"Right. When I realized you had no idea what I was talking about, I called the cops."

"I'm assuming your furnace is in the basement?" Wes asks.

"It is," Garrett answers with a sigh, "but I was so fucking stupid."

"What do you mean, Gar?"

"Before you and I talked, he came to my door and told me there was a disconnect between the furnace itself and the thermostat. Some bullshit about efficiency or something. Clearly, I'm no thermodynamics expert, so I believed him. He fucked around with the one in my living room and said he needed to see the one in your place."

"Oh my God . . ."

"So, you let him in?" Wes prompts.

"Yep. Then I got a call from *Prodigy's* director and had to run downstairs. The heating guy went back to the basement and then upstairs to your place again. I didn't think much of it until we spoke."

"What did you do?" I ask.

"I called the cops first. I'm sorry I didn't call you back right away. I kinda just tossed my phone and ran to intercept the fucker. The cops told me to wait at my place, but I wanted answers."

"And did you get them?" Wes asks.

"Yeah . . . after I broke his nose. And possibly his jaw."

"Oh my God!" Even I get goose bumps from the shrillness of my voice. "Who is he? What did he want?"

Garrett doesn't answer for a moment, causing my blood to run cold.

"Tell me, Gar."

"I found him in your bedroom, Leens."

"Doing what?" Wes snaps, lurching to his feet.

"He was looking under her bed. Clothes were all over the floor, telling me he'd already gone through her dresser drawers . . ."

Wes paces the room. "So, he wanted something specific?"

"Right. He found her jewelry box and pocketed most of it."

"Oh, God," I whimper. "Gram's jewelry is in there."

"I know, Leens." He sighs heavily. "That's why he came."

"What?"

"I jumped him from behind and brought him down in the hall. I hit him a few times . . . forced him to talk . . . I'm so sorry to tell you this, Leens—"

"Just tell me."

"Your father hired him to steal your grandmother's jewelry."

"No," I sob. "Please tell me you're joking."

"Honey, I wish I was, but no," Garrett mutters. "He said your dad spent the rest of your parents' savings on bail after this DWI. He needed the money for his legal fees. He claimed the rubies are rightfully his."

"Jesus Christ," Wes growls. "So, he hired some fucker to break into his daughter's home? What if he fucking hurt her?"

"My thoughts too, man. Lemme go, the cops are calling. Love you, Leens. Bye."

Wes sets the phone on the dresser. A cold sweat chills my skin. The room starts spinning and tremors seize my frame. I rush into the bathroom and kneel in front of the toilet. Clutching the seat, I empty the contents of my stomach. Acid burns my throat as tears sting my cheeks.

Wes rushes to my side. "Are you all right, love?"

"No," I sob, dry heaving over the bowl. "I am *not* all right."

He squats behind me, gathers my hair into a ponytail, and places a cool washcloth on the back of my neck. I can barely breathe through the agonizing ache in my chest.

Wes gently rubs my back—the act more comforting than any words could ever be. I sit on my heels and look up at him. Beneath a deeply furrowed brow, compassion wars with the fury in his gaze.

"Come here," he murmurs, pulling me into his arms. "The floor's too cold."

I melt into the embrace, focusing on his warmth, strength, and the quiet comfort of his presence. He tugs me into his lap and holds me, softly stroking my hair.

I rest my head on Wes's chest. We traded the bathroom's cold tile for the bed. I trace my fingertips over the phoenix tattoo on his wrist, outlining each detailed feather. He'd gotten it with Isla on her eighteenth birthday. Symbolic of her kidney transplant and subsequent freedom from dialysis, it's a colorful reminder of their bond—bright, caring, and vivid. *How family should be. Not dark and fucked-up like mine.*

"Your mind's racing. Talk to me, sunshine."

"He's my *father*. He's supposed to protect me—not hurt me," I whisper, wiping my cheeks. "He's the one man who's supposed to love me unconditionally, keep me safe and happy."

"He betrayed you instead."

"Over and over again. I didn't think he could hurt me more than when he tried to frame Garrett, but he has. What if that guy had a weapon on him? What if he hurt Garrett?" I meet his gaze. "Or killed him?"

"Better yet, what if *you* were home?" Wes clenches his jaw. "When I think of what could've happened to you—"

"I wouldn't have let him in."

"What if he barged in?"

"I would've kicked him in the balls."

"I'm not denying your feistiness, and I certainly don't intend for this to sound sexist, but a grown man could easily overpower a woman of your stature. And if he had a weapon . . ." He squeezes his eyes shut. "I used to hate the idea of you having a male housemate, but now I'm glad Garrett's there."

"Yeah, me too. He'd die before he'd let anyone hurt me," I say solemnly. "And I have a feeling he'd *kill* for me, if it came down to it."

Wes grips my chin. "So would *I*."

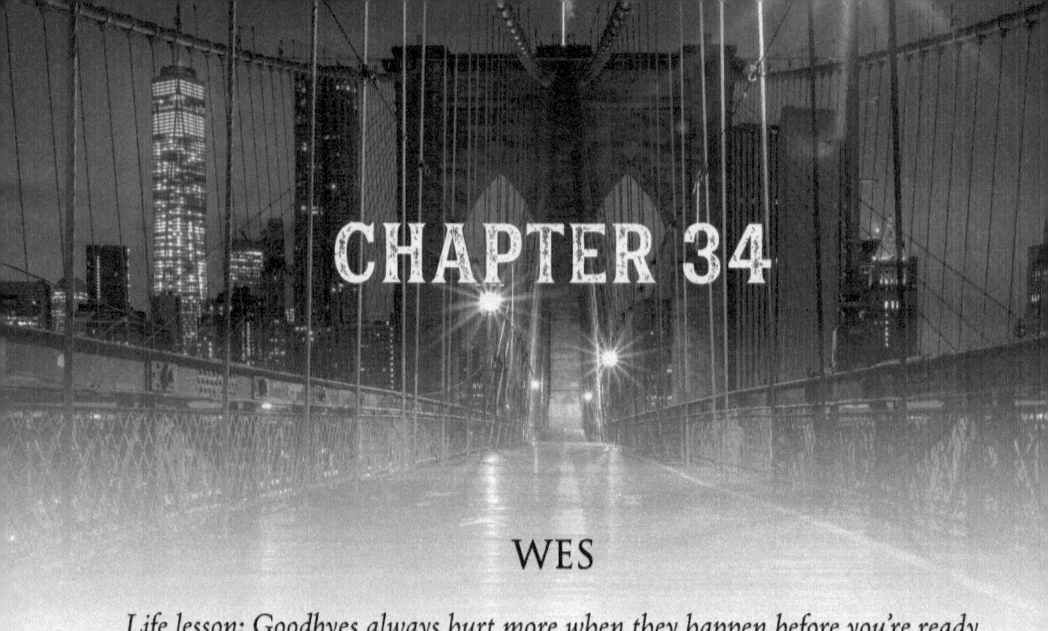

CHAPTER 34

WES

Life lesson: Goodbyes always hurt more when they happen before you're ready.

I turn the TV on after a shitty night's sleep. I tossed and turned for hours, thinking about the incident at Lena's. I flip through the channels while she dozes beside me. Desiring something on the light-hearted side, I settle on reruns of some random American sitcom. The guy's nasally voice and meddling mother make me chuckle. They say laughter's the best medicine—and I need a strong dose of something.

I glance at the clock. *Too early for whiskey.* I don't need alcohol. No, what I need is to punch someone. Preferably that fake heating company dick. As grateful as I am to Garrett, I envy his opportunity to lay the fucker out. I envy Garrett's proximity, his ability to protect Lena . . . *I should be the one protecting her.*

I can't fathom what Lena's father did. A betrayal so deep, it made her physically sick. My heart breaks for her. The alpha inside me paces, teeth gnashing, a growl rumbling in my chest. *How the fuck does a man do that to his daughter?*

"You're scowling, Ace."

"Not scowling," I feel my expression soften, "just stewing."

"Me too." She stretches and nuzzles against me. "I'm sorry you had to witness that."

I roll Lena onto her back, pinning her hands at her shoulders. "Did I just hear you apologize?"

Lids puffy from crying, her red-rimmed jade eyes meet my gaze.

"Yeah. My family drama ruined our day and cut my visit short. Surely, that warrants an apology."

"Lena, you have *nothing* to apologize for." Releasing her hands, I nip her earlobe. "Nothing. Do you understand me?"

"Yes," she whispers, her beautiful eyes welling. "Thank you for being there when I needed you. I love you so much, baby."

"I love you more than you know," I pin her with my gaze, "and I meant what I said . . . I'd kill someone in a heartbeat if it kept you safe."

"I know," she whispers.

"Do you?" I lean in so the tips of our noses touch. "Because I need you to understand that I'd stop at *nothing* to protect you. It kills me that I have to be away from you. It fucking kills me."

"Promise me we'll talk regularly," she says, her voice soft and vulnerable.

"Every day. Either we'll text, call, video chat, or some combination of those. I'll make sure ya know my press-tour itinerary and the time difference at each stop. You call me *any* time, day or night, and I'll answer the phone."

She nods instead of answering, her soft lips quivering in her attempt not to cry.

"I mean it, sunshine." I brush my lips over hers. "After the premiere, you'll see me regularly. Until then, I'm only a phone call away."

"I hate the thought of saying goodbye to you . . . even if it's temporary."

"I don't do goodbyes, love." I kiss her lower lip. "I prefer 'until next times.'"

"Then I need you to do something for me to hold me over until next time."

I brush the hair back from her face. "Anything."

"Make me forget about what happened. Make love to me, Wes," she whispers, peering into my eyes. "Slowly. Like we have no schedules, conflicts, or responsibilities. Like we're the only two people in the world and nothing can come between us. Like I'm yours and you're mine. *Only* mine."

"I feel that way every time we're together, sunshine."

"Then show me. Make me feel it too," she bites her lip, "because I feel so lost right now."

I brush the hair from her forehead and cradle her face in my hands, thumbs stroking her cheeks. "Close your eyes. Picture the night sky in Alaska—the constellations, the North Star. Remember how bright it was up there?"

Her eyes flutter closed. "Yes."

"You're *my* North Star. Focus on me—on us—and shine for me, love. Let me find you again."

I lower my lips to her face, pressing soft kisses from her cheeks to her forehead. I trail them to her mouth, her lips parting as I lick the seam. My tongue sweeps in, a tentative advance. Lena clasps the back of my neck and deepens our kiss. I nudge her legs apart, settling between her thighs. I harden as we kiss. Finding the hem of her tank top, I break the kiss just long enough to pull it off her. A moment later, her panties glide over her hips to her ankles.

I shove my boxers off and lift my T-shirt over my head before meeting her lips again. Lena wraps her legs around me, pulling me closer.

"Easy, sunshine. You wanted it slow, remember?"

"Changed my mind."

I nip her earlobe and lick her neck. "Too bad."

"Keep doing that." She tilts her head to the side. "Please kiss my neck."

My lips and tongue find the hollow of her throat while my hands roam from her breasts to her hips and thighs. She reaches between us and guides my cock to her body.

I press inside her, softly groaning once fully seated. "Your body's paradise."

She tightens her legs around me and grips my back as I move with slow, deep strokes. I bury my face in her neck and kiss her while I thrust.

"Gonna give me a hickey, Ace," she says on a gasp.

"Good." My breath warms the spot I just kissed. "When you see it, you'll think of me and remember this moment." I roll my hips and deepen my strokes. Firm, yet tender, I feel my measured thrusts bring her higher.

Her fingers thread into my hair. My hips pick up speed, my body coiling tighter.

"Look at me and kiss me," she moans. "I wanna see your eyes when we come."

I lift my head and bring my lips to hers. With our eyes locked, I bring her over the edge. Back arching, she focuses on our kiss, on my gaze. I see my reflection in her eyes. Our love. My future. I see her reverence, the depth of her passion.

She whispers my name and climaxes, her body fluttering around me. I kiss her harder, my tongue matching my thrusts.

"Lena . . ." Eyes never leaving hers, I release inside her with a deep groan.

I roll to my back and pull her on top of me, arms locked around her, chest heaving with our breaths.

She rests her cheek against my chest and clings to me, to this moment. A perfect moment in time with no noise, no distractions, just us.

I run my fingers through her hair and hold her close. "More than words."

Her eyes well. "Love you too, Wes."

LENA

Paul lifts my suitcase. "I'll bring this out to the car so you two can say your goodbyes."

"Until next times," Wes corrects him. "I don't do goodbyes."

"*Arrivederci*, bon voyages, whatever you call them. I'll be back in a few." He gestures to me. "Security's a bitch and you don't wanna miss your flight."

"I'll be ready when you come back."

Not.

Paul leaves the suite, and the door's click behind him feels like a timer. Ticking away, counting down the minutes I have left with Wes.

No amount of time seems like enough. Yes, I'll see him in under three weeks, but still, it feels like an eternity.

Wes pulls me into his arms. "Some animal gave ya a hickey."

I laugh and touch my neck. "I'll allow it this time."

He smirks. "You'll allow it anytime I give it."

"We'll see about that." I kiss his neck. "Maybe you'll have to try again *next time.*" My voice wavers on the last two words.

"No maybe about it, love. There *will* be a next time, and I'll be counting down the seconds until we see each other again."

"Me too," I whisper, clenching my jaw against the tears that threaten to come. *I won't cry. I won't cry. I won't—*

A tear rolls down my cheek. Then another.

Wes brushes them away and kisses me. Knotting my hands in his hair, I pour my soul into the kiss. My heart. My everything.

He does the same, clinging to me with a desperation that defies the morning's relaxed vibe. He breaks the kiss and meets my gaze. My heart clenches at the mist in his eyes. "If you need me . . . I don't care what time zone I'm in—you call me. Any time of the day or night. Do you understand?"

"Yes."

He clenches his jaw and squeezes his eyes shut. A tear appears from beneath his lashes. "You're everything to me," he whispers. "I hope you realize that."

"I do."

"Don't doubt me, Lena, all right?"

"I trust you, baby." I grip the sides of his face and kiss him. "With my heart and soul."

Paul knocks on the door.

"One minute, mate." Tears roll down Wes's cheeks as he kisses me. "Be safe, sunshine. Let me know when you arrive."

"I will," I promise, hugging him tightly.

He wipes his cheeks. "Look what you're doing to me."

I blink back my tears because wiping them away means letting go of him. "You started it, Ace."

He kisses me once more. "Until next time, sunshine."

"Until next time."

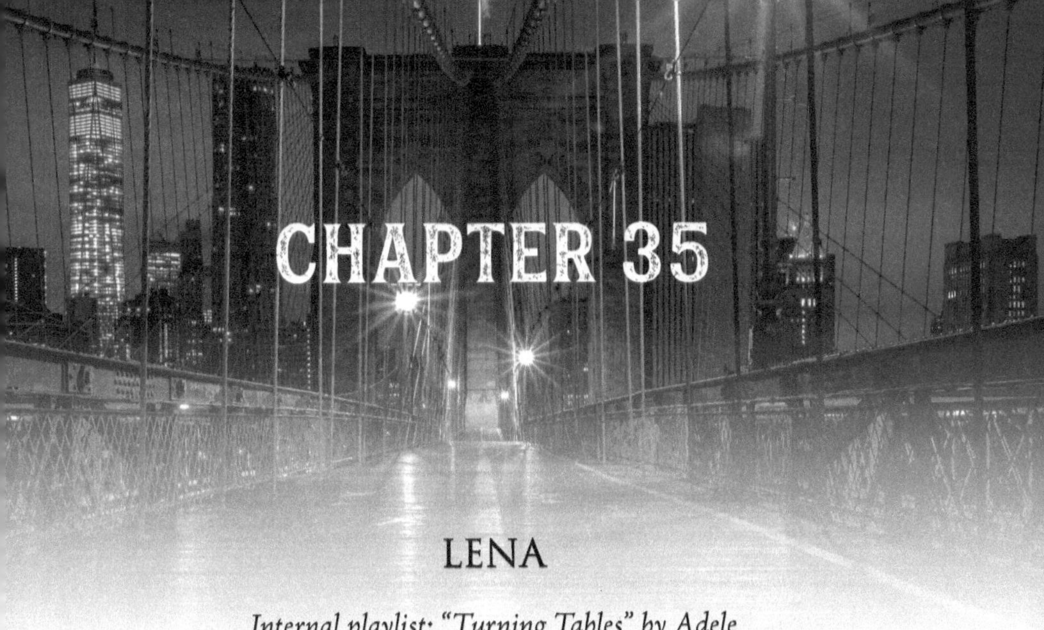

LENA

Internal playlist: "Turning Tables" by Adele

Garrett lifts my suitcase from the baggage claim and drags it behind us as we make our way through the terminal at JFK airport.

"You hungry?" he asks once we reach the sidewalk.

"No."

Garrett stops walking. "Let me rephrase. We're getting food before we go to the police station."

"Fine," I mutter. "Where'd you park?"

"First row over there." He points.

I follow him to his Jeep. A streetlight illuminates his hands as he lifts the back hatch to put my suitcase inside. I snatch his wrist and eye his battered knuckles. "Jesus."

He smirks. "The fucker's lucky he still has a face."

"Do you think he'll press assault charges?"

He shrugs. "Pretty sure attempted robbery negates some of that—and he had a knife on him."

"What?"

"Blade exceeded the legal length, so the odds are in my favor."

Tears prick my eyes. "You could've been killed."

"Yeah, but I wasn't." He closes the hatch and looms over me. "Connor's installing a security system this week."

His cousin Connor is a computer mastermind with a background in security and law enforcement. He currently works as an independent contractor with the FBI's intelligence unit. Garrett has been trying to get me to agree to an alarm system for years, but I always hated the idea of living in a fortress. Now, the thought comforts me.

"You sound like Wes."

"Wow, I expected pushback on that one. You're finally gonna do it?"

"Yeah. This scared the shit out of me, Gar."

"I know." He gestures to the passenger door. "Let's go."

I climb inside and fasten my seat belt while Garrett hops in the driver's seat. He rubs his hands together to combat the chill.

"You wouldn't be cold if you wore a jacket."

"I hate jackets."

I chuckle. "Some things never change."

"Speaking of changes . . ." He wags his brows. "You once swore you'd never let someone give you a hickey."

I feel myself flush. "He did it on purpose."

"Ah, claim staking. Kinda like that kiss."

I cock my head. "Huh?"

"You mean to tell me you haven't seen it?" He snorts. "You're famous, Leens."

"Oh, God . . ."

"*Celebrity Buzz* had pictures of Emerson's tongue down your throat at a cozy rooftop café."

I shake my head. "No, I haven't seen it, yet. He did that on purpose too." I glance at him. "Did I look all right? I mean . . . we didn't look awkward, did we?"

He laughs. "You two were classic old-Hollywood, kinda like Ingrid Bergman and Humphrey Bogart in *Casablanca*. Or John Wayne and Maureen O'Hara in *The Quiet Man*."

"Funny, that's how it felt." I elbow him. "Aren't you glad I made you watch all those old movies? Otherwise, you'd never be able to describe it properly."

He cocks a brow. "I'm more than capable of describing sex."

I roll my eyes. "We're talking about a kiss. I didn't fuck him on a rooftop, Gar."

"But you wish you did." He starts the engine and adds, "Kissing is tongue sex."

I snort. "You just gave me a gross visual of a pair of tongues lying in bed together. One's smoking a cigarette, while its partner is giving him the side-eye."

He laughs. "A wee bit tongue-in-cheek this evening, aren't we?"

"It's my coping mechanism at the moment."

"In all seriousness, have you given any thought to how you'll respond to this?"

"Yeah, and I'm at a loss."

"What does Emerson think? He sounded as pissed off as I was yesterday."

"He was. I think it was hard for him to wrap his mind around it. His family's so close, you know? He insisted we install a security system and offered to pay for it—which I told him wasn't necessary. I lost it after we spoke. Literally puked my guts out."

"I'm so sorry, Leens. It broke my fucking heart to tell you, but I'm glad you had him with you."

"He's so good to me, Gar . . ." I stare out the window for a moment.

"But?" When I glance at him, he adds, "There's more, isn't there?"

"I'm embarrassed. I feel like I come from trash. I mean, he must have all kinds of shit running through his head. What will his family think of me and all my fucking drama?"

"I thought you said you hit it off with his sister?"

"We did. Isla's amazing, and I already adore her."

"Then what are you so worried about?"

"His brother."

"Hmm. I expected you to say his parents."

"Them too." I sigh and pick at my nails. "But mainly Reed. A drunk driver caused the accident that ruined his life. *My* father is a repeat offender. Reed will automatically associate me with disaster." I bite my lip. "So will the media, Wes's fans, the rest of the world . . ."

Garrett squeezes my knee. "You're getting ahead of yourself. Wes loves you. He doesn't judge you for your piece of shit father's behavior, and that's all that matters."

"I know."

He pulls up outside Chipotle. "Burrito?"

"I'm really not hungry."

"Tough titties. You're getting steak tacos."

I salute him. "Aye, aye, captain."

He chuckles and climbs out of the Jeep. "Be right back."

I pull out my phone and send Wes a text letting him know Garrett picked me up and we're heading home.

His reply is immediate.

> **Wes: Good. Miss you already, sunshine. Did you eat something yet?**

"Jesus Christ, they're tag teaming me," I mutter while typing my response.

Wes sends a picture of our famous kiss.

> **Wes: I miss your lips.**
>
> **Lena: Miss yours too, Ace. I love you.**
>
> **Wes: Love you. Call me before you go to sleep.**
>
> **Lena: Will do. Talk to you later, baby.**

I study the picture. Garrett's right. It's old-Hollywood glamour for sure. My heartrate picks up speed. I download the image and make it my phone's new wallpaper.

Garrett returns with the food. "You're smiling. What's up?"

I hold out my phone. "He sent me this."

"Told you it looked hot."

Unable to speak, I stare across the desk at the detective.

"Ms. Hamilton, we need to know how you want to proceed with this," he says gently. "We've got Mr. LaGrange on weapons possession and attempted burglary. His lawyer claims he will *not* pursue assault charges against Mr. Casey, which surprised me, given the extent of his injuries." He glances at Garrett, then turns his attention back to me. "We planned to press charges against your father."

"Don't bother," I whisper.

Garrett's head jerks in my direction. "You can't let him get away with this!"

"He's already facing the DWI. He tried to *steal* from me to pay for that. What good can come from pursuing this? It'll further smear the Hamilton name. Besides, I don't want revenge or his fucking money—I just want him out of my life."

"So, you're okay with sweeping it under the rug?" Garrett challenges, crossing his arms over his chest. "Letting him put you in danger because he values antique rubies over your fucking safety?"

"If I thought it would keep him out of my life, I'd *give* him the goddamn rubies." I swipe at a tear.

"What kind of message does that send?" Garrett sputters. "Go ahead, stomp all over me, Dad—just like you stomp on the whole family to get what you want." He motions to the detective. "Roger Hamilton is a fucking piece of shit and *something* needs to be done about it."

"Calm down, Mr. Casey."

"With all due respect, sir, I will *not* calm down. You don't know that man's brutality. I've seen it firsthand. I've seen how he battered her mother, and I watched him hit Lena and slam her into a wall. Then he sends some shady motherfucker into her house with a *knife*? Over some fucking jewelry?" He slams his fist on the desk. "What if I wasn't there? What if LaGrange hurt her?"

A pair of officers approach Garrett from behind, but the detective waves them off. "Mr. Casey, I understand where you're coming from, but as the owner of the property and the intended target, Ms. Hamilton is the one who has the final say."

Garrett glowers at me. "What's it gonna be, Leens?"

"I want my father out of my life."

"You can file a restraining order," the detective suggests. "That will keep him away from you *and* your property."

"I'll do it," I turn to Garrett, "if you also file one."

"I don't need a restraining order," he protests. "I can handle my shit."

"I'm well aware of that, Gar, but I don't want my father retaliating against you. File it, or I *will* give him the rubies."

Fire flashes in his lion-like gaze. "Fine. I'll file orders against the whole town of Windham if it keeps you from being that fucker's doormat and handing over your inheritance."

"Then it's settled. Restraining orders against Roger Hamilton." The detective scrawls something on a piece of paper.

Garrett leans in. "I want provisions on Lena's that include *any* of her father's past, present, or future associates."

The detective shakes his head. "Can't do that. An order of protection is specific to the person to whom it's served."

"Then what's to stop him from hiring another thug to bully her?"

"Unfortunately, we can't prevent that."

I peer at Garrett where he stews on my couch. "I know you're pissed at me."

His gaze flickers to mine. "I'm pissed at the situation, not you."

"Me too, but what am I supposed to do? File charges and have a huge court case? If the media gets wind of this, it'll be a firestorm. I'm already in the fucking spotlight."

"I dunno," he mutters, shaking his head. "But I want you to promise me you'll have the security system installed and change the locks." He touches my hand. "Your mom shouldn't have a key, Leens."

"This isn't about her."

"No, but he could easily bully her into handing it over."

I nod and blink back tears. "I know."

"I realize this is painful for you, but he crossed a line, Leens. There's no going back from this, and as long as your mom continues to stay by his side, she's a risk to your safety as well."

"I feel like I've lost my entire family."

He scoots closer and wraps an arm over my shoulder. "You'll always have me."

"I love you, Gar."

"Love you too, Leens." He flashes me a sheepish smile. "This will probably piss you off, but I called Trevor and filled him in."

I lean back and groan. "Why would you do that?"

"Because he's your brother, and he deserves to know what's happening on this side of the world."

"How'd he take it?"

"He's furious with your father."

"Not surprised by that."

"He's flying in tomorrow."

My head jerks up. "What?"

"You heard me."

"Why?" I let out an exaggerated groan and bury my face in a couch pillow. Trevor's bullshit is the last thing I need right now.

"Because, despite being a royal dick, Trev loves you. I think with the Alaska ordeal, and now *this*, he wants to make the effort to have a relationship with you."

I roll my eyes. "Yeah, okay."

"Leens, he sounded sincere." He squeezes my knee. "But don't worry, he's only staying for a day or two. Then he's going upstate to try and sort things out with your mother."

"Whatever. Hopefully, he'll talk some sense into Mom."

Garrett cocks a brow. "You think that's possible?"

"I don't know what to think anymore."

CHAPTER 36

WES

Life lesson: Control what you can.

I look up as Reed enters my hotel room in Singapore. He'd flown in from Sydney for the Asian leg of *The Aegean's* press tour. I already miss Lena tremendously—even though it's only been five days since I last saw her. It relieves me to learn she filed a restraining order against her father and changed the locks on her doors. Garrett's cousin installed a security system, which makes me feel much better about the whole situation.

I smile at my brother and think about Lena's brother's surprise visit. He stayed a few days longer than she expected, but she said their time together was actually quite pleasant. That makes me happy. With a father like hers, she needs all the family she can get. If I remember correctly, Trevor was supposed to fly back to Japan this morning.

"How was your flight, mate?"

"Long," Reed mutters, crossing the room. "Fucking babies crying the whole time."

I hug him and pat his back. "Good thing ya love kids so much."

"I don't get it." Reed snorts and limps to his bed. "Why do people insist on bringing their fuck trophies on vacation?"

"Did you just call them *fuck trophies?*"

"Loin fruits, crotch droppings, whatever you wanna call them."

"Christ, mate. That's foul. I know you don't want kids, but I hope if I ever have kids, you won't think of them that way."

Reed smirks. "I might consider tolerating yours, but I can't make any guarantees."

"I guess I'll have to accept that." I flop onto my mattress. "What's new?"

He tosses a magazine onto my bed. "You tell me."

I lurch upright and gape at Lena's face on the cover. "Son of a bitch."

"You have no bloody idea." He presses his lips into a grim line. "Wait until you read it."

My heart freezes in my chest. I flip to the article which details the incident at Lena's home, her father's criminal past, and her mental health history. Someone has leaked *everything*—from her father's brutality, her living arrangement with Garrett, the workplace strangulation assault, to her recent forced medical leave. Everything is there—in great detail.

Reed cocks a brow and gestures to the magazine. "This is the first time you're seeing this? I've already fielded six calls from people wanting to hear your thoughts on your new woman's sordid backstory."

"You know I don't read this shit," I snap. "Tell anyone who calls to fuck off. I refuse to add to her pain and humiliation. This will fucking destroy her. Call Murphy. I want the article retracted."

If anyone can help the situation, it's our family lawyer. Come hell or high water, I need to fix this before Lena falls apart.

Reed shakes his head. "You know I have no control over what's put out there. Tell me something, mate. Are you sure you wanna be mixed up with the likes of her?"

"What did you just say?"

"You heard me." His whiskey-colored eyes lock with mine. "Sounds like she's off her bloody rocker. At the very least, she's got some serious daddy issues."

I heave the magazine across the room and jump to my feet, rounding on Reed. "*Never* speak about her that way again," I snarl, my voice low and dangerous. "Do you hear me?" When he doesn't answer, I grab him by the collar and roughly shake him. "Do you fucking hear me?"

Reed nods and looks away. "Hope she's worth the trouble, that's all."

CHAPTER 37

LENA

Internal playlist: "Love Me Anyway" by P!nk (featuring Chris Stapleton)

I burrow beneath the blankets while my phone rings in the distance—like it has been doing all day. I don't want to talk. Not to Trevor, not to Garrett, not even to Wes. Fresh tears burn my cheeks, soaking my pillow. I curl into a tighter ball and try to breathe.

Garrett enters my room and thrusts the phone in my face. "Answer him, damn it."

"Don't wanna talk."

"Tough shit." He sits on the edge of my bed and answers, "Lena's phone, Garrett speaking."

"Yeah, she's home." Garrett sighs. "Hiding in her bed right now. Said she doesn't feel like talking."

"I'm with you, Emerson." He snorts and nudges my foot. "Wes said to cut your shit and talk to him."

I don't even look at Garrett. Instead, I burrow tighter, hoping to escape all of this.

"Doesn't look like that's happening," Garrett mutters to Wes. "I like your style." The phone beeps and he places it near my face. "You're on speaker, Emerson. Later."

"Thanks, mate."

I silently give Garrett the finger.

"You're welcome." He squeezes my shoulders and leaves.

"Lena . . . listen to me. This changes nothing between us." Wes's voice fills my room, causing the tears to fall harder. "Please don't cry, love."

"How can you want anything to do with me? I'm a fucking mess."

"Remember what I told you in Alaska? I want more than your light, sunshine. I want your darkness, your scars, your rough edges—not just the easy shit."

I wipe my nose. "I'm making you look like a fool for being with me."

"You think I care what anyone thinks?" When I don't reply, he adds, "Let me make this abundantly clear. I don't give a flying fuck what anyone thinks, and neither should you. I love you, Lena. That's all that should matter to ya."

"I love you too, Wes. I'm just . . ."

"Gutted some stranger's exploiting your pain?"

"Yes," I whisper. "I'm mortified, and the fact they uncovered those details makes my skin crawl."

"Sunshine, those details weren't uncovered . . . they were *leaked*. By someone close to you."

"Who would want to hurt me like that?"

"I dunno, but I'm sure as shit gonna find out and make them pay."

Hours later, after nearly force-feeding me, Garrett studies my face. "Do you think Marc had something to do with this?"

I shake my head, curling my legs beneath me on his couch. "He wouldn't stoop that low."

"I dunno, Leens . . ."

"No. I *know* Marc. He's a better man than that."

"Who else could it be? Your father?"

"But why would he smear his name?"

Garrett crosses his arms over his chest. "Why would he hurt your mom? Why would he slam you into a wall? Why would he try to frame me for kidnapping you? Why would he hire a thug to break into your house? Need I continue?"

"You're right." I pause and rub my chin. "It's his retaliation for my restraining order."

He nods. "Makes sense, doesn't it?"

"How the fuck did I come from this dysfunction? Better yet, how am I not fucked-up like them?"

Garrett grips my shoulders. When he speaks, his tone is fierce. "Because we left, Leens. We got the fuck out of there, away from the toxicity, and started over. Who knows what would've happened to us if we stayed?"

"Now what? How do I deal with this while the whole world watches?"

"Like Wes said, ignore it. Keep living your life and let it blow over. They'll lose interest eventually."

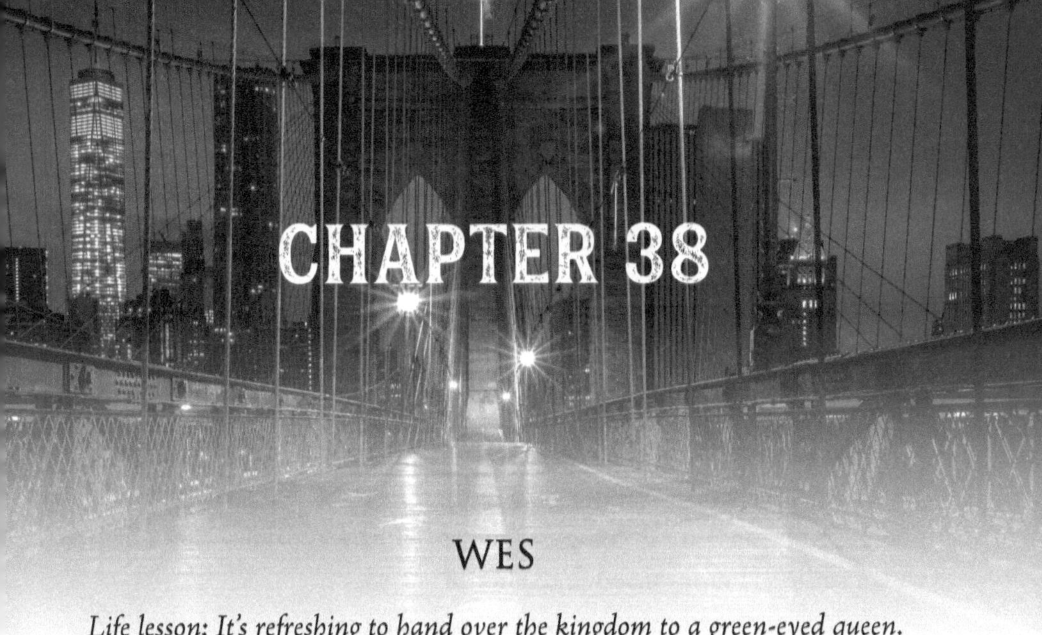

CHAPTER 38

WES

Life lesson: It's refreshing to hand over the kingdom to a green-eyed queen.

Over the past few weeks, Lena and I have fallen into a steady rhythm of long-distance communication, with ample texts and calls. Mindful of the time difference, we schedule daily video chats before she goes to bed. Since I'm home in Australia for a few days, that falls around my lunchtime, but I can't think of a better way to break up my day.

The tabloid leak was traced back to her father. Lena won't take legal action against him, which is a damn shame. That bastard should pay for hurting her. Despite Reed's protests, I went on the record in Lena's defense, giving *People* magazine an exclusive interview singing her praises. My brother isn't happy with me, but I don't give a flying fuck—he wouldn't let this shit happen to Cora.

I stretch and glance at my watch. It's almost time for our video chat. Lena promised something extra special since today's my birthday. I glance at the enormous box that was delivered a few days prior. She made me swear not to open it yet, but I'm dying to know what's inside. Anticipation courses through my veins when my phone finally vibrates.

"Good evening, sunshine."

"Howdy, Ace." Lena grins. "Happy birthday, my sexy Halloween man."

"Thank you. I miss you so much."

"I miss you too. Can you call me back from your iPad or computer?"

"Sure, love."

"Excellent. You're gonna want a big screen for this . . ."

My breath leaves me in a rush as I power up my laptop. "Are you planning to do a striptease or put on a sexy costume?"

"You'll see," she singsongs. "Grab the box and head to your bedroom. Oh . . . and I recommend you lock your doors and close the blinds."

My cock hardens in an instant, straining against my zipper. "If you're trying to turn me on, it's already a success." Honestly, the woman could prance around in a hazmat suit and I'd still be hot for her.

"Well, since I couldn't be with you today, I wanted to give you the next best thing." She winks and then promptly ends our video chat. I scramble, punching buttons on my computer to get her back on video. She answers with a smile as I move through the house.

I close my bedroom door, lock it, and place the box on my bed. "You said you wanted to give me the next best thing. What, exactly, might that be?"

"A curated journey of the senses. Here's the deal. For the remainder of this chat, I'm in charge. You'll do what I ask, when I ask it—no exceptions. Do you think you can handle that?"

"Yes."

"Good. You may run the show when we're together, but right now, consider me your alpha."

I bite the inside of my cheek to curb my grin. She looks so serious right now and it's damn cute. "I'm listening."

"All right. First things first, I want you to strip down to your boxers and get on the bed."

I quickly follow her directive, shedding and tossing my clothes aside. I settle onto my bed and peer at the screen. Dressed in a bathrobe with her hair in a braid, Lena appears comfortable. Relaxed. Sexy as hell.

"Open the box," she commands. "You'll notice several smaller boxes inside. See those labels?"

I study the contents of the big box. Five smaller boxes are wrapped with gold paper and numbered. "Yeah."

"Take them out and line them up in numerical order, but don't open them yet."

I nod and follow her instructions, noticing how the size, weight, and shapes of the boxes vary.

Lena continues, "When I was thinking about what to get you, I must admit I struggled. What does one give the man who has everything? But then the answer came to me a couple weeks ago. Instead of *things*, I decided on an experience. And by that, I mean a *shared* experience. I want to make this a birthday to remember."

"I'm bursting at the seams, love."

"Good." Lena grins wickedly. "When I'm done with you, there won't even be a thread."

My breath wooshes out of me. She's so fucking sexy I want to scream. She removes her bathrobe in a slow tease. Beneath it, she's wearing red silk pajamas.

"I love the red, sunshine. I see you painted your nails too."

Lena wiggles her fingers. "Oddly enough, this polish is called red hot sex. Seemed fitting for the occasion." She licks her lips and motions to the boxes. "Grab box number one and open it. We'll call this the gift of scent."

I unwrap the box to discover a jar candle. I remove the lid. Closing my eyes, I lower my nose to the wax and inhale deeply. Warm, sultry vanilla with a hint of spice—exactly how Lena smells. And fuck, the scent hardens my cock. I glance at the jar. There isn't a label or any identifying marks. I raise a brow. "How'd you do this?"

"I had a candle made using my perfume," she explains. "Now, I want you to put it on your dresser and light it."

I carry the jar to my dresser, locate a box of matches, and light it as instructed. Quickly, the heady scent fills the room, making me want to nuzzle her neck and hair.

"Open box number two," Lena commands in a tone that makes my cock twitch. "Behold the gift of sound."

I unwrap the package and withdraw a small speaker and a mini-MP3 player. In addition, a handwritten note.

"I made a some playlists with songs that remind me of us as a couple. The first one is called 'Northern Reflections,' which is mainly lovey-dovey songs. I listed them out on that page."

I scan the collection of songs, recognizing a few titles, including Ray LaMontagne's "Shelter," and the Chainsmokers & Coldplay's "Something Just Like This." My gaze comes to rest on John Legend's "All of Me."

"I see you put our dancing song on here."

"Of course. I listen to it all the time now, and I can almost feel your arms around me, us swaying in the suite. Candles lit, rose petals everywhere."

I smile. "You liked that, huh?"

"It was the most romantic day of my life."

"Mine too." I touch the screen, wishing I could run my fingers through her hair.

Lena clears her throat. "Back to your gift. Stop distracting me."

"Right, sorry."

"The second playlist, which I've titled 'Lioness,' is mainly sexy songs that come to mind when I think of you. I've preloaded both playlists on that MP3 player. I want you to turn the speaker on and select 'Lioness.'" She shimmies her hips. "I'm thinking we need a little background music."

I move quickly to do as I'm told, and a sultry female voice fills the room. I don't recognize the song, so I glance at Lena's list. This is a J. Lo song entitled, "Come Over." I set the speaker on my nightstand and peer at the screen expectantly.

"Box three. The gift of taste. Open it."

Growing more excited by the second, I tear the paper and withdraw a small box of chocolates, a bottle of caramel syrup, and a little velvet bag.

"Put the bag aside and open the gold box—those are *Giorgio's* truffles," she explains. "Best chocolates in New York. Go ahead, eat one."

I bite into the chocolate as Lena opens her own box of truffles and eats one.

"Wow." The decadent chocolate melts in my mouth. "This is divine."

"I know. They're my favorite—so smooth and sweet." She finishes her truffle and holds up the same bottle of caramel syrup as the one she sent me. "But *this* stuff is nectar of the gods. I put it on ice cream, in my coffee, in various baked goods." She reaches for a banana and peels it. "I make this amazing dessert called Bananas Foster. It's my favorite. I'll make it for you sometime. Go ahead, squeeze some into your mouth."

No joke, the syrup is the most delicious thing I've ever tasted. I actually moan when the sticky sweetness coats my tongue. "My God, this is amazing."

"Yeah. The next time we see each other, you're going to lick it off me," she purrs. "And I'll be sure to return the favor."

My jaw drops open as she drizzles syrup on the banana and licks it. Then, with her eyes locked on mine, the sultry vixen deep-throats it.

"Holy fuck." My cock throbs and my balls tighten. "Lena, you're killing me."

"I'm just getting started, Ace." She sets the banana, syrup, and chocolates aside. "Box number four. The gift of sight. Open it."

"Wait, you forgot the little black bag."

"That's for you to open later. When it's quiet and you're missing me a little."

My gaze flashes to hers. "And what if I open it now?"

"Then you'll miss out on the rest of the gift. I'm in charge, remember?"

"At least tell me what's inside. Otherwise, I won't be able to focus." I flash a wicked grin, knowing she'll take the bait.

"Those . . ." Lena brings the screen closer to her face so I can watch her lick her lips. Slowly. Deliberately. Exactly how she'd rub her tongue on the head of my cock. "Are butterscotch hard candies for you to suck on." She flutters her lashes. "I seem to recall you comparing a certain part of my body to those confections."

My cock jerks at her words. That's it. I'll suck every lolly in this bag dry before tonight is over. The next time I see Lena, I'll make her sit on my face. Then I'll lick her until she screams.

"Lena, you're gonna get it when I come to New York."

"Get what? The hard fuck and spanking you owe me?" She bites her lip. "If that's not what you mean, then I'm sorry, I'm just not interested."

"I've never wanted you as badly as I do right now."

She raises a brow. "Never?"

"*Never.*"

"We'll see about that." She winks. "Open box four."

I open the fourth box and lose the ability to breathe. A lacy, red bra and silk panties are nestled inside. I pull them out and rub the material between my fingertips. Staring at the screen, I watch Lena slowly unbutton and remove her pajama shirt. Beneath it, she's wearing the same lace bra. She bites her lip and slides the pants over her hips, exposing identical silk panties. I clench the material in my hands.

"Noticing a theme yet, Ace?"

I can't answer. My eyes are riveted to the screen. Lena loosens her braid. Her silken hair cascades over her graceful shoulders and lace-covered breasts. My chest heaves. My cock grows impossibly harder.

Lena smiles and slides the straps over her shoulders, then reaches around and removes her bra. She trails her fingertips down her neck, the bright red nail polish contrasting with supple, porcelain skin. Dusky pink nipples peek out from behind strands of caramel-colored hair. She tosses the locks over her shoulder and cups her breasts. Her nipples harden to mouthwatering peaks as she brushes her thumbs over them. A soft moan escapes her throat.

I'm on fire with lust, completely in flames. Even with an ocean between us, my hands remember the soft fullness of her breasts. I'd give anything to touch Lena. Kiss her. Make love to her. Instead, I'm a desperate voyeur, burning with the heat of my desire, forced to watch the scene unfold across continents and time zones.

She slides her hands lower and, eyes on mine, hooks her fingertips in the waistband of her panties. She tugs them off and tosses them aside.

I clench my jaw. "You are so beautiful."

Slowly spinning in a circle, she lets me see all of her. My eyes travel from her breasts to her hips, to the curve of her arse, to that wet, tight pussy I can't wait to be buried inside.

Lena settles onto the bed and repositions her laptop. "Enjoying the view?"

"You have no fucking idea."

"Good." She licks her lips. "Now watch closely, Ace." Trailing a hand down her stomach, she finds her clit and strokes it. She gasps, her eyes fluttering closed. "First, I'm going to let you watch me make myself come."

Gaze glued to the screen; I struggle to breathe watching her massage her clit in circles. She pleasures herself slowly at first, then much faster. Soft moans and gasps reach my ears. Lena brings herself to the edge, back arching, hips flexing in rhythm with her touch.

"I'm almost there." Her moan reverberates to my balls.

I clench my hands in the lingerie she sent, the lace in jeopardy of being shredded. Now, I've seen porn a time or two in my day, but nothing compares to this lust coursing through my veins. *Nothing.*

"You're so fucking hot, Lena," I growl the words. "I wanna fuck you senseless."

Glossy lips parted, chest heaving, cheeks flushed, Lena is a goddess. She moans my name loudly as she orgasms, and I watch her ride the waves of her release.

"Box number five," she gasps the command. "The gift of touch."

I snatch the box and rip it open to find a bottle of lube.

Lena gestures to me. "Get naked. Now, it's my turn to watch."

I strip out of my boxers and glance at my cock. I seldom stroke myself, and I have *never* done it in front of a woman.

"Angle your screen so I can see you."

Hands shaking, I tilt the screen, then squeeze some lube into my palm. I firmly grip my cock. Eyes locked on hers, I begin to stroke myself, the liquid cooling my overheated skin.

"Use both hands. Hold it tighter," she says in a husky whisper. "Like when my body squeezes you."

Tightening my grip, I rub myself harder and groan. "You're killing me, sunshine."

"Keep stroking it, baby." To my shock, Lena holds up a red dildo and flashes a sultry smile. "I'm gonna join you," she purrs. "This doesn't come close to you, but I'm going to close my eyes and imagine it's you deep inside me."

"Oh, fuck, Lena . . ." I groan. "I want you so badly."

"I want you too, Wes. Now, I need you to *feel* yourself inside me."

She slowly slides the toy inside her pussy. My cock jerks in my hands, toes curling in ecstasy. Her eyes flutter closed as she strokes the dildo in and out.

"Match my rhythm." She alternates fast and slow strokes, and I keep pace with her, stroking and tugging my cock. "Do it harder, Wes . . ." she hisses. "I want you to fuck me."

Lena consumes my senses. The scent of her perfume fills my head. My ears indulge in the sultry music beneath her gasps and moans of my name. The lingering taste of the caramel caresses my tongue. My gaze remains locked on the screen. From her eyes, to her breasts, to her hips and thighs, to that red toy she's thrusting in and out of herself, she is perfection. I tighten my grip and increase the pace, seconds from release.

"Feel me, Wes," she moans. "Feel it and come for me."

I lose it.

With a feral groan, cock jerking and spurting, I come hard. "Oh, *fuck*. Lena . . ." I keep moving my hands until I can't take it any longer. Moments later, Lena follows with her release. Hips bucking, she writhes on her bed and wails my name.

I stare at the screen in disbelief. For a moment, I *was* thrusting inside her, not an ocean away. We stare into one another's eyes and bask in the afterglow.

"Happy birthday, Ace."

"Lena, I . . . you just . . . I fucking can't . . ." I shake my head.

Lena chuckles. "Was it good for you?"

"You own me, sunshine," I rasp. "You fucking *own* me."

I stroll along the beach and cast a wistful glance at the sea. I left my shoes behind so I could feel the waves lapping at my feet. Closing my eyes, I breathe the salty ocean air. The late afternoon sun warms me, and a gentle breeze ruffles my hair.

This is nirvana. Too bad I can't surf.

Sighing, I tug on the sling. I hate the bloody thing, but Lena insisted I wear it a little longer since I haven't been consistent. I smile at the thought. I'll do anything she wants me to.

Lena has transformed me. She opened my eyes on every level, and I pray I'm a better man for it. I love her more than I ever thought possible. My cock hardens, remembering the birthday surprise she'd given me hours earlier. The experience was mind-blowing. Not only had I never stroked myself while someone watched, but I never had cybersex in any capacity. She is the *only* woman I've ever done bareback, and no one fits me like she does. *All these firsts with Lena.* I can't wait to kiss her, taste her, and sink deep inside her. Over and over again.

My eyes flutter closed at the memory of her face. She's so exquisitely beautiful it steals my breath. I ache to hold her in my arms, kiss her soft lips, make love to her. The amount of thought she put into my gift blew me away. Not only was it creative as fuck, but no one has ever done anything like that for me. I've been listening to the playlists all afternoon. It touches my heart knowing she selected each song with me in mind.

While I still have a few more work obligations, I plan to fly to New York next week. The producers will release *The Aegean* on Wednesday. I groan at the thought of all the events I'm required to attend. Especially the fucking premiere. The idiots scheduled it two days *after* the film actually releases. I wish I could skip it and be at Lena's side for Jake's gala, even though Garrett is going as her date. *Lucky bastard.*

I squint in the sunlight at the figure approaching in the distance. Sighing, I return my attention to the waves and watch them crest and crash over the rocky jetty that extends into the sea. The sound soothes me. *Lena soothes me more.* The fact that she surpasses the ocean's soul-settling ability tells me I need more of her. So much more.

I think about my career and the direction my life has taken. It's not that I'm unhappy, just weary and disenchanted. The role of Ares has served as both a blessing and a curse. I have more money than I know what to do with, and thanks to future royalties, finances will never be a concern. Thankfully, Reed manages my investments. But the money doesn't matter to me. Time has become a currency more precious than the dollar. The strain over the past few years has been relentless. The stifling pace saps my time and energy. And that needs to change. If there's one thing I learned in Alaska, it's that life is too bloody short. I want to spend my time with Lena and my family, not filming.

I have a project lined up for the spring, but after that, I plan to step back and be more selective with the productions I take on. I don't need to torture myself with this marathon career. If a project doesn't speak to me on a creative level or if it doesn't enrich my life, then I don't want any part of it. I want more quiet strolls and fewer races.

I cringe, recognizing the person who continues to approach.

Shit.

Somehow, I managed to avoid the petite redhead at Gwen's funeral, but it seems my luck has run out.

Cora's cousin closes the distance between us. "Hey, Wes."

"Hello." I continue to walk.

She hustles to keep stride with me. "Knew I'd find ya here."

"Yeah? And how's that?"

"Let's see, you're in town and the sun's shining. I swung by your flat and didn't see your car. Where else would ya be? Although I expected to see you out there with your board," she states with a self-satisfied smirk.

"Didn't realize I'm so predictable."

She ignores my statement and looks me over. "You look good. And happy birthday, by the way."

"Thanks."

"Why the sling?"

"Fractured my collarbone and dislocated my shoulder. Hence the absence of a surfboard."

She nods. "Good thing your brother married a physical therapist."

I think of Cora. "She's a drill sergeant, but yeah."

"Cora knows what she's doing. Maybe you ought to pay attention." She smiles sweetly. "So, what's new?"

I stop walking and study her face. "Why're ya here, Rachel?"

"It's a public beach. I'm taking a walk."

"I might buy that if you hadn't already told me you stopped by my flat."

"Fine. I wanted to talk to you."

"What's there to discuss?"

"Oh, I dunno, maybe the fact that you were lost in the wilderness? Or that ya nearly died?" She stares up at me. "Surely, those are pertinent topics."

"It was a life-changing adventure; let's leave it at that. I don't have the energy to go into detail."

This feels like one of those old arguments when she wanted to know every detail of my life and wouldn't stop pressing me—one of the reasons we broke up all those years ago.

"Believe it or not, the thought of you mauled by a bear or dying of starvation was upsetting to me. Your disappearance affected many people, especially your brother. Cora told me he was devastated."

"I know," I say, feeling a twinge of guilt. "And I'm sorry about your aunt."

"Thank you. It happened so fast. My mum hasn't stopped crying," she murmurs. "I just don't understand how with all the advances in today's medicine, they still haven't found a cure. She endured so much, you know? Chemo, radiation, surgeries, nausea . . . all of it. And even so, it claimed her." She sniffs and brushes away a tear. "I'm sorry to get worked up. I still can't wrap my head around it."

"Don't apologize, Rach. Gwen was an incredible woman who fought to the end."

"That's the other reason I came to see you. Cora told me what you did for the Australian Cancer Foundation."

"It was supposed to be an anonymous donation." I pinch the bridge of my nose and shake my head. "Cora talks too much."

"Stop it. She adores you. Five million's worth mentioning, Wes."

"Didn't do it for a mention."

"Well, regardless of your motives, thank you. Your gesture means a lot to our family. It means a lot to *me*. I wanted you to know that."

"You're welcome."

"You hungry?" she asks.

"Not really," I lie. Just then, my traitorous stomach growls. Rachel arches a brow and I grin, crunching the hard candy in my mouth. "All right, maybe a little."

"What're you chewing on?"

"It's a butterscotch lolly."

"I never knew you liked those."

"There's a lot you don't know about me, Rach."

"Wanna grab a birthday burger at Benny's? As friends," she adds. "It would be nice to catch up on each other's lives. You can tell me some of the stuff I don't know about ya."

I study her face. I haven't seen her in years, and she's been through a lot. "Yeah, we can do that," I reply with a smile, thinking of the beachside burger joint.

Surely, it won't hurt to catch up.

CHAPTER 39

LENA

Internal playlist: "Water Under the Bridge" by Adele

Miniature tornadoes of dead leaves scuttle past me as I walk the few blocks to Ralph's Tavern. Naked oaks and maples reach skyward, their barren branches paying homage to the full moon. My phone buzzes in my pocket.

I smile. "Hey, Ace."

"Hi, sunshine. What're ya up to?"

"On my way to Ralph's to grab burgers with Garrett and Jake. I'm running late."

"How come?"

"My therapy session ran over, so I told the guys I'd meet them there."

"Well, I don't wanna hold you up, but I figured I'd call and tell you about my talk with Reed."

"The guys can wait." I settle on a park bench. "I always have time for you, babe. How'd it go?"

"It was good."

"Wait, why do you sound like you have marbles in your mouth?"

He chuckles. "I may or may not be indulging in part of my birthday gift."

"I have another box for you here."

"Good—I'm almost done with the ones you gave me."

"Already?"

"Well, you said to have one whenever I missed ya . . ."

"I miss you too."

"I can't wait to see you, sunshine. And you were right."

"About what?"

"Everything." He clears his throat. "I told him I felt like I stole his life."

"And what did he say?"

"He said, 'I passed the torch to you, and you ran with it. You kept that flame alive and took it places I couldn't. I'm happy to watch you succeed and I'm proud of who you've become.' He said that seeing the attention I deal with made him happy to be living the quiet life." Wes sighs again. "All these years I've felt disgusted by my success, you know?"

"I know, babe. But it must be a relief knowing he doesn't see it that way."

"It is. I told him I felt responsible for the accident."

"I wondered if you'd go there." The wind picks up and I brush the hair back from my face.

"Yeah. He never blamed me for that either. Told me he accepted his reality and moved forward and that I need to do the same. Said I need to make peace with myself."

"He's right."

"I know, love. I'm working on it."

"I'm proud of you for getting it off your chest. I know how hard it was for you."

"Thanks for giving me the kick in the arse I needed."

"Anytime, babe."

"Also, Reed reminded me that Cora came out of the situation and he couldn't imagine his life without her."

"It was a blessing in disguise, a silver lining."

"He channeled Memphis and called it his *destiny*." Wes chuckles. "I swear those two must sit around with candles and crystals. Always talking about chance, serendipity, and twists of fate."

"Well, maybe they're on to something."

"Whaddya mean?"

"I mean the universe works in funny ways. Our meeting was a cosmic encounter, don't you think?" I muse, twirling a strand of my hair. "You said it yourself in Alaska. 'We were destined to spark and catch fire.'"

"We're more than a coincidence, love."

"I think so too. So, what are you doing for the rest of the day?"

"Stopping by my parents' place to have lunch with Mum and Isla."

"Did your mom make pie?"

"Yes, and I'm ready to gorge myself. Anyway, we'll talk more later. I love you. Until next time, sunshine."

"Love you too, Ace. Until next time . . ."

I stand and pocket my phone. After a few minutes, I arrive at Ralph's and find Jake and Garrett sitting at the bar.

Garrett points to his watch.

"I know. I'm sorry. Dr. Turner was running behind and then I was on the phone with Wes." I hug both men.

"No worries, Lena-Bean," Jake says. "We were starving, so we already ordered."

"I got you your usual," Garrett adds, sipping his seltzer.

"With curly fries, I hope?"

"Yeah. And an extra pickle." He snorts. "This isn't my first rodeo, woman."

"You're the best. Thanks."

Jake and I listen as he describes the *Prodigy* audition and his cast-mates. Positioned on the bar near Garrett's elbow, my phone lights up with a text.

Garrett cocks a brow. "Why the fuck is the number one LDP texting you?"

"No clue."

"Thought you ripped him a new asshole after he pulled that shit with the flowers?"

"I did."

"I'm lost. Who are we talking about? What's LDP?" Jake asks.

"Her ex, Marc, aka Limp-Dick-Pussy Numero Uno," Garrett explains. "I hate that stupid fuck."

Jake snorts a laugh. "You don't mince words, do you?"

"I'm not Willy Wonka. I don't see the point in sugarcoating things." Garrett smirks. "People always know where they stand with me. Right, Leens?"

"Yep."

He points to my phone. "You'd better not answer him."

"It may be work-related." I unlock my screen.

"You're on medical leave. Tell him to fuck off."

I open the message and freeze. The floor drops out from beneath me and it feels like I'm falling.

Down, down, down.

Faster and faster.

Eyes glued to the screen, I can't think or breathe. I just keep falling.

"What's wrong?" Garrett's voice echoes in the distance.

My reply comes out as a strangled whisper. "No . . . please, no . . ."

He grabs my phone to look. "Are you fucking kidding me?"

Jake leans in. "I'm confused. What's going on?"

He thrusts the device at Jake. "Who the fuck is *this*?"

Jake's mouth falls open. "That's Rachel, his ex," his gaze flashes to me, "but it may be an old picture."

"Explain the sling," Garrett demands with narrowed eyes.

"He wore that shirt on his birthday . . . Excuse me," I whisper. Blinking back tears, I rush to the ladies' room.

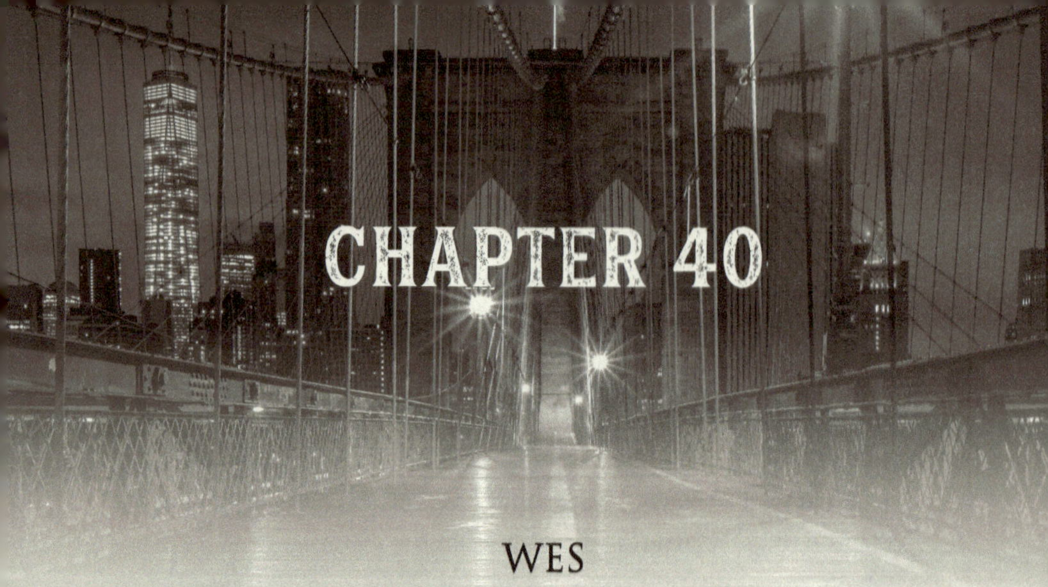

CHAPTER 40

WES

Life lesson: Always trust your gut.

"Thanks for making time for us." Mum squeezes my shoulder and sets a plate in front of me.

"Of course, Mum. I wanted to see ya before I head out," I answer, taking a bite of apple pie.

"How come he always gets pie?" Isla asks.

I bat my eyelashes at her. "Because I'm the favorite."

"I don't have favorites," Mum insists. "But if I did, it would be Reed."

I laugh and elbow my sister, who sticks out her lip in a mock pout. My phone chimes from its position on the counter between us.

"Who's texting you? Is Lena sending nudes?" Isla waggles her brows.

"Isla! Your mother's present." Mum laughs.

I snatch the phone. "No, it's Bennett."

The message is still downloading since service isn't great at my parents' place.

"If Jake's sending nudes, I wanna see them," Isla insists cheekily.

"Shut it, Imp." I chuckle. "Remember, Bennett's off-limits."

"Why?"

"Because all my friends are." I furrow my brow at the device. "Looks like he *is* sending pics." The first message comes through.

Jake: Are you out of your fucking mind?!?! Really, dude? WTF?!

I narrow my eyes. Horror replaces my confusion when the first picture loads. I stare open-mouthed at a screenshot of Rachel and me walking along the beach. Four more pictures appear. The last one bears the gossip site's headline, "Wes Emerson, safe from wilderness nightmare, rekindles old flame on his birthday. Lena Hamilton, who?"

My lungs stop working.

Another picture appears, which Jake captioned, "YOU'RE A STUPID FUCK." This one—which shows me in a passionate lip-lock with Rachel in front of her car—is the final nail in my coffin.

My blood drains to my feet and I feel like I'm going to chuck my guts up.

Jake: Someone just sent these to Lena's phone. WHAT THE ACTUAL FUCK IS WRONG WITH YOU?!?!?!?!?!?!

I slam my fist on the counter. "Motherfucker!" I leap from the stool and knot my hands in my hair. "Son of a *fucking* bitch!"

"Wesley James! What the hell's the matter with you?" Mum breathes.

I kick the stool and grip the counter. Chest heaving, I white-knuckle the granite. A muscle in my jaw pulses violently. I can't see through the haze in my vision.

Isla snatches my phone. "What the hell did you do?"

"Not what it looks like," I sputter. "Swear to God."

"What were you doing with *Rachel?*" Her face twists in horror.

"Talking."

"You're kissing her, fuckwit." Isla points to the screen. "*That's* not talking."

"Give me my phone. I need to call her."

"Who? Rachel?"

I round on my sister. "I want *nothing* to do with Rachel!" I scream in her face like a raving lunatic.

Grabbing my phone, I storm outside. I call Lena and it goes straight to voicemail. I hang up without leaving a message. I dial Jake, who answers on the second ring.

"Wes, what the fuck?"

"I swear, it's not what it looks like. Put her on the phone."

"She's in the bathroom crying," Jake snaps. "What possessed you to go on a date with Rachel?"

"It wasn't a fucking date!" I roar.

Mum stares out the kitchen window at me, a look of utter shock contorting her features. Isla's face appears beside her.

Jake grunts something.

"What?"

"I said Lena's coming back."

"Put her on the phone." I pace my parents' driveway. I hear Jake say something to Lena in a muffled tone.

He addresses me, "She said she'll call you later."

"I wanna talk to her *now!*" My shout echoes across the property, sending a flock of birds into flight.

I hear Jake mumble something else, and then Lena's voice in the background. Jake speaks up, "Not gonna happen right now, man."

"What did she just say?"

"She said she's not concerned with what you want." Jake sighs. "Look, I'm not playing middleman, so you're gonna have to wait 'til she calls you. Sorry." He hangs up.

I stare at the phone in disbelief. I sit on a retaining wall near Mum's car and try to breathe. The paparazzi fuckers must've been lurking in the bushes near where I parked. I'd gotten so accustomed to the privacy of the wilderness I forgot my reality.

Scumbag Troy Reynolds is behind this.

The media snake's team of photographers will stop at nothing for the perfect shot, even if that means ruining lives. This isn't the first time I've been featured on *Celebrity Buzz's* homepage, but it's certainly the most explosive story the gossip rag has ever run about me. Maybe I'll pay Troy a visit and demand he retract everything. I shake my head.

No, can't do that. I'll wind up assaulting the fucker.

Instead, I march inside, nearly barreling into Mum and Isla. They scatter like mice when I snatch a bottle of bourbon from my father's stash, crack it open, and park my arse at the kitchen table. Now I'm going to call Murphy and every other lawyer in the fucking country until I get those pictures—and fabricated story—retracted.

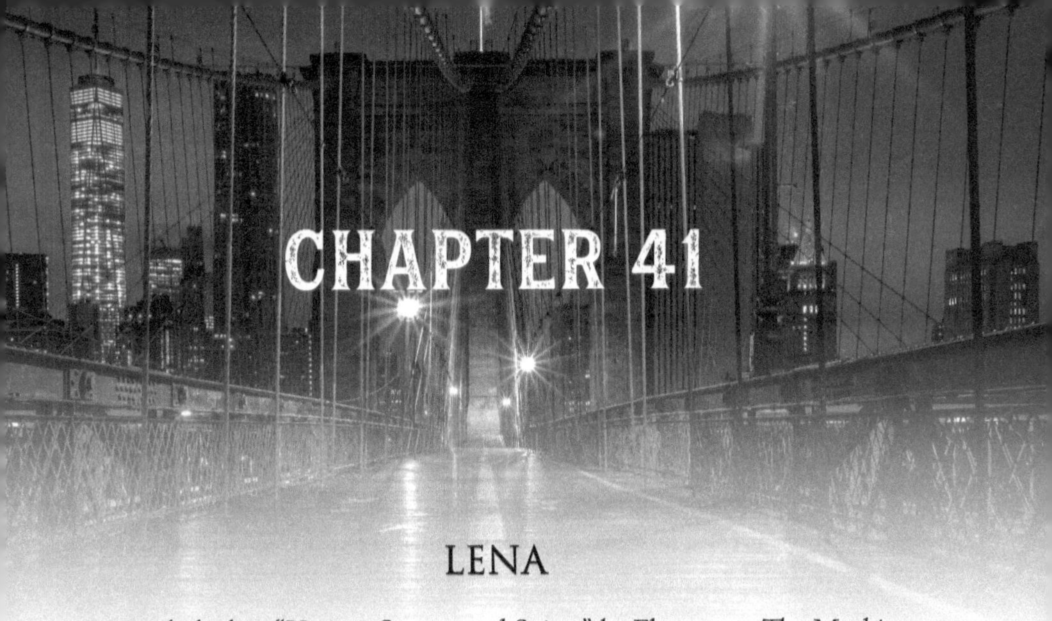

CHAPTER 41

LENA

Internal playlist: "Various Storms and Saints" by Florence + The Machine

I push the food around my plate. Rachel. It makes no sense. Wes has given me over a dozen reasons why she was a terrible partner. *But pictures don't lie.*

No matter how incriminating those photos may be, I'm going to give Wes the benefit of the doubt. There has to be an explanation.

Unless . . .

"Jake," I murmur, "let me ask you something. I want the truth, even if you think it'll hurt me." I pause as I meet his chocolate-brown gaze. "Does he . . . love her?"

"Absolutely not. He loves *you*." He squeezes my hand. "Call him."

"I'll call him when I'm good and ready. Regardless of what Wes thinks, I do things on my terms. I'm not gonna drop everything when he barks an order just because he got caught with his pants down. He can wait." I guzzle my beer. "And he damn well better explain himself."

Hours later, I climb the oak staircase to my apartment. Garrett told me to be ready by nine tomorrow morning for a spa day upstate. He took the day off from work to pamper us.

I slip into my pajamas, take a steadying breath, and dial Wes's number.

He answers on the first ring. "Why'd it take ya so long to call?"

"Excuse me?"

"You knew I wanted to talk," he mutters, "but made me wait over three hours. Inconsiderate, don'tcha think?"

Is he fucking serious right now?

"Asked you a question."

"I heard you, Ace. I'm trying to think of a response that doesn't include fuck off."

"The truth works."

"Look who's talking," I snap. "And perhaps my delay had something to do with your *considerate* tongue down another woman's throat."

"Got an explanation for that."

"Oh, I'm sure you do." I shake my head in frustration. He sounds defensive, combative. Which makes no sense given that I am the one who's been wronged. "I'm listening."

"You don't trust me," Wes states.

"I called to hear what you have to say. If I didn't trust you, I would've taken what I saw at face value and not given a fuck about your explanation."

"You still interested in what I gotta say?"

"Did I not just call you? And I could do without your attitude."

"Not givin' ya one."

"Whatever, Wes. Just tell me what happened."

"Went for a walk on the beach. Still can't surf, obviously. But I wanted to hear the waves and feel the sand. Rachel went to my place to talk and wish me a happy birthday. I wasn't home, so she went to my favorite beach and found me there. She asked about 'Laska and if I wanted to get a burger. I was hungry, so I went with her. Afterward, I walked her to her car 'cause it was dark out. Prolly shouldn't have hugged her."

"So, why did you?"

"She was upset."

"Do you usually comfort your exes?"

There's a pause. "Really?"

"Well? Do you?" I probe. "I'm trying to get into your head here."

"Her fuckin' aunt just died," he snaps.

"Don't bark at me, Wes. Explain the kiss."

"She kissed *me*," he insists. "Not the other way 'round."

"You looked pretty involved to me."

"Funny thing 'bout zoom lenses and rapid shutter speeds," Wes growls. "I wasn't involved."

"Why were your hands on her shoulders?"

"You have a fuckin' microscope?"

"Nope. Just my eyes. Why are you getting so defensive about this?"

"'Cause you're interrogatin' me!"

"I'm asking a simple question based on something I saw. They photographed you kissing another woman—hours after I gave myself to you in our video chat. You're out of your mind if you think I'm okay with that. We've talked several times and you didn't mention it. Put yourself in my shoes, Wes. I think I deserve an explanation."

"I wasn't kissing her!" he roars.

I hold the phone away from my ear in shock. "What the hell's your problem?"

"This is my life. I deal with this shit every day. You know this—you've seen it, for fuck's sake. People hide with their cameras, so they can make shit up and fuck me," he sputters. "I need the people I love to trust me, to believe *me*, not the tabloid shit."

"I *do* trust you," I insist. "I was out for dinner and received pictures of you in a lip-lock with your ex-girlfriend. I'm just asking for an explanation here."

"You don't trust me, Lena. You don't fucking get it. How can this ever work? What's the point?"

"Have you lost your goddamn mind? *Listen* to what I'm saying."

"Rachel didn't trust me. Reed almost fucking died. Can't do it again."

"Do *what* again?"

"Make the same fuckin' mistake twice," he slurs. "Can't do it."

I clench the phone as a sickening realization washes over me. "Are you *drunk?*"

"No."

"Don't lie to me. I can hear it in your voice."

"Givin' me shit about that too?" he mutters. "Rachel all over again."

"Don't you *dare* compare me to her."

"Actin' just like her." Something glass shatters in the background. "Fuck." More muttered curses float down the line.

"What the hell was that?" No answer. "Wes?" I peek at the phone to make sure the call didn't drop. "Hello?"

When he finally speaks, his tone is hollow. "Can't do this. Won't go through it again."

"What are you saying?"

"Can't do this . . . I'm sorry."

My mouth goes dry. "Wes, I don't understand . . ." My eyes well as the room spins.

"Can't do it."

"Is this you ending things?" Shocked tears spill over, burning my cheeks as they fall. My scalp prickles. Air refuses to fill my lungs.

"Yeah . . ."

"Wes, no."

"Goodbye, Lena. I'm done."

I squeeze my eyes shut. "Well, I hope you find someone who's content to live on eggshells—" My voice breaks on a sob. "Because I deserve better than that."

I hang up and throw the phone across the room. It skids to a stop beneath my dresser.

The floodgates break. The fucking pillowcase doesn't stand a chance.

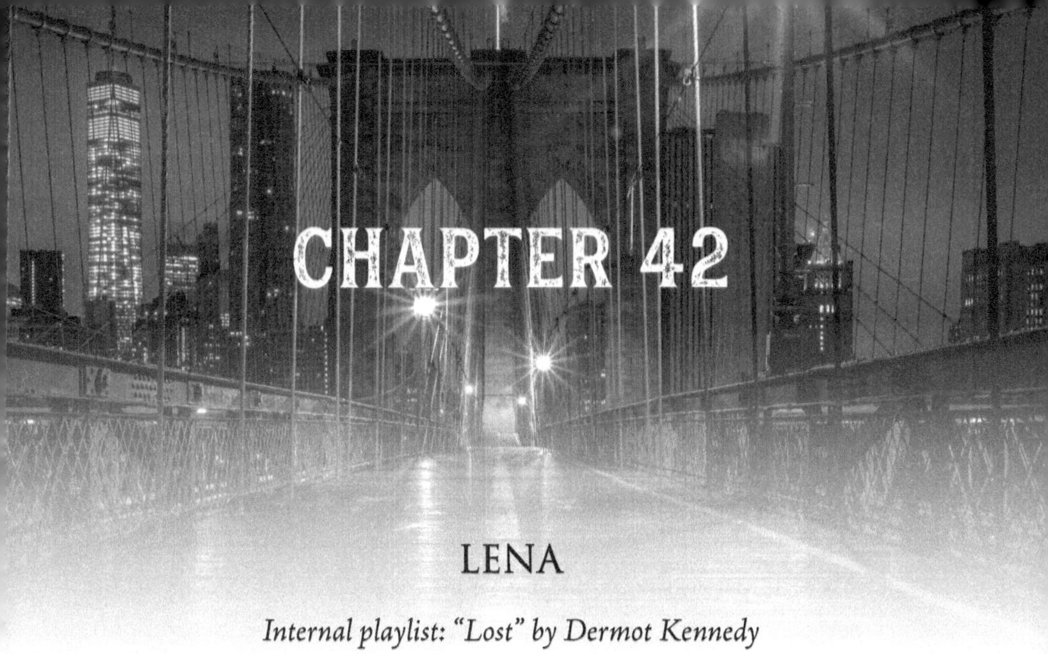

CHAPTER 42

LENA

Internal playlist: "Lost" by Dermot Kennedy

I pile on more under-eye concealer—not that it helps. After hiding the dark circles to the best of my ability, I accentuate my eyelids with a smoky, gilded shimmer and sweep on a few coats of mascara. I apply blush to my cheekbones and finish with a rich red lipstick. I admire my reflection. Yesterday's blissful relaxation did wonders for my appearance. You'd never know I cried through both massages and my facial. Or maybe it has something to do with the six pounds of makeup on my face.

I ease into the forest-green gown, which showcases my shoulders and a scandalous amount of cleavage. My caramel tresses cascade over my shoulders and glint in the light. With its sequins and intricate beadwork, the scintillating garment takes my breath away. Especially since the last time I wore it, Wes was inside me.

"Leens, you almost ready?" Garrett calls out.

"Be right down."

I dab cover-up on my scars, slide gold stilettos on my feet, and shove extra tissues into my clutch.

"The driver's here. Let's go."

I drape a shawl over my shoulders and descend the stairs to the foyer. Garrett stares open-mouthed as I glide to the front door. He holds it open and takes my arm to guide me down the stoop.

"You're like Helen of Troy. The face that launched a thousand ships."

"Thanks, Gar. You look sexy too."

A luxury SUV idles at the curb. I climb inside and Garrett slides onto the leather seat beside me. The driver eases from the curb and begins the trek to Manhattan. My belly flutters in anticipation. I've never attended a black-tie event, let alone a star-studded gala. Everyone who is anyone in the entertainment industry will be there. I peer out the window at the Manhattan skyline.

We reach the venue in no time. The posh hotel is a known gathering place for the rich and famous. The driver parks our SUV and jumps out to open the door for us. Garrett gets out and reaches for my hand to follow.

With a deep breath, I emerge like a rare orchid blossoming in the sun. I step onto the pavement. Suddenly, all eyes are on me. Several photographers begin snapping pictures of us. Garrett leads me into the hotel with a possessive hand at the small of my back as if protecting me from the paparazzi vultures.

We enter the ballroom. Absorbing decadence beyond my wildest dreams, I suck in a breath and allow Garrett to take the lead. He's much better in these situations than I am. He's grown accustomed to the spotlight during his years on stage. Heads turn at our approach. I hear the whispers of, "Who's that?" and feel the weight of stares on me. I glance at Garrett. He looks divine.

Garrett's eyes have always reminded me of a lion. The color is a rich, burnished amber with flecks of gold. Glossy onyx waves brush his collar. He selected a forest-green shirt to match my gown. An inky black suit showcases his strong musculature. Olive skin, a shadowed jawline, and plush lips complete the package. As he smiles and nods at people he recognizes, he displays a perfect set of teeth. I smile up at him. He winks and tightens his grip on my waist.

We spot Jake at the far end of the venue. He's the picture of rugged sophistication in a fitted, navy suit. Tousled chestnut waves fall haphazardly over his forehead. His facial hair is neatly groomed to a thick stubble. He sips from a flute of champagne and chats with a pot-bellied man in a tuxedo.

Jake's chocolaty eyes light up when he notices our approach. He excuses himself and rushes over to us. "Lena-Bean, you look *stunning*."

"Thank you, my dear."

He turns to Garrett and shakes his hand. "Long time no see. I'm so glad you guys could make it."

"Thanks again for the invite." Garrett smiles. "This place is incredible."

"Seemed like an appropriate choice for the occasion," Jake explains. "I'm glad you're here to save me from the stuffy old duffers holding me captive."

Garrett snorts a laugh. "We've got your back, Bennett. Just make sure the duffers keep their paws off Lena."

"Lena, you look gorgeous," Jake repeats, shaking his head in appreciation.

"Thanks, Jake, you're making me blush."

"Can I get you guys some champagne?"

"No, thank you," Garrett replies. "I'm good with water."

"Yeah, I'd love some," I answer. "I'm way out of my element and could use something to help me relax."

"This way." Jake motions for us to follow him to the bar—a colossal fixture flanked by ice sculptures. He greets the bartender and orders our drinks before turning to Garrett. "I meant to ask this the other night, but I was," he glances at me, "sidetracked. Have you given any interviews for *Prodigy*?"

Garrett shakes his head. "No, not yet."

"Good. I'll make some introductions then."

I touch Jake's arm. "I can't thank you enough for inviting us here tonight. I appreciate you going out of your way to connect Garrett with theater people."

"My pleasure, Lena-Bean. I'm just glad you came after . . . well, everything. You all right?"

"Yep."

GARRETT

Lena points to the ballroom's entrance. "I need to use the ladies' room. Be right back."

I watch her cross the dance floor, then turn to Jake. "She almost didn't come tonight, but I used my powers of persuasion on her."

Jake nods. "I'm glad you convinced her. How's she been?"

"Not good." I sigh. "Question for you."

"What's up?"

"What the fuck's his problem?"

Jake cocks his head. "What do you mean?"

"You talk to him?"

"No, I've been swamped prepping for this thing. Why? What's up?"

"He broke up with her the other night when she called him back after dinner."

"Are you fucking kidding me?" Jake sputters. "No, that can't be possible. Austin told me he's flying in."

"Wait, I thought Lena said the premiere's tonight."

"According to Austin, he's skipping it."

I raise my brows. "Skipping the *premiere?*"

"Yep. Dumb move, I know." Jake glances at his watch. "He should've landed at JFK an hour ago."

"This is gonna be interesting," I mutter. "Please don't mention that to Lena. She'll run out of here. She finally just stopped fucking crying."

"I don't get it. What was his reason?"

"Apparently, she asked for an explanation and he flipped out. Compared her to his ex."

"Lena's *nothing* like Rachel. She had Wes by the balls and treated him like shit. I dunno what his problem is. She deserved an explanation."

"She said he sounded drunk, which is a real sore spot for her."

"The stupid fuck probably was."

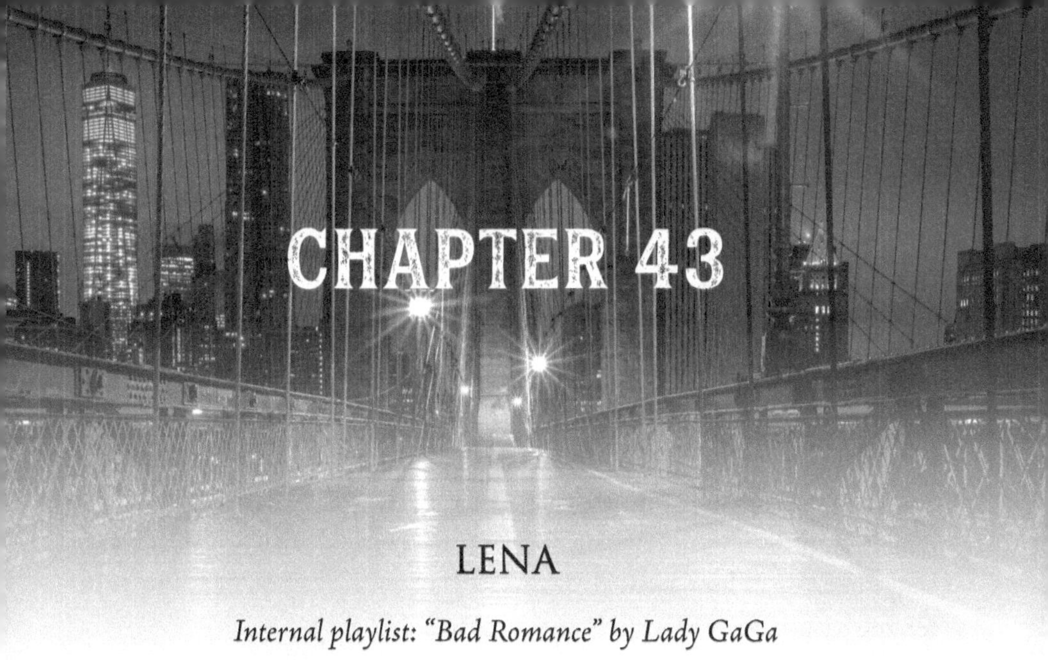

CHAPTER 43

LENA

Internal playlist: "Bad Romance" by Lady GaGa

Garrett, Jake, and I place our drinks on a cocktail table we claimed for our group. A photographer seizes the opportunity to snap a few pictures. Across the ballroom, a tuxedo-clad jazz quartet serenades the crowd. The sultry wails of the saxophone match the champagne's slow warmth easing through my system.

Jake makes his way to the front of the ballroom for his speech. Accepting the microphone offered to him, he discusses his foundation and the coming year's goals. Donations received at the gala will fund a community arts center. Jake speaks passionately about the arts and their impact on today's youth.

"This is our chance to shape the future, make our world more beautiful. Thank you all for coming. Eat, drink, and be merry. A DJ will take over soon, and I expect to see everyone on that dance floor," he finishes with a broad grin.

Garrett and I join in the applause. Jake bows to the audience and makes his way over to our table, shaking hands and nodding as he goes.

"How'd I do?" he asks.

I grin. "You were wonderful, Jake. I know I said it in Alaska, but thanks for not being a dick."

Jake laughs and hugs me. "Lena-Bean, I love you."

Across the room, the jazz quartet packs up their instruments. A DJ begins to set up her equipment. I down another flute of champagne. *Was that my second or third? Fuck it, who cares?* It's been a long time since I let loose and danced.

Various photographers mill about, documenting the evening's highlights. Most are nondescript males who blend with the surroundings; however, there is one who's captured my attention. This photographer is wearing a scarlet, curve-hugging gown. She has an exotic Mediterranean appearance, complete with mocha-colored waves, olive skin, and full, red lips. Her eyes are the same turquoise as the Caribbean Sea. She possesses a sultry confidence and familiarity with many gala attendees. As the photographer saunters in our direction, Garrett's sharp inhale snags my attention.

I peek up at him, noticing his heated gaze is locked on her. "Put your tongue back in your mouth. It's not nice to stare."

He grins and brings his lips to my ear. "We both know I'm not a nice boy." His whisper drips of sin and sex.

The mystery woman instructs us to pose for a group photo. Jake joins us at my other side. She snaps a few pictures, casts a lingering glance in Garrett's direction, and sashays across the ballroom.

He stares after her—no doubt mesmerized by the voluptuous curve of her ass. I chuckle to myself. My best friend is very much an ass man, and this woman boasts a booty that could turn a holy man to sin. Hell, even I want to pinch it.

I elbow Garrett in the ribs. "Take a cold shower."

"Won't work," he replies. "I'd need the Arctic."

The DJ begins to play some upbeat music and summons people to the dance floor. I snag another glass of champagne from a passing tray.

"Pace yourself, Leens. You haven't eaten much."

I toss back the contents in one gulp. "I feel great. Dance with me." I lead him by the hand to the dance floor.

The DJ plays a salsa-infused number. Hands gripping my hips, Garrett bends me to his will. He's good at many things, but moving his body tops the list.

"Easy there, cowboy!" I laugh as he dips me.

"You wanted to dance." He grins, pulling me close. "You should've known what you were asking for." He presses the small of my back and tugs me against him. "Close your eyes and let the rhythm take over."

I weave my arms around his neck. "Show me how it's done, Enrique."

"You got it, Leens. Now try to keep up."

Garrett makes dancing easy. His strength and fluid carnality come to life with the music. All eyes are on us—especially a set of Caribbean blues.

The DJ switches gears, and John Legend croons, "All of Me." I squeeze my eyes shut, forcing myself to breathe. A wave of emotion threatens to drown me. Suppressing memories of Wes, I cling to Garrett. Always my rock, my best friend holds me as we sway to the music with a dance floor full of other couples.

"You all right?"

"No, but I will be," I whisper.

He tightens his arms around me and nudges my head closer.

Someone taps Garrett's shoulder. "Mind if I cut in?"

My head darts to the side. "Austin!"

"Lookin' mighty fine, darlin'."

Austin's wearing a fitted charcoal suit with a burgundy shirt and tie. Clean-shaven, with his signature pompadour and sparkling baby-blues in full force, he grins and wraps me in a hug.

"You too. Hot damn, Memphis." I look him over. "Austin, this is Garrett, and Gar, well, you know who *he* is."

Austin shakes Garrett's hand. "Nice to meet you, man. Feel like I already know you."

Garrett smiles. "Nice meeting you too. Thanks for looking out for her in the woods."

"Are you kiddin'? She's the one who kept us alive."

"How are you? How's Katie feeling?" I scan the ballroom. "Is she here?"

"No, she sat this one out. The nausea's been givin' her a run for her money." Austin grins. "Oh, and by the way . . . she said yes."

"Congratulations," I squeal and hug him. "I was hoping to meet her."

"Congratulations," Garrett adds.

"Thanks so much. Don't you worry, you'll meet her soon enough."

"You two dance," Garrett says. "I need a breather." He strides to our table and rejoins Jake and a few others.

"Talk to me, baby girl. What's new? What have you been up to?"

"Not much." I sigh. "Took an extended leave of absence from work. I go back the first week of January. I'll do three twelve-hour shifts a week. That'll free up some time so I can focus on other things."

"Good plan." He lowers his voice. "What happened with Wes?"

"Ask *him*. I'm at a loss."

"I already asked him. Now I want your side."

"He broke things off the other night. Told me I was acting like Rachel because I wanted to know why he was photographed kissing her. Mind you, hours earlier, he'd claimed he wanted to spend the rest of his life with me."

"Jake told me what happened at dinner. I talked to Wes this morning. Did he call you?"

"No clue. I was too upset to deal with my phone. It's in my bedroom somewhere with a dead battery. Why would he call me?"

"To smooth things over. He set a bunch of lawyers loose on the guy who owns the tabloid site."

"Why?"

"To make him retract the story and admit it was fake. You know Wes though. He wanted to beat the shit out of him and the photographer."

I roll my eyes. "Big surprise there."

"Got plastered instead," Austin reveals.

"Had a feeling he was drunk when we spoke."

"Yeah, he drank a bottle of bourbon while waitin' for your call."

I squeeze my eyes shut. "Yeah, I heard it in his voice."

"He didn't know what he was sayin', Lena."

"Booze is no excuse though. I've seen my share of drunken battles—my father's an alcoholic and he's hurt me more than you can imagine." I shake my head. "The difference is, I'm *not* spineless like my mother."

"Just hear what he has to say," Austin suggests. "Give him the benefit of the doubt."

"Tried that the other night. He crossed a line. Drunk or not, his behavior was uncalled for." I meet his gaze. "Austin, I love him, and I know he's your best friend, but I deserve better than that."

"Fair enough." The song changes to one of Austin's, an upbeat track that's all the rage in the club scene. "How 'bout we crank this up to a respectable level?" He grins and spins me dramatically.

"I'm down." I throw myself into the surging fray on the dance floor.

A few songs later, I excuse myself to the ladies' room. After taking a moment to study my reflection, I dance my way into a stall and hike up my gown.

Suddenly, I feel the beginning of a panic attack. *What the fuck? Not here, not now.* I plow from the cramped stall and rush to the sink. Cold water on full blast, I wash my hands and hold my wrists under the icy stream. It should calm me, but it doesn't. I can't catch my breath or think. I frantically dig through my miniature purse to discover I forgot my anxiety meds at home.

Shit. Plan B. I need another drink.

I make a beeline for the bar and nudge my way to the front.

"What can I get you, miss?" the bartender asks.

"A kamikaze, please." I glance at Garrett, who's watching me like a hawk. I need to squash the panic before Grandpa puts the kibosh on me. I saw his disapproving glance when I chugged my champagne. *If he knew I ordered a kamikaze . . .* The last time I got wasted on kamikaze shots, it ended with my near rape in an alley behind a Manhattan karaoke bar—an incident Garrett prevented and nearly wound up behind bars over.

He leans in and says something to Jake. Then, both men watch me. Still a little overheated from my near panic attack, I quickly weave my hair into a braid to get it out of my way. It also gives me something to focus on—other than Garrett's scowl—while I wait for the drink I shouldn't be having.

The bartender places the glass in front of me. "Here you go, Miss."

"Thanks." I hand him a tip and peer over my shoulder.

Austin has joined them. Now, all three are gawking. I smirk and wave. Garrett cocks a brow. I put the glass to my lips, tip my head back, and swallow the contents. Slamming it down onto the bar, I cast a defiant glance in his direction. From across the room, the weight of his golden glare sits heavy on my shoulders. He slowly shakes his head.

"I'll take another, please." I grab a cocktail napkin and distractedly twist it into knots. The bartender sets the glass in front of me. "Thanks."

"You drinking to loosen up?" Caribbean-Sea-Eyes asks, setting her flute of champagne on the bar. Pivoting toward me, she rests her elbows on the edge. Glorious mocha waves flow over her shoulders, cascading down her back.

She's sex on legs.

I stare, lost in the tropical blue of her gaze. *I love men, but she could turn me.* The thought comes unbidden and I flush. The other woman looks at me expectantly.

Right. She asked me a question.

"No, I'm drinking to forget," I reply.

"There's a notion I can get behind." She sips her champagne and stares at the gyrating masses on the dance floor. "Except, sometimes what you're trying to forget is part of your soul."

"I can relate," I mutter, forcing the image of Wes from my mind. I finish my drink and set the glass on the bar.

"I'm Ella."

"Lena."

Lady Gaga's "Bad Romance" begins to play, with its subversive lyrics and intoxicating bass.

Ella takes my hand. "Come dance with me."

I follow the femme fatale to the dance floor and lose myself in the rhythm of the music.

GARRETT

I grit my teeth and watch Lena dance with the vixen in the red dress. The ebb and flow of their hips is sex personified. The brunette makes eye contact with me and whispers something in Lena's ear. Lena beckons me to the dance floor with a curved finger and a come-hither stare.

Austin chuckles. "Uh oh, you're in trouble."

"Jesus Christ," Jake breathes the words, "there's a sight to dream about."

As someone who has battled alcohol dependency, I'm well-versed in the signs of inebriation, and Lena is heading down that road fast. *Time to go.*

"Hate to cut this short, but I need to get her home before she embarrasses herself," I mutter.

"Wait, don't leave yet." Jake scans the ballroom and glances at his watch.

I shake my head. "He missed his opportunity."

Austin motions to the women. "She's just dancing, man."

"You call it dancing, but I watched her drink two kamikazes. I'm not trying to get arrested tonight." I wave Lena over, but she ignores me. "She's so fucking stubborn."

"We got a taste of that in Alaska." Austin chuckles. "Gave Wes a run for his money."

"I bet she did," I say darkly, making no attempt to hide my feelings.

"I know you hate him, but he's not a bad guy," Austin insists. "He fucked up."

"Ever since she came home, I've been busy picking up the pieces. He needs to make up his mind and stop fucking with hers."

Austin nods and turns to Jake. "Where is he?"

"I dunno, Memphis," Jake mumbles. "Garrett, please hang a little longer. I still want to introduce you to some people."

I glance at Lena and sigh. Laughing and smiling as she dances, she seems to be having a great time. *She deserves a night out.*

"Fine. If you tell your bartender to cut her off. She's eaten very little today and barely ate dinner last night."

Jake nods and strides to the bar.

Austin eyes me as he swirls the bourbon in his glass. "You're protective of her."

I meet his gaze. "Wouldn't you be?"

"Absolutely."

"Lena's my family. Can you understand why your boy isn't high on my list?"

Austin nods. "You meet Ella yet?"

"Who's Ella?"

"Lena's dance partner."

I grin wickedly. "Not yet, but I plan to."

Jake returns with a pair of theater bigwigs. Gesturing to me, he says, "Gentlemen, it's my pleasure to introduce you to the face of *Prodigy*, Mr. Garrett Casey."

CHAPTER 44

WES

Life lesson: Go big or go home.

I ignore the photographers' requests for posed red-carpet shots and hurry into the ballroom. Thanks to flight delays, I'm over two hours late for Jake's gala. The place is packed. Loud music thumping, the dance floor is a mass gyration. I scan the room but don't see Lena.

"Emerson," a female voice purrs. "So nice of you to join us."

I make eye contact with Jake's photographer friend. "Hey, Ella. Long time, no see."

"Rough day?" Camera strapped around her neck, she sips from a flute of champagne and studies me curiously.

"You have no idea," I mutter. "Have you seen Jake or Austin?"

"Sure thing." Ella points a fiery red fingernail toward a group that has congregated in the corner of the ballroom. "They're over there rubbing elbows with important people."

"Thanks." I make my way across the room, scanning the crowd.

Austin is engrossed in conversation with another man and doesn't seem to notice my approach.

Jake taps his watch. "Where the hell have you been?"

"My flight to Chicago was delayed. Missed the connection to New York. Big clusterfuck all around." I meet his gaze. "Where is she?"

Jake gestures to the dance floor. "Out there dancing with Ella."

I shake my head. "No, she's not. I just talked to Ella."

He scans the packed dance floor. "Oh. Maybe she went to the restroom."

"You sure Garrett didn't drag her out of here?" Jake's lips curve into a smirk, but he doesn't answer. I step closer to him. "I asked you a question, Bennett."

The man talking to Austin speaks up, "Believe me, the thought crossed my mind, Emerson."

My jaw drops open. *That's Garrett?*

Aside from being the most important figure in Lena's life, the other man is a prime physical specimen. It occurs to me I've never seen pictures, and Garrett far exceeds my expectations. Despite Lena's description of him as a fighter, I'd imagined a smaller man, more on the geeky side.

I size him up, searching for weakness, but it quickly becomes clear I need to reevaluate my approach. At nearly the same height, heavily muscled, and brooding with lethality, Garrett is *not* a man who can be intimidated. Shoulders back, chest puffed, his territorial stance irritates me, so I curl my lip.

Garrett raises a dark brow. "Got a problem?"

Something glints in his freaky gold eyes that has me narrowing mine. "Where's Lena?"

"Dancing."

I stalk to the dance floor and weave through the crowd. Drunken women grab at me, but I brush them off. They mean nothing to me. All I can focus on is Lena, and she isn't here. After a few minutes of searching, I march back over to Garrett.

"Where's Lena?" I repeat.

He scans the crowd, brows furrowing. "Probably vomiting by now."

I bristle. "Why? Is she drunk?"

"Dunno about drunk, but I watched her guzzle a couple kamikazes."

"And ya didn't think to stop her?"

"I made them stay," Jake chimes in, grabbing my arm. "I expected you sooner."

Garrett sets down his glass. "Thought about it, but if the woman wants to drown her sorrows, then who am I to stop her? Besides, she's probably danced off most of the liquor by now, anyway."

I clench my jaw. "That's great. Now, where the fuck *is* she?"

Garrett steps closer, his freaky eyes darkening. "Might wanna rein in that hostility, Emerson."

I glare in response. I don't care how much MMA training he's had; I'll gladly lay the fucker out.

Jake turns to his cousin Vanessa, who stands nearby. "Hey, Ness, can you do me a favor?"

"What's up?" she chirps.

"Please swing into the ladies' room and check on my friend Lena. She's the one in the dark green dress."

"Sure thing." Vanessa heads across the ballroom.

"You want a drink, man?" Austin asks me.

"No. I'm done with that shit."

Bourbon fucked up everything. I shake my head. *No, I fucked up everything.* What was I thinking, agreeing to have dinner with Rachel in the first place? I walked her to the car because it was the right thing to do, but I was an idiot for not anticipating the outcome. Rachel gripped my face and shoved her tongue into my mouth before I even realized what was happening. I was so stunned, that it was a hot minute—or, rather, a hot five *seconds*—before I came to my senses and pulled away. Of course, *that* was the hot minute the paparazzi captured on film. That was the hot minute that threatens to ruin everything I've built with Lena.

They say a picture's worth a thousand words. How about half a million dollars? That's what I paid motherfucking Troy Reynolds to get him to take down the story and pictures. Five hundred thousand dollars. Money that could've been channeled into a charity or environmental agency.

Stewing, I knocked back a bottle of bourbon while waiting for Lena's call. And when she finally called, I lost my bloody mind and broke things off. I still can't believe what I did. I tried to reach her to apologize all day yesterday, to fucking grovel if I had to. I left dozens of messages *begging* her to call me, but she didn't.

Vanessa returns a few minutes later. "She's not in the ladies' room. I checked the lobby and peeked outside too."

Garrett stiffens and yanks his phone from a pocket.

"She doesn't have her phone, man," Austin informs him. "Told me the battery was shot so she left it in her bedroom."

"Son of a bitch." Garrett points to the bar. "There's the woman she was dancing with."

Jake waves Ella over and a chill goes down my spine like always.

Maybe if I weren't so worried about Lena, I could appreciate the way her red dress clings to her curves, but I have zero interest in the seductress. There's no doubt about it, Ella Sammons is attractive in that dangerous way, like a siren who lures a sailor to his ruin. The men around me all seem to notice—especially Garrett. If I gave a fuck about him, maybe I'd warn him off. Tell him she's bad news.

Despite several close encounters, nothing has ever happened between Ella and me. Mainly because there's just something about her that rubs me the wrong way. Something almost . . . sinister. Bottom line, I don't trust the woman, so I'd never involve myself with her.

You trust Lena with your life. My brain offers the contrast like it's something I don't know. Like losing Lena hasn't ripped my fucking heart to shreds. Like I didn't wake up Thursday morning and cry like a baby to my mum about what I'd done.

No, Ella is nothing like the woman I love. I watch her approach, my mind and gut churning over Lena.

She sidles up between me and Jake. "Well, well, well . . . if it isn't the Three Musketeers." She glances at Garrett. "With a new sidekick, I see."

"Hey, El. Have you seen my friend Lena?" Jake asks.

They've been friends since college, and for whatever reason, he's blind to her darkness.

Ella cocks her head to the side and her full, red lips curve into a smile. "My dance partner left with some guy a half hour ago."

"*What?*" Garrett and I say in unison.

She glances at us over her flute of champagne. "Seemed to know him."

"Motherfucking déjà vu right now," Garrett says through a clenched jaw.

"Who was he?" My voice is a low growl.

Ella arches a brow at me, her turquoise eyes glittering with amusement. "I wasn't introduced. But like I said, she seemed to know him."

"What did he look like?" Garrett asks.

"Why are you two acting like you're her brothers?" Ella counters.

"Answer the question, El," Jake commands. "It's important."

Ella glances at Garrett. "Oh, I dunno, a bit shorter than you, dark hair, dark eyes . . . nice body . . ."

"That's all you've got?" Garrett narrows his lion eyes, pinning her with a glare. "You're a photographer. I think you can do better than that."

Ella arches a brow. "Excuse me?"

"I'm asking for a better description," Garrett clarifies slowly, like he's trying to force the hard edge from his tone.

"Why?" Hands on her hips, Ella eyes him, sweeping her gaze up and down. "You gonna cock-block her?"

"Give him a fucking description!" Ella flinches at my snarl. Her widened gaze snaps to mine and she takes a step back, making me feel guilty for scaring her. "Look, Lena has been drinking, and she could be in danger. If someone hurts her, there's gonna be a lot more than cock-blocking to worry about." *Like murder.* She's still staring at me like a deer in headlights, so I try again, "Please tell him what the man looked like."

Ella nods and turns to Garrett. "About six foot, well-built, scar on his jawline—"

"Son of a bitch," Garrett interjects, going ramrod straight. "Jake, do you know your guest list?"

"Some of them," he says. "Hang on, I'll grab a copy from the coordinator." He strides toward the lobby.

"Who is it?" I growl.

Garrett doesn't answer, just stares at the dance floor in broody silence.

I step closer. "You hear me?"

"Wes, chill," Austin commands.

I advance on Garrett, our chests bumping. "I'm talking to you."

Garrett lifts a brow. "I suggest you back the fuck up." His lips twist into a cocky smirk. "Or we can go for a walk if you'd like."

I want to punch the smirk off the fucker's face. Beat the shit out of him.

"Wes, back up," Austin snaps, pulling my arm. He doesn't let go until I take a step back.

Jake returns with a sheet of paper and hands it to Garrett. "She doesn't have the guest list on her right now, but these are the organizations that were invited. Hopefully, that helps."

Garrett scans the names and tenses. "I thought this was mainly entertainment people?"

"Primarily, yes. But money's money. I want this community center done by July, so I'll take donations from whomever wants to give them. Why?"

"What's Fosters United?"

"That's a charity group for foster children. It's run by a bunch of former foster kids who've been successful in life."

Garrett turns to Ella. "What did Lena say to this guy?"

"She wasn't thrilled to see him but agreed to talk. He was sorry about something, but I couldn't hear what."

Garrett nods. "Thanks, that's all I needed to know." He turns to Jake. "I'm heading out. I'll be in touch."

"Where ya goin'?" I demand.

Garrett ignores me and marches from the ballroom.

I turn to Ella. "What else was said?"

"I couldn't hear him over the music." This time she answers right away. I should feel bad about scaring her, but I don't. Not even a little.

"Anything else?" I probe.

She shifts her weight. "I dunno, maybe something about flowers?"

I stiffen and meet Jake's gaze. "You invited her ex?"

"Uh, no, I did not. I gave them my list of people and told them they could add organizations as they saw fit."

I turn back to Ella. "You *sure* she left with him?"

"Watched her get into his Porsche," she whispers.

I see red and it has nothing to do with Ella's gown. "I'm outta here."

"Where the fuck you goin'?" Austin demands.

"I'm going after Lena. But first, I'm gonna have a chat with Garrett."

"Not tonight, you're not," Jake insists. "She's had a few drinks and you're itching for a fight."

"I don't think that's a good idea, man," Austin adds, gripping my shoulders. "You don't wanna fuck with him."

"I don't give a fuck what you—or anyone else—thinks right now. I'm gonna find Lena and make this right. Garrett doesn't wanna fuck with *me*."

Storming from the building, I locate Garrett where he stands at the curb, eyes riveted on his phone.

He spins around to face me as I stalk across the pavement. "Where is she?"

"I dunno."

"But she's with Marc?"

He nods. "Description fits."

"Would he hurt her?" My gut churns with the possibility of Lena in danger.

"No," Garrett shakes his head, "not physically, at least."

"Would he take advantage of her?"

"Doubtful. He barely touched her when they were together."

"What's his last name? Where does he live?"

"Not answering that."

"Why not?" I demand. "She said you hated him."

"Doesn't mean I'm gonna give *you* any information. And for the record, you're not high on my list, either."

"I'm not concerned about your fucking list," I snap. "I want to know where she is."

Garrett steps closer and clenches his fists at his sides. "And *I* want to know why you're here. You plan to fuck with her head some more? I finally got her to stop crying over you. Why should I tell you anything?"

"You're not gonna fucking keep her from me!" I snarl, seconds from losing my shit and smearing him across the sidewalk.

"You're insinuating *I'm* possessive?" He shakes his head. "Lena's her own woman. She wouldn't allow me or any man to control her. Am I protective? You bet your ass I am. Wouldn't you be?"

I don't answer.

"That woman is my family. If you fuck with her, you fuck with *me*," he delivers the warning on a low growl. "And you don't wanna do that." He cocks his head to the side. "I'll ask you again. Why are you here?"

"That's none of your business."

Garrett rubs his jaw. "See, there's where you're wrong. Lena's health, safety, and happiness will *always* be my business. I don't expect you to understand our relationship, and I don't care either way. If you're serious about her, *I'm* not a threat to you." He closes the distance between us, bumping his chest against mine, mirroring my move from inside. His gold eyes burn into mine. "But understand this, Emerson . . . If you hurt her again or try to keep me from her, I *will* become that threat. And I'll come at you like a motherfucking freight train."

"If I weren't serious about her, I wouldn't be here right now, facing legal and financial ramifications for breach of contract. I blew off the fucking premiere. I've been going out of my mind trying to reach her. I didn't come here to argue with you. She won't take my calls, so I came here to confront her face-to-face. I know I fucked up, but I wanna make it right."

"Then you're gonna need to wait until tomorrow when she sobers up."

"I wanna talk to her *now.*"

"Well, she doesn't have her phone and hasn't reached out to me. I know she isn't home because I checked with our neighbors."

"Did he take her to his place?" I demand.

He takes a step back. "I dunno. But I'm gonna find out."

My vision blurs at the thought of her ex putting his hands on her. "And drag her out of there?"

"Not my place to do so. Besides, Lena doesn't take orders from me."

"So, you'd fucking let her stay with *him?*"

"If that's what she wants, yes." Garrett shakes his head. "You don't get it, do you? This isn't some random fucker getting handsy in an alleyway. They have a history and a professional relationship. I'm not about to charge in there like a fucking caveman. Not sure how you operate, but I respect her judgment—even if I hate him."

"She's fucking drunk. She can't possibly know what she wants!"

Garrett raises a brow. "Sound familiar?"

"Yes, I was drunk. I fucked up. I didn't mean any of it." I knot my hands in my hair. "I swear to Christ, I didn't mean it."

"Save your explanation for tomorrow morning when you talk to her."

"I'm talking to her tonight."

A black SUV pulls up to the curb. The driver emerges and opens the door for Garrett.

"Don't walk away from me," I snarl. "I'll be on your doorstep in a fucking hour."

Garrett meets my gaze. "If you show up on our doorstep tonight, I'll have the cops there before you even have a chance to press the buzzer. Don't test me, Emerson," he growls, murder flashing in his eyes. "I won't let you bulldoze her. You'll have to wait until the morning to see her. Maybe try to be sober this time, *Ace.*"

"Who the fuck do you think you are? Her fucking gatekeeper?"

"You're goddamn right, I am."

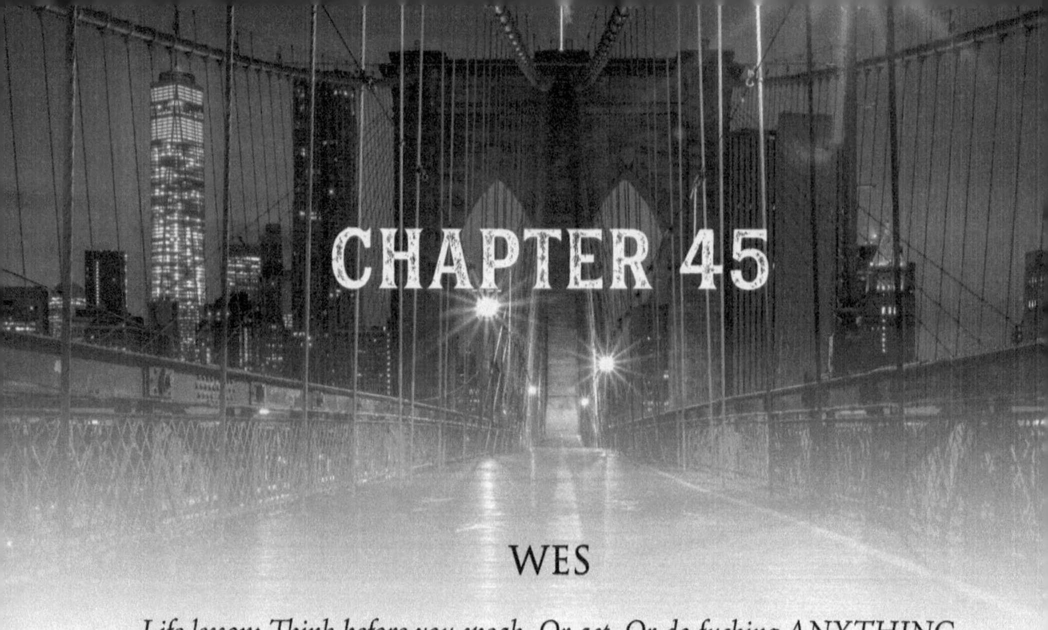

CHAPTER 45

WES

Life lesson: Think before you speak. Or act. Or do fucking ANYTHING.

I lean against the balcony railing outside my hotel room. I have no idea what time it is, and I don't care. The crisp November wind gusts through my hair and chills my skin. I watch the lights and chaos of the street below, a bustling labyrinth of energy. But it isn't energy I feel. It's a mixture of possessiveness, fear, and regret. I want to comb the city and hunt for Lena.

I clench the railing. The caveman inside me wants to break down Marc's door, drag my woman home, and make damn sure she knows who she belongs to. I want to ease the pain I caused her. Apologize. Beg for forgiveness. Fall at her feet. I'll do *anything* to fix this. *Anything.* Instead, I'm forced to do nothing. Forced to wait until morning. Garrett has me by the fucking balls and there's nothing I can do about it. I picture the other man's cocky smirk and clench my fists tighter.

Fucking Garrett.

Ella promptly emailed Jake her pictures, making a point to attach dance floor footage. I snatched the phone before Jake had the chance to delete it. I didn't expect the volcanic jealousy the footage triggered, especially the slow song. Taunted by the image of Lena's arms woven around Garrett's neck and his low grip on her waist, it was all I could do to control myself. My mind replays a continuous loop of the sensuous arch of her body when Garrett dipped her. Austin had to pry Jake's phone from my grip.

But she didn't leave with Garrett . . . she left with Marc.

A man who'd already taken steps to win her back.

Marc is the true threat.

I turn my attention skyward. The full moon cloaks the scene in an ethereal sterling glow. I think about Lena's smile. Her sass. Her stubbornness. Ella had captured moments of laughter, broad smiles, and the vivid jade of Lena's eyes. I envision her in that green dress and clench my jaw. I remember making love to her in our hotel room. She is so exquisitely beautiful that it takes my breath away. And she's out there somewhere with another man. All because I was too drunk to listen. *I'm no better than her father.*

My cell rings. Hope surges, only to dissolve when I see who's calling. Reed. I've been ignoring his calls for hours, but sooner or later I need to face my actions.

"What?" I snarl.

"Where the fuck are you?"

"In New York."

"Chasing that woman?"

"I'm not chas—"

"You're off your bloody rocker, mate!" he bellows into the phone. "Do you have any fucking idea what you've done?"

"I know what I'm doing."

"Oh, do you? That's funny. Did you forget you have a contract?"

"Nope." I clench my jaw. "Is there a purpose to this call?"

"You skipped the premiere."

"I'm aware."

"This isn't you, mate. You're being reckless. You breached the most important contract of your career."

"Fuck my career," I bark, regretting the words the moment they leave my lips.

"Fuck your career, eh? Yeah, fuck all those opportunities. Fuck following your dream when others can't. Who gives a fuck about acting anyway?" The coldness in his tone turns my blood to ice.

"Reed, I'm sorry. I didn't mean—"

"I saw the account—you shelled out five hundred grand to Troy

Reynolds to protect that woman's image. Now you're kicking your responsibilities to the curb like some callous, pussy-whipped cunt. For what, Wes?"

My blood comes to a rolling boil. "I did what needed to be done."

"Oh, yeah? I thought Rachel was bad for you—"

My vision blurs. "Don't go there, Reed."

"I'm serious. I hope your train wreck of a girlfriend will stick around when no one wants to hire you for a job."

"Don't you fucking dare talk about her that way!" My roar reverberates against the surrounding skyscrapers.

Austin and Jake burst through the door onto the balcony.

"Grow the fuck up, Wes. You can have any girl you want. Don't waste your time on tras—"

A battle-cry rips from my chest as I heave my phone over the balcony. Moments later, a crash from twelve stories below tells me it landed.

Jake and Austin don't move or speak.

I'm so enraged, I couldn't speak if I wanted to.

CHAPTER 46

LENA

*Internal playlist: "Say Something" by A Great Big World and
Christina Aguilera*

Pouring more syrup on my pancakes, I peer across the table at Marc.
He slices his omelet with a surgeon's precision.

"What?" he asks.

"You think those eggs are gonna run away?"

He chuckles. "Not if I can help it." He takes a generous forkful and
smiles while he chews.

My ex-fiancé is the last person I expected to see at Jake's gala. Evidently,
he's a benefactor for some charity organization for foster kids. Who knew?
When he approached Ella and me on the dance floor and begged me to hear
him out, I was tempted to tell him to fuck off. But I didn't. Mainly because
I was starving, and he offered to feed me.

"I love pancakes," I mumble. "Thanks for taking me for dinner."

"This hardly qualifies as dinner, but you're welcome."

"It's the first thing I've eaten all day."

His eyes soften. "Why aren't you eating?"

"I dunno. Just . . . stuff."

"When are you coming back to work? We miss you."

"January third."

Marc nods. "Dr. Soteris mentioned you declined that promotion."

"Yep. It's not for me."

"I disagree," he says, taking a sip of his coffee. "You're more than qualified."

"I may be qualified, but I don't want the pressure. After everything that happened, the added stress isn't worth it to me."

"I'm glad you're safe."

"I know."

Marc meets my gaze. "I, uh, I was so worried about you . . . I asked Garrett to keep me in the loop." He shakes his head. "He didn't, of course. Not that I expected him to."

"You know Gar," I begin. "He's—"

"He hates me." Marc squeezes my hand. "It's all right. I'd hate me too." He sighs heavily. "Listen, Lena, I'm sorry . . . for everything."

"It's fine, Marc—"

"Hear me out." He pauses. "Please."

"Go ahead. You have my full attention."

"I realize I wasn't good to you. I was so fucking stupid. I . . . I loved you, Lena. Please know that. I still do. I just don't know how—"

"I know, Marc." I squeeze his hand back. "You loved me to the best of your ability. I know you didn't intend to hurt me, but you did."

"I'm sorry," he whispers. "And I'm sorry about the flowers. I don't know what came over me. I wanted to reach out but didn't have the balls. And I read the card he sent and I—"

"Yeah, that was pretty fucked-up."

"I'm sorry," he repeats. "And I'm sorry I sent you those pictures. You didn't need that thrown in your face."

"Maybe you did me a favor," I mutter, toying with the end of my braid.

"Are you guys together?"

"Not to my knowledge. He made that clear when I questioned him."

"You said you loved him," Marc starts.

"I *do* love him."

"Then, where is he?"

I sigh. "At his premiere, I assume."

"Do you love me?"

His question catches me off guard, so I drop my fork. It takes me a moment to formulate an appropriate response. "Marc, I care about you and always will. For four years, I loved you with all my heart. But you can't give me what I need." I slowly shake my head. "I won't settle for less than I deserve. I'd rather be alone."

"What if I changed? Would you give me another chance?"

"I gave you years' worth of chances. You forgot my birthday, Marc."

"What do you want? I'll buy it—"

"I didn't want *something*, I wanted *you*. But you were never there for me. I wanted your time, your attention, your affection. I wanted you to talk to me, listen to me. I wanted you to hold me, kiss me, make love to me . . . but you were always too busy. I was never your priority, Marc. I was an afterthought. And I deserve better than that."

"What if I scale back at the hospital?" he offers. "Give me a chance to show you I can change."

"If you'd come to me over the summer, it would be different. I would've given you another chance, but I can't now. I'm sorry."

"Why?"

"Because I'm in love with someone else. I've felt what it's like to be respected, worshiped, and loved, and there's no going back for me."

"Even if he's out of the picture?"

"Yes." I meet his gaze fiercely. "I love him even if he doesn't want me. I care about you, Marc, but I don't love you anymore. I can't. It's not healthy for me."

"I really fucked you up, didn't I?" He looks down at his hands. "Lena, I'm so sorry I hurt you. I loved you then, and I love you now. If you change your mind, you know where to find me."

We finish our meal in silence. I feel lighter after finally baring my heart to Marc, but I just want to go home.

"May I please use your phone? I need to call Garrett." I glance at the clock on the wall and grimace. It's after four a.m. "Or a cab."

"Why?"

"To go home."

Marc sighs. "I'll drive you home, Lena. You don't need to wake him or call a cab."

"Thank you."

Marc pulls up in front of the brownstone and cuts the engine. Gaze riveted to my face, he watches as I unfasten my seat belt.

"Thanks for dinner and for bringing me home."

"My pleasure, Lena," he murmurs. "I meant everything I said."

"I know." I reach for his hand and squeeze it.

"So, this is goodbye?"

"I'll see you when I come back to work," I insist.

"You know what I mean."

"Yes, this is goodbye."

Marc nods. "May I please hug you?"

"Of course." I wrap my arms around him. "I love hugs."

Marc hugs me tightly and I feel the emotion in his embrace. *Maybe if he'd hugged me like this when we were together, I would've stuck around.*

Then, he cups my face and kisses me slowly and deeply. I try, but I can't force myself to kiss him back. Feeling my hesitance, Marc clasps the back of my neck and pulls me closer. I yank from his hold and gasp, wrapping my arms around myself.

"Fuck! Lena, I forgot," he admits, raking a hand through his hair. "I'm sorry."

"How could you forget something like that, Marc?" I sputter. "How could you forget that a man squeezed my neck and tried to kill me? This is exactly what I mean. I'm an afterthought."

"Lena, I—"

"No! Please don't." I shove the car door open. "Goodnight, Marc."

Slamming it behind me, I run up the stoop without looking back. Marc speeds away as I fish for my keys inside my clutch.

The front door is yanked open from the inside. Garrett appears in the doorway, a dark expression on his face.

"Where the fuck have you been?"

"Gar, please. I can't do this right now." I push past him into the foyer.

He steps aside and closes the door. "You ghost out of the fucking gala with no call, no text—"

"I forgot my phone. I'm sorry." I rush up the stairs.

"I went to his place, but you weren't there." He follows, taking the steps two at a time. "Where'd he take you?"

I shove my key into the lock. "How'd you know I was with Marc?"

"Don't underestimate me, Leens."

"Look, nothing happened—"

"Then why are you crying?" he snaps. "Did he hurt you?"

"No, he didn't hurt me." I enter the apartment with Garrett on my tail. "He came up to me on the dance floor and wanted to talk. We couldn't hear over the music. He asked if I was hungry, and I was. We went to the diner and talked."

"For four hours?" He follows me into the kitchen.

"We had a lot to say," I insist, finally meeting his gaze. "Plus driving time."

"Why are you crying?" he repeats.

"I'm not."

"Don't bullshit me. You have tears on your cheeks."

"Because he just fucking kissed me, okay?" I snap, flailing my arms in exasperation.

"I knew he'd come crawling back."

"Garrett, enough." I wave a finger in his face. "I don't have the energy for this right now. I'm sorry you were worried."

He snatches my wrist. "Don't put your hand in my face, you know I hate that." His expression softens. "I just dealt with you being lost in the wilderness . . . Then I have to relive the karaoke fiasco? You have no idea what kind of shit crossed my mind."

"I'm sorry. I should've told you where I was going."

"I wasn't the only one who was worried."

I sigh. "Yeah, I know. I'll call Jake tomorrow."

He tilts his head to the side. "Not talking about Jake."

I prop my hands on my hips. "Gar, I've been up all night. Spare me the riddles."

"Emerson."

"What?" I breathe. "Who the hell called *him*?"

"Nobody called him, Lena. He blew off the premiere and showed up at the gala."

"*What?*"

"You heard me."

I clutch my chest. "Why?"

"For *you*, Leens. He broke his contract and flew across the country for you."

"Why would he do that? He said he was done with me . . ."

Garrett rubs his jaw. "Had a change of heart, I guess."

I stare at his face and try to make sense of his words. Wes came after me. *He came for me.*

"Gotta tell you, he's more hotheaded than you described. Nearly had to kick his arrogant ass . . . and I still might."

"What happened?"

"He was hell-bent on hunting you down and killing Marc, so—"

"Oh my God," I croak, sinking to a kitchen stool. "Wes knows I left with Marc?"

"Sure does." Garrett leans a hip against the island. "And he wasn't happy about it."

"Nothing happened, Gar. I swear to God," I sputter. "We just talked. I mean, Marc kissed me in the car before, but I didn't kiss him back. I couldn't. I felt *nothing*, absolutely nothing. And he knew it. He even grabbed my neck and tried to pull me closer, but I freaked out."

Garrett pops his brows. "He knows better than to touch your neck."

"Yeah." I force a dark laugh. "He said he *forgot*."

"He forgot?" He narrows his eyes. "How the fuck did he forget that?"

"Right," I say bitterly. "He went on about how he wants me back, promising to cut his hours, do whatever it takes to fix it. Said he realized he wasn't good to me and wanted to prove he's changed." I toss my braid over a shoulder. "I think he meant it and part of me wanted to believe him, you know? But obviously, nothing's changed. It's one thing to forget my birthday, but he can't remember I was *assaulted?* Four years together and he doesn't remember the nightmares, the panic attacks?" I shake my head. "I told him I wasn't in love with him anymore. He can't give me what I need."

"And how'd he respond?"

"Better than expected. But then he asked about Wes."

"Did you tell him anything?" He crosses his arms. "Or was the fucker pleased with himself for sending those pictures?"

"I would've seen them eventually, Gar," I insist, my shoulders slumping in sadness. "But at least he apologized for rubbing it in my face."

"Well, that's big of him."

"Yeah." I sigh. "I told him I'm in love with Wes. Even if it's not recip-rocated, even if he's out of the picture . . . I'll always love him. Wes changed me. Now I know what it feels like to be a priority, even if it was only for a little while." I bite the inside of my cheek in an effort not to cry. "Gar, I won't let myself be anyone's afterthought. I won't go down that road again. I deserve better—even if that means being alone."

"How quickly you forget that you're *mine*, sunshine."

CHAPTER 47

LENA

Internal playlist: "My Kind of Love" by Emeli Sandé

I spin around with a gasp and nearly fall off my stool. Wes is leaning against the living room doorway, arms crossed over his chest, gaze locked on my face.

"Have you been here this whole time?" I sputter.

"No. I teleported in. You didn't see that flash of light a few minutes ago?"

Fucking Garrett didn't think to warn me? I shoot my best friend a death glare, and the bastard has the audacity to smirk.

Wes approaches the island and stands over me. "Apparently, I didn't make myself clear enough."

"You were crystal-clear on the phone. You know, when you told me it was over. For a man who never says goodbye, you sure said it loud and clear."

"I didn't mean any of that."

I raise an eyebrow. "I thought you don't say things you don't mean?"

"Lena, I was drunk, and I fucked up. I've been trying to get ahold of you since Thursday. I would've hunted you down last night, but your guard over there wouldn't allow it." He glances at Garrett.

"I told him he could talk to you in the morning after you'd sobered up," Garrett explains. "Asshole was banging the door down at four-thirty."

"You said morning," Wes replies smoothly. "It's morning."

"I'm surprised you let him in." I arch a brow at Garrett. "You're on my shit list, by the way."

"It may have been that sliver of compassion in my cold Grinch heart, but for whatever reason, I get the feeling he's serious about you." Garrett grins. "Could also be the fact that he *begged*."

He begged? I can't picture Wes Emerson begging anyone for anything, but he'd begged Garrett. *To get to me.*

I meet Wes's gaze. "Marc kissed me, but nothing else happened."

"I know. I heard everything you said. Lucky for you, Garrett insisted on being the one to meet ya at the door." He clenches his jaw. "I would've lost my shit if I saw him kiss you."

"Imagine how it felt to see similar pictures and then get your head ripped off when you tried to ask someone for their side."

"I'm sorry." Wes touches my shoulder. "Like I said, I was drunk."

"For the record, I don't care if you were drunk, high, or under a spell. Bourbon's no excuse for hurtful behavior. *Never* speak to me like that again." I step closer and narrow my eyes. "I've witnessed my share of hearts broken by alcoholism. Mine won't be one of them."

"It won't happen again, love," Wes insists. "I'm so sorry."

"That was the one and *only* time I'll allow you to use booze as an excuse. Unlike my mother, *I* won't put up with it. Don't test me."

"It won't happen again," he repeats.

"See, Leens? Everyone's happy now, and I saved you the hassle of being interrogated. You're welcome." Garrett grips my chin and turns my head to face him. "You're on my shit list too. Thanks to your antics, I didn't get to acquaint myself with that photographer."

"Jake's already planning to introduce you," Wes says. "Wants Ella to score the first interview for *Prodigy*."

"Good to know." A wicked smirk transforms Garrett's face. "She might get more than she bargained for."

"You're gross. Go home," I command.

Garrett grins. "I'm taking my suit to the dry cleaner's when they open. Gimme your dress."

I glance at myself. *I must've been quite the sight in that diner.* Eager to remove the heavy garment, I nod.

"That works, thanks. I'm gonna change into comfortable clothes. Be right back." I head for my bedroom.

"I wouldn't bother with clothes, love," Wes calls out.

I turn on my heel and march back into the kitchen. Hands on my hips, I stop in front of Wes. "I don't think so, Ace. You and I need to talk. You're in for a rude awakening if you think I'm gonna let you touch me anytime soon."

"Oh, I think you will."

Garrett chuckles.

"And I think *you're* delusional," I snap, rounding on Garrett. "Don't encourage him." I storm from the kitchen and bound up the stairs.

"Keep stomping, sunshine," Wes shouts after me.

He's infuriating.

I quickly change into yoga pants and a flannel and head for the kitchen. Both men smirk as I enter and plop the gown in Garrett's arms.

I wave a finger at Wes. "Keep it up, and I'll stomp you."

Wes glances at Garrett. "Told you she doesn't take any of my shit."

"And I'm not about to start."

"Atta girl." Garrett squeezes my shoulders. "All right, I'm out." He kisses my forehead. "Love you, Leens." He turns to leave but pauses in the doorway. "Later, *Ace.*"

"Garrett, thank you," Wes says quietly.

He gives a curt nod. "Just don't fuck up."

"I won't."

"Two words." Gesturing to himself, Garrett adds, "Freight. Train."

"Got it."

Garrett smiles and leaves the apartment.

"Freight train?" I probe.

Wes sighs heavily. "Sunshine, it's a *long* story."

"I'm listening."

"He threatened my life if I hurt you or try to keep you from him."

"Sounds like Garrett. Tell me the rest. What happened with Rachel?"

"I don't even know where to start."

"Try the beginning."

"I walked Rachel to her car after we got a bite to eat. She cried about her aunt, so I hugged her, but then she grabbed me and kissed me. I took a moment to react because I wasn't expecting it. I mean, she'd just gotten through telling me about her fiancé at dinner. When my brain finally kicked in, I pulled away and told her about you. Rachel apologized and left. I didn't think anything of it and went home. I didn't know we were being followed by paparazzi."

"You know, Wes, if you'd called me and said, 'Hey, I ran into my ex and grabbed food. She unexpectedly kissed me when I walked her to the car,' this would've played out quite differently."

"You can't honestly tell me you would've been fine with that," Wes protests.

"No, I wouldn't have been thrilled, but I would've appreciated the fact that you came to me and told me. Instead, Marc sent me the pictures in a text, with a snarky message that read, 'Isn't this your new man?'"

Wes grabs my hand and rubs his thumb across my knuckles. "I'm sorry."

"And when I tried to be reasonable and give you the benefit of the doubt, you treated me like shit. I asked for your side of things because that's what matters to me, not some gossip nonsense. I trusted you enough to come to you when my instincts screamed for me to walk away." I narrow my eyes. "Then you accuse me of being jealous and insecure. And you know what? Maybe I *am* jealous and insecure, but I'm *nothing* like Rachel. I won't come between you and your family, or your career. I'll do nothing but love and support you, push you forward, and encourage you. I don't do guilt trips or ultimatums—I ask questions. Big difference. Don't compare me to *her*."

"I'm sorry, love."

"I know you overheard me telling Garrett, but here's what happened. I *forced* myself to go to Jake's gala because he's my friend and I wanted Garrett to make some connections. Marc came up to me when I was dancing with Ella. We couldn't hear each other, so we left and went to the diner. I should've told Garrett, but I didn't want any of his shit." I sigh. "Anyway, we talked for a few hours, which morphed into him saying he wanted me back. I told him I couldn't do it. I was going to call Garrett to come get me, but Marc insisted on bringing me home. You know the rest."

"What if it had been someone else you left with? Would we be having the same conversation?"

"Maybe not." I shrug. "But the difference is, we're having *this* conversation. I'm answering your questions and telling *you* to your face what happened. Not waiting for you to get it secondhand."

Wes nods.

"Anything else you'd like to know?"

"Why would ya wanna forget about me?"

"Because you gave up on me. You didn't trust in *me* enough to hear what I was asking. All you heard was someone questioning you. Then you equated me to Rachel. This is all new to me—the spotlight, the attention, the paparazzi, all of it. I'm doing the best I can and trying to adjust. Don't *I* deserve the benefit of the doubt too? Isn't there a learning curve here? Don't I deserve an explanation when pictures like that surface?"

"That's why I'm here."

"Wes, I can't believe you skipped the premiere. Won't that cause issues?"

"According to Reed, some legal and financial trouble, but I really don't give a fuck." He shrugs. "It's not like they can cut me out of the film." He grips my chin. "You're more important than some fucking red-carpet bullshit."

"I've brought enough drama into your life—I don't want to be the reason for career drama too."

"Sunshine, you're the only reason I'm alive right now."

"You know what I mean, Wes." I run a hand over my face. "Your brother probably hates me."

"I don't care what Reed thinks and neither should you. Listen, I know I fucked up and I'm sorry. If you let me, I promise I'll fix this. After all we've been through, I'm not lettin' ya go." His eyes bore into mine. "And I'll be damned if I let someone take you from me. We both know you're mine, sunshine." He trails his fingertips down the column of my throat. "Even your body knows it. No one else can touch you like this."

My eyes flutter closed. "Only you."

"Can anyone else do this?" He dips his head and kisses my neck.

"No."

"Then tell me you're mine," he commands, his lips at my ear.

"It's a two-way street, Ace."

He kisses my ear. "Whaddya mean?"

"I won't be yours unless you're *mine*. And I don't think you have what it takes."

"Whaddya want from me?" He nips my lobe. "Spell it out."

"Stop kissing me and pay attention."

Wes meets my gaze. "I'm listening."

"I need us to be equals."

"We are, love."

I hold a finger to his lips. "I don't share well. I'll share you with your family, your friends, your career, and your fans. But I will *not* share you with another woman. Not under any circumstance. I'll trust you and give you the benefit of the doubt, but when I ask a question, I expect an answer. I expect the answer before I need to ask the question. I want *you* to come to me. Tell me what happened. No matter how trivial or insignificant it may seem. And if I feel the need to question you, I don't want any of your shit. *That* is what it means to be mine."

Eyes clear and focused, his gaze doesn't leave my face.

"If you can't handle that, or if you *truly* believe I'm like Rachel, then you need to walk away right now." I grip his chin. "Because I won't settle for pieces of you, either. I need you to make a serious commitment to me, Wes. Point blank, I want a family one day. I want forever with you. If you can't give me that, then turn around and walk out the door."

He doesn't move.

"Did you hear me?" I grit my teeth. "I told you to walk away. Do it now so we don't waste each other's time." I draw in a slow breath and whisper, "Walk away."

Wes grips my shoulders and crushes my body to his. Hands knotting in my hair, he swallows my gasp of surprise. I close my eyes and absorb the ferocity of his kiss. Deep, plundering, and intense, his tongue surges into my mouth. I clasp his neck, pulling him deeper, kissing him with a desperation of my own.

He breaks the kiss. "I'm not going anywhere, sunshine. I'll do whatever it takes to show you how sorry I am. I need you. I'm fucking *lost* without you. I'll travel to the ends of the Earth for ya, but I swear to God, I'll never walk away from you again." He strokes his thumbs over my cheeks. "You've seen me at my worst. Now I'm begging you to let me give you my best."

I stare into his gorgeous eyes. "I want all of you, Wes, not just your best."

He smiles and kisses me. "I love you, sunshine."

"I love you too," I whisper. "Where do we go from here?"

"I'm a man of action, so we solidify our commitment with action." Lifting my hand to his lips, he presses a kiss to my knuckles. "I'm yours, love. Mind, body, heart, and soul, I belong to you."

"But your home's an ocean away," I remind him. "And you love to surf."

Wes flashes a wicked grin. "I'd rather ride you than any wave."

I roll my eyes. "You know what I mean."

"For me, home isn't a place, it's a feeling. You're that feeling. *You* are my home, Lena. I want to be where you are, wherever that path leads us. I don't care where we live."

I pull his lips to mine and pour my heart into the kiss.

After a few minutes, Wes pulls back. "You realize what all this means, right?"

"What?" I whisper.

He brushes his lips on my ear. "Make-up sex."

"Not right now, Ace. I've been up all night."

"Me too," he insists. "We can sleep afterward. Right now, we're going to hunker down in this flat and pick up where we left off. No distractions . . . and no interruptions. I'm gonna take my time and show you what I've wanted to do since I first laid eyes on you. I'm gonna give it to you the right way."

"We'll see about that." I turn to leave the kitchen.

Wes seizes me around the waist. "Where ya goin'?"

"To take a nap."

"No, sunshine, you're taking off your clothes." Wes prowls to the front door. Eyes locked on mine, he slides the deadbolt. "Did ya hear me?" His voice is a husky rumble that hardens my nipples.

"Heard you just fine, Ace." I cock a brow at his approach. "Got two words for you . . ."

He looms over me. "I'm all ears, love."

"Make me."

"Was hoping you'd say that." He focuses below my waist, licks his lips, and dips his head. His teeth graze my ear. "I'm gonna make it impossible for you to forget me, sunshine."

I inhale sharply and Wes advances. A countertop blocks my retreat. I grip the edge as he trails his fingertips from my collarbone to the curve of my breast. He kisses the side of my neck and I squeeze the granite tighter.

"I want you." He lifts me onto the counter and grasps the end of my braid. Gaze burning into mine, he removes the elastic and shoots it across the kitchen. He slowly unravels the strands and runs his fingers through my hair. "Tell me you're mine."

I bite my lower lip. "Make me."

Wes clears the counter with a swipe of his arm. The fruit basket flips, bananas go flying and several apples thud to the floor. Without skipping a beat, he presses my torso back and climbs onto the island. He seizes my mouth and straddles my hips. I savor the delicious weight of his body.

Lips traveling to my neck, he kisses and licks. The scrape of his stubble intensifies the wet heat of his mouth. His breath gusts over my throat, sending shivers down my spine.

"Oh, God, Wes," I moan.

"I'm just getting started, love."

Wes takes his time unbuttoning my shirt, his fingertips brushing my skin. Halfway down, he grips the flannel and tugs it open. Buttons pop off and land alongside the fallen fruit. I gasp as he yanks the material from my shoulders and shreds it.

"You won't be needing that," he growls.

He flings the shirt, which lands on the ceiling fan. He moves aside and slowly slides the yoga pants over my hips to mid-thigh, then yanks them the rest of the way off. He tosses them on the floor and grips my ankles. With a flick of his wrists, my socks are gone. The interplay between his slow, deliberate motions and primal aggression ignites me, and the anticipation of his next move is nearly as enticing as the actions themselves.

Wes slides my bra straps over my shoulders, tugs it to my waist, then unclasps and chucks it across the kitchen. Warm palms cup my breasts. He dips his head and licks at the lower curve of my right breast before slowly flicking his tongue over the nipple. His thumb mirrors the action on my other breast, causing me to moan and squirm beneath him. I feel his smile as he continues to unravel me. On my back beneath the heavy weight of his body, I try to dig my fingertips into the cool granite.

Wes rears up. His molten gaze comes to rest at my navel, then lower. He strokes his hands down my sides to my waist, sliding his fingertips beneath the waistband of my panties. Clenching the lace, he swiftly rips them down the center. I gasp and clutch the countertop. He shreds the panties and launches them across the kitchen. "You definitely won't be needing those," he growls, leaning down to kiss me.

Tongues melding, I fist my hands in his hair and pull him closer. His dress shirt's smooth material brushes against my breasts. The denim of his jeans strokes me lower. I dig my heels into his ass, drawing him closer.

Wes pulls back and hops from the counter. He walks across the kitchen, flings the pantry door open, and returns with a bottle of caramel syrup.

I gasp. *How'd he know that was in there?* "That'll make a sticky mess."

His eyes darken in response to my weak protest. "Good thing we've got running water, sunshine."

Standing at the island between my legs, he grips behind my knees and yanks my body to the counter's edge. He flashes a wolfish grin, drizzles syrup on my thighs and lower abdomen, then sets the bottle aside. He drags a stool over. Metal scrapes the tile as he positions it in front of me.

Oh my God, he's pulling up a fucking chair.

Gripping my hips, he yanks me closer and trails his tongue up my thigh. He licks and sucks the syrup off, moaning against my skin. I gasp as he repeats the motion on the other side. Then he slowly sinks onto the stool and nips at my kneecap, guiding my legs over his shoulders. Face between my thighs, he turns his attention to the caramel on my belly, swirling his tongue lower and lower. Pausing just above my clit, he meets my gaze and I feel his hands tighten on my ass.

"Get comfortable, sunshine. We're gonna be here awhile."

My body bows off the counter when he puts his mouth on me. My sweat-slicked hands skid on the granite. Holding my hips in place, the rasp of his stubble brushes my inner thigh. He pleasures me with sensual, swirling licks, then squeezes my ass and spears his tongue inside me. Moaning, I grip his biceps. He groans and it reverberates to my core. Hips bucking in his hold, Wes brings me to the edge with his tongue's merciless crusade.

He surrounds my clit with gentle suction and slowly eases one finger inside. He rapidly flicks his tongue and adds another finger. It never ceases to amaze me how quickly he can make me come. The wanton moans that escape my throat spur him on. A third finger joins the others, his thrusts matching the rhythm of his tongue.

I moan his name, fracturing into a million scintillating pieces. His marauding mouth continues its quest, and my clit is defenseless against the onslaught. His fingers thrust inside me, stretching me, preparing me for him.

"Oh God, Wes," I wail. "I can't take it . . ." I orgasm again, this one more intense than the first. Hips thrashing in his hold, my entire body trembles with the aftershocks of the climax.

And still, he doesn't stop.

He's gonna burn me alive.

My body arches off the granite. A stack of mail goes flying, some clementines fall, and glass shatters on the floor. I don't give a fuck. Wes groans into me and thrusts his fingers. The third orgasm steals my breath. I can't scream, can't move.

Finally, he relents.

My hands slide over the countertop as he climbs to his feet and kicks the stool aside. It crashes to the floor and skids a few feet before it stops. He stands between my legs, grabs my wrists, and yanks me upward. He brings those plush lips to mine in a bruising kiss, giving me a taste of caramel and myself.

"Ready for me, love?"

I can't answer through my gasps.

"I'll take that as a yes," he growls, hoisting me off the island.

Wes tosses me over his good shoulder and carries me upstairs. When we enter my bedroom, he kicks the door closed, pausing at my full-length mirror. He grins at our reflection. I stare at him in shock. Then, he tightens his arm over my thighs and slaps my bare ass.

Crying out, I grip his back. He holds me in place and slaps the other cheek. And again. And once more.

"I seem to recall someone requesting a spanking."

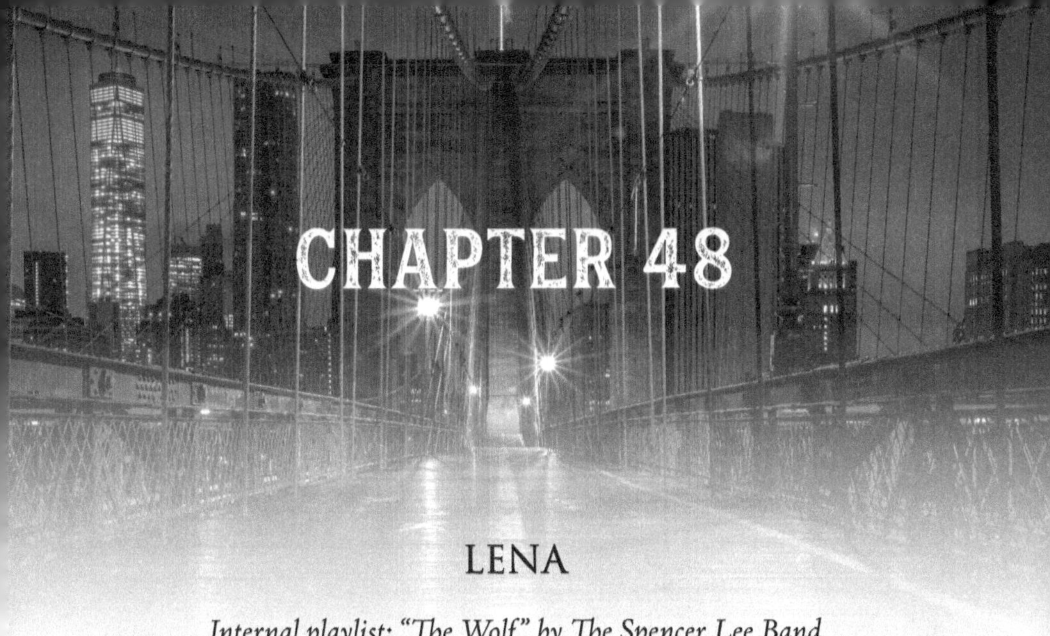

LENA

Internal playlist: "The Wolf" by The Spencer Lee Band

In the mirror, I watch as Wes trails his fingertips up the backs of my thighs. Gaze locked on mine; lust rolls off him in waves. He prowls across the room, settles on the foot of the bed, and positions my body facedown on his lap.

"Do you remember that conversation, Lena?"

"Yes," I moan.

He holds me in place with an arm across my back. Smiling at our reflection, he feathers his touch over my exposed cheeks.

"Don't think I heard ya," he murmurs with an ass slap.

"Yes!"

"Good." His eyes darken. "I wanted to make sure that wasn't one of the things you hoped to forget about me . . . Is this what you had in mind?" He lightly smacks my rear.

I gasp. My fantasy has come to life—and it is hotter than I could've ever imagined.

"Or this?" He gives my ass a hard strike.

"Oh, God, Wes," I moan, clutching his jeans.

"You want a sting?" He traces the curve of my spine. "I'll give it to ya." He slaps my ass again, hard.

"Oh, *fuck.*" His hand comes down again. "Wes!"

"Now I'm gonna give you that hard fuck you've been asking for, sunshine."

In one swift motion, he flips me over and tosses me onto the bed. Off comes his shirt. His belt hits the floor with a clunk. He kicks off his jeans, sheds his boxers, and stands at the foot of the bed, hard as a rock and fucking huge.

Wes prowls up the bed to me. "You ready to get fucked through this mattress?"

He shoves my legs apart, kneels between them, and lifts my ankles to his shoulders. Then, he grips my hips and plunges deep inside. No prelude, no slow ease in. The power in his first thrust makes me scream.

His hands clench my ass as he works his hips in a driving rhythm. My spine bows off the bed, and I wail his name, spurring him on. The slap of his body against mine is evidence of the determination in his thrusts.

"Tell me you're mine."

"Make me." I gasp, flexing my hips to meet him.

He groans and slams into me, increasing the speed and intensity. Like always, he brings me over the edge in no time.

"Wes, oh, God, yes!"

The power in his thrusts forces my ankles from his shoulders. Surging forward, he kisses me, his tongue in rhythm with his strokes. Then he pulls out, flips me onto my stomach, and yanks my hips back. Pressing my shoulders into the mattress, he thrusts deep inside, and knocks me off-balance. I scream into the mattress. He clamps his hands on my hips and pulls me back up, holding me in place while he thrusts.

"Tell me you're mine," he repeats on a growl.

"I'm yours," I moan, fisting the comforter. "Fuck me."

The guttural sounds that leave his throat mix with my moans. I orgasm again. Legs shaking, knees giving out. Wes moves in a brutal rhythm, pausing every now and then to slap my ass. After a few strikes, he pulls out and flips me onto my back once more. A picture of savage lust, he surges inside me and buries his face in my neck. The angle and his wild thrusts trigger another intense orgasm.

"Let me hear you." He sucks on my throat. "Fucking scream for me."

My cries echo through the bedroom, my inner muscles spasm and clench around him.

Wes groans. "Oh, fuck, Lena . . ."

The raw, animalistic lust that drives him is relentless. Incandescent. Clawing his back and shoulders, I absorb the power of his thrusts as he gives me everything he has.

Finally, he passes the point of no return. Guttural shouts and gasps fill the room as he releases the entirety of his soul into me.

"You're killing me, woman," Wes sputters, collapsing on top of me.

Gasping, I cling to him and trail my fingertips down his back. We stay like this for several minutes. Our bodies still joined; we hold on to one another for dear life.

"I love you so much, Lena."

I tighten my arms around him. "I love you too."

He meets my gaze. "Are you all right?"

"Yes, I'm all right. Thank you for coming after me," I whisper, lips swollen from his kisses. "I never want to lose you again."

"You won't lose me, sunshine. I wanna spend the rest of my life making you mine." He kisses me in a slow, deep tango of tongues. "I'm never lettin' ya go."

"I won't let go, either." Reaching up, I run my fingers through his hair. "I'm yours, Wes. No matter what the universe throws at us. We were destined to spark and catch fire, remember?" I kiss his lower lip. "Now we need to keep burning."

"I'll always burn for you, love. I'm so happy I found you."

"We found each other, Wes."

After our four-hour nap, Wes and I venture into the kitchen for food. I survey the mess, hands on my hips. Clementines litter the island and the fruit bowl lies broken on the floor. Several utility bills are smeared with caramel syrup. Hermione has gnawed the top of a pineapple off and is currently retching in the corner. Cue the cat vomit. I snatch a roll of paper towels and clean it up.

"Is that normal?" Wes asks. "I've never had a cat before."

"For her, it is." I sigh. "Maybe if she didn't eat everything in sight, we wouldn't have issues."

Hermione chirps in response and sashays from the kitchen. Wes chuckles and begins to gather the fallen fruit. He holds up a smushed banana. "Well, fuck. This didn't stand a chance."

I flash him a grin. "If you mean well-fucked, I concur."

He laughs and tosses the banana into the trash can. Reaching up, he pulls the scraps of my shirt from the ceiling fan.

I hold up the shredded panties and chuckle. "You're going to have to buy me a new wardrobe if you keep destroying my clothes."

"I'll buy you anything you want."

Smirking, I fill a pot with water for pasta. I switch on the stove and pour us both large glasses of water. After gathering what remains of the fruit, Wes leans against the island and watches me intently.

"Why are you looking at me like that?"

"You're a supernova. I'm just . . . I . . . fuck." Shaking his head, he runs a hand through his hair and over his face.

"Likewise, big boy." I wink and open a jar of pasta sauce. I pour some into a saucepan and still feel the weight of his gaze on me.

"I love you, Lena. Please don't ever doubt me again."

"I won't. But you can understand why I did, right? Imagine yourself in my shoes."

"It's not your shoes I'm imagining myself in," he replies with a wolfish grin.

I roll my eyes and pour a box of spaghetti into the pot. "You know what I mean, Ace."

"Lena, I'll give you anything you want. I wanna show you the world, and I will do whatever it takes to prove myself to you."

"You're all the world I need, Wes. I just want you. All of you," I say steadily.

"It's yours. Everything that I am and everything I have belongs to you. I am yours." He smiles, reaches into his pocket, and withdraws a box. My eyes flash to his. "I know you don't wear anything around your neck, but I had this made for ya." He places the box in my hand. "I hope you like it."

I lift the lid to find the most exquisite necklace I have ever laid eyes on. The platinum and diamond pendant sparkles in the light.

"Wes, it's gorgeous. Thank you."

"May I?" he asks, reaching for the box.

I hand it over. He removes the necklace and gently places it around my neck. The weight of the pendant rests against my breastbone as Wes fastens the clasp.

"It's Polaris, the North Star," he explains.

"It's breathtaking. I love it, Wes. Thank you," I whisper. "But I'm surprised you chose a star."

He cocks his head. "How come?"

"Well, you always call me *sunshine*."

He grins. "Is the sun not a star?"

I smile and kiss him. "You surprise me every day, Wes. I love you."

Wes presses his lips to my neck and whispers, "You're my true north, sunshine."

EPILOGUE

(2 days later)

LENA

Internal playlist: "I Won't Give Up" by Jason Mraz

Humming to myself, I pull a pan of chicken parmigiana from the oven and prepare a salad. Jake and Garrett are due to arrive in thirty minutes. The front door opens. Footsteps head in my direction.

"Smells great in here, Leens." Garrett settles on a stool.

I glance at the clock. "You're early."

He shrugs. "Didn't feel like working."

"Must be nice to make your own schedule," I muse.

"They don't call me boss man for nothing." He looks over his shoulder. "Where's lover boy?"

"Showering."

"That's a good place for him."

"Gar, please don't be a dick tonight." I sigh. "I need you guys to be on good terms. It's important to me."

"I'm never a dick."

Yeah, okay.

I return my attention to the salad. As the two most important men in my life, I need them to get along. They don't have to be best buds—hell, I'll settle for amicable tolerance—but I don't need a warring pair of alphas pounding their chests either. In truth, I'm more concerned about Garrett's response to Wes. I invited Jake, mainly because I adore him, and he'll make a good buffer if necessary.

Garrett filled me in on the details about his altercation with Wes at the gala. It sounded like the clash of the fucking Titans and the fact that I missed the drama relieves me. Temper wise, I've seen them both in action. Wes's hotheaded, fly-off-the-handle approach, and Garrett's calculated detonation makes for a volatile mix. Last thing I need is a brawl.

"The wheels are turning," Garrett murmurs.

I cock my head. "Huh?"

"I see you over there, stewing." He chuckles. "Steam coming out your ears and everything."

"I'm not stewing," I protest. "I'm just—" I tense when I hear Wes come down the stairs. I flash a warning glare in Garrett's direction. "Behave."

"I always do."

"Where'd ya put my clothes, love?" Wes enters the kitchen wearing only the towel he wrapped around his hips. Droplets of water glisten on his chest and chiseled abdomen.

He catches sight of Garrett and his gaze darts to the clock above the sink. Smiling, he sticks out his hand. "G'day, gatekeeper."

Garrett shakes his hand. "Howdy, Ace."

"Pick a different nickname, mate." Wes grins. "She calls me that in bed."

"*Wes!*" I chuck a piece of carrot at him, which hits his shoulder and bounces to the island.

"She calls you *that* too." Garrett snorts. "Got any suggestions?"

I laugh and shake my head. "Is nothing sacred?"

"Depends on your definition of sacred." Garrett smirks and picks up the piece of carrot. He crunches on it while rubbing his jaw. "Also heard a few 'Oh, Gods' mixed in."

Wes laughs.

"I've endured Wailing Wanda and Yowling Yolanda for *years*." I elbow Garrett. "Suck it up and deal."

"I'm dealing, Leens. And it's Lisa and Anya, by the way."

"Whatever their names are."

"My clothes, love?" Wes repeats with a chuckle.

"Just took them out of the dryer. Basket's in the living room."

"Thanks." He turns to leave the kitchen.

The scratches and welts on his muscular back aren't lost on Garrett. "You fall onto a cactus or something, champ?"

Wes spins around and flashes a megawatt grin. "Brooklyn is prime lioness habitat." He eyes me hungrily. "Wild, vicious creatures."

At that, he bounds upstairs to dress.

"Good for you, Leens." Garrett helps himself to a seltzer. "Godiva territory, right?"

I'm too flustered to answer. *I really did a number on him.* The redness appears more prominent after a hot shower. My eyelids flutter closed. Other than our quick field trip to the outside world so Wes could purchase a new phone, we've been sequestered in my apartment, going at it like horny teenagers. Unhinged, unrestrained, raw fuckery. Wes is a bona fide alpha wolf.

The man—and beast—staked his claim on my body, branding me with soft kisses and hard thrusts. I love seeing his loss of control, feeling his hands clamped on my hips, the weight and heat of his body. There aren't words to describe the ecstasy. If that's what our make-up sex is going to be like, I'll make it a point to fight him.

The weekend has been one for the record books. I lost count of my orgasms. I lost count of the ways I love him.

Wes returns a few minutes later wearing the jeans and a fitted black shirt he arrived in. He uncorks a bottle of wine and opens several cabinets in search of glasses.

Garrett points. "Far cabinet on the left."

"Thanks, mate." Wes withdraws three wineglasses. He eyes Garrett, who holds up his seltzer.

"I'm good."

Wes nods and pours some Shiraz for me, Jake, and himself. He comes up beside me and hands me the glass. "Need any help, love?"

"No, I'm good, thank you. You sit and relax."

Wes takes the seat next to Garrett. From their position at the island, the men watch me gather silverware and napkins.

"Why are you two staring at me?"

"Because you're beautiful," Wes says.

Garrett grins. "I'm not staring."

I attempt to place the cutlery beside each man, but I drop Wes's knife, which clatters to the floor at my feet.

"Shit. Sorry." I toss the soiled knife into the sink and grab a fresh one.

"She's nervous," Wes mumbles to Garrett under his breath. "She always drops things when she's nervous."

"Yep," Garrett agrees, "it's a pattern, for sure."

I prop my hands on my hips. "You know I can hear you, Ace." Tossing my hair over a shoulder, I continue, "I'm glad you guys have me all figured out. I'm not nervous, thank you very much. I'm just—"

"Nervous," Wes interjects with a snort. Garrett snickers. "Sunshine, you worry too much." He sips his wine and grins. "If we were gonna fight, it would've happened at the gala."

"He's right," Garrett says. "If I weren't so worried about you, I would've kicked his ass."

Wes laughs. "I would've kicked yours, mate."

"And *I* am going to kick both your asses if you keep it up. Don't test me."

"Relax, love." Wes reaches for my hand and I clasp his warm palm. "We've moved past it."

"We're fine, Leens." Garrett nudges Wes. "As long as Dundee over here keeps his head on straight."

Wes chuckles. "Nope. Pick another one, mate. She calls me that too."

"Running out of options, Emerson."

"Emerson works. Use that one."

"Nah, that's boring." Garrett perks up and slaps his knee in self-satisfaction. "Kangaroo Jack."

I punch his arm. "Garrett!"

"What? It's a good nickname."

"No, mate. If you're going down that road, you'd better get it right." Wes shakes his head. "Jack refers to a lone, male kangaroo. That's more fitting in reference to you." His lips curve into a smirk. "You can call me Boomer."

Garrett tilts his head. "Boomer?"

Wes flashes a cocky grin. "The alpha male."

"Yeah, fuck no." Garrett snorts. "Emerson it is, then."

I laugh in spite of myself. "You two are infuriating."

"But you love us," Garrett singsongs.

"You're both lucky that I do." I put the plates in front of them. "Or you'd be going hungry tonight."

"Thanks, love."

"Thank you." Garrett glances at Wes. "First time with her chicken parm?"

"Yeah."

"Oh, you're in for a treat."

"Thanks, Gar." I smile. "I already won him over with my omelets."

"Won me over long before that, love."

The doorbell rings, signaling Jake's arrival.

"Wes, please let Jake in."

Wes heads for the door and they come in a few moments later.

Jake claps Garrett's shoulder. "Hey, man."

"Welcome to Casa Hamilton." Garrett bumps fists with him.

He wraps me in a hug. "Lena-Bean, it smells amazing in here."

"Thank you. I hope it doesn't disappoint. Okay, guys, you're all here and dinner is ready. Have a seat, Jake." I place a generous portion on each man's plate before settling on a stool.

Wes takes a bite of the chicken parm. "This is *amazing*."

"Fucking delicious," Jake adds.

"You already know how *I* feel about your chicken parm, Leens. Put it this way, you didn't disappoint."

I feel myself flush. "Glad you like it."

Jake turns to Garrett. "Ready for your date on Wednesday?"

Garrett shrugs. "I wouldn't call it a date."

"Why not?" I ask.

He elbows Jake. "This guy's gonna be there. Threesomes aren't my thing."

Wes chuckles. "You may be thankful for the buffer, mate."

Jake laughs. "I was going to say the same thing."

Garrett eyes them. "What do you mean?"

"We mean, Ella can be a little . . ." Wes rubs his jaw while pondering his word choices. "Intense."

Garrett's expression darkens. "I'll see her intensity and raise her mine."

"Just be careful with her," Wes warns.

I study him. "Why do you say it like that?"

"She's a nice girl, but she's got a dark side." He sips his wine. "Ella the enigma. Camera-wielding destroyer of men . . . and women."

Jake shakes his head. "Don't say that. She doesn't have a dark side—she's just a little misunderstood."

"I *understand* that she's a master puppeteer, and I'd hate to see him tangled up in that." Wes meets Garrett's gaze. "Don't let her bedroom eyes steal your wits, mate."

Garrett's lips curve into a smile. "It's a little too late for that."

Jake punches Wes's arm. "Dude, stop making her sound all sinister and shit. I've known Ella a long time. She's a nice person."

Wes's new phone buzzes and he peers at the screen. "Sorry to be rude, but I need to take this." He glances at me. "It's the realtor."

I nod. "Take your time, babe."

He kisses my forehead and leaves the room.

Garrett cocks a brow. "Realtor?"

"Yeah. Wes has been looking for a place to buy and is considering a brownstone on Jake's block."

Jake swallows a sip of wine. "Which one? Two of them recently went up for sale."

"He said it's directly across the street from your place," I answer.

Jake grins. "Congratulations. That place is gorgeous—rooftop gardens and shit."

Garrett shakes his head. "I'm confused. If you two are gonna shack up already, why not have him stay here? Why would he buy a place a few blocks away?"

I laugh. "Because it's not for us."

"Who the fuck's he buying houses for, and when can I get mine?" Garrett asks with a snort. "Or do I have to spend the rest of eternity listening to you two fuck my light fixtures through the ceiling?"

Jake snickers. "Word on the street is you earned that, my friend."

"Damn right, he did." I high-five Jake.

"I'm with Garrett, though. Why's Wes buying the place across from me? Doesn't make much sense. Who's it for?"

"Actually, it makes perfect sense." I smile at Jake. "Isla accepted an internship at the Fashion Institute. She's moving to New York in December."

Shiraz shoots out Jake's nose and spurts from his mouth, staining his white dress shirt. He coughs and sputters, clenching the granite countertop.

I hand him a napkin and continue, "Wes didn't want her living alone in midtown Manhattan, so—"

"Our boy Jake's getting a new neighbor?" Garrett claps Jake's back.

"That's the plan," I reply sweetly.

Jake stares, red-faced and watery-eyed, his mouth opening and closing like a fish. He runs a hand over his face. "Did I hear you correctly?"

"You sure did." I squeeze his hand. "Surprise."

"You knew and didn't tell me?"

I shrug. "Wasn't my news to share."

"I think this qualifies for an exception, Lena-Bean."

"Maybe. Or maybe I don't like fucking with fate." Grinning, I lean in close. "Oh, I almost forgot. Isla had a message for you when I saw her in LA."

The color drains from Jake's face. "And that was?"

"She said to tell you she plans to take you up on your offer."

"My offer?" he croaks.

"The one where you told her she could stay with you for a while," I bat my lashes, "you know, when you show her around the city."

"I *did* say that," Jake whispers, hands knotting in his hair. "Holy. Fuck."

Garrett jerks his head toward the living room. "I'm curious. Does Dundee know you wanna bone his baby sis?"

"Garrett!" I shoot him a warning glare. "Keep your mouth shut or I'll fuck you up."

"Never said I wanted to bone her." At Garrett's cocked brow, Jake sighs. "But, no. And it's gonna stay that way. He'd cut off my balls and feed them to me. Then, he'd fucking kill me."

"Not if Lena has anything to do with it." Garrett nudges him. "She has a way with this type of thing."

"It doesn't matter though," Jake mutters. "Isla isn't interested in me."

I smirk. "Oh, I wouldn't be so sure about *that* one, Jake Bennett."

"Wait a minute, Lena-Bean, have you been playing matchmaker behind my back?"

"Who? Little old me?"

Jake shakes his head. "I *knew* it."

I flash a wicked grin and—knowing damn well both men will understand the theater reference—I purr, "Trust me, honey, Dolly Gallagher Levi ain't got *nothing* on me."

"I see some forbidden fruit on your horizon, brotha." Garrett rubs his hands together in excitement. "Looks like the northern and southern hemispheres are about to collide."

Wes enters the kitchen at that moment with a broad smile on his face. "Great news—the sellers accepted my offer!"

The End

Stay tuned for Jake's story in book three of the Compass Series:
**HORIZON*

Stay tuned for Garrett's story in book one of the Prodigy Series:
**MASQUERADE*

PLAYLIST FOR NORTH STAR

"Awake" by Josh Groban

"Something Just Like This" by The Chainsmokers & Coldplay

"Remind Me" by Emily King

"Shape of You" by Ed Sheeran

"Lioness" by Sarah Fimm

"Tapes" by Alanis Morissette

"Drops of Jupiter" by Train

"Cosmic Love" by Florence + The Machine

"Unsteady" by X Ambassadors

"No Light, No Light" by Florence + The Machine

"Remain Nameless" by Florence + The Machine

"Faded (Restrung)" by Alan Walker

"Hear Me" by Kelly Clarkson

"FutureSex/LoveSound" by Justin Timberlake

"Consider Me" by Allen Stone

"A.D.I.D.A.S. (All Day I)" by Ro James

"Ride" by SoMo

"Kisses Down Low" by Kelly Rowland

"Hurts 2B Human" by P!ink

"You Have No Idea" by Josh Groban

"Surrounded" by Chantal Kreviazuk

"I Don't Care" by Ed Sheeran & Justin Bieber

"Versions of Violence" by Alanis Morissette

"Seven Devils" by Florence + The Machine

"The Hard Stuff" by Justin Timberlake

"Turning Tables" by Adele

"Love Me Anyway" by P!ink (feat. Chris Stapleton)

"Water Under the Bridge" by Adele

"Various Storms and Saints" by Florence + The Machine

"Lost" by Dermot Kennedy

"Bad Romance" by Lady GaGa

"Say Something" by A Great Big World (feat. Christina Aguilera)

"What Have I Done" by Dermot Kennedy

"My Kind of Love" by Emeli Sandé

"Power Over Me" by Dermot Kennedy

"The Wolf" by The Spencer Lee Band

"I Won't Give Up" by Jason Mraz

"All of Me" by John Legend

Thanks so much for reading my words! It means the world to me. If you enjoyed North Star, please leave me a review.

Up next: *Horizon* (Jake's book!)

Please subscribe to my newsletter for updates and new releases!

Website: www.ariawyatt.com

Facebook: www.facebook.com/AriaWyattAuthor

Join my readers' group on Facebook: Aria Wyatt's Speakeasy at www.facebook.com/groups/ariawyattsspeakeasy

Instagram: www.instagram.com/ariawyatt_author

TikTok: www.tiktok.com/@ariawyattauthor

Twitter: www.twitter.com/AriaWyattAuthor

OTHER BOOKS

Compass Series:
True North
North Star
Horizon
Symphony (forthcoming)
Title TBD (forthcoming)

Busy Bean Standalone:
Afterglow

Prodigy Series
Masquerade
Prodigy (forthcoming)
Supernova (forthcoming)

Devil in the Details

PROLOGUE

ISLA ROSE EMERSON, AGE 18

Internal playlist: "Waiting in Vain" by Annie Lennox

It's no secret that tightly woven fabrics excite me. Bonus points awarded if they're stretchy. Today, as I scan the packed private beach, my love affair with Spandex has never been more relevant. In fact, I'm considering a ménage with nylon and polyester. Maybe even Lycra. If anyone needs me, I'm building a mental shrine for the people who design men's bathing suits.

All around me, blokes wearing Speedos and jammers parade their sculpted bodies across the sand. As a girl who grew up toddling in the Pacific Ocean, one would think I'd be used to seeing so many muscles in one place. Nope. Still gets me.

My brothers' mates are hot. Like, *really* hot. A salty breeze ruffles my hair as the Australian sun sets over crashing waves. Music is blasting. People are laughing, drinking, and surfing. Someone built a huge bonfire. The crackle of burning wood is barely audible over the surf. Leaping orange flames mesmerize me almost as much as the abundance of rippling abdomens and toned arses . . . *not*.

I sip my wine cooler and smile. My oldest brother's birthday bash is the last place I expected to find myself tonight, mainly because I wasn't invited to the bloody thing. That is, according to Reed, middle child, and resident party-planner. His decree didn't sit well, so I went over his head and asked Wes. It's *his* birthday, after all. As the youngest, and the only girl in the family, I'm used to getting what I want—especially from Wes. This time was no exception. So here I sit, feasting my eyes on a delicious buffet of scantily clad musculature.

Across the fire, Reed's still glowering at me. Nothing new. I get it—we're ten years apart and he can't stand me, but that's his problem. Our relationship has never been a close one. Truth be told, it bothers me sometimes. As far as I know, my greatest offense to him was being born. You know, something I had zero control over. I blow him a kiss, and he curls his lip.

My gaze drifts to Wes. I still can't believe he's thirty. Standing near a shed that houses surf equipment, waxing his surfboard, the scar from five years ago stands out against the bronze of his skin. My fingers instinctively trace along my matching scar—the one that represents our bond and my freedom from dialysis.

It doesn't seem possible I've had his kidney for half a decade. It took years for the doctors to figure out a diagnosis. When they finally did, it was too late—lupus nephritis landed me in renal failure at age twelve.

Movement in the parking area draws my attention. The party has been going since noon. Everyone who was supposed to come is here. A Jeep rolls to a stop, and the driver's door pops open. A man emerges, silhouetted by the sunset. He walks across the sand, approaching Wes from behind.

Who's this?

I squint and blink a few times, holding up a hand to shield my watery eyes. *Where the hell are my sunglasses?* Lupus makes me extremely photosensitive, which is why I chose to arrive closer to sundown. Even with ample protection, my skin and eyes can't handle sunlight for more than a couple hours.

Mystery man claps my brother's shoulder, causing him to spin around.

"Bennett!" Wes's surfboard hits the sand, wax landing in the shed, as he throws his arms around his best mate.

Jake Bennett.

I stare open-mouthed at the man I've loved since he built sandcastles and splashed in the waves with me when I was a child. We collected seashells, played Barbies, and he endured endless games of hide and seek. I taught "my Jake" everything I knew about hopscotch.

Now, my Jake is a multi-platinum singer-songwriter with the sexiest voice I've ever heard. I have the audio file for every song he's put out, and I adore listening to his smooth, deep baritone on repeat. I especially love falling asleep to the ballads. Thanks to his touring schedule, I haven't seen him in almost three years.

Jake.

My Jake. Is. Here.

Aviator sunglasses obscure his eyes, but I can picture those warm chocolaty irises like I saw them yesterday. Dressed in a plain, gray T-shirt and khaki shorts, with a charcoal hoodie draped over his arm, Jake's muscled physique heats my insides. Forget the blokes in Speedos, my reaction to him surpasses sparks, bordering on a wildfire. Factor in his tousled chestnut waves and stubbled jawline, and I'm done for. I've crushed on Jake my whole life, but nothing could've prepared me for this tidal wave of longing.

He doesn't see me yet. Just as well—I need a few minutes to cool down. I duck behind the surf shed. Careful to stay hidden, I peek around the corner to where the men are standing.

Wes grins. "Holy fuck, mate; I didn't think you could make it. I thought you were still on tour."

"I am, dude. Got another six months, but I had a few days off between shows, so I hopped a plane." Jake glances at his watch. "I can hang for a couple of hours, but I need to fly out in the morning."

I spy like the quintessential little sister that I am. Perhaps it has something to do with Jake being the speaker, but their conversation is perfectly audible from my vantage point.

Austin "Memphis" Pines, pop star and tonight's chef, jogs over to Jake and Wes. Austin is their other best mate, and the one who brought all the guys together as kids. "Bennett, you made it." He turns to Wes and grins. "Surprise."

Jake hugs Austin. "What's up, Memphis? You save me any food?"

"Yeah, man. The ribs are almost done, and I made my famous honey-bourbon wings. Saved you some bourbon too."

"Sweet, thanks." Jake runs a hand through his waves. "I could use a drink after that flight."

"Screaming babies?" Wes asks.

Jake nods. "Triplets."

Wes chuckles. "Ah, the Three Musketeers, like us."

Jake, Austin, and Wes are affectionately known in the entertainment industry as the Three Musketeers. Instead of swashbuckling swordsmen, two singers and an actor comprise this inseparable trio. With Austin hailing from Tennessee, and Jake being a Brooklyn, New York native, their globe-spanning friendship has been going strong for two decades.

Wes's fame is still weird for me—especially the way women throw themselves at him since his lead role in the Olympus Fire franchise. To the rest of the world, Wes is Ares, the Greek god of war. To me, he's just my big brother. The bikini-clad group of giggling women following him around are clearly enthralled by the Ares persona. Since our cousin owns this section of beach, and details about the party were kept under wraps, the paparazzi haven't shown up. *Yet.*

"The flight was awful." Jake shakes his head. "The babies were in the row in front of me. At one time or another, they were barfing, shitting, and screaming."

Wes cocks his head. "You didn't fly first class?"

"It was booked."

Wes grins. "Thanks for suffering to come to my party."

Jake claps his shoulder. "I'm happy to be here, man."

Austin points to the coolers. "I'll grab you a drink. Be back in a min."

Reed makes his way over to them and gives Jake a fist bump. "Glad you could make it, mate."

I edge my body away from the shed's corner and peek through a crack instead. If Reed spots me, he'll gladly blow my cover. He fucked up every game of hide and seek we played.

Austin returns, handing Jake a shot of bourbon. "Bottoms up, brotha."

Jake smoothly knocks it back. I watch his throat move on a swallow, jealous of the amber liquid. I glance at the pina colada wine cooler I'm holding. I can't drink hard liquor but wish I could do shots with the guys.

"What's new? How's the family?" Jake asks Wes and Reed.

"Everyone's good, mate. Mum and Dad are on a trip." Wes points to a group of people up the way. "And Isla's here somewhere."

"Really?" Jake scans the beach. "I haven't seen Sprite in years."

Sprite is the nickname he gave me when I was a kid because I'd flit around like a bird or a fairy. It's one of my more endearing pet names.

"Yeah, Bird Brain's crashing the party, like always," Reed grumbles.

"Don't call her that, mate." Wes shakes his head. "I said Imp could come. Besides, she's not bothering anyone." He smirks. "Other than *you*."

Austin chuckles. "Yeah, be nice to Flight Risk. She brought dessert."

Bird Brain, Flight Risk, and Imp. Talk about a shitty nickname trifecta. It's not that they're wrong—I'm flighty—but if dialysis taught me anything about myself, it's that I hate being caged.

Jake nudges Reed. "I see nothing's changed in the Emerson family."

"Don't remind me," Reed mutters. He shields his eyes, scanning the beach once more. "I swear, she was just here."

I press my body to the weathered building, praying no one spots me. Given my penchant for eavesdropping, I should probably pursue a career in espionage instead of fashion design.

Down the beach, someone calls Wes to help with their surfboard.

"Be right back." He jogs across the sand.

Reed limps after him. The familiar wave of sadness crests in my heart. It's no wonder he's miserable. A drunk driver shattered his acting career, along with his leg and vertebrae, when he was my age. He hasn't been the same since. The only positive to come of it was Cora Priest, his physical therapist girlfriend. Only Cora sees Reed's soft side. Much as his distance hurts me, I'm grateful he has her to turn to.

Jake tells Austin about music industry stuff. I continue to eavesdrop, hanging on every word that leaves his lush lips.

Cora catches sight of me after retrieving a dry towel from her car. She cocks her head at my position behind the shed.

I hold a finger to my lips and wave her over.

"Why're ya hidin' out here, love?" she whispers.

"Oh, uh . . . well, I—"

Her knowing smirk stops me as heat floods my face. "He's only gonna be here a few hours, so you'd better make it count." She winks.

"Please don't tell my brothers," I whisper.

She wraps her little finger around mine and tightly squeezes. "Pinky promise."

Cora is the big sister I've always wanted, and our bond makes up for what I lack with Reed. We've been sharing secrets for years, sealed with our signature promise.

"Thank you." I meet her emerald gaze before gesturing to my bikini. "Do I look all right?" I smooth my hair and show my teeth. "Any lettuce?"

Cora giggles. "No. You look stunning, as always. Is that a new bather?"

"Yeah."

"Yellow's your color." She motions to my chest. "The halter makes your boobs look bigger *and* shows off your new ink."

"Good. That's what I was hoping for."

Despite my nicknames, I like birds. So much, that I got a huge phoenix tattoo on my eighteenth birthday. Situated on my upper back, the colorful bird's wings stretch across my shoulders. Wes has a much smaller one on the inside of his left wrist. Matching scars, tattoos, and eye color are just a few things I have in common with my favorite brother.

I touch my scar. "Does this look bad?" Cora cocks a brow, and I backpedal. "Yeah, yeah, I know. Battle scars and all."

"Your beauty's soul deep, little bird. Now, get your arse over there before your brothers cock-block ya."

I snort. "I don't think Moody Melvin would give a shit either way, but Wes may be an issue."

"That's an understatement, love." She grips my shoulders. "You know damn well he's fierce about you."

I sigh. "At least one of them is."

Cora bites her lip. "Reed loves you. He's just—"

"Reed."

"Right. Where is he, anyway?"

I pick up a conch shell near my feet. "He's up the way helping Wes with somebody's board."

"Still pouting?" she asks.

"Of course."

"I can't do anything about keeping Wes occupied, but I'll try to keep Reed out of your hair tonight." She squeezes my shoulder. "Call me tomorrow with details."

"I will." I watch Cora leave before I make my way toward Jake.

The hot sand burns my feet, quickening my pace. In my hurry to hide, I left my thongs by the bonfire. I slide the yellow shoes back on and summon my inner wild child.

Pre-transplant Isla didn't take risks. I followed the rules and did what was expected of me. My reward? I was chained to dialysis for over a year. Now I live my life by my rules. I follow my heart—and my dreams—like they could be shattered at any moment. Should I do more looking and less leaping? Probably. But being careful didn't save my kidneys.

Austin's at the grill, brushing more sauce onto his famous chicken wings. Jake stands near the coolers, tapping out a text on his phone.

Now or never.

I stop in front of Jake and touch his arm. "Hey."

He turns to face me; and his brow furrows, his gaze searching my face. "Hey . . ." He slides his phone into a pocket.

I can't blame him for not recognizing me. Let's be real, I've come a long way from the dorky, awkward version of myself he'd last seen. I'm taller. My skin's clear. Teeth are straight, and I finally have boobs—sort of. Wes does his best to shield me from the spotlight; and social media isn't my thing, so I haven't posted a picture in ages.

I hand Jake the shell. "It's been a while."

His frown deepens as his palm closes around it. "Uh, thanks."

"Put it with Malibu Stacy." I wink. Years back, I'd given him one of my Barbie dolls. According to Wes, he'd kept her.

His brows shoot upward, and his jaw drops open. He blinks a few times before shaking his head. "Isla?" My name leaves his lips on a husky whisper, and everything inside me catches fire.

"Was starting to think ya forgot me."

"No, I . . . uh—" Jake clears his throat and looks me over. It feels like a physical touch. He swallows tightly. "I . . . I didn't recognize you." His gaze snaps to mine and redness creeps across his cheeks, spreading to his neck and ears. "You've grown up."

"You too." I realize how lame I sound, but my mind is incapable of a better reply. "I mean, obviously you've *been* an adult—"

Smirking, he motions to my wine cooler. "You're drinking?"

"Good observation." I don't mean to be snarky, but his statement amuses me.

Jake rubs the back of his neck. "Let me rephrase. Why are you drinking?"

"You sound like my brothers. I'm of age, ya know."

"Yeah." He steps closer to me. "I know."

"Which means a wine cooler's a perfectly acceptable refreshment."

His gaze wanders to my scar and lingers, making me feel more exposed than if I'd skipped the bather entirely. "It's acceptable for someone other than you."

"It's my first one. Besides, my liver's fine." I lift the bottle to my lips. "One wine cooler won't kill me."

In a lightning bolt move, he snatches my cooler before I realize what's happening and tilts the bottle on end. "I'd rather not take that chance."

Cool liquid spatters my ankles and soaks into the sand at my feet.

My hands fly to my hips. "Excuse me, do ya mind?"

"Actually, I do." He looms over me. "You need to take care of yourself. Don't be reckless with your health, Sprite."

I cross my arms over my chest. "I'm *not* reckless."

He cocks a brow and holds up the empty. "Fine. We'll call it nonchalance."

I clench my jaw and stare at the waves. I'm not some foolish ankle-biter in need of a scolding. And while I take some risks, I'm not irresponsible. The last thing I'd do is jeopardize my transplanted kidney. I endured dialysis for over a year while my family went through a battery of compatibility tests. Wes was the only match, and our surgeries were the day after his twenty-fifth birthday. He gave me a new life like it was as simple as sharing chips with me. I'm forever grateful for his sacrifice and furious Jake thinks I'd take it lightly.

Jake tilts my chin to face him. "Don't be mad, Sprite. I'm looking out for you."

That's the problem. Everyone's always looking out for me. People treat me like I'm a bloody fuckwit hanging out at the edge of a cliff, incapable of self-preservation. I'm not some fragile little girl who can't hold her own—I'm a fucking survivor.

"Who said I'm mad?"

His plush lips quirk into a smile. "A hunch."

"I wanted the freedom to celebrate my brother's birthday like a normal person. For the record, my doctor said it was fine." I point to the empty bottle. "I chose a wine cooler with the lowest possible alcohol content. That's the only one I've had, and I nursed it for over an hour."

Then you show up and have the balls to dump it in the fucking sand.

He holds his hands up in surrender. "Okay, I'm sorry. Didn't mean to upset you."

"I'm not." At his raised brow, I stiffen my spine. "And I'm not reckless *or* nonchalant. I can look out for myself."

"Hey." He sets down the empty and grips my shoulders. "No one's questioning that."

"You're insinuating I'm a birdbrained lush."

He tightens his grip, fury flashing in his gaze. Framed by thick, dark lashes, the chocolaty depths unravel me. "You know damn well that's not what I meant." My lungs hold oxygen captive as he steps closer. "No one's questioning your ability to look out for yourself, Isla Rose Emerson. Especially, not me."

I nearly moan when his deep voice rumbles my full name. The air between us crackles. His pupils dilate, telling me he feels it too.

Jake consumes my senses—every sight, every sound, every scent. Crashing waves fade into the background, replaced by our breaths. The bonfire's smoke dissipates, and I savor his woodsy clean scent. As I stand before the boy who I've known my whole life, I drink in his muscles, his stubbled jaw, his heated gaze. My eyes flick to his dimples—visible even when he's not smiling. Thick waves fall over his forehead. I want to thread my fingers through them, pull his face to mine, and kiss him with everything I've got.

He releases my shoulders and clears his throat, taking a step back. "Let's start over. How have you been?"

His sudden distance brings me back to reality. I'm his best mate's little sister—not one of the beautiful women ogling him from across the fire. So help me God, if they start following him like they've been doing to Wes, I'll lose my shit.

I draw a calming breath and come back to center. "Great. I signed up for university next year."

"You still interested in fashion design?"

"Yes." I cock my head. "I'm surprised you remember."

"I remember everything," he murmurs. "It's a gift and a curse."

"There's my favorite imp!" Wes bounds over, stopping beside Jake, who takes another step back and stuffs his hands inside his pockets. Wes ruffles my hair with one of his huge paws and flashes me a grin. "Thought you went home already."

I strike a pose. "Nope. I'm still here in all my glory."

Something flares in Jake's gaze, and he looks out at the ocean.

"Good. I was worried Reed made you leave." Wes glances at Jake. "You eat yet, mate?"

"Nah, I'm good, thanks."

"All right, well, don't be shy. Memphis made more food than we know what to do with."

Jake nods, plopping on a log near the fire.

Needing some distance between us before I combust, I settle across the way and peer at him through the flames. His molten gaze never leaves mine, even as people gather around the fire, laughing, singing, and sharing memories. Elbows resting on bent knees, fingers steepled in front of his lips, Jake watches me with an intensity that defies his laid-back demeanor. No one's ever looked at me like this. He's certainly never looked at me this way.

I shift on the log and brush sand off my ankles, gritty, yet sticky from my spilled drink. I rub it between my fingers and picture the sandcastles of my youth. We didn't have much growing up; but our family spent a lot of time at the beach, especially when Austin and Jake visited from the States. Before his motorcycle accident, Reed was an avid surfer. He and Wes spent hours riding waves, and even attempted to teach Austin. Jake was never interested in surfing—content to watch from a distance and build castles with Mum and me.

Jake let me use the shovel to dig, while he used his hands. Our castles were never sprawling structures; instead, they were tall. He showed me how to use wet sand as plaster to make them structurally sound, but ours still teetered precariously. That was part of the excitement—seeing how tall we could make them before they fell. Then we'd start again with a new one rising from the ruins of the last.

I remember sloshing back and forth with buckets of seawater to fill the moat. We always had a moat—a requirement of mine. Once the foamy moat water was deep enough, we'd set sail a fleet of boats. I called them guard boats, for the purpose of protecting the princess, of course. He'd laugh when I insisted we decorate the castle with seaweed and shells, but he let me do it. We'd stroll along the beach collecting shells, bits of coral, and sea glass. He'd carry the bucket when it got too heavy for me.

The boy in the red swim trunks had messy chestnut waves. I peer across the fire into the eyes of the man he's become.

The man I want.

He stares, gaze swirling with unnamed emotions. *What's on his mind? Is his head taking him on a trip down memory lane too? Does he feel this magnetism, this inexplicable pull between us? Does he sense this attraction that started long before either of us knew what it was?* Warmed by memories and the heat in his expression, I smile.

He smiles back at me, stealing my breath. My sanity. My heart. My hand instinctively flies to my chest.

He's mine. He's always been mine.

The soul-deep realization floors me. Veins thrum with knowledge. My heart hammers against my ribcage. As each shaky inhale expands my lungs, I fight the urge to throw myself in his lap.

The breeze picks up, and I shiver. I should've brought something to change into, but I was excited to come and forgot. I briskly rub goosebumps on my arms, willing them away.

Jake frowns and climbs to his feet, walking over to me. He shrugs out of his Brooklyn hoodie and holds it out. "Put this on, Sprite."

I pull it over my head. "Thank you."

He nods and returns to his spot—hard nipples visible beneath his thin T-shirt.

Cloaked in his warmth, my body relaxes; and the chills stop. I glance down at the maroon, block lettering and slide my hands into the pockets. They close around something metal—his keys. I make a mental note to tell him before he leaves. Another thought punches my gut.

He's on tour for six more months.

The pain surprises me. I burrow deeper into the heavy sweatshirt and breathe in his scent, my eyes fluttering closed. It's decided—he's not getting it back. I'll wear it until it's threadbare.

Three hours later, Jake glances at his watch and stands to hug my brother. "Happy birthday, Wes. I'm gonna head back to my hotel."

My heart sinks. I've been dreading this moment since he arrived.

"Thanks for making the trip, mate. Means a lot."

"Anytime, man."

Jake bids everyone goodbye and makes his way to me. "It was good seeing you, Sprite."

"You too," I whisper. "Good luck on the rest of your tour."

"Thanks. Good luck with college. Make us proud."

"I will." *Please tell me I'll see you before then.* "Wait, don't forget your shirt." I tug at the hem.

"Keep it." He stops me with a hand on my shoulder and a devastating smile. "It looks better on you."

"Thanks." My throat is thick with emotion. I want to say more, but words won't come.

Jake squeezes my shoulders, his warmth radiating through the sweatshirt. "Promise you'll take care of yourself, Isla Rose."

I clench my jaw and nod. He gives everyone a wave and trudges across the beach toward the parking area.

I meet Cora's gaze across the fire. Her compassion-filled smile is enough to make my tears well. Thank God, my brothers are oblivious. I stare at my feet and shove shaking hands inside my pockets.

His keys.

I leap to my feet and hold them up. "He needs these." I sprint after him.

Standing in the dark lot near the Jeep he'd rented, Jake tries the door handles and searches his pockets.

"Wait!" I catch up and wave the keys. "You forgot these—" My foot snags on a rock, launching me into him. Our collision sends him stumbling backward against the car.

"Whoa. Easy, Sprite." He holds me to his chest.

"Sorry." I clutch his shoulders. "Didn't see that rock."

"You need to be more careful. You'll break an ankle if you keep running in the dark. This isn't what I meant when I told you to take care of yourself."

I grip the front of his shirt. "I don't want you to leave."

"Isla, I—"

Our eyes meet. Once again, the rest of the world disappears. We're alone in this perfect, electrifying moment. I feel him from my scalp to my toes—a soul-deep awareness that leaves me breathless.

"Don't go." I lick my lips, and his eyes track the movement. "Please."

His gaze flickers to mine and darkens, pupils dilating. "Why?"

Now or never.

I grip the sides of his face, pull his lips to mine, and kiss him like my life depends on it. Every breath, every heartbeat begins and ends with him. I want to spend the rest of my life kissing him.

Only him.

A groan escapes his chest. His thick, strong arms tighten around me; and he deepens the kiss, sweeping his tongue into my mouth.

I clasp the back of his neck and pull him closer. He groans again and spins us, pressing me against the vehicle. Leaning into the kiss, his muscular thigh wedges between my legs, the friction making me moan. The rock-hard length of him presses into my belly. Fire spreads through my veins, burning a path from my head to my heart and beyond. My hips flex, deliberately rubbing him.

Jake weaves his hands into my hair, fingers tugging the strands. Our tongues stroke and slide against each other with a desperation that surpasses anything I've felt. This isn't my first kiss, but so help me God, I wish it were. Now I *know* what I've been missing. I know beyond a shadow of a doubt nothing will *ever* compare to this.

He's mine. He'll be my first.

The thought unleashes a flood of heat between my thighs. I've had plenty of boyfriends, but I've never done the naughty—never really wanted to. Knees weak and palms sweating, I want nothing more than to feel him inside me. Holding me. Loving me. Whispering my name in the darkness. The thought consumes me until Jake is all I know. His masculine scent. His warmth. His kiss, with the brush of lips and scrape of stubble. The weight and heat of his body pressed against mine. His fingers tugging my hair, pulling me closer, deeper.

Jake jerks his lips from mine and jumps back like I'm a leper. Chest heaving, his expression's a mix of shock and horror that rips my heart in two.

"What's wrong?" I gasp.

"I have to go," he grunts, knotting his hands in his hair.

"Let me come with you."

He squeezes his eyes shut. "No."

"Jake, please—"

"I've gotta go." His voice is cold and distant, like we're strangers. Like he didn't just kiss me into oblivion. "I'm sorry."

I watch in bewilderment as he yanks the door open, hops inside, and guns the engine.

He rolls down his window. "Please take care of yourself, Isla."

"Jake—" My voice breaks. "Don't leave."

"I'm sorry, Sprite." He speeds away, taking my heart with him.

ABOUT THE AUTHOR

Aria Wyatt is a pharmacist mom who spends the inhumane predawn hours with a cup of coffee and her laptop, gleefully indulging in her passion for romance. Her novels range in heat from steamy to scorching, and she doesn't shy away from writing flawed characters with real life issues.

She resides with her husband and two children in New York's picturesque Hudson Valley, near the Catskills and iconic Woodstock. The avid reader balances marriage, motherhood, her pharmacist career, and her romance author dream. When not writing, she dabbles in photography, using the natural beauty of the region to her advantage. She's a self-proclaimed cat lady who cannot live without coffee, chocolate, music, and books.

Author of True North and the Compass Series, Aria has a soft spot for those who are searching, yearning, and ultimately, finding. Whether on a mission to find themselves, find love, find forgiveness or solace, she believes the answer is out there somewhere.

"Journey to Love."

ACKNOWLEDGEMENTS

I'm ridiculously fortunate to have a tribe of amazing friends and family who support and encourage me on this crazy author journey.

To all of my Danas: **Dana Fisher** and **Dana Kragh-Swingle**, thank you for always believing in me. You've listened to my ramblings for decades. Somehow, you keep coming back for more. The Dana sandwich is everlasting, and I cherish the hell out of our friendship. (Sorbet x 2, + September + JTT = a whole lotta . . . you know.) **Dana Marchetti**, thank you for pimping my books and for being so damn funny. You're my sister from another mister and I adore you! Last, but certainly not least, **Dana Schechter**. Confession time: I saved you in my phone as "Boss Dana" for a reason. Notice how I never inadvertently messaged you any of the ramblings intended for the rest of my Dana harem? Guess what! Now you can experience my full spectrum of inappropriateness in a book. Thanks for embracing my side hustle. Love you!

Karen Harris, aka Care-Bear-Bo-Baggins, you're the original superstar. I'm beyond grateful we connected on that rainy day in the general admissions line for 98Degrees. Who would've thought one conversation would set so much in motion? Keep singing, my love. "Forget Me Not" is apropos in so many ways. I love your enthusiasm, your heart, and your outgoing personality. Thanks for supporting me, shouting your love from the social media rooftops, and helping me figure out TikTok. I adore you.

Krista Villielm and **Jen Liese**, thank you for being my cheerleaders. You make me feel a hundred feet tall and I love you both to pieces!

To all my girls in the **Bitches Love Books Book Club**: I call for a resurrection! Let's make it happen, shall we? Thank you for being part of my True North release party. It meant the world to me.

Lydia Amamoo, I live for the funny. You're a goddess through and through.

Elma Omeragic-Waldo, Melissa Young, and **Judy Moy,** you helped me keep my sanity in pharmacy school, and now you're showing love for my side hustle. I adore you. We need a reunion STAT.

Ian Maroney, your unique brand of hilarity nurtures my soul. Like I told you on many occasions, don't be surprised to find your funny AF sayings in one of my books. Thanks for the laughs and the psyche check-ins. You're an amazing friend and I love you! (I know, I know . . . as I should.)

Amanda Madsen, please re-read the dedication. I love you and your cute southern accent. Yeah, I went there.

Kristie Wolf, I'm beyond grateful to have you in my life. Thanks for being my author bestie, birthday sister, and sounding board. You motivate and encourage me, even when I'm whining. Thanks for being both the voice of reason and a kindred spirit. I love reading your words and can't wait to watch you succeed. I love you!!

Ashley Haile, Marly Tulimero, Meghan Mercier, Stephy Sit, Amanda Schermerhorn, Erin Anderson, Samantha Blakeney, Nesa Amamoo, and **Kristel Storm**, thanks for going out of your way to enthusiastically spread the word. I appreciate it more than you know.

To my pharmacy family: I love you all. Thanks for embracing your favorite dirty-minded pharmacist and for giving me so much material to work with.

A big shout-out to my beta-readers and author friends: **Cassandra Cripps, Becca L'Amour, Liz Schille,** and **Aria Peyton,** I appreciate everything you do for me!!! Your feedback is invaluable, and I can't imagine writing a book without you. **Lilian Harris**, thanks for your support and for having phenomenal taste in music. When Dermot comes back to NY, we're going. **Wren Murphy**, I'm so happy to have a fellow pharmacist in my tribe. I'm super excited for your debut, and for when we bring pharmacy representation to romance.

Thank you to my editors, **Silvia Curry** and **Eve Arroyo**, for making my words shine. To my proofreaders, **Virginia Tesi Carey, My Brother's Editor**, and **Amy Briggs**, thanks for catching the little stuff.

Wander Aguiar, as always, your photography is amazing. To my cover designer, **Lori Jackson**, thanks for your talent and patience. A special thanks to my formatter, the brilliant **Stacey Blake** of Champagne Book Design, for perfecting my book innards.

Linda Russell and team at Foreword PR & Marketing: thank you for everything you do!! Especially the handholding. Linda, your support and encouragement means the world to me. #Teamwork

To **my family**, I love you more than words. Thanks for believing in me.

Last, but certainly not least, to **my readers**: I appreciate each and every one of you! I'm humbled and honored that you've taken the time to read my words.

Much love,